AFRAID

Books by Jo Gibson

OBSESSED

TWISTED

AFRAID

And writing as Joanne Fluke

Hannah Swensen Mysteries

CHOCOLATE CHIP COOKIE MURDER
STRAWBERRY SHORTCAKE MURDER
BLUEBERRY MUFFIN MURDER
LEMON MERINGUE PIE MURDER
FUDGE CUPCAKE MURDER
SUGAR COOKIE MURDER
PEACH COBBLER MURDER
CHERRY CHEESECAKE MURDER
KEY LIME PIE MURDER
CANDY CANE MURDER
CARROT CAKE MURDER
CREAM PUFF MURDER
PLUM PUDDING MURDER
APPLE TURNOVER MURDER
DEVIL'S FOOD CAKE MURDER
GINGERBREAD COOKIE MURDER
CINNAMON ROLL MURDER
RED VELVET CUPCAKE MURDER
BLACKBERRY PIE MURDER
JOANNE FLUKE'S LAKE EDEN COOKBOOK

Suspense Novels

VIDEO KILL
WINTER CHILL
DEAD GIVEAWAY
THE OTHER CHILD

Published by Kensington Publishing Corporation

AFRAID

JO GIBSON

KENSINGTON PUBLISHING CORP.
www.kensingtonbooks.com

KTEEN BOOKS are published by

Kensington Publishing Corp.
119 West 40th Street
New York, NY 10018

Compilation copyright © 2014 by Kensington Publishing
Dance of Death copyright © 1996 by Joanne Fluke
The Dead Girl copyright © 1993 by Jo Gibson

All Kensington titles, imprints, and distributed lines are available at special quantity discounts for bulk purchases for sales promotion, premiums, fund-raising, and educational or institutional use.

Special book excerpts or customized printings can also be created to fit specific needs. For details, write or phone the office of the Kensington Special Sales Manager: Kensington Publishing Corp., 119 West 40th Street, New York, NY 10018. Attn. Special Sales Department. Phone: 1-800-221-2647.

Kensington and the K logo Reg. U.S. Pat. & TM Off.
KTeen is a trademark of Kensington Publishing Corp.

ISBN-13: 978-1-61773-242-3
ISBN-10: 1-61773-242-7
First Kensington Trade Paperback Printing: August 2014

eISBN-13: 978-1-61773-243-0
eISBN-10: 1-61773-243-5
First Kensington Electronic Edition: August 2014

10 9 8 7 6 5 4 3 2 1

Printed in the United States of America

Contents

Dance of Death

This book is for Ann Reit.

With many thanks to Amy and Lisa.

Prologue

It was hard, being the new girl in school, Donna Burke thought as she flipped her notebook open to a fresh, blank page. She was in her room, seated at the desk her parents had bought for her when they'd moved to Jefferson City, two months ago. The walls were painted her favorite color, a pale sky blue. The white curtains at the window matched the canopy over her new bed, her dresser and nightstand were exactly the style she'd always wanted, and there was a new braided rug on her floor. Donna's room was perfect, the room she'd always dreamed of having. There was only one thing wrong. Her room was in Jefferson City. And Jefferson City was over two hundred miles away from her friends.

Donna sighed and glanced at the clock. It was four o'clock on a dreary Friday afternoon in October, and she wasn't looking forward to the weekend. It would be like all the other weekends she'd spent in Jefferson City. The phone in her room wouldn't ring. It never did. She'd read, do her homework, watch a little television, and end up being bored silly for the next forty-eight hours.

Donna's classmates had gone to Clancy's, the local burger place and after-school hangout She could imagine them there, crowded into one of the big, fake-leather booths in the back and sharing a giant plate of fries. Donna knew she could have tagged along. They would have squeezed together to make her a place, offered her some fries and been perfectly friendly, but she wouldn't have been a real part of the group. Donna's classmates had a history together that went back to the first day of kindergarten. And even though Donna had been at Jefferson High for over six weeks, they still called her the new girl.

Donna had done her best to be accepted. She'd taken all the jobs the popular girls didn't want; usher for the fall play, head of the cleanup committee for school activities, student helper in the library, and ticket seller for football games. None of it had done any good. The other students smiled and said hello when they saw Donna running the ticket booth or tacking up notices on the library bulletin board. But no one had invited her to a single party, or called to talk about an assignment, or asked her for a date.

All that was going to change very soon. Donna squared her shoulders and picked up her pen. The former editor of the *Jefferson High Gazette,* one of the most popular girls in the senior class, had transferred to another school. Instead of simply appointing a new editor, Miss Adams, the faculty advisor, had decided to hold a contest. The entries would be published in the school paper, and the student who wrote the best article would be the new editor.

There was a frown on Donna's face as she stared down at her blank notepaper. She simply had to think of something! She brushed back her curly brown hair, which always got in the way when she was trying to work, and stared down at her notebook again. What could she write about?

Donna tried to remember what the students talked about in the halls. Sports wasn't taken and that was always a popular subject. Donna considered it for a minute, and then she shook her head. There was no way she could write an article about football when she wasn't even sure what a fullback was.

An in-depth profile of someone at school? Donna thought about it for a moment and then rejected that idea, too. It might work, but there wasn't enough time to do the research.

Thinking some music might help, Donna got up to turn on

her stereo, but the local station, K-TOP, didn't give her any ideas. Neither did looking out her window at Steve Harvey's house.

Steve Harvey. Donna sighed again, but this time it was a soft sigh of longing. Steve was easily the best-looking guy in the senior class, the quarterback on the football team, the class president, and the boy voted most likely to succeed by the faculty. To top that off, he wasn't a bit conceited. Of course, there was one small problem with Steve Harvey. He was practically engaged to Tammy Peters, the daughter of the man who owned Jefferson Plaza, and Jefferson Towers, and Jefferson Country Estates. Steve Harvey was taken, and Donna knew her chances with him were less than zero.

Thinking about Steve wasn't getting her article written. Donna picked up her pen and held it poised, at the beginning of the first blue line. She simply had to be the new editor! It was her only hope of becoming accepted by her classmates.

Making a list might help. Donna began to jot down ideas, one on each line. Classic blues. She knew a lot about the blues since it was her mother's favorite music, but she didn't really think that the students at Jefferson High would be interested in reading about Blind Lemon Jefferson or Otis Rush. No, she needed a scoop, a real heartstopper.

The phone rang and Donna put down her pen. Saved by the bell. Just in case it was one of her classmates, Donna put on a smile as she reached for the phone. Her grandfather always claimed he could hear a smile over the phone, and there was no sense in taking chances.

"Hello?" Donna spoke past her smile. And then the pasted-on smile turned into something warm and genuine as she recognized the voice on the other end of the line. It was Steve Harvey! And he wanted to know if she was going to the school carnival tomorrow night!

"Yes, I'll be there." Donna was so excited, her voice was shaking. She'd heard a rumor that Steve and Tammy weren't getting along, but she hadn't really believed it. What if Steve had broken up with Tammy? This could be the moment she'd been dreaming of, ever since she'd taken the seat next to his in history class. Steve Harvey was going to ask her for a date!

But when Steve explained why he'd called, a frown began to spread across Donna's face. It wasn't a date at all. Steve said he was expecting an important letter, but he'd be busy all day tomorrow, helping to set up booths for the school carnival. If his letter was delivered, he wanted Donna to bring it to the carnival with her.

"Yes, Steve. I'll be glad to do it." Donna hoped she didn't sound too disappointed. "I'll check your mailbox right before I leave. And if it's there, I'll bring it."

Donna's frown faded as she hung up the phone. At least Steve had called her. And he'd given her the perfect excuse to see him at the carnival. Maybe it wasn't exactly a date, but they *had* agreed to meet by the Ferris wheel at eight o'clock. And that was better than nothing, wasn't it?

One

She was early. Donna glanced at her watch as she stood in front of the ticket booth. It was seven forty-five and she wasn't supposed to meet Steve until eight. Donna didn't really mind waiting at the school carnival midway. She smiled as she watched the lights on the Ferris wheel make graceful circles. She could imagine riding the big wheel with Steve, holding his hand tightly as they started to rise up into the deep night sky. They might be lucky enough to stop at the very top, too high for anyone to see them, too far away to hear the noises of the crowd. If she happened to shiver from the cool breeze that swept over the hills, Steve might drape his arm around her shoulders and hold her close.

Donna clutched her purse tightly. Steve's letter was tucked inside and she knew it was from the state university. Their logo was in the upper left-hand corner of the envelope, and Donna had received a similar letter just last week. Her letter had contained very good news. Her application had been accepted and next year she'd be enrolling as a freshman. Steve had applied, too, and everyone at Jefferson High knew that he was hoping for a football scholarship. If Steve got his scholarship, they'd be on the same campus together!

Waiting for Steve to open his letter was agony. From the first moment Donna had taken it out of his mailbox, she'd had the urge to hold it up to the light to see if she could read the letter inside. She hadn't done it, but Donna had been careful to think positive thoughts all day. If Steve got his scholarship, he'd feel like celebrating. And since Donna was the one who'd brought him the news, Steve might ask her to be his date for the rest of the evening—if he'd really broken up with Tammy.

"Hey, Donna! How's it going?"

"Hi, Jerry." Donna turned to smile at Jerry Taylor. Jerry was Steve's best friend and he was on the football team, too.

"Hey . . ." Jerry cocked his head to one side and grinned at her. "You look great, Donna! Are you waiting for somebody?"

Donna nodded and hoped she wasn't blushing. "I'm supposed to meet Steve here at eight o'clock."

"Uh . . . Donna?" Jerry looked very uncomfortable. "You don't have a date with Steve, do you?"

"No, Steve just asked me to check his mailbox and bring him a letter."

Jerry looked very relieved. "That's good. I just saw him by the game booths with Tammy."

It was difficult, but Donna managed to keep smiling. It was still possible that Steve and Tammy had broken up. Maybe they'd decided to be friends.

"Looks like we're making some money here, huh?" Jerry glanced around at the crowded midway. "I just walked past the merry-go-round and there's about a hundred kids in line."

Donna nodded and pointed out a group of kids who were racing down the midway, clutching cotton candy and hotdogs. "I think the food booths are doing good business, too."

"Hey, Donna! Jerry! Wait up!"

Donna turned to see Steve making his way through the crowd toward them. She reached in her purse, pulled out the letter, and handed it to him the moment he arrived at her side.

"Thanks, Donna." Steve slipped his arm around her shoulders and gave her a little hug. "I really appreciate this."

Donna noticed that Steve's hands were shaking slightly as he held the letter. She knew exactly how he felt. Her hands had been trembling when she'd opened her own letter from the university. "I really hope it's good news, Steve."

"So do I!" Steve grinned and turned to Jerry. "Hey, Jer—did you get yours?"

Jerry shook his head. "Not yet, but if you got your scholarship, maybe I'll get mine. Come on, man—open it!"

"Okay, here goes." Steve ripped the letter open and glanced inside. And then he let out a whoop of excitement. "I got it! A full scholarship!"

Jerry grinned. "It's celebration time!"

"Come on." Steve took Donna's arm and marched her along the midway. "Everybody's waiting at the Duck Pond."

Donna felt like she was walking on air as she hurried down the midway with Steve and Jerry. Steve's hand was still on her arm and, as they passed a group of girls, several of them turned to stare. Rumors would be flying through the halls of Jefferson High on Monday morning, but they wouldn't mean a thing if Steve was still going with Tammy.

Her grandfather had always said to enjoy the moment, and that's exactly what Donna tried to do. The carousel was playing "Someday My Prince Will Come," and Donna knew she'd always remember that song. Every time she heard it, she'd think of the brightly painted horses revolving slowly and the wonderful feeling of Steve's warm fingers on her arm.

But as the three of them approached the Duck Pond, Donna saw Tammy, tapping her foot impatiently.

She looked gorgeous! Tammy's long, golden blonde hair was swept up into a barrette tonight, and it tumbled down her back in a cascade of perfect curls. She was wearing an outfit that Donna had never seen before, white suede pants and a matching jacket that was decorated with flowers made of brightly colored beads. Donna suddenly felt drab and ordinary. Why would Steve bother to look at her when Tammy was so beautiful? She'd been silly to hope that he'd take her on the Ferris wheel. And she'd been absolutely crazy to think that he might ask her for a date!

"What took you so long?" Tammy frowned as they approached.

"Aren't you going to ask if I got my letter?" Steve asked.

"Of course I am." Tammy put on a smile as she took Steve's arm. "Don't keep me in suspense, Stevie. Did you?"

"Yes, I got it. And . . . I *got it!*

"That's wonderful, Stevie." Tammy stood on her tiptoes to kiss his cheek. "I knew you would. And if you're really nice to me, I'll buy you a present."

Steve turned to Donna to explain. "That means she wants to go shopping. And I'll get stuck, carrying everything she buys."

"Of course. That's what boyfriends are for." Tammy grabbed Steve's arm and pulled him toward the row of vendors. "Come with us, Jerry. Let's go see if they've got anything worth buying."

"The queen speaketh." Jerry turned to Donna and extended his arm. "Come on, Donna. I'll carry your stuff if you buy anything."

Donna hesitated. Tammy had deliberately excluded her. But Jerry had invited her and she really wanted to go.

"Donna? Come on. It'll be fun."

Steve turned around to motion to her, and Donna took Jerry's arm. "Okay. But don't worry, Jerry. I'm not going to buy anything so you won't have any packages to carry."

"Hey! Wait up!" Jerry hurried to catch up with Tammy and Steve. "Donna says she's not going to buy anything."

Steve smiled at Donna. "Maybe Donna's a little more sensible than some people I could name."

"Stevie!" Tammy frowned at him. "That wasn't very nice. And you wouldn't like a sensible girlfriend. They're boring! Isn't that right, Donna?"

Donna shrugged. "I guess they could be. I've never really thought about it before."

"And of course Donna's going to buy something." Tammy gave her a condescending smile. "She won't be able to resist. We've got over fifty vendors here tonight."

Donna didn't say anything at all. She just smiled. Tammy was

so self-centered, she didn't even wonder why Donna wasn't going to buy anything. It took money to go shopping, and Donna
had a total of $15.65 in her purse. The $15 was next week's
lunch money, and Donna wasn't about to spend it on something
she didn't need.

The area they'd named Vendors' Row was at the far edge of
the football field, next to a grove of trees. They wandered past
several booths of costume jewelry, a display of handmade leather
purses and wallets, and a booth with hand-thrown pottery. As
they rounded the corner between two tents, Tammy stopped and
pointed to an unusual display. "Oh—look! There's a totally fantastic booth!"

Donna nodded. The booth really was fantastic. The sign read
MAGICAL FOOTWEAR, and the vendor had used a big oak tree to
display the wares. A huge tent draped with oriental carpets was
set up under the tree, and shoes and boots hung from the
branches.

"Let's go, Stevie!" Tammy grabbed Steve's hand and began to
push to the front of the crowd. "I'm going to be in the fall play
and I want a pair of totally incredible shoes to wear."

Donna managed to hide her smile of amusement. She was an
usher for the fall play, and she'd attended a few rehearsals.
Tammy didn't need new shoes; she needed to learn her lines!

"You guys better keep me company." Steve turned back to
Jerry and Donna. "This could take hours. Tammy loves shoes."

Donna nodded. It was clear that Tammy was an impulse
buyer, and she had plenty of money to indulge herself.

By the time they'd made their way through the crowd and up
to the counter, Tammy was already talking to the woman who
ran the booth. She looked as if she'd stepped from the pages of
a storybook as the evil stepmother, or the wicked witch. She was
dressed in black, from her head to her toes, with a skirt so long,
it swept the floor of the tent. There was a heavy black cape
around her shoulders, and the way it flapped around her arms
when she moved reminded Donna of a huge, black crow.

Tammy pointed to the sign on the wall of the tent. "It says
you make your own shoes. Is that true?"

"Yes, young lady." The old woman nodded. "From the finest materials, each pair an original."

"Good. I need a totally gorgeous pair of shoes. I want the best that money can buy, and it's very important that no one else has a pair just like them."

"This is for a special occasion?" The old woman's eyes began to gleam, and Donna was sure she was going to charge a fortune for any pair of shoes that Tammy chose.

"Yes." Tammy brushed back her hair and gave a proud smile. "I have the lead in the fall play, and my shoes have to be spectacular, not like the ordinary ones out here."

"Of course, young lady. Would you like to see my private collection in the back?"

"All right." Tammy grinned. "But I don't have all night, so hurry!"

Donna frowned slightly. Tammy was being quite rude, but the old woman didn't seen to notice. She just led them to the back of the tent and pointed to a shelf where several beautiful pairs of shoes were displayed.

"That's more like it!" Tammy reached out to touch one pair. Even from several feet away, Donna could tell that the shoes were beautifully colored. "These are nice, but I've seen dozens just like them. Don't you have anything really—"

Tammy stopped in mid-sentence and pointed to the shelf where a pair of red shoes was displayed in a glass case. "That's exactly what I mean. Those red shoes are perfect! Take them out so I can try them on!"

"No, young lady." The old woman shook her head. "The red shoes are not for sale. They are for display purposes only."

"That's ridiculous!"

Tammy started to frown, and Donna could tell that she didn't like being denied. The shoes in the display case really were spectacular. They were made of soft, shining satin that was almost luminescent.

"I am sorry, young lady. If you would like to place an order, I can make you a pair of shoes just like them."

"No way!" Tammy's frown deepened. "I need them for opening night next Friday. And I said I want originals, not a copy of something else. Get them down for me. If they fit, I'll buy them. And I'll pay you double the asking price!"

The old woman shook her head again. "No, young lady. I told you before. I cannot sell you the red shoes."

"Why not? I said I'd pay double!"

A crowd was starting to gather, and the old woman pulled them to the side of the tent, where there was a little alcove. "You seem like a very nice girl, and that is why I cannot let you have the red shoes. You see, they are dangerous."

"Dangerous?" Tammy raised her eyebrows. "How could a pair of shoes be dangerous?"

The old woman lowered her voice so that only Tammy and her group could hear. "If you will listen, I will explain. This particular pair of shoes is cursed."

"Cursed?!" Tammy started to giggle. "Well, I don't care if they're cursed or not—I still want them!"

Donna was so curious, she stepped forward and touched the old woman on the arm. When the woman turned to her, she blurted out her question. "Please—could you tell us about the curse?"

The old woman smiled, and Donna stepped back instinctively. It was a chilling smile.

"It's an ancient charm that has survived over the centuries. Any girl who wears the red shoes will be blessed with incredible talent, but there is a terrible price to pay. She will also be cursed with bad luck."

"That sounds good to me!" Tammy laughed so hard, she had to lean on Steve's arm. "I could use some incredible talent for opening night, and I'm certainly not afraid of a silly curse. Now, take those shoes down or I'll talk to the principal and have you removed from the carnival!"

Donna winced. Tammy was really being awful. She moved a little closer and tapped Tammy gently on the arm. "Tammy? Maybe she's right and you shouldn't try on those shoes. What if there *is* a curse?"

"Really, Donna!" Tammy burst into laughter. "You don't actually believe in curses, do you?"

Donna was blushing as she shook her head. "No. Not really. But . . . there could be something about the shoes that might be dangerous."

"I'll take my chances." Tammy turned back to the old woman again. "Well? Are you going to get them down, or not?"

The old woman shrugged. "If you insist. But I have done my duty by warning you."

"Okay, I'm warned." Tammy laughed as the old woman took the red shoes out of the case. It was clear she wasn't one bit worried about the curse. "This is going to be fun! I'll tell everyone that I'm wearing cursed shoes, and it'll be great publicity for the play. People will come from miles around to watch me act!"

When the old woman handed her the shoes, Tammy sat down to try them on. Donna crossed her fingers and hoped that they wouldn't fit, but when Tammy stood up again, she was smiling. "Look! They fit me perfectly!"

"Yes, I knew that they would." The old woman nodded. "But you must promise to be very careful when—"

"How much?" Tammy interrupted what was sure to be another warning.

The old woman frowned. "I do not know. Since the red shoes have never been for sale, I have not put a price on them."

"A hundred dollars." Tammy opened her purse. "That ought to be plenty. So what do you say? Is it a deal?"

The old woman looked as if she was about to refuse, and Tammy spoke up quickly. "Two hundred. That's four times what you're asking for any other pair of shoes. And I'll give you cash!"

Donna tried not to gasp in shock. Two hundred dollars was a fortune to pay for a pair of shoes!

"Let me think for a moment." The old woman stared at Tammy for a few seconds, and then she nodded. "Yes. I can see that you are destined to have the red shoes. I will sell them to you for two hundred dollars."

Tammy pulled out a roll of twenty-dollar bills and began to count out the money. "And then we're all going on the Ferris wheel. I promised the gang we'd meet them there."

Donna took a deep breath for courage, and then she stepped forward. "Tammy? Do you really think you should?"

"Don't be an idiot, Donna!" Tammy gave her a look that would turn a puddle of water into a solid sheet of ice.

"Don't waste your breath." Steve gave Donna a little pat on the shoulder as they walked out of the tent. "Nobody can change Tammy's mind, and she'll just get mad at you if you try. She's been like this ever since her parents got divorced last year."

Donna began to feel a little sorry for Tammy. "That must have been hard for Tammy."

"It was." Steve nodded. "Come on, Donna. We'll get in line for the Ferris wheel and buy the tickets."

As they turned onto the midway and hurried to take their place in the Ferris wheel line, Donna glanced up at Steve. He didn't look very happy for a guy who'd just earned a full football scholarship. Perhaps it was Tammy's reaction to the news. She'd acted as if it wasn't the least bit important to her.

"Steve?" Donna smiled up at him. "Congratulations on your scholarship. I think it's really fantastic!"

"Thanks, Donna. You're going to college, aren't you?"

Donna nodded. "Yes, I'm going to State, too. I just got my letter of acceptance last week."

"Hey! That's great!" Steve gave her a hug, and then he turned his attention to the ticket seller. "I'll take ten, and we'll use two of them right now."

A huge smile spread over Donna's face. Steve was going to take her on the Ferris wheel! The first of her dreams had actually come true.

"Hey, Donna." Steve took her arm. "What do you say we go for a spin while we wait for everybody else to show up?"

Donna nodded. "Sure! The Ferris wheel is my absolute favorite ride!"

The giant wheel stopped, and Steve and Donna got on. A moment later, they were rising up into the night sky.

Donna smiled as they neared the top of the wheel. "I love it up here!"

"So do I. You can see the whole city."

Donna held her breath and wished with all her might. They just had to stop at the top! And another of her wishes came true, because they did!

"King of the Mountain . . . right, Donna?"

"Right!" Donna laughed out loud. She'd seen the neighborhood boys play King of the Mountain when she was a child. They'd rush up a big snowbank and the first one to get to the top would yell out that he was King of the Mountain. Then he'd try to push the other boys back down as they tackled him to become the next king. "I'll bet you were always king."

Steve shook his head. "Not always. Sometimes Jerry would knock me down. It's going to be great if Jerry gets his scholarship. Maybe the three of us can take some of the same classes and study together."

"That's a great idea." Donna smiled happily. But then she remembered Tammy. "What about Tammy? Isn't she going to State, too?"

"Tammy? At State?!" Steve gave a little laugh. "Her father's sending her to some expensive Ivy League college in the East—if he can buy her way in. Tammy's grades aren't very good."

Donna nodded and tried to keep from showing how excited she was. Tammy wouldn't be going to college with Steve. But *she* would!

"Donna?" Steve looked very serious. "It was really nice of you to be so concerned about Tammy . . . especially after the way she treated you."

Donna nodded and kept her lips firmly sealed. Her grandfather always said the best thing to say was nothing at all when you weren't sure how the other person felt.

"Tammy used to be nice until her parents split up. Then they both felt guilty and they tried to buy her off with money. Her mother takes Tammy shopping every time she visits, and she buys Tammy everything she wants. Her father sees all the stuff her mother bought, and he increases Tammy's allowance. It's like a contest. They both want Tammy on their side and they don't realize what they're doing to her. And now Tammy's got the idea that money will buy her anything, even friendship and love."

Donna nodded again. She was impressed with Steve's insight, but she wasn't about to open her mouth for fear she'd say the wrong thing.

"Tammy's really not as awful as she seems. She's just confused. She's hurting and she never thinks about how anyone else feels. I know that's hard for you to understand, Donna. You're such a caring person."

Donna began to blush, and she was glad it was dark. Steve really seemed to like her!

"Anyway," Steve said as he put his arm around Donna's shoulders, "I wish that Tammy could be as nice as you are."

This time Donna knew exactly what to say. She smiled up at Steve, and said quite simply, "Thank you, Steve."

Two

Donna was feeling great when she walked into the Jefferson High cafeteria at noon on Monday. She'd finally decided on a subject for the school newspaper contest. The title of her article was "Curses and Superstitions," and it would be all about Tammy's red shoes. She'd spent most of the weekend making notes, describing the carnival booth and the beautiful red shoes in their glass display case. She'd even written down exactly what the old woman had said about the ancient curse.

"Hi, Donna!"

Lisa Jensen, one of the first girls Donna had met at Jefferson High, waved at her. Donna waved back and walked quickly to Lisa's table. "Save me a spot, will you, Lisa? I'm just going to grab a salad and something to drink."

Lisa nodded. "Okay. I heard you were with Tammy's crowd at the school carnival."

"I was." Donna shrugged. "But I'm not really part of Tammy's crowd. And I'd much rather sit with you."

Lisa smiled and her whole face lit up. She was sitting alone, eating a sandwich she'd brought from home. Lisa always sat alone so she could study at lunch. She was very serious about her grades and she was hoping to get an academic scholarship to State next year.

As Donna went through the line of students waiting for their lunches, she thought about Lisa. Lisa was small and pretty, with long dark hair. Her father drove a tow truck for the city and her mother was a file clerk at night. Lisa worked as a waitress to help out her family, and she never had time to attend any school functions.

Lisa wasn't part of Tammy's crowd. At first Donna thought it was because she was always busy. When Lisa wasn't waiting tables, she was taking care of her younger brothers and sisters. But Donna was wiser now that she'd been at Jefferson High for almost two months. She knew the real reason why Lisa wasn't accepted. Lisa's family had no money. There was no way that Tammy and her friends would invite Lisa to one of their parties.

"Hey, Donna . . ." Jerry tapped her on the shoulder. "I hear you're writing an article about Tammy's red shoes."

"That's right." Donna began to grin. News certainly traveled fast in the halls of Jefferson High! She'd just signed up to write about the red shoes this morning and Jerry already knew about it.

"So where are you sitting?" Jerry picked up his tray and waited for Donna to pay the cashier.

"With Lisa Jensen. She's over there by the windows."

"Okay." Jerry nodded. "Do you think she'd mind if I sit with you? I've seen her around, but I don't know her very well."

Donna began to grin. Jerry was very popular and he wanted to sit with them. That ought to raise some eyebrows!

"Lisa won't mind." Donna picked up her tray and led the way across the crowded cafeteria to Lisa's table. "Lisa? You know Jerry, don't you?"

"Uh—sure!" Lisa looked so surprised, it was almost comical.

"Hey, Lisa." Jerry sat down directly across from her. "You sure blew the top off the curve on the calculus test! I don't know if I should talk to you, or not."

Lisa began to blush. "I—I'm sorry."

"Why?" Jerry grinned at her. "If you've got the brains, flaunt 'em, right?"

"I—I guess so." Lisa still looked very uncertain. "But messing up the curve doesn't get you many friends."

Jerry laughed. "Oh, I don't know about that. You could be

very popular with me if you helped me study for next week's test. How about it, Lisa? Will you?"

"Well—yes. I could do that." Lisa began to smile. "There's only one problem. I work after school."

"Where do you work?" Jerry looked interested.

"I'm a waitress at Shelly's Coffee Shop on Fourth Street. It's right across from the hospital."

"I don't think I've ever been in there." Jerry frowned slightly. "What kind of place is it?"

Lisa laughed. "It's ptomaine central. At least that's what the interns call it. We send them most of their patients."

"Ptomaine? As in ptomaine poisoning?" Jerry cracked up when Lisa nodded. "I was going to say I'd come in for a burger, but I think I'll pass. What time do you get off?"

"Nine. That's when we close. But then I have to go home and baby-sit. My mother works late, and my dad's on call most nights."

"I could come to your house if your parents wouldn't mind. Would that be okay with you, Lisa? I don't want to blow this next test."

Lisa hesitated, and Donna thought she knew why. Lisa had mentioned that her family lived in a small, rented house on the edge of town. She was probably embarrassed and didn't want Jerry to see it.

Jerry leaned across the table. He looked very serious. "Come on, Lisa. Please help me out."

"Well . . . okay." Lisa gave him a shy smile. "I guess we could study tonight, if that's all right with you."

Jerry nodded, and then he stood up to wave at someone who'd just gone through the lunch line. Donna turned and began to blush as she saw that it was Steve.

"Hey, Steve! Over here!" Jerry waved once more and sat down again. And a moment later, Steve came over to their table.

"Hey, Donna . . . Lisa." Steve set down his tray and pulled out a chair. "Any news on your scholarship, Jer?"

Jerry nodded. "I got it—but they weren't exactly thrilled

when they saw how I was doing in calculus. Of course that's going to change now that Lisa's come into my life."

"I'm tutoring him." Lisa was blushing as she explained.

"Great!" Steve gave her a warm grin, and then he turned to Donna. "I beard about your article this morning. It's a really good idea. Everybody's waiting to read it."

Donna frowned slightly. "Everybody except Tammy, right?"

"Wrong." Steve shook his head. "Tammy thinks it'll bring more publicity for the play, and all that stuff."

"But my article's not due until the end of next week and the play opens this Friday."

Steve nodded. "I know. That's why Miss Adams is going to ask you to do a flyer about the cursed shoes. Tammy wants to send some to every school in the county so they'll come to see her in the play."

"Oh." Donna tried not to show how upset she was. Tammy was trying to sabotage her article! Miss Adams would expect Donna to use all the best lines from her article in the flyer. And then, when "Curses and Superstitions" was published in the school paper, the students would have already read part of it.

Steve seemed to know exactly how she was feeling because he reached out to take her hand. "Look, Donna, I know you'll be using some of your best stuff in the flyer, but it could be almost like a serial in a magazine. You know—the first part will come out and everybody'll read it. And then they'll be holding their breath, waiting for the next part."

Donna nodded. What Steve said was true. Perhaps she could turn Tammy's dirty trick to her advantage.

Just then, there was a sharp rise in the noise level. It seemed like everyone in the cafeteria was talking at once. Donna turned toward the door to see what was happening, and she saw Tammy coming in with a group of her friends.

"Attention everyone!" Tammy clapped her hands and the talking died down to a whisper. She walked to the front of the room and stood there, smiling. And then she reached into her large leather purse and pulled out the pair of red shoes.

"I thought you'd all like to see these. They're genuine cursed shoes and I bought them at the school carnival. Some of you probably saw the tent made out of carpets. It had a sign that said Magical Footwear."

Most of the students nodded. Everyone had noticed the unusual booth.

"Remember the old woman who ran the booth? She was dressed all in black and she looked like a witch. She swore up and down that these were cursed shoes! I'll be wearing them in the fall play, so I want all of you to come on opening night."

There was a round of applause. Tammy had certainly gotten their attention.

"So what's the curse?" Somebody called out the question, but Donna couldn't see who it was.

"It goes like this . . ." Tammy lowered her voice and it was so silent in the cafeteria, you could hear the sound of the motor on the soft drink machine. "Any girl who wears these red shoes will be blessed with incredible talent. But there's a terrible price to pay. She'll be cursed with bad luck! So come to the play to see if I'm blessed with incredible talent."

There were whistles from several tables, and then someone called out. "Right. And then we can watch you have bad luck!"

Donna turned to see who'd spoken, but there was such a crowd in the cafeteria, she couldn't tell. And then Tammy held up her hands for silence again.

"The new girl is writing a flyer for me."

Donna was so surprised her mouth almost fell open. She wasn't writing a flyer for Tammy. She was writing an entry for the school newspaper contest! But Tammy went right on speaking.

"It's going to be all about my cursed shoes, so watch for it on the table outside the *Gazette* office. I want you to help me put it up in every shop window in Jefferson City. Let's make this the best fall play we've ever had!"

Some of the students who were in the play started to cheer, and Donna sighed. Tammy really was an incredible ham. And then Tammy picked up her red shoes, stuffed them inside her purse, and headed straight for Donna's table!

"The queen cometh." Jerry glanced at Steve. "And she does not look pleased."

When Tammy arrived at Donna's side, she smiled. To everyone else it might have looked like a friendly smile, but Donna saw the dangerous glitter in her eyes. "Donna—I do hope you'll get started on that flyer right away. As you can see, I've just recruited everyone to help pass them out."

Donna nodded. What else could she do? "So you're really going to wear the red shoes in the play?"

"Of course. I said I would, didn't I? And don't start in about that silly curse! Just remember—if I don't wear the shoes, you won't be able to write your entry for the contest!"

Donna's sense of duty made her speak up. "My entry doesn't matter, Tammy. Just be very careful."

"Oh, sure." Tammy waved Donna's concern away. It was clear she wasn't worried about the curse. And then she turned to Steve. "You're not going to give me any grief about the shoes, are you?"

There was a definite challenge in Tammy's voice, but Steve just smiled. "No way, Tammy. I know how stubborn you can be."

"Well, maybe sometimes." Tammy giggled. "But that's only because I'm always right. Let's go now, Stevie. I'm not eating lunch."

But Steve shook his head. "Sorry, Tammy. I *am* eating lunch and I'm not through yet. I'll catch up with you in class."

The moment Tammy had left, Lisa turned to Donna. "Do you really believe in that curse?"

"Not really. But my grandfather used to have a saying about not tempting fate, and I can't help thinking that's what Tammy is doing."

"You don't have to worry about Tammy." Jerry gave a little laugh. "She's too stubborn to let a little thing like a curse get to her."

Lisa nodded. "And that story about the curse can't be true. The old woman probably made it up so she could sell the shoes for more money. It's really a very clever sales gimmick."

"Wasn't there a story about red shoes?" Steve looked thoughtful. "Something about a dancer who wore them and danced herself to death?"

Jerry snapped his fingers. "You're right! I remember reading it when I was a kid. But Tammy's not going to dance in the play, so we don't have anything to worry about . . . right, Donna?"

"Right." Donna nodded, but she knew that she *did* have something to worry about. It had absolutely nothing to do with the curse of the red shoes, but it was still very dangerous. She'd seen how angry Tammy had been when Steve had refused to leave with her. And if Donna had read the look in Tammy's eyes correctly, she'd just made one nasty enemy!

Three

It was six-thirty on Friday night and Donna was in her room getting dressed for the fall play. Tonight was opening night, and they were sold out. Her flyer had been a huge success and several of the surrounding schools had called to order blocks of tickets.

In previous years, the ushers had worn white blouses and dark skirts, but this year the policy had changed. Tammy had suggested that the ushers dress up in formal clothes to add a touch of elegance to their production. But Tammy had made her suggestion this morning, and that left Donna in big trouble.

Donna didn't have any formal dresses. Most of her clothes were school clothes and they were much too casual. Her best dress, a light blue silk that she wore for special occasions, was at the cleaners. It was too late to buy something new, and Donna frowned as she examined the contents of her closet. There had to be something she could wear . . . but what?

She did have a black velvet jacket that she'd made last year, for the Christmas concert. Everyone in the chorus had worn black velvet jackets, but that had been at her former school, and no one at Jefferson High would know that it had been part of a chorus uniform. With a pair of black slacks and a white silk blouse, the velvet jacket might be perfect.

Donna dressed quickly, and stood in front of the mirror. She was supposed to look elegant, but her outfit was much too plain. She needed some accessories to dress it up, and there was a whole box full of costume jewelry in her great-grandmother's trunk.

The wooden trunk was under her window with cushions on top to make a window seat. Donna took off the cushions, lifted the lid, and took out the antique jewelry box. Great-grandmother Anna must have been very fond of pins because there were dozens of brooches inside. Perhaps she could attach them to her jacket and make her own design. With all the glittering, multicolored stones, her jacket might pass for elegant.

Donna took off her velvet jacket and hung it on the back of a chair. She was smiling as she pinned on a butterfly made of green and blue stones. A heart with fake rubies was next, and then a cat made of rhinestones with yellow eyes. There was a turtle made of pearls, a horseshoe with double rows of purple stones, and a large daisy with pink glittering petals. Donna covered the front and the back of the jacket with pins of every shape and color. Then she slipped it on and stood in front of her mirror again.

It was perfect! Donna smiled at her image in the mirror. And it was also an original. No one else had a jacket like hers.

A love song was playing softly on the radio, and Donna sighed as she sat down at the dressing table to fix her hair. Steve and Tammy were still going together, but the rumors were flying fast and furious. They weren't about Steve and Donna. Donna hadn't seen him since their lunch on Monday. The rumors were about Tammy, and how she'd be bound to ditch Steve if she made it to instant stardom.

Tammy had announced in the cafeteria on Wednesday that the curse was working. She'd been wearing the red shoes to rehearsal and her acting had really improved. She reminded everyone that Keith Michaels, Jefferson High's most famous graduate, was coming to the play on opening night.

Lisa had leaned close to whisper in Donna's ear. Keith Michaels was a director in Hollywood, and he always attended their fall play. He'd be in town anyway, for his mother's birthday, and he did it as a favor to their drama teacher, Mr. Carlson.

But Tammy's next announcement had shocked even Lisa. Tammy had told them that if Keith Michaels was impressed with her, he'd promised her a part in his next movie!

At first, no one had believed Tammy. Keith Michaels had never offered any Jefferson High student a part in one of his movies before. But Mr. Carlson had confirmed Tammy's story. Keith Michaels was casting a teenage actress, and Tammy would be auditioning for him on opening night.

The whole school had been buzzing about Tammy's good fortune, and that worried Donna. She'd seen Tammy in rehearsal, and Tammy hadn't been that good. What had changed her? And how could such a change happen overnight? Did it mean that the curse of the red shoes was true?

The wind was blowing as Donna walked down the street and turned the corner toward the school. It was a cold, bitter wind and there was a sense of evil in the air as it kicked up the dry leaves and rustled them across the sidewalk like scurrying demons. The clouds were low, whisking across the full moon like ghosts.

After her cold, solitary walk, it was a relief to step into the heated lobby of the theater. Donna hung her coat on a hook behind the concession stand, and took a deep breath of warm air. The smell of the theater was a pleasant change from the dank, foggy air outside. Donna was glad that she was here, behind closed doors, where the wailing wind was only a whisper and the bright lights chased away the shadows.

It was a perfect night for a curse. Donna shivered slightly, even though the lobby was almost too warm. Her grandfather had always said not to borrow trouble, and that was exactly what she was doing. Instead of thinking about all the dire and horrible things that could happen, Donna took out the packages of cookies the home economics classes had made and began to arrange them on a tray. They were selling punch and cookies at intermission, and she was in charge of the concession stand.

There was a faint burst of laughter from backstage, and Donna could imagine the cast of the play putting on their makeup before lighted mirrors and checking their lines one last time. The boys had one large dressing room, and the girls had another. Of course Tammy wouldn't be in the dressing room with the other girls. Since she had the lead, Tammy was entitled to use the private dressing room with the gold-painted star on the door.

How did Tammy feel about the curse? Was she getting a little nervous, now that opening night had arrived? Donna doubted it. She suspected that Tammy wasn't even giving the curse a second thought. If Tammy was nervous at all, it was about impressing Mr. Michaels and getting a part in his movie.

The play was scheduled to start at eight-thirty and people began to trickle in around eight. There was a flurry of activity at eight twenty-five. Mr. Michaels and Mr. Carlson took their seats at eight-forty, and then the curtain, predictably late, rose at eight-forty-five.

Donna slipped into her seat in the darkness. She shut her eyes, and wished with all her might that nothing bad would happen to spoil the performance. Then she opened her eyes to watch as the lights began to come up on the set.

"You really look great tonight, Donna," someone whispered in her ear. She turned, and then smiled as she realized that Steve was sitting next to her. "Hi, Steve. I thought you'd be in the front row."

Steve didn't say anything. He just shook his head, and that made Donna wonder. She'd heard that, traditionally, at Jefferson High, girlfriends and boyfriends of the cast watched the opening night performance from the front row. Did Tammy know that Steve wasn't there? And would she see him sitting in the back row with Donna?

A doorbell sounded on stage, and Donna turned her attention to the play. There was a moment of silence, and then it rang again.

"Who's there?" It was Tammy's voice and Donna's eyes widened. She was much better than she'd been in rehearsal! Tammy was supposed to sound as if she'd awakened from a sound sleep, and she actually did!

Tammy gave a very realistic groan, and then she began to sit up from the couch. Since the audience could only see the couch from the back, this was a very funny scene. Tammy had never managed to get it right in any of the rehearsals that Donna had seen, but tonight she was perfect. First one arm came up, and then the other. They weaved slightly, as if it was too much effort to lift them, and then Tammy's right arm threatened to slide back down again. Her left arm caught it, pulled it back up, and then the back of Tammy's head appeared. She turned very slowly so the audience could see her face, stared at the door with an expression of pure disgust, and then flopped back down on the couch again. "I don't care who it is. Go away!"

The audience reacted with a swell of laughter, and Donna turned to whisper to Steve. "Tammy's really good tonight!"

"I know." Steve whispered back.

"Maybe I'm crazy, but it makes me worry about the curse."

"I'm a little worried, too." Steve nodded.

"I've watched a couple of rehearsals and Tammy's never been *this* good before!"

As the play went on, both Steve and Donna were spellbound. Tammy had turned into a fantastic actress. Every line was perfect, every gesture was flawless. It was really a commanding performance. When the curtain went down and the lights came up for intermission, there was a thunderous round of applause.

Donna glanced at Mr. Michaels, and then she turned to Steve. "I think Tammy impressed Mr. Michaels. He's still applauding."

"She'll get the part in his movie. And she deserves it. She really *was* great."

"I'll see you later." Donna got up from her seat. "I have to run the concession stand."

"I'll help you." Steve stood up, too.

"But don't you want to go backstage to congratulate Tammy?"

Steve shook his head. "Tammy can't see anyone between acts. Mr. Carlson said that her dressing room is off-limits. He wants Tammy to stay in character."

"Oh." Donna lifted the shelf to duck behind the concession

stand, and Steve took his place beside her. A line had already started to form, and Donna was so busy serving customers, she didn't have time to ask the question that was burning in her mind. Was Steve sitting with her because Tammy didn't want him in the front row? Or was it just another one of Mr. Carlson's rules to keep Tammy in character?

Tammy leaned back in her chair and propped her feet on the dressing table. She knew she was doing a fantastic job and she was sure she'd get the part in Mr. Michaels' movie. She wiggled her toes and grinned as her shoes caught the light. Their brilliant shade of deep red reminded her of rubies. Perhaps she had the charmed ruby slippers that Dorothy had worn in *The Wizard of Oz*.

The thought was so funny, Tammy laughed out loud. She didn't believe in magic, or charms, or curses. But she did believe in good luck, and her luck was fantastic tonight. The first act had gone perfectly, even better than her wildest hopes. She hadn't blown a single line and the audience had adored her. When she'd looked at Mr. Michaels, right before the curtain had fallen, he'd been smiling and clapping right along with the rest of the audience. And then Mr. Carlson had raised his hand and made a little circle with his thumb and forefinger. It must mean that Mr. Michaels had liked her.

She'd seen Steve, sitting in the back row with Donna. Tammy couldn't understand what Steve saw in her. Of course, that was none of her business now. She couldn't care less who Steve dated.

Right before the play had started, Tammy had broken up with Steve. Now that she was going to be an actress, she needed to be seen with someone more important, someone rich and famous. There was no way Tammy wanted to be linked romantically with a small town, high school football player like Steve!

It was time to get ready for the second act. Tammy glanced down at her red shoes and her eyes widened in surprise. She'd planned to take them off for the second half of the play. She'd been sure that they'd clash with her costume, but the beautiful ruby red color had darkened to a shade of bronze that exactly matched the dress she was wearing.

How strange! And how wonderful! Tammy's face lit up in a smile. She didn't actually believe that the red shoes had helped her acting, but now there was no need to take any chances. She'd wear them, just in case.

Tammy checked her makeup. She was ready, and she could hardly wait for the next act. But when she tried to open her dressing room door, it wouldn't budge. The knob turned and the latch clicked, but the door simply wouldn't open.

"Oh, great!" Tammy glared at the door. When she didn't appear backstage, someone would be sure to come. But Tammy didn't want to wait to be rescued by one of the stagehands.

Luckily, the door opened out. It was against fire regulations, but the maintenance man hadn't gotten around to fixing it. Tammy put both hands on the door and shoved, but nothing happened. It really *was* stuck, and that made Tammy so angry, she kicked it.

That was when something totally unexpected and awful happened. Although Tammy didn't kick that hard, her red shoe connected with the door with incredible force. There was a loud snapping sound, and for the briefest of moments, Tammy was puzzled. Then she felt a rush of blinding pain, and she started to scream.

Tammy fell to the floor, writhing in agony. Her leg was broken! Her last thought, before she lost consciousness, was about the red shoes. She should have believed the old woman. And she should have listened to Donna's warnings. The red shoes really *were* cursed and this was her bad luck!

There wasn't time to talk during the fifteen-minute intermission. The concession stand was swamped with people, and Donna and Steve served punch and cookies until they'd sold out. They'd just finished wiping the counter when the lights flickered for the start of the second act.

"Let's go." Steve lifted the shelf and held it up so Donna could step through to the lobby. "If we hurry, we won't miss any of the second act."

But there was no need to hurry. Donna and Steve sat in the darkened theater for a full five minutes and the curtain still hadn't risen. And then Donna heard it, the wail of a siren in the distance, coming closer and closer to the school.

Donna didn't think. She just reached out to take Steve's hand. "Oh, no! I hope nothing bad has happened!"

There was a low murmur in the audience that grew louder and louder as people began to talk about the delay and the siren they'd heard. By the time the murmuring had grown to a loud buzz of excited voices, Mr. Carlson walked out on the stage.

"Please bear with us." Mr. Carlson's voice was shaking slightly. "There's been an accident backstage. Our star, Tammy Peters, has broken her leg."

There was another murmur from the audience, and Donna exchanged worried looks with Steve. What had happened? And exactly *how* had Tammy broken her leg?

Mr. Carlson held up his hands for silence. "If you'll give us five minutes, our production will continue. Miss Rondelle Green, Tammy's understudy, will play the lead."

There was a smattering of polite applause and Mr. Carlson left the stage. The loudspeakers began to play some soothing classical music, and Steve pulled Donna to her feet. "Let's go, Donna. We've got to find out what happened!"

As they rounded the corner of the school, they saw the flashing red lights of the ambulance. It was just backing away, and Steve ran to catch it.

"What hospital?" Donna heard him shout. And then he ran back to her side again. "They're taking her to County General. Come on. My car's this way."

As she ran to keep up with Steve's long strides, Donna felt her heart pounding hard. It wasn't from the exertion. Donna's heart was pounding in fear. They had to get the red shoes away from Tammy before something even more horrible happened!

Four

Steve drove directly to the hospital, but they arrived too late to see Tammy. Her doctor told them that she was being taken to a private hospital, several hundred miles away.

"Will she be all right?" Steve looked worried.

"Yes. She's in stable condition and her vital signs are good." The doctor gave Steve a comforting pat on the shoulder. "But we took an X ray and several bones in Tammy's leg are shattered. It's the worst break I've seen in a long time, and we're not equipped to handle it here. They're going to have to do a series of complicated surgeries to repair the bones before she can walk normally again."

Donna felt terribly sorry for Tammy. "How long will Tammy have to stay in the hospital?"

"It'll be quite a while. I talked to the head surgeon by telephone. After the surgeries, she'll need several months of physical therapy. They're going to have to teach her to walk, all over again."

"But will Tammy be able to graduate with us?" Steve started to frown.

"I wouldn't count on that. But the surgeon said that they have tutors on the staff. Tammy can keep up with her studies and they'll have her ready for college in the fall."

Donna took a deep breath. She wasn't sure how to ask, but they had to know. "Did Tammy take her shoes with her?"

"Shoes?" The doctor looked completely puzzled.

Steve nodded. "They were red, and she wore them in the play."

"I see." The doctor smiled. "They were part of her costume and you're here to collect them?"

"That's right." Donna nodded. She was glad she didn't have to explain about Magical Footwear and the curse of the red shoes.

"Tammy wasn't wearing any shoes when I examined her, but you can check with the paramedics at the emergency room. They may have removed them."

It took several minutes to find the team of paramedics who'd brought Tammy to the hospital. The driver didn't remember the shoes at all, but his partner did.

"She was wearing shoes. I think they were orange, or red."

Steve nodded. "That's right. They were part of her costume for the play."

"I removed them when we put her on the stretcher. There's a lot of swelling with leg injuries and it's a standard precaution."

"A precaution?" Steve looked puzzled.

"If the shoes were too tight, we'd have to cut them off. It's easier and safer to remove them before the swelling starts."

"What did you do with them?" Donna held her breath and hoped that he remembered.

"I put them on the table in her dressing room. They're probably still there."

"Thank you." Donna grabbed Steve's hand and pulled him toward the door. "Let's go, Steve. We've got to find the red shoes before someone else decides to wear them!"

Rondelle Green was so happy she felt like she was floating on a cloud of pure joy. She'd never thought she'd get to play the lead in the fall play, but thanks to Tammy's broken leg, she'd just received a standing ovation. It had been a night of incredibly good luck for her. Rondelle had finally gotten a chance to show what a good actress she was.

Tammy's red shoes were still on the dressing table where the paramedics had left them. Rondelle smiled as she reached out to stroke the satin. She was sure the shoes weren't cursed, and they certainly weren't to blame for Tammy's accident. If anything was to blame, it was Tammy's almost legendary temper.

Mr. Carlson had told them all what had happened. The dressing room door had stuck, and Tammy had been so angry, she'd kicked it. But Tammy had kicked much too hard. She'd hit the door with so much force, she'd shattered the bones in her leg.

The red shoes were beautiful. When Rondelle picked them up, they felt warm, almost as if they were alive. Rondelle giggled. Of course she was imagining things, but she just couldn't resist trying them on.

She slipped on one shoe and then the other. They seemed to fit her perfectly. She was just admiring the way they looked, when there was a knock on her dressing room door.

Rondelle frowned. It was probably her best friend, Alice Mayfield, coming to congratulate her on her performance. Alice loved to gossip, and Rondelle didn't want to be accused of wearing Tammy's shoes without her permission. She slid her feet under the dressing table, where they couldn't be seen, and put a smile on her face. "Come in."

But when the door opened, it wasn't Alice. It was Mr. Carlson and Mr. Michaels. Both of them were smiling and Rondelle smiled back. "Did I do all right, Mr. Carlson?"

"You did a fine job, Rondelle."

"Wonderful!" Mr. Michaels nodded. "It takes a real trouper to come in at a moment's notice and take over someone else's part."

Rondelle blushed. She'd just received a compliment from Mr. Michaels!

"Would you like to read for me, Rondelle?" Mr. Michaels looked very serious. "I may have a small part in my movie for you."

Rondelle was so shocked, her mouth dropped open. Everyone had thought that Mr. Michaels would offer Tammy a part, but now he was interested in her!

"It won't take long." Mr. Michaels smiled at her kindly as he handed her several pages from a script. "And there's no reason to be nervous. You'll be reading for the part of Betsy. She's a bubbly, energetic high school student, the younger sister of the lead. Just take a few moments to go over your lines and I'll cue you."

Rondelle's hands were shaking as she read over the lines. Mr. Michaels had said there was no need to be nervous, but he didn't know how important this was. She simply had to get the part! It was the chance of a lifetime!

"Ready?"

Rondelle nodded, even though she'd never been good at cold readings. She took a deep breath, prayed that her voice wouldn't shake, and then she read her first line.

The next five minutes were a blur. Mr. Michaels cued her, and Rondelle delivered her lines. Even to Rondelle's critical ears, the reading went very well. Her voice was clear, her gestures were perfect, and she seemed to sense exactly what emotion Mr. Michaels wanted her to portray. When they were finished, Rondelle stood there in the middle of the dressing room, waiting to hear what Mr. Michaels would say.

"Didn't I tell you she was good?" Mr. Carlson looked very proud.

"You were right." Mr. Michaels smiled as he turned to Rondelle. "Well, Rondelle . . . you're a very talented young lady, and you have the part. I'll be contacting you when I come back in December."

"Thank you, Mr. Michaels." Rondelle was so excited, she wanted to hug him. "I'll do my best, I promise."

Mr. Michaels smiled. "I'm sure you will. I'll call your parents in the next week or so and we'll work out the details of your contract."

Rondelle managed to contain herself until Mr. Michaels and Mr. Carlson had left. Then she hugged herself and twirled around, beside herself with joy. Mr. Michaels had said she was talented, and he'd given her a part in a major movie!

As she twirled around, Rondelle caught a glimpse of the red shoes. They seemed to glow from the overhead lights, and she began to frown slightly. She knew she'd read much better than usual. Had the red shoes given her new talent?

Rondelle had seen the flyer the new girl had written. Anyone who wore the red shoes would be blessed with incredible talent, but there was a terrible price to pay. She would also have very bad luck.

"Oh, sure!" Rondelle laughed. Mr. Michaels had been impressed with her performance in the play, and she hadn't worn the red shoes on stage. They had nothing to do with the part he'd given her in his movie, nothing at all.

But the red shoes were very pretty, and wearing them made her feel special. Rondelle didn't want to leave them here, where the janitor would probably throw them away. What was to stop her from keeping them? Tammy couldn't use them in the hospital and Mr. Carlson had said it would be months before she could walk again. There was really no reason why Rondelle shouldn't have them as a souvenir of this wonderful night. Of course, she wouldn't tell anyone that she had them. She didn't want to be accused of stealing Tammy's expensive shoes. She'd just take them home to wear in the privacy of her room, and no one would ever know.

"There's a light inside. Somebody must be here." Steve hammered on the theater door again.

"It's Mr. Parks." Donna peered through the glass. "He heard you, Steve. He's coming."

The janitor grumbled as he unlocked the door, but when he saw Donna, he smiled. Most of the students didn't even bother to talk to him, but Donna always said hello.

"Hi, Donna. Did you forget something?"

"Yes, Mr. Parks. Is it all right if we go backstage? It'll just take us a minute."

"Sure, go ahead." The janitor turned to Steve. Steve was another friendly student, and he'd watched a couple of football games. "How's your girlfriend? I heard they took her to the hospital."

Steve nodded. "Tammy shattered the bones in her leg. She's going to be all right, but she won't be coming back to school this year. And she's not my girlfriend, Mr. Parks. We broke up before the play tonight."

Donna drew in her breath sharply. That was news to her!

Mr. Parks looked just as shocked as Donna, but he recovered quickly. "Well, Steve . . . I'm sorry Tammy got hurt, but I'm not sorry you two broke up. What you need is a girl like Donna. She's perfect."

"You're right." Steve turned to wink at Donna. "Donna is perfect."

Somehow, Donna managed to wink back. She knew that Mr. Parks had been teasing, but it was still a little embarrassing. As they walked past the silent rows of seats, Donna's mind was whirling with unasked questions. Had Steve been the one to break up with Tammy? Or had Tammy broken off with him? And was he simply being polite, or did he really think that she was the perfect girl for him?

It didn't take Donna long to write another page for her article. She described Tammy's awful accident and then she put down her pen. They'd gone to the star's dressing room to search for the red shoes, but they hadn't been on the dressing table where the paramedic had said he'd placed them. Donna and Steve had looked in every nook and cranny of the dressing room, but the shoes were nowhere to be seen. It was as if they'd disappeared into thin air.

Steve had suggested that Rondelle might have them since she'd used the dressing room after Tammy. They'd gone to the wrap party to talk to her, but Rondelle had told them she hadn't seen the red shoes.

Something about the way Rondelle had avoided their eyes made Donna doubt her word. The pretty redhead had been very nervous, and that could have been a sign of guilt. But when they'd checked, they'd found out that Rondelle had worn her own shoes in the play. The red shoes had vanished, and no one at the wrap party had known where they were.

Donna closed her notebook and rubbed her eyes. It was almost midnight and it had been a long day. She switched off the lights, got into bed, and stared up into the darkness. What was Steve doing right now? Was he in his bed, staring up at the darkness, just like her?

She reached out and pulled up the shade just a bit, so she could see Steve's window. It was dark and that told her nothing. He could be sleeping. It was after midnight and he had football practice every Saturday morning. Or perhaps he'd gone out again, after he'd dropped her off at home.

Even though the night air was cold, Donna raised her window a couple of inches. Then she got back in bed and fell asleep, wondering if the cursed red shoes were out there somewhere, preparing to claim their second victim.

Five

The house was dark when Rondelle got home, and she took off her shoes to tiptoe up the stairs. When she'd told her parents about Mr. Michaels and the part she'd landed in his movie, they'd given her permission to stay late at the wrap party.

Rondelle grinned as she walked past her parents' bedroom. Her father was snoring loudly. Dad wouldn't try any of the special pillows or the mouthpiece that was supposed to help him stop snoring. And even though Rondelle and her sister had tape-recorded his snores one night, he still claimed he didn't snore!

Her father's snoring was one of the reasons Rondelle closed her bedroom door. Who could sleep through all those deep, irregular snorts and rumbles? Rondelle's little sister, Janie, was the second reason why Rondelle closed her door. Janie was a snoop and she loved to go through Rondelle's things. There was no privacy with a little sister like Janie, and even though Rondelle had begged her parents to put a lock on her bedroom door, they'd just told her to be patient until Janie grew out of it

At least she wouldn't have to worry about her privacy tomorrow. Rondelle smiled happily. Her parents and Janie were going away, to visit her aunt and uncle. Since Aunt Pat and Uncle Roy lived four hours away, they were leaving early on Saturday

morning. And they weren't coming back until Sunday afternoon!

For the first time in her life, Rondelle had convinced her parents that she could be trusted to stay by herself overnight. Of
course she'd obey *most* of their rules. She'd be on restriction
until she was an old lady if she didn't. She wouldn't have boys in
the house, she'd do all her homework before they got back on
Sunday, and she'd clean her room while they were gone. But
there was one rule that Rondelle planned to break. She had a
date with Craig Ellison tomorrow night and she was going to
stay until the party was over, even if it lasted all night!

Rondelle was excited about her date with Craig. He was incredibly handsome, and he drove a fire-engine red 1955 Thunderbird.
His father had completely restored it and put it up on blocks the
day Craig was born, and he'd given it to Craig on the first day of
his senior year.

Her luck had been absolutely fantastic tonight! Rondelle
flicked on her stereo and smiled when her favorite song came
on. She'd been wanting to date Craig since junior high, and
tonight he'd asked her to be his date for the party.

Rondelle tossed her clothes on a chair, and got ready for bed.
She was just turning back the covers when she remembered the
red shoes. Steve and that new girl Donna had asked about them
at the wrap party, and she'd lied and said she hadn't seen them.
No one could know that she had them, and that meant she didn't
dare leave them in her room. Even if she hid them under the mat-
tress or high on the closet shelf, Janie would be bound to find
them. She had to think of a hiding place that her little sister
would never discover.

The attic. The moment she thought of it, Rondelle grabbed
the flashlight she kept by her bed. She didn't like the idea of
going up to the attic at night, but it couldn't be helped. Janie
hated the attic and she never went up there. She said it gave her
the creeps. It also gave Rondelle the creeps, but it was the one
place her sister wouldn't snoop.

Rondelle wrapped the red shoes in her oldest sweatshirt, and tiptoed up the stairs. Her flashlight didn't shed much light, but she knew exactly where to hide them. There was a freestanding, antique wooden closet against the back wall, and it was the one place her little sister would never dare to look. Janie was terrified of the old-fashioned wardrobe.

Rondelle moved a moth-eaten fur coat, and hid the red shoes in the very back. Even if her sister outgrew her fear of the attic, she'd never find them there. The red shoes were her secret. No one would ever find them in the back of the wardrobe. And no one would ever know that she'd lied about taking them.

Her alarm clock rang at seven o'clock, and Rondelle almost shut it off and went back to sleep. But the moment she remembered what day it was, she jumped out of bed with a smile on her face. Janie and her parents were leaving. It wouldn't look right if she didn't get up to say good-bye.

It took ages for them to get ready to leave. Rondelle stifled a yawn as her father rechecked the map. She helped her mother make sandwiches to take along on the trip, answered Janie's questions about what she was going to do while they were gone, and helped them carry their luggage to the car.

"Okay. Let's hit the road." Rondelle's father smiled and gave her a hug. There were hugs and kisses all around, along with last-minute instructions for Rondelle, and then they drove away.

Rondelle sat down on the front porch swing and waited five minutes, just to be sure. Then she went inside and locked the door. She was free! And now she could do anything she wanted!

She wandered around the house for a few minutes, exploring her options. But there wasn't really anything that Rondelle wanted to do. The house seemed strange with everyone gone. She'd never noticed the way the floorboards creaked, or how the furnace boomed when the heat kicked in. It wasn't exactly frightening. After all, it was morning and the sun was shining brightly. But it was strange to be in the silent house all alone.

Rondelle checked the front door again, to make sure it was locked, and then she climbed the steps to her room. She hadn't bothered to make her bed and the rumpled blankets looked very inviting. Perhaps she'd stretch out for a minute and close her eyes. She hadn't had much sleep last night.

What if Craig called and she was asleep? Rondelle frowned slightly, but her phone was right next to her bed and she was sure she'd wake up if it rang. She'd just catch a quick nap so she'd have plenty of energy to be the life of the party tonight.

It was two-thirty in the afternoon when Rondelle woke up, and Craig hadn't called. He'd probably gone out to the lake to make last minute preparations, and he'd call when he got back to town.

Rondelle smiled in anticipation. The Ellisons' cabin was a perfect place to hold a party. There was a huge stone fireplace and a massive family room that was great for dancing. Rondelle could hardly wait. Craig's party was always the biggest event of the year—everyone in school was always invited.

But what if her parents found out she'd gone without asking permission? She knew she was taking a chance, but she really didn't think they'd call the house to check on her. Even if they did, she could always make up some kind of excuse.

As the minutes ticked by and the phone didn't ring, Rondelle decided to start getting ready. She had a slinky red dress that she'd bought last year on sale and she'd never worn it before.

Rondelle slipped on the dress and glanced in the mirror. She looked great! The dress clung to her like a second skin and Craig was bound to be impressed. This might be her first date with him, but Rondelle was sure it wouldn't be her last. She'd take her red leather shoulder bag, it would match the dress perfectly, but which pair of shoes should she wear?

Rondelle tried on every pair of shoes in her closet, but nothing looked right with the red dress. She even raided her mother's closet, but she didn't find anything she could use. That was when she remembered the red shoes. Could she get away with wearing them? They weren't really that unusual, and she could always say that she'd bought them at the mall.

The afternoon sun was beginning to dim as Rondelle raced up the stairs to the attic. Since there were only two high narrow vents at either side of the attic to let in air and light, it was already quite dark. Rondelle shivered as she stepped carefully across the loose boards. She'd never been afraid of the attic before, but today she felt uneasy.

"There's absolutely nothing up here to hurt you." Rondelle spoke out loud. And then she gave an embarrassed laugh because she'd been talking to herself. Perhaps she'd done it because she was all alone. Their neighbor, a widower in his eighties, talked to himself all the time. When she walked by his house and his windows were open, Rondelle could hear him carrying on imaginary conversations with the pictures he'd hung on the walls.

As she stepped further into the attic, Rondelle shivered. The wind whistled through the vents, and since the attic wasn't heated, it was cold! As she stood in front of the wardrobe, Rondelle could almost understand why Janie was so afraid. Its claw feet looked real in the dim light, and the carvings of leaves and branches on the doors seemed to reach out to try to grab her!

"It's just my imagination." Rondelle spoke out loud again. She reached inside, and then she almost screamed as her fingers brushed a spiderweb. Just what she needed! Now she'd have to take another shower before Craig came to pick her up!

The red shoes were right where she'd left them, tucked in the very back of the wardrobe. Rondelle unwrapped them and sat down on an old steamer trunk to try them on. They were very comfortable, almost as if they'd been made especially for her, and she stood up and twirled, careful not to bump into any of the old furniture. The red shoes were perfect! She could dance in them all night.

There was an old oval mirror against the wall, and Rondelle checked her reflection. Her image was wavy and covered with cobwebs, but she could see that the red shoes matched her dress.

"Great!" Rondelle clapped her hands in delight But just as she'd turned to head for the door, she heard a sound like gunshot.

"What was that?!" Rondelle whirled around and frowned as she realized what had happened. The old oval mirror had cracked in half, from the top to the very bottom. Could it have been the change in temperature? It had been warm and sunny today, but now that night was falling, it was turning very cold.

Rondelle shrugged. It didn't really matter. The mirror was so old, the silver was peeling away from the glass, and the wooden stand was broken. If her mother decided to use it downstairs, she'd have to get it repaired anyway. But there was something strange about the mirror, something that drew Rondelle closer to peer directly into its depths.

On the right side of the crack, her image was beautiful, just the way it had been before. But on the left, where the silver was starting to peel away, she looked like something out of a nightmare.

"Nooooo!" Rondelle's voice was a terrified whisper as she stared at her gruesome reflection. Her left leg looked broken, as if someone had chopped it with an axe. The bone actually seemed to be sticking up through her pale, gray-colored skin. Her left arm was wrenched from its socket, hanging uselessly at her side, and the fingers on her left hand looked like claws with long yellow fingernails curling in to scratch at her palms.

Rondelle blinked, trying to banish the awful sight. But when she looked in the mirror again, nothing had changed. On the left side of the mirror, her dress was tattered, with bits of soil clinging to its folds. She looked as if she'd been exhumed from a grave!

Rondelle swallowed hard and tried not to panic. The light was dim. She was imagining things. But she screamed a scream of pure unadulterated terror as she caught sight of her face!

In the left side of the mirror, her flesh hung loosely from her skull and bits of shiny white bone were visible. Her eye was gone and a hollow socket was in its place. On the left side, her lips were swollen and purple, grinning around broken and jagged teeth.

As Rondelle stood there, paralyzed with terror, a cold gust of wind blew through the attic. It smelled of decay, a sickeningly sweet, putrid odor that made Rondelle gag and start to cough. She wrenched her eyes away from the awful sight, and forced her feet to move. One step. Two steps. And then she was running to the attic door, tripping and stumbling in her haste to escape the awful apparition she'd seen.

She was only a few steps from the door when there was another burst of wind. It was cold and bitter, and it whipped Rondelle's hair into her eyes. She staggered to a stop, blinded by the stinging pain. Then came a loud bang that made Rondelle jump in fear, and the attic door flew shut.

Rondelle raced for the door. She had to get out of there! Her hands were shaking as she grabbed the knob and twisted hard. But as Rondelle pulled on the knob, desperately trying to escape, it came off in her hand!

Frantically, Rondelle tried to reattach it. She knew how. The doorknob in her bedroom was the same type, and it came off every month or so. But in her haste to get out of the attic, Rondelle pushed the knob back in place much too hard.

There was a hollow thump from the other side of the door, and Rondelle cried out in dismay. The outside knob had fallen to the floor of the landing and the latch wouldn't work unless both knobs were in place. She was trapped in the attic, with no way out!

She hammered at the door and screamed for her parents. They had to come and rescue her! She pounded until her knuckles were battered and bleeding, and then she remembered. Her parents and Janie were gone.

Rondelle sank to the cold, wooden floor, whimpering in terror. The last light of day was fading fast, and she was trapped in the attic. There was no way out, and not one single person knew where she was!

Six

"Yes, Steve. I'd love to go with you." Donna hung up the phone. Her first date in Jefferson City! And it was with Steve! He'd just called to invite her to Craig Ellison's party.

Steve had apologized for not asking her sooner. He'd been planning to help his father fix up their guest room and they'd planned to paint it tonight. But his mother had decided that she preferred wallpaper, and the pattern she wanted wouldn't be in until next week.

Even though Donna had never met Steve's mother, she immediately liked her for choosing a pattern that was backordered. Now Steve was free for the evening, and he'd asked her for a date!

Donna sat on the edge of her bed for a moment, smiling in anticipation. Craig's party was an annual October event. The Ellisons were rich, and their lake cabin was incredibly beautiful. Donna had heard that Craig's mother always hired caterers to serve Hawaiian food on the beach, and everyone in the school was invited. She'd planned to go alone, but now that she had a date with Steve, it would be much more fun.

Rondelle opened her eyes as the telephone rang. It was dark, and for one brief moment, she didn't know where she was. Then she remembered, and icy panic washed over her in waves. She was locked in the attic! And she couldn't get out!

But where was the phone? There was a faint beam of light coming up through the rafters, and Rondelle crawled toward it on her hands and knees. The ringing sound got louder as she got closer to the light and when she put her eye to the crack, she saw the inside of her bedroom. The light was on. She must have forgotten to turn it off when she'd come up here. She had been complaining about the crack in her ceiling for several months now. Thank goodness her father hadn't gotten around to fixing it!

Looking through the crack soothed Rondelle. It was almost as if she were down there again, getting ready for her date.

"Oh, no!" Rondelle groaned loudly. Craig had promised to call her, and he could be on the other end of the line right now, listening to the empty ringing. He'd think she wasn't home and he wouldn't come over until it was time for their date. But he would come over. Rondelle was sure of that. She'd told him that she might go shopping, and he'd agreed to pick her up at eight.

But what would Craig do when she didn't answer the door? Rondelle wasn't sure. Somehow, she had to get his attention and let him know she was trapped up here.

The vent. It faced the front of the house. The moment Rondelle thought of it, she felt much better. When Craig came up to the front door to ring the doorbell, she'd call out to him. He'd hear her, crawl through one of the windows, and come up to the attic to let her out. All she had to do was be patient and try not to panic. Craig would be here very soon and then she'd be free.

The ceiling in her bedroom was low, and the phone was only a few feet below her. But those few feet might as well have been hundreds. There was no way Rondelle could reach through the crack to answer the phone.

The answering machine kicked in on the fifth ring, and Rondelle held her breath as she listened to the outgoing message. *This is Rondelle. I'm not here right now, but leave a message and I'll get back to you as soon as I can.* Then there was a beep, and she heard Craig's voice.

Rondelle? Where are you? It's almost seven and I'll be there in an hour. Maybe I'd better call Alice and see if you're over there.

Rondelle frowned. The last thing she wanted was for Craig to call Alice, especially since Alice was dying to date him, too. Would Alice be a true friend? Would she say that Rondelle wasn't there and hang up? Or would Alice take advantage of the situation to flirt with Craig and try to get him interested in her?!

There was a creaking sound from the far corner of the attic, and Rondelle's eyes searched the shadows. A faint light was coming in through the slatted vent, and she could see huge, looming shapes in the darkness. Nothing was moving. There was no need to panic. Old houses always creaked and groaned at night. There was absolutely nothing up here to hurt her.

The mirror! Rondelle almost screamed as she remembered the hideous reflection she'd seen. She started to panic, her heart pounding fearfully in her chest, but somehow she managed to calm herself. The reflection had been horrifying, but it had been a trick of the light and her own imagination. It wasn't real, and things that weren't real couldn't possibly hurt her.

The phone rang again and Rondelle turned back to the crack in the floor. Once again, the answering machine picked up on the fifth ring. *This is Rondelle. I'm not here right now, but leave a message and I'll get back to you as soon as I can.*

Rondelle? It was Alice's voice. *Craig just called to see if you were here and I said you weren't. I told him you were probably in the shower, and you didn't hear the phone. Since my car's not working right, he said he'd give me a ride to the party, if that's okay with you.*

"That's not okay and you know it!" Rondelle shouted the words, even though she knew Alice couldn't hear her. Giving Alice a ride was worse than not okay, it was a complete disaster! If Alice went to the party with them, she'd want a ride home. And that meant Rondelle would have absolutely no time alone with Craig!

There was another noise from the far end of the attic, and Rondelle whirled around again. Something was there! She was sure of it! But what?

That was when she heard it, the sound of scurrying feet scraping against the rafters. Rats! And Rondelle was deathly afraid of rats!

Fighting panic, Rondelle pressed her eye to the crack again. She concentrated on the safe haven of her bedroom, only a few feet below. So close, and yet so far. Could she somehow make the crack bigger? Big enough to jump through? Rondelle didn't like the idea of falling all the way to the floor below, but it wasn't as frightening as staying here, locked up in the attic with rats!

Rondelle clawed at the crack until her hands were bleeding, but she only succeeded in widening it an inch or two. And then she heard the phone ring again.

Rondelle? It's Craig. Call me back when you get this message. Alice thought you were in the shower or something, but you must be out by now. What's going on anyway? We've got a date, don't we? I mean—are we still on for tonight, or what?

Rondelle winced. Craig sounded angry, and she wished that she could call him to explain. If she'd thought to bring the remote phone with her, all her problems would be solved. But she'd only come up here to get the red shoes. She'd never expected to get locked in the attic.

There was another rustling, scampering sound, and Rondelle convinced herself that it was only squirrels, running across the roof. This was a nice house, in a nice neighborhood, and her mother kept it very clean. They couldn't possibly have rats.

Time seemed to stand still in the darkness, but Rondelle knew the minutes were ticking by. And then the phone rang again.

Rondelle? It's Alice. Where are you? You just went out shopping or something, right? I mean, I know your parents wanted you to go with them, but you didn't, did you?

"No! I'm here!" Rondelle swallowed hard. But Alice was still speaking.

Look, Rondelle—you really blew it if you went with your parents and you didn't tell Craig. He thinks you stood him up, so he asked me to go to the party with him. If you don't call me back in the next ten minutes, I'm going to say yes!

"No! Craig's my date!" Rondelle almost screamed the words.

Both Craig and Alice thought she wasn't home, but she was! And Craig wouldn't come to pick her up if she didn't call him back. Alice wouldn't bother to come over to check. She'd always wanted to go out with Craig, and this was her golden opportunity!

The seconds ticked by, and Rondelle tore frantically at the crack in the floor. She just had to get to the phone! And then it rang again, and she heard Craig's voice.

Rondelle. If you went with your parents and didn't tell me, don't bother to apologize. I wouldn't ask you out again on a bet! I'm a fair guy so I'm going to drive by your house to check. If the lights are off, I'll know you're gone.

Rondelle breathed a deep sigh of relief. The light was on in her bedroom. Craig would see it and come to the door. And then she could call out through the vent to explain that she was locked in the attic.

But Rondelle's relief was short-lived. The lamp in her bedroom flickered once and then it went off. The bulb had burned out. If Craig didn't see any lights, he'd drive right by without stopping!

Rondelle rushed toward the vent in the darkness. As she stared out through the slats, she gave a deep sigh of relief. The street was deserted, and she had some time. It would take Craig at least ten minutes to drive to her house.

What could she do to let Craig know that she was locked in the attic? Rondelle knew she needed some sort of a signal. She planned to scream, but it was a cold night. If Craig's windows were closed and his car stereo was on, he'd never hear her.

She could wave a flag. The moment Rondelle thought of it, she felt her way back to the corner where her father stored his fishing poles. The tip of a pole would be thin enough to stick through the vent.

Rondelle opened the wardrobe and pulled out the first piece of clothing she could find. It felt like one of her grandfather's old silk shirts, and her fingers were shaking as she tore off one arm. She tied the end of the fishing line around it and poked it through the vent to dangle down, in front of the house. She'd jerk it up and down when Craig drove by and he'd be bound to see it—if the porch light was on.

But the porch light wasn't on! Her mother had turned it off this morning, and the timer was broken. All Rondelle could do was hope that Craig's headlights would sweep across the front of the house.

Rondelle held her breath as she heard a car turning onto her block. She peered out the vent and her heart beat desperately in her chest as she saw that it was Craig. She jerked the fishing pole frantically. He just had to see her signal! She'd die if she had to spend all night in the attic!

Craig's red Thunderbird slowed as he turned the corner, and Rondelle jerked the fishing pole in a frantic bid for his attention. But she jerked it too hard and the line snapped, sending her makeshift flag fluttering to the ground. Her signal had failed, and there was only one thing to do. Rondelle leaned forward, close to the vent, and screamed at the top of her lungs. "Craig! Up here! Help me! I'm locked in!"

But Craig didn't stop his car. He just drove slowly past her house. And then he was gone, the sound of the Thunderbird's powerful motor fading to a whisper in the distance.

"Nooooo!" Rondelle stood at the vent, clutching the metal slats so tightly, her knuckles turned white. Craig was gone. He was driving to Alice's house right now, to take her to his party!

A tear rolled down Rondelle's cheek, and she slumped against the wall in utter despair. There was no hope for her, no hope at all. There was no way she could get out of the attic and she'd be locked in until her parents came home on Sunday afternoon . . . unless one of the neighbors heard her screaming and called the police.

Rondelle stood up and took a deep breath. And then she screamed, over and over, until her voice was hoarse. When she couldn't scream any longer, she banged against the vent with the fishing pole, but it didn't do any good. The night had turned very cold, and all the neighbors had closed their windows.

There were tears in Rondelle's eyes as she turned away from the vent. She was stuck in the attic with no one to help her, and she was shivering with cold. She had to keep from freezing, and that meant she had to find something warm to wear.

Rondelle didn't look at the mirror as she stumbled to the wardrobe. Even though it was dark, she was still afraid of what she might see. She pulled the door open, grabbed the old fur coat, and wrapped it tightly around her shivering body. Then she crept across the floor to huddle against the attic door where a little warmth was seeping up the stairs.

Rondelle knew she should try to sleep. It was the only way to get through the night. But the moment she closed her eyes, she pictured Alice at the party with Craig.

They'd eat in the tent that was set up on the shore, and the thought of all that delicious food made Rondelle's stomach grumble with hunger. When dessert had been served and everyone had raved about the marvelous dinner, they'd go into the living room to dance to the music of the live band.

Staring up at the darkness, Rondelle could almost see Alice, dancing with Craig. Alice would purr like a kitten when Craig held her close and she'd snuggle into his arms. They'd dance every dance and when the band left, they'd relax on one of the leather couches, the stereo playing softly and Alice's head nestled tightly against Craig's chest.

Jealousy was too tame a description for the emotion that Rondelle felt. Alice had stolen her date and, at that moment, Rondelle hated Alice with every fiber of her being. But then something happened that made Rondelle forget all about Alice and Craig. Something was moving, in the far corner, and it was coming closer. She was trapped in the dark attic, and she was not alone!

Her heart pounding frantically, Rondelle began to whimper. Every sound was magnified in the blackness, all the scratching, and creaking, and rustling noises she'd heard earlier. There were rats in the attic and they were after her!

Rondelle shuddered. What would happen if the rats attacked her? Could she fight them off? She grabbed the heaviest object she could reach, an old metal lamp with a broken shade, and held it in her hand. How many rats were there? And how could

she fight them if she couldn't see them? She had to protect herself from their razor sharp teeth!

The old fur coat would help. The rats couldn't bite through
the heavy fur. Rondelle wrapped it tightly around her body, and
tucked in her feet and arms. Then she started to rock back and
forth. If she kept moving, it might scare the rats away.

Rocking made Rondelle feel much better. It reminded her of
how her mother had rocked her when she was a baby. She'd felt
so safe, cradled in her mother's arms, and she needed to feel that
safe again. The rocking motion calmed her fears, and without
really thinking about what she was doing, Rondelle began to recite a nursery rhyme.

*"London Bridge is falling down, falling down, falling down.
London Bridge is falling down. My fair lady."*

Rondelle stopped abruptly, and frowned. *"My fair lady."* She
was fair, but Alice wasn't. Alice had stolen her boyfriend. Alice
was horrible, and she deserved to be punished for what she'd
done.

As Rondelle sat there thinking about punishing Alice, the
scratching, scrabbling noises started again. They seemed louder
and much more ominous, and Rondelle's eyes went wide with
terror. The rats were moving again! They were coming closer
and closer, and she had to do something to stop them!

But the rats had been quiet when she'd recited her nursery
rhyme. Rondelle didn't take the time to wonder why. She just
started to recite again.

*"There was an old woman who lived in a shoe. She had so
many children, she didn't know what to do."*

The moment Rondelle started reciting again, the noises
stopped. It was working! The rats liked nursery rhymes! If she
kept on rocking and reciting, she could keep them away!

Rondelle recited on and on, into the night, huddled in the old
fur coat. She recited every nursery rhyme she could remember:
*Old Mother Hubbard, Jack Be Nimble, Hey Diddle Diddle,
Mary Had a Little Lamb,* and *Jack and Jill.* When Rondelle had
gone through every nursery rhyme she knew, she started all over

again. She recited hour after hour, afraid to stop for even a moment, rocking back and forth like a pendulum.

The rats stayed away as long as she recited and rocked, even though her voice faded to a hoarse whisper. And in the middle of one of her favorite nursery rhymes, something snapped in Rondelle Green's mind.

Seven

Steve pulled up in front of Donna's house at five minutes before midnight. The party had been wonderful, with incredible food and a really great band. Donna had danced with Steve all night, and now they were here, in front of her house. Donna wasn't quite sure how she should end their date. Would Steve want to kiss her? And should she let him?

"You look worried, Donna." Steve sounded amused. "Were you wondering if I was going to kiss you?"

Donna felt her cheeks grow hot and she knew she was blushing. But Steve was right, and she nodded. "Yes, I was."

"Well, you can stop worrying." Steve sounded even more amused. "I just saw your mother pull back the curtains so I'd better walk you up to the door."

Donna waited until Steve had walked around the car to open her door. He was old-fashioned that way and she liked it. Even though she was entirely capable of opening it by herself, it made her feel special when he did it for her.

They walked up the steps to Donna's front door, and Steve reached out for her hand. "So what are you doing tomorrow afternoon?"

"Not much." Donna felt her heart beat faster. Was Steve going to ask her for another date? "I don't really have any plans. I was just going to hang around the house."

"Let's drive to Rondelle's house and ask her some questions. I talked to a couple of people at the party, and they were sure the red shoes were still in the dressing room when she used it."

Donna frowned slightly. "But will it do any good to confront Rondelle?"

"We won't confront her. We'll just say we know she had a lot of other things on her mind, playing the lead in the play, and then landing a part in Mr. Michaels' movie."

"You're right," said Donna. "With all those other things on her mind, she probably forgot about seeing the red shoes. But now that she's had a chance to calm down from all the excitement, she might remember."

"Exactly! We'll be giving her an excuse she can use. Rondelle might have lied to us deliberately, but this'll give her a second chance to tell the truth."

"What do you really think, Steve?" Donna was very serious. "Did Rondelle take the red shoes?"

Steve shrugged. "They were there when she used the dressing room, and they were gone when we checked it later. Mr. Parks said that Rondelle was the last person to leave the theater, and the red shoes couldn't walk away all by themselves."

"I don't know about that." Donna couldn't resist teasing him. "You're forgetting that the red shoes are cursed, and cursed shoes could have magical powers. They might have danced off into the night."

Steve laughed. "Right. If you believe in magic, I guess that's possible, but I'm willing to bet that Rondelle knows exactly where they are."

"And if Rondelle thinks she won't get into trouble for taking them, she might give them to us?"

"It's worth a try." Steve nodded. "I'd better let you go in. It's getting cold out here."

He was right. It was a cold night. But Donna hadn't even felt the cold before Steve had mentioned it. Perhaps it was because he was still holding her hand.

"I'll pick you up around three. Rondelle and her parents should be home by then."

"Okay." Donna smiled. And then something popped right out of her mouth before she'd had time to think. "If my mother wasn't watching, would you kiss me?"

Steve laughed. "You bet I would! Mr. Parks was right. You're wonderful, Donna."

"You're wonderful, too." Again, the words popped out before she'd had a chance to think. Was it wrong to tell a boy that he was wonderful? Donna wasn't sure, but Steve was still smiling and he looked as if he liked what she'd said.

The curtain fluttered again. Steve noticed, and he grinned at Donna. "Your mother's still watching."

"I know." Donna nodded.

"Let's show her what a nice guy I am." Steve was still grinning as he bowed from the waist and raised her hand to his lips. He kissed it lightly and then he released it. "Thank you for a very enjoyable evening, Miss Burke."

Donna giggled. And then she held out the corners of her skirt and curtsied, something she'd only seen in the movies. "Thank *you*, Mr. Harvey."

"Until tomorrow?" Steve backed down the steps, grinning all the way.

"Until tomorrow." Donna answered him. Then she opened the door, stepped inside, and smiled all the way up the stairs to her room.

The night seemed endless. Rondelle huddled in the old fur coat and recited to the rats until her eyes closed in exhaustion. But every time she fell asleep the rustling sound would awaken her and she'd have to recite some more. Finally, a faint gray light began to filter in through the attic vents. Morning was here, and she was sure she'd read somewhere that rats only fed at night.

She could sleep now. There was an old couch against the far wall, but Rondelle was too tired to drag herself across the attic floor. She stretched out by the door where she'd be sure to hear her parents when they came home, and tried to go to sleep.

But Rondelle couldn't sleep. Her eyes snapped open every

time she thought of Alice with Craig. Alice had stolen her boyfriend. Her best friend had turned into her worst enemy.

What could she do to punish Alice? Rondelle sat up, her back propped against the attic door, and thought about it. But her thoughts were so jumbled, nothing seemed to make sense.

Rondelle was still thinking when the first rays of sun came in through the vent. They streamed across the floor, almost blinding her, stopping directly at her feet. The red shoes glowed brilliantly in the bright stream of light, the red shoes she'd stolen, the red shoes that some people thought were cursed.

"The red shoes!" Rondelle's hands were shaking as she reached down to take them off. She didn't know why, but she was sure that the red shoes were responsible for everything bad that had happened. Rondelle was about to toss them away, in the farthest corner of the attic, when she had a wonderful idea. She'd give the cursed red shoes to Alice.

"Hello?" Alice's voice was groggy with sleep when she answered the phone in her room. But she sat up straight and began to smile as she recognized the voice on the other end of the line. "Hi, Craig! What's going on?"

As she listened to Craig's voice, Alice glanced at the clock. She'd slept all morning, and it was already one o'clock in the afternoon!

"Sure. I'll be there." Alice hung up and jumped out of bed. She had to hurry. She'd promised to help Craig clean up after the party, and he wanted her to meet him at the cabin in an hour!

Alice was singing as she turned on the water and stepped into the shower. She'd had a fantastic time last night, thanks to Rondelle. Alice really couldn't understand why Rondelle had left town without a word. Maybe her parents had forced her to go, but why hadn't she called Craig to cancel their date?

As she washed her hair, Alice sang at the top of her lungs. She knew she didn't get the melody right, but that didn't bother her at all. And even though the Jefferson High chorus director had asked her not to sing so loudly at their concert next week, Alice intended to ignore his advice. She liked to sing and enthusiasm should count for something. After all, chorus was supposed to be for everyone.

Alice frowned slightly as she began to get dressed. Rondelle would be furious when she got back to town and found out that she'd gone to the party with Craig. But Alice wasn't about to let a little thing like friendship stop her from enjoying her date this afternoon. It was all Rondelle's fault, and Alice didn't feel one bit guilty.

Rondelle was smiling as she put the red shoes in a shoe box, but it wasn't a nice smile. It was more of a grimace with her lips drawn back from her teeth, and her eyes glittering dangerously.

When Rondelle's father had heard her pounding on the attic door, they'd all rushed up the stairs. Her mother had stood by, wringing her hands, while her father had taken the door off its hinges. Even Janie had been very subdued, and the first thing she'd asked her older sister was whether the attic monsters had hurt her.

Rondelle had concentrated on one thing and one thing only. She had to convince everyone that she was fine so they'd leave her alone. She'd told her parents that they didn't have to worry about her. Of course she'd been bored, all alone in the attic, and her back hurt from sleeping on the floor. What she really wanted to do was take a nice, hot shower and stretch out on her bed for a long nap.

Perhaps she really was a good actress. Rondelle gave a small, bitter laugh. She'd been so convincing, she'd persuaded her parents to go right on with their plans to take Janie to a friend's birthday party. Janie hadn't wanted to go. Questioning her big sister about the terrors of the attic was much more interesting than watching someone else open birthday presents. But Rondelle had promised to tell Janie all about it when she got home, and Janie and her parents had left.

It didn't take long to wrap Alice's package. Rondelle used silver paper and tied a beautiful red bow on the top. It looked very professional, as if it had been wrapped by a shop in the mall. Then she printed Alice's name on a card and taped it to the box.

The moment she was through, Rondelle raced for the door. Alice lived over two miles away, but she ran almost all the way there. Rondelle placed the package in front of Alice's door, and then sprinted down the sidewalk, as if the rats in the attic were chasing her.

By the time Rondelle got home, she was exhausted. She flopped down on the couch, curled up into a ball, and began to rock slowly back and forth. The red shoes would work. They would punish Alice, and she wouldn't have to do a thing.

Eight

"You look great, Donna!" Steve turned to smile at her as he started his car.

"Thanks, Steve." Donna's eyes sparkled. She was wearing another of her instant creations, a tan jumpsuit her father had brought back with him when he'd inspected a pipeline the government had built in Alaska. The jumpsuit was standard issue. All the government inspectors had worn them. But Donna had shortened the legs and sewn wide elastic around the waist. She'd added a bright blue belt, tied a long blue scarf around her neck, and now the jumpsuit looked like something she'd bought at the mall.

They talked about the red shoes on the way to Rondelle's house. Steve was sure they had nothing to do with Tammy's accident, and they weren't really cursed at all.

"I hope that's true." Donna looked a little worried. "I'd like to believe it was only a coincidence. But something very strange is happening."

Steve reached out to squeeze her hand. "Go on, Donna. I'm listening."

"I talked to Lisa this morning. She told me that Rondelle's been wanting to date Craig for years. We were right there when he asked her to his party and Rondelle said yes."

"I know." Steve nodded. "But I heard that she had to go out of town with her parents."

"Maybe that's true, but Rondelle didn't call Craig to cancel their date. She just stood him up. Don't you think that's a little strange?"

Steve nodded. "Definitely. It only takes a minute to call."

"I've been thinking about it all morning, and I'm sure Rondelle has the red shoes. If she was wearing them the night she read for that part in the movie, it would explain why Mr. Michaels was so impressed with her. What if Rondelle didn't go with her parents? What if she stayed home? And what if she wore the red shoes?"

"We'll know soon." Steve squeezed Donna's hand, again. "Rondelle's house is right around the next corner."

Steve parked in front of the house, and they got out. As they walked up the sidewalk to the door, Donna felt very anxious. She was really worried about Rondelle.

It seemed to take forever for someone to answer the door, but at last they heard footsteps approaching. And then it opened, and Rondelle stood there in the light.

"Rondelle?" Donna's mouth dropped open. Rondelle looked awful! There were dark circles under her eyes and she was swaying back and forth as she held on to the doorjamb. "What's the matter? Are you sick?"

Rondelle swayed again, and Steve grabbed her arm to steady her. But Rondelle just smiled a strange smile, and shook her head. "I'm fine, just fine. I've never been better."

Donna exchanged glances with Steve. It was clear that Rondelle wasn't fine.

"Come in, come in." Rondelle's voice was hoarse, and she leaned heavily on Steve's arm as she led the way to the living room. "I was just sitting here reciting a poem. Do you know *London Bridge is Falling Down?*"

Steve exchanged another glance with Donna. There was something very wrong with Rondelle. "Sure, we know it. Are your parents home, Rondelle?"

"No, not yet." Rondelle sank down on the couch. "I'm so tired of *London Bridge*. I had to recite it to the rats all night, to keep them from eating me. I was locked in the attic and they were very hungry."

"I . . . see." Steve nodded, as if he understood. And then he looked at Donna. His message was clear. Rondelle had flipped out, and he wasn't sure what to do next.

Donna took a deep breath for courage. She hated to ask Rondelle about the red shoes, but if the curse was responsible for Rondelle's condition, she might feel better if she gave them up. "We need the red shoes, Rondelle. Could you give them to us, please?"

"No, I can't." Rondelle began to rock back and forth. "I can't . . . I can't! *One, two buckle my shoe!*"

Donna put her arm around Rondelle's shoulder and, gradually, Rondelle stopped rocking and chanting. Donna spoke again, very softly. "Why can't you give us the red shoes? We really need them."

"Because I had to give them to her! She went to the party with Craig. She stole my date, and she has to be punished!"

"She must mean Alice." Steve reached out for Rondelle and held her tight, before she could start to rock again. "Listen to me, Rondelle. How did you know that Alice went to the party with Craig?"

"The answering machine told me." Rondelle's eyes glittered strangely. "I heard it through the crack in the floor. So near and yet so far. I could see it, but I couldn't reach it. And I tried soooo hard."

Rondelle started to rock again, faster and faster, and Steve reached out to calm her. "Donna? You'd better call Alice and tell her what's happened."

Donna looked up Alice's number in the phone book, then dialed it on Rondelle's phone, but no one answered. "She's not home."

"Keep trying. We can't drive over there now. We have to stay with Rondelle until her parents get home."

Donna dialed Alice's number over and over but no one answered. "She's not home, Steve. Or she's not answering the phone."

"Okay." Steve nodded. "I guess we should take a run over there after Rondelle's parents get home. I want to make sure that Alice is all right."

Rondelle started to rock again, so hard that she bumped her head against the wall. "Alice? Who's Alice?"

"Rondelle . . . take it easy." Steve pulled her into his arms. He held her for another few minutes, and then they heard a car pull into the driveway.

"They're home." Steve got up from the couch. "You stay with Rondelle, and I'll go out to meet them."

Rondelle was rocking again, and Donna reached out to hold her close. She was quiet for a moment, but then she started reciting *"One, Two, Buckle My Shoe"* in a hoarse, whispering voice. The first line was right, but then Rondelle changed the words in a very frightening way.

"One, two, buckle my shoe. Three, four, the curse locked the door. Five, six, I couldn't get it fixed. Don't look back, the mirror just cracked."

"Rondelle . . . you've got to calm down." Donna tried to hold her, but Rondelle just jerked away. She seemed possessed by the awful rhyme she was chanting.

"Craig drove by, and I started to cry."

Donna wasn't sure what to do, so she tried to reason with Rondelle. "Don't worry, Rondelle. It's all right now."

"No, it's not! I can't stop! The rats are still here, and they're very near. Three, four, five. They'll eat me alive!"

"No, Rondelle. The rats are gone." Donna did her best to soothe Rondelle, but it didn't work. Rondelle shook her head, and kept on rocking.

"Seven, eight, Alice took my date. Nine, ten, she'll die in the end! The cursed shoes are red, and Alice is dead!"

The frightening words that Rondelle chanted made the hair stand up on the back of Donna's neck. The night in the attic had taken its toll. Rondelle's mind had snapped.

As Donna held Rondelle, she felt her suspicions grow.

Tammy had worn the red shoes, and now it would take painful months for her to learn to walk again. And when Rondelle had worn them, she'd lost her mind. Were the red shoes to blame? Donna still wasn't sure, but the evidence was stacking up. She just hoped they'd be able to convince Alice that the red shoes were dangerous before they claimed their third victim!

Alice was in such a hurry, she almost tripped over the gift-wrapped package on her porch. She picked it up and admired the wrapping, beautiful silver paper with a large, red bow. There was a card on the top with her name. It was a gift for her. And Alice knew of only one person who'd send her a beautiful gift like this. It was from Craig!

"How sweet!" Alice's fingers were shaking in excitement as she tore off the paper and opened the box. Craig had given her a pair of red shoes. It seemed like a strange gift, but the shoes were *beautiful*.

The moment Alice slipped them on, she began to smile. They looked absolutely wonderful and they fit her perfectly! Craig must have asked one of her friends for her shoe size.

Alice stood up and twirled around. The shoes were comfortable and they were gorgeous. She could hardly wait to thank Craig in person!

In no time at all, Alice was heading down the road in her old green Chevy. When she saw the blue and red sign for Eddy's Drive-In in the distance, she had an absolutely brilliant idea. Craig had told her he was crazy about the stuffed mushroom appetizer they served at Eddy's, and it wouldn't take long to go through the line at the drive-up window. Craig would be impressed that she'd remembered, and it would be a nice way to thank him for her gift.

There were only two cars in line as Alice drove in. She gave her order to the crackling voice on the speaker, and drove up to the window to park behind the other cars. While she was waiting, Alice turned on the radio and smiled as she heard her favorite song. She was so happy, she started singing right along with the music.

Alice was delighted as she belted out the lyrics to the song. She really sounded good, much better than she had in the shower. All the notes were right and her voice soared out the open window. Their chorus director was crazy. She had a fantastic voice!

Alice was still singing as another car pulled up behind her. The driver heard her singing, and he leaned out his window to stare at her. Alice sang even louder. If he didn't like her voice, that was just too bad. But the driver was smiling as he got out of his car and walked up to hers.

Alice kept right on singing, but she raised her eyebrows in surprise. Something about him was very familiar. When the song had ended, Alice stuck her head out the open window. "Did you want something?"

"Yes." The man smiled. "I want you."

"Excuse me?" Alice started to laugh. It was a great pickup line, but she was taken.

"I'm serious. We just lost one of our backup singers, and we need to replace her." The man reached in his pocket and handed Alice a card. "You sounded really good, and I want you to audition. How about coming down to The Hot Spot around eight tonight?"

Alice glanced down at the card. And then she almost fainted in shock. No wonder he looked so familiar! She'd seen his face on CDs and posters, all over town. It was Shane Summers, and his band was in Jefferson City for a concert!

"Well? How about it?" Shane leaned against her car. "The audition's just a formality. I'd hire you right now, but I'd like the rest of the guys to meet you first."

Alice was so excited her head was spinning, but she decided to play it smart. She shrugged very casually and smiled at him. "Why not? I guess I could be there at eight."

After he'd thanked her and gone back to his car, Alice took out his card and stared at it again. She had an audition with Shane Summers tonight! This was incredible luck!

Alice pulled up to the window to pick up the stuffed mushrooms. She set them down on the passenger seat, and drove out onto the highway. Alice could hardly wait to tell Craig what had happened.

Alice zipped along the highway, lost in her dreams of fame and fortune. If she was a singer with Shane Summers' band, she'd go on tour and meet all sorts of fascinating people. Maybe she'd even marry someone incredibly talented like Shane Summers, himself.

The turn for the lake was just ahead, and Alice was so excited, she took it much too fast. Her tires slid on the gravel road and she hit the brakes, fishtailing to a stop. She had to be careful. The gravel road around the lake had lots of tight curves and they hadn't graded it recently. They would scrape it smooth before next summer, but the ruts were deep at this time of the year.

As she put the car into gear again, Alice laughed out loud with delight. There was absolutely no doubt in her mind. She'd really sounded fantastic at the drive-in and she would be sure to get the job. In the space of an hour, her singing had improved a thousand percent!

But why did she suddenly sound so good? Alice remembered the curse of the red shoes. Any girl who wore them was supposed to show incredible talent, but there was a price to pay. She'd have incredibly bad luck.

Alice glanced down at her feet, and then she shook her head. There was absolutely no reason to worry. Her red shoes weren't cursed. How could they be when they were a present from Craig?

Donna and Steve took turns calming Rondelle while her parents called the doctor. He wanted to see her at the hospital right away, so they helped to get Rondelle settled in the backseat of her parents' car. The moment they had driven away, Steve grabbed Donna's hand. "Come on, Donna. Let's go."

As they drove to Alice's house, Donna began to think about what had happened. "Poor Rondelle. She seemed totally insane. Do you think it's because of the red shoes?"

"I don't know. It could have been the night in the attic. She must have been terrified, all alone in the dark."

Donna shivered. It wasn't pleasant to imagine being trapped in a dark, spooky place with no way to get out. "When Rondelle was making some kind of sense, in between all that other stuff she said, she told me she saw something horrible in the attic mirror."

"Was she wearing the red shoes?"

Donna nodded. "It was right after she put them on."

"We're here." Steve said a few minutes later, when they pulled up in front of a pink stucco house. He shut off his engine. "I'm pretty sure that Rondelle sent the red shoes to Alice. And even if they're not cursed, I think we'd better get them back."

Donna held her breath as Steve rang the doorbell, but no one came to the door. He rang it again, with the same result, and Donna sighed deeply. "Alice must have left."

"What's this?" Steve pointed to a box by the side of the door. It was the size of a shoe box and there was a torn piece of silver wrapping paper beside it.

Donna knelt down to look at the box, and she saw the white card stuck to the paper. "Here's a card with Alice's name, but there's no message. Do you think it's from Rondelle?"

"I know it is. She's the only person I know who dots her *i*'s with a circle. And if Rondelle gave this package to Alice, you can bet that the red shoes were inside."

"But the box is empty!" Donna swallowed hard. "Do you think Alice is wearing the red shoes?"

"I wouldn't be surprised. I just wish we knew where she was."

"Last night at the party, I heard her tell Craig she'd help him clean up. Do you think she could be out at the cabin?"

"It's worth a try." Steve grabbed Donna's hand. "Maybe we're making something out of nothing, but we'd better drive out there to make sure that Alice is all right."

Alice stared down at the red shoes on her feet and they seemed to gleam dangerously. But that was ridiculous. These shoes were from Craig, weren't they?

But Craig hadn't signed the card and she'd only assumed that the shoes were from him. What if someone had sent her that package and tricked her into believing that it was from Craig? She could be wearing the cursed red shoes!

Alice glanced down at the shoes again. They had stopped gleaming, and now they looked perfectly harmless. But when she raised her eyes to the road, the fence posts were speeding by at an alarmingly fast rate.

What was happening?! Alice glanced at the speedometer and gasped. The needle was hovering at just below fifty, and that was much too fast for a gravel road in poor repair!

Alice tried to ease up on the accelerator, but something was terribly wrong. Her foot was stuck, and with each passing second, it was pressing down harder and harder.

The needle on the speedometer rose to fifty-five and then to sixty. And even though Alice struggled to pull up her foot, it just wouldn't budge. She *was* wearing the cursed red shoes! And one of them was tromping down on the accelerator, trying to kill her!

Nine

Steve knew a shortcut and they took a back road to the lake. As they turned onto the gravel road that led around the shoreline, Donna clutched her hands together to keep them from trembling. Alice just had to be at the cabin. And she had to be all right!

The lake sparkled in the afternoon sun. It was a beautiful shade of blue that she would have appreciated at any other time, but now she was much too worried about Alice to give it more than a passing glance.

"Only four miles to go." Steve looked at his watch, and Donna could tell that he was just as worried as she was. "Hang on, Donna. This gravel road is really rough."

As they drove over the ruts made by heavy summer rains, Donna held onto the edge of her seat. Steve's car was old and a spring poked her every time they bounced over a rut, but the last thing Donna wanted was for Steve to slow down. The faster they got to the cabin, the quicker they could talk to Alice. If she was wearing the red shoes, they simply had to convince her to take them off!

As they rounded a corner, they heard a loud bang. Steve stopped the car by pumping the brakes, and they both got out to look.

"It's flat." Steve frowned as he pointed to the right rear tire. "We must have picked up a nail or something."

Donna nodded. "Do you have a spare?"

"Sure. Don't worry, Donna. It'll only take a couple of minutes to change. You can wait in the car if you want to."

"No way!" Donna walked around the car with him and waited until he'd opened the trunk. Then she reached inside and grabbed the jack. "I'll jack it up while you roll out the spare."

It didn't take long to change the tire with both of them working. Steve lowered the jack, put it back in the trunk, and handed Donna a clean rag. "Thanks for helping, Donna. I hope you didn't get too dirty."

"Only a little and that'll wash off." Donna smiled at him as she wiped her hands on the rag.

Less then five minutes later, they were turning onto the long winding driveway that led to the cabin. Donna held her breath as they passed the tall, stately pines and the cabin came into view.

"Craig's here." Steve rounded the corner, and parked next to Craig's Thunderbird.

Donna nodded, but she felt her heart sink down to her toes. Craig's car was the only one in the driveway. There was no sign of Alice's Chevy.

Steve seemed to read her mind, because he turned to give her an encouraging smile. "Alice might be here. She could have parked in the garage."

They rang the doorbell and a moment later, Craig opened the door. "Hi, guys. What are you doing out here?"

Donna crossed her fingers for luck. And then she took a deep breath and blurted out the question. "Is Alice here?"

"Not yet." Craig looked a little disgruntled as he motioned for them to come inside. "She told me she'd be here by two, but she's late. She probably had car trouble. That old wreck of hers doesn't go more than ten miles without breaking down. Which way did you come?"

"We took the shortcut." Steve turned to Donna. "Let's show Craig that card."

Donna pulled the card out of her purse and handed it to Craig. "We found this with a gift-wrapped box on Alice's front porch. Did you send her a present?"

"No. Not me." Craig looked puzzled as he examined the card.

Steve nodded. "That's what we were afraid of. We think Rondelle might have sent Alice the cursed red shoes."

It took Steve and Donna several minutes to tell Craig what had happened to Rondelle. When they were finished, Craig looked shocked.

"And you think that Rondelle sent the red shoes to Alice for revenge?"

Donna nodded. "But we won't know for sure, until we can talk to Alice."

"This stuff about cursed shoes is crazy, but she *is* really late." Craig started to frown. "Let's give her another five minutes. If she's not here by then, we'll go out and try to find her."

The needle on the speedometer was hovering at seventy, and Alice felt panic wash over her in waves. She couldn't lift her foot off the gas pedal, and the road ahead climbed steeply. At the top of the hill was the most dangerous curve on the road. It was deceptively sharp and very steep, with a rock-filled ravine on one side. It had been the scene of several fatal accidents, and everyone called it Deadman's Curve.

She had to do something before she got to Deadman's Curve! Alice began to tremble with fear. If she couldn't slow down, she'd skid off the road and crash into the ravine.

But only her right foot was stuck. Alice picked up her left foot and stomped down hard on the brakes. Her car slowed for a brief instant, but then the sole of the red shoe slipped right off the brake pedal, as if it had been greased. The red shoes had control of her car, and they were going to kill her!

That was when Alice started to scream, a high thin wail of pure horror. But screaming wouldn't help. She had to stay calm. Alice clamped her lips tightly shut, and forced herself to think. There had to be some way to stop her car, but what was it?

The emergency brake! Alice reached down and pulled up on the handle with her hand. And then she sobbed in relief as the brake engaged and her car began to slow. Thank God she'd thought of it in time!

The acrid smell of burning rubber filled the car. Alice began to cough, but she didn't release her hold on the emergency brake. It was her only chance to stop.

The burning smell got worse with each second that passed. The smoke that filled the interior of the car made Alice's eyes water, but it was working! Her car was slowing down.

Alice could see the speedometer through the haze of choking smoke. The needle had gone down to fifty, even though her right foot was still pressing down on the accelerator. She was going to defeat the curse of the red shoes!

As she watched through painfully stinging eyes, the needle sank slowly to forty. Alice laughed out loud, she was so relieved. The red shoes couldn't kill her. The moment her car stopped, she'd take them off and throw them right in the lake!

Her speed went down to twenty, and then to fifteen miles an hour. The needle was almost at ten when Alice heard a loud grinding noise. The noise got louder and louder until it turned into a high-pitched screech. And then there was a horrible snap and the handle on the emergency brake pulled off in her hand.

"Oh, no!" Alice stared down at the broken handle for a moment, and then she raised her eyes to the speedometer in fear. The emergency brake had broken and the needle on the speedometer was climbing again. The cursed red shoes had won! She was going to die!

Alice watched in horror as her car hurtled forward, down the gravel road. Even though she was wearing her seat belt, she still bounced up and down in her seat. Her head hit the top of her car with a painful thump. She was going too fast to steer the car and the most dangerous curve of all was only a mile ahead.

She was going to die. Alice dropped her hands from the wheel as her car charged forward toward the curve, faster and faster until the trees whipped past with a dizzying speed. Alice no longer heard the thumps and the rattles, and the high keening sounds of the engine. The terror of knowing that she was going to die filled her mind.

But a sound like a gunshot brought Alice back to the present with a jolt. One of her rear tires had blown out! Alice reached for the wheel and began to steer again. She couldn't just sit there passively, waiting for her car to crash. She had to do something, and she had to do it fast!

A high, tinkling sound claimed Alice's attention, and she glanced down to see what it was. Her key chain. It was rattling against the metal post of the steering wheel, tinkling like wind chimes, as the car bounced over the ruts.

The key! Alice reached down to grab the key, and she pulled it out with one swift jerk. The sound of the motor stopped abruptly, and Alice sobbed in relief. She'd done it! Now all she had to do was wait until her car coasted to a stop.

But Deadman's Curve was coming up fast! Would she slow down in time? Alice gripped the wheel so hard, her knuckles turned white. She was still going over fifty miles an hour. Could she steer around Deadman's Curve that fast?

The yellow curve sign flashed by her window, and Alice felt her heart jump up to her throat. Deadman's Curve was posted at a maximum speed of thirty, and even though her car was slowing down, she was still going much too fast. How fast could she take Deadman's Curve?

Alice held her breath as she went into the curve, her tires skidding on the gravel. Her car fishtailed, swerving dangerously close to the edge, but Alice fought the wheel and somehow managed to stay on the road.

She'd made it! Alice laughed out loud in triumph. There was nothing but straight road and gentle downhill curves for the next two miles. Without any power, her car would stop, and she would be safe from the curse of the red shoes!

That was when she heard it, another sound like a gunshot. Her second rear tire had blown out. Alice jerked the wheel, fighting to keep from going into a skid, and again, she managed to stay on the road.

A glance at the speedometer told her that she was only going forty, and Alice began to relax slightly. And then something happened that Alice had never anticipated. There was another loud bang that sent her car swerving to the left side of the road. And then another, as both of her front tires blew out in rapid succession.

Alice's old green Chevy swerved sharply and sideswiped the guardrail. The glancing impact sent her careening across the road to crash into the thin metal barrier on the other side. For one brief moment, Alice thought the guardrail would hold. But it didn't, and she and her car hurtled into space, rolling over and over, finally landing upside down on the jagged rocks at the bottom of the ravine.

The wheels spun around and around, gradually slowing to a stop. Then there was silence, but Alice didn't hear it. She had entered a much deeper silence, the permanent silence of death.

Flames licked up under Alice's wrecked car, flicking their way to the gas tank. They hovered there for a moment, and then there was a mighty explosion. The tremendous force turned the old green Chevy into a pile of twisted metal that glowed and burned with tremendous heat, igniting the surrounding trees in a towering funeral pyre.

Ten

They were just getting ready to leave when they heard a loud explosion across the lake. Donna turned to Steve with fear in her eyes. "What was that?!"

They rushed to the deck to get a better look. What they saw made them shudder. There was a giant fireball leaping up toward the sky and, as they watched, it ignited several pine trees.

Steve was the first to recover. "I'll go call it in. The pines are dry this time of year, and a fire this big could spread fast."

Donna and Craig stayed on the deck, staring at the fire, which was growing larger with each passing moment. A slight wind was blowing in from the north, and several more pine trees started to burn before Steve came back.

"They're on their way." Steve looked very worried. "A couple of other people reported it, too. I was the third call."

They heard the high-pitched wails of several sirens, and Donna drew a deep sigh of relief. "Here they come!"

"Let's take a run over there." Craig motioned to them. "I've got a really bad feeling about this."

Steve and Donna climbed in Craig's Thunderbird and they peeled out of the driveway. Normally, Donna would have enjoyed a ride in the classic car, but right now she was too worried about the fire.

"I wonder what started it?" Donna frowned slightly. "A gas line explosion?"

Craig shook his head. "There aren't any gas lines out here at the lake. My mother wanted a gas range and they told her she'd have to get electric."

They were flagged down by a fireman when they were still about a mile away. Craig rolled down his window and leaned out to talk to him. "Do you know what started the fire?"

The fireman nodded. "Somebody lost control coming out of Deadman's Curve. The car crashed through the barrier and it exploded when it hit the bottom of the ravine."

Steve exchanged worried glances with Donna. And then he asked the question that was uppermost in all their minds. "Do you know what kind of car it was?"

"It was burning too hot to get very close, but we found a hood ornament up by the guardrails. It looked like it came from a Chevy."

"Any idea what color it was?" Craig's face paled.

The fireman seemed impatient, but when he noticed how worried they were, he nodded. "My guess is green. There was a scrape of green paint on the post that held the rail."

"How about the driver?" Steve's voice was shaking slightly.

The fireman shook his head. "I don't think the driver made it. You couldn't walk away from a crash like that, and no one called for an ambulance."

They didn't say anything on their way back to the cabin. They just rode in silence, each lost in private fears. When they were back inside, Craig headed straight for the phone. "We're probably worrying for nothing. I'm going to call Alice."

The phone rang several times and then a deputy sheriff answered. The news he gave them wasn't good. Alice's old green Chevy had crashed through the guardrail on Deadman's Curve, and Alice was dead.

They were back in town, parked in front of her house, when Donna finally asked the question. "Do you think Alice was wearing the red shoes?"

"I don't know." Steve frowned. "I'll try to find out and I'll call you, later tonight."

Donna was glad her parents weren't home as she climbed the stairs to her room. There were tears in her eyes, and she knew she'd break down if they'd asked her a single question.

Even though she didn't want to think about it, Donna sat down at her desk and worked on her article. It was due on Friday and she'd be disqualified from the contest if she didn't turn it in by the deadline.

As she wrote about what had happened to Rondelle, tears threatened to spill from Donna's eyes. The red shoes were cursed; she was sure of it now. What else could explain the awful things that had happened to Tammy and Rondelle?

When she came to the part about Alice, Donna began to cry. A tear dripped down on her article, leaving a messy blot. Another tear fell, and Donna put down her pen, sobbing quietly to herself. She felt terribly guilty about everything that had happened, and she was sure she could have prevented the tragedies if she'd just tried a little harder.

She'd made her first mistake the night of the school carnival. She should have dragged Tammy away from Magical Footwear and stopped her from buying the red shoes. Her second mistake had happened right after the play. She should have confronted Rondelle at the wrap party and demanded that she give up the cursed shoes. Then there was her third mistake, just today. She should have stayed with Rondelle and told Steve to go find Alice. If he'd found Alice in time, he could have stopped her before she'd put on the red shoes.

Donna swallowed hard and wiped her eyes with a tissue. Tammy was in the hospital, Rondelle's mind had snapped, and Alice was dead. It was all because of the cursed red shoes, and one thing was very clear. Donna had to find them and destroy them before someone else was hurt!

The phone rang and Donna reached out to pick it up. She was so miserable, she barely smiled when she heard Steve's voice. "Hi, Steve. Did you find out about the red shoes?"

Donna held her breath as Steve told her what he'd learned.

He'd called his older sister, who was dating a deputy sheriff, and he'd found out that Alice's car had been completely destroyed. If Alice had been wearing the cursed red shoes, they had certainly gone up in smoke.

"Are you sure they're gone?" Donna held her breath. But Steve seemed very sure when he told her that nothing in Alice's car had escaped the flames. The deputy would be there tomorrow, to sift through the wreckage, and he'd promised to tell Steve if he found even the slightest trace of the cursed red shoes.

Donna was smiling as she thanked Steve and said good-bye. She felt so much better, she even managed to finish writing about what had happened to Alice. But after she'd climbed into bed and turned off the lights, Donna began to feel uneasy again. What if the red shoes had somehow survived the wreck? If someone found them and put them on, the curse might claim a fourth victim!

Things seemed much better in the morning. The sun had been shining when she'd climbed out of bed, and Donna had felt much more in control.

Steve had called his sister during lunch, and he'd come back to the cafeteria with very good news. Her boyfriend had examined every inch of Alice's car, and he'd found no trace of the cursed red shoes.

That had made Donna relax a little, and the rest of the day had gone very well. When she'd turned in the new pages of her article, Miss Adams had said they were perfect. Steve had walked her to every one of her afternoon classes, and her classmates had begun to call her Donna instead of "the new girl." And now she was sitting with the crowd at Clancy's, sharing the biggest fake leather booth.

"I'm so glad I'm not working!" Lisa gave a deep sigh as she slid into the booth next to Donna. "This is the first day I've had off for over three weeks!"

Jerry reached out to take Lisa's hand. "And you've got Friday night off, too, right?"

"That's right." Lisa nodded. "Shelly says no one should have to work on their birthday, and I even get paid for taking the night off. Isn't that great?"

"So you'll go to the fall dance with me?" Jerry looked hopeful.

"Oh—uh—sure!" Lisa smiled the biggest smile Donna had ever seen. "I'd love to, Jerry!"

"You'd love to do what?" Steve came back with a giant plate of fries just in time to hear the end of Lisa's sentence.

Lisa laughed. "Go to the fall dance with Jerry. You're going, aren't you?"

"Sure, but I haven't asked Donna yet." Steve turned to Donna and held out the plate of fries. "How about it, Donna? I'll give you the biggest fry if you'll go to the fall dance with me."

"You just made me an offer I can't refuse." Donna reached out to grab a long, crispy fry and popped it into her mouth.

"Do you want to double?" Jerry turned to Steve. "Your Olds is nicer than my Nissan."

Steve shrugged. "That's fine with me. How about it?"

Donna and Lisa nodded. A double date would be fun.

"Great!" Jerry gave a relieved sigh. "That means I won't have to clean out my car!"

Jerry's comment prompted a series of jokes about the Nissan and how Jerry hadn't cleaned it out since he'd bought it used, two years ago. Donna smiled and laughed right along with the others, but she noticed that Lisa had begun to look a little worried.

"Lisa?" Donna motioned her over so that they could talk privately. "What's wrong?"

"Nothing, really. It's just that I said I'd go to the dance with Jerry, but I don't have anything to wear. I can't afford to buy clothes like yours."

Donna leaned closer to Lisa and lowered her voice. "I don't buy my clothes, Lisa. I just . . . well . . . I make them up. There's a thrift store in town, isn't there?"

"Sure." Lisa nodded. "That's where I buy all my clothes. But they don't have anything fancy enough for the dance."

"That's no problem. We'll go down there right after school

on Friday. I know we can find something we can use. Then we'll go to my house and put together some fantastic outfits. It'll be fun, Lisa."

Lisa's eyes began to sparkle and she looked very excited. "You wouldn't mind helping me?"

"Of course not. The guys can pick us up at my house."

Lisa's face lit up in a grin. "Thanks, Donna. I can hardly wait!"

Donna smiled. She felt fantastic, even though she'd just given away the secret of her designer outfits. It was a small price to pay to see Lisa so happy.

Eleven

Charlie Jensen slowly approached the scene of Alice Mayfield's fatal accident. This job wasn't going to be easy. When the sheriff had called to say he was releasing the car, he hadn't mentioned that it was at the bottom of the ravine!

It was late Thursday afternoon and Charlie was tired. He'd been working since eight that morning and his regular shift was over. He could have told the sheriff that he'd haul the car in the morning, but the city paid time and a half for overtime and he wanted to earn enough money to buy his daughter a nice birthday present.

When Charlie got out of his tow truck, one of the deputies waved him over. He handed Charlie a clipboard and a ballpoint pen that said *Property of the Bannard County Sheriff's Department* on the side. "Hey, Charlie. Sign here and this one's all yours."

"Thanks." Charlie signed on the dotted line. "What took so long with this one?"

The deputy shrugged. "Search me. I guess Sheriff Berg suspected something. He made us sift through every bit of the wreck."

"Did you find anything?" Charlie was curious. Alice Mayfield had been Lisa's classmate.

"Nothing. She must have taken the curve too fast and lost control of her car."

Charlie nodded. "The kids should know better than to speed on this road. Deadman's Curve is tricky."

"I know. We tell 'em that, every year. We even go to the school and show them pictures of the wrecks. It works for a day or two, but then they forget. The sheriff's got a theory about that."

"Yeah?" Charlie leaned against the tow truck and let the deputy talk.

"They don't think it can happen to them. It's always the other guy, you know? They just can't picture themselves lying out on the road, covered by a bloody sheet. It's part of being a teenager. They really believe they'll live forever."

Charlie nodded. What the deputy said was true.

"We do everything we can. We post that curve with warning signs, and the PTA puts up little white crosses for every teenager that dies. The kids drive right past, but it doesn't sink in."

Charlie glanced down at the clipboard again, and then he raised his eyebrows. "I thought you guys were through with this wreck, but this says I'm supposed to haul it to the impound lot."

"Right." The deputy nodded. 'We're trying something new. There's a big dance at the high school tomorrow night. They're going to dismiss the kids early from school and bus them out to the lot. The sheriff wants every teenage driver to see the wreck. He figures it might do some good."

Charlie glanced down at the charred wreck, and then he nodded. "It's sure worth a try. My daughter's going to that dance and I worry when she's on the road."

When the deputy had driven away, Charlie climbed down the bank with the cable. If he didn't get started soon, he'd be hauling the wreck in the dark.

It took twenty minutes to attach the cable to the frame of the wreck. Charlie scrambled up the steep bank and held his breath as he fired up the winch. It was a heavy-duty cable, but the rocks were sharp and the cable could break.

The noise was deafening as the cable tightened and the wreck began to move, scraping and sliding against the side of the bank. It seemed to take forever, but at last the wreck came up over the crest of the bank. When it was on level ground, Charlie used the winch to pull it up on the platform, and then he got into the cab to raise the platform off the ground. It was a good thing he'd brought the best tow truck in the yard. The others didn't have a lift and there was no way he could have dragged the wreck all the way back to town.

Charlie flicked on the headlights and the flasher, and put the truck into gear. He was just pulling away when the twin beams of his headlights illuminated something red in the bushes. Charlie stopped the truck and got out to see what it was.

"Well . . . I'll be!" Charlie reached out to pick up a beautiful red shoe. It looked brand-new and he searched through the bushes to see if he could find its mate. The other shoe was nearby, and Charlie grinned as he carried them back to the truck. They were made of fine, shining satin and they might fit Lisa.

Charlie put the red shoes on the passenger seat and drove-away. He'd compare them to a pair of Lisa's shoes and, if they were the right size, he'd give them to her for a special birthday present.

The red shoes seemed to glow from the light of the dash, and Charlie was glad he'd found them. Lisa would love these shoes, and there was no reason to tell her he'd found them by the side of the road, tossed out like a piece of trash. He'd wrap them up and say he'd bought them at the mall. The little white lie would be his secret, and Lisa would be thrilled with her beautiful birthday present.

Donna shuddered as she walked past Alice's car. She knew why the sheriff had brought the seniors here, but the sheriff didn't know the whole story. Alice hadn't died because she'd been reckless, and she hadn't been speeding deliberately. The cursed red shoes had killed her.

"Are you okay, Donna?" Steve reached out for Donna's hand.

Donna swallowed hard. "I'm all right. It's just seeing Alice's car like this. I can't help thinking I should have warned her."

"I know." Steve squeezed her hand. "I've been thinking the same thing. But we couldn't leave Rondelle. We did our best, Donna."

Donna nodded, but she was silent as they climbed on the bus and rode back to the school. They'd done their best and it hadn't been good enough. Alice was dead. Nothing could change that.

When they got back to the school, Lisa and Jerry met them on the sidewalk. Lisa's face was very pale and Jerry had his arm around her shoulders.

"Do you girls want a ride home?" Steve turned to Donna.

"No, thanks. Lisa and I are going shopping, and I wouldn't want you to get stuck, carrying our packages."

"That's okay. I don't mind."

Donna turned to stare at Steve in shock. "But I thought you hated to carry packages!"

"I used to hate it, but I wouldn't mind carrying them for you."

Jerry burst into laughter. "Oh, man—you're hooked!"

"No, he's not." Donna grinned. "He's off the hook because Lisa and I don't need him. We're just going to buy one thing apiece, and we can handle that."

Steve nodded. "Okay. The dance starts at eight, so I'll pick up the two of you at seven-thirty. Then we'll come and get you, Jerry."

"That's fine." Jerry glanced up at the sky. "I'll bring a couple of umbrellas. The weatherman said it's supposed to turn cold and rainy tonight."

The rain started to fall just as Donna and Lisa were putting the final touches on their outfits. Donna turned to see how Lisa was doing, and she nodded in approval. "I really like the contrast of that bright red braid against the black. Are you going to wear black shoes?"

Lisa smiled as she shook her head. "My parents gave me a pair of red shoes for my birthday. I'm wearing them."

"Red shoes? What *kind* of red shoes?"

Lisa started to laugh. "Relax, Donna. These aren't the cursed red shoes. My Dad got extra money for working overtime, and he bought them for me at Delano's at the mall."

"That's a relief!" Donna laughed, too. "For a minute, you really had me worried. I still have nightmares about those red shoes."

"That's because you're writing that article for the contest. They're always in your mind. The shoes are gone, Donna. They burned up in the wreck."

Donna nodded. She didn't want Lisa to think she was crazy for still worrying about the red shoes.

"We'd better get dressed. We don't have much time." Lisa slipped on her dress and glanced at her reflection in the mirror. "I look all right, don't I?"

"You look gorgeous." Donna smiled at her friend. "And we finished just in time. Steve'll be here in less than ten minutes."

Lisa looked out the window. "It's raining. I'm going to wear my old shoes until we get to the dance."

"Good idea." Donna nodded. "Come on, Lisa. Let's get our coats."

They were ready when Steve rang the doorbell, and he whistled as he noticed their outfits. "Hey! Both of you look really fantastic!"

"Thanks, Steve." Donna smiled as they hurried out to Steve's car. He'd pulled up, under the carport by the side of the house, so they wouldn't get wet.

"Isn't it a lovely night?" Lisa sighed happily as she got into the backseat.

Steve and Donna exchanged glances and then they both cracked up. The rain was pelting down in sheets, lightning was flashing, and thunder was rumbling loudly overhead.

"What do you think, Donna?" Steve grinned at her. "Do you think it's a lovely night?"

"Absolutely!"

Twelve

Donna was amazed when she caught her first glimpse of the gymnasium. The art classes had decorated it, and they'd really done a great job. The scene was an enchanted forest, and in the center of the dance floor was a beautiful, arched bridge that spanned a pool of real water.

"The bridge looks good, doesn't it?" Steve was grinning so proudly, Donna knew he'd worked on it in shop class.

"It's beautiful." Donna smiled back at him. "Can we walk on it?"

Steve nodded. "There's a spot at the top where you can toss in a coin and make a wish. We'll go up there later, but you have to promise to tell me your wish."

Donna didn't say anything. She just snuggled a little closer to Steve's side. She wasn't sure what her wish would be. Right now, it seemed she had everything she'd ever wanted.

"Let's find our table."

Steve took her arm, and they walked past the tables. They were arranged around the edge of the dance floor and each one had room for two couples.

"Here's ours."

Steve pulled out a chair and Donna sat down. She read the names on the other place cards, and she began to smile. "Oh, good! We're sitting with Jerry and Lisa!"

"That's right." Steve nodded. "I thought you knew we'd be sitting with them."

Donna shook her head. How could she have known that? Then she glanced around and realized that they were sitting at the head table. "Steve! This is the head table! Why are we sitting here?"

"Because I'm the class president. Did you forget?"

"Oh, Steve! I *did* forget!" Donna began to blush. And then a worried expression crossed her face. "Does that mean we have to do something special?"

"Not really. All we have to do is head up the reception committee, and start the first dance."

"Oh, my!" Donna gasped again. "But . . . the only time we've ever danced together was at Craig's party. And it was a lot darker then!"

Steve laughed. "Relax, Donna. You're a great dancer and you look really beautiful tonight."

"Thank you." Donna blushed again. "How long will we have to dance alone?"

"Only a minute or two. Then they'll introduce Jerry and Lisa, and they'll join us for the rest of the dance."

Donna was puzzled. "Jerry and Lisa? But why?"

"Because Jerry's the class vice president."

Donna nodded. Thank goodness they'd worked so hard on their outfits, because when they got up for the first dance, everyone at Jefferson High would be staring at them!

It turned out that all Donna's fears were groundless. Everyone had applauded and whistled when they'd danced the first dance. Lisa and Jerry had joined them, and a few minutes later, everyone else had come out on the dance floor.

"That wasn't so bad, was it?" Steve pulled Donna close and wrapped his arms around her waist.

"It was fun." Donna smiled up at him. "And Lisa seemed to be enjoying it, too."

The song ended, and Steve took her arm. "How about some

punch? They're serving it in that hollow tree, over in the corner, and I think I see Jerry in line."

Donna smiled as they approached the hollow tree. Two freshman girls, dressed like elves, were serving the punch. "Hi, Jerry. Where's Lisa?"

"Out there." Jerry pointed to the dance floor. "Craig asked her to dance and I said that was fine with me. Lisa loves to dance, and she practically wore me out on that last set."

Donna was puzzled. Lisa had never mentioned that she loved to dance. As a matter of fact, she'd told Donna she was worried she'd step on Jerry's toes. "Is Lisa a good dancer?"

"She's fantastic! Before we got out on the floor, she warned me that she'd never done much dancing, but she's the best dancer I've ever dated!"

Donna nodded. It was clear that Lisa had been worried for no reason. Perhaps all she needed was a little self-confidence.

Jerry turned to talk to Steve, and Donna watched the dance floor, trying to catch a glimpse of Lisa. It took a few moments, but Donna finally saw her, dancing with Craig. They were dancing to a slow, mellow song, and Craig had the reputation of being the best dancer in the senior class. He and his older sister had competed in ballroom dance contests.

Craig and Lisa did a graceful turn and then a dip so low, Lisa's hair brushed the floor. Donna was so impressed, she almost started to applaud. Lisa was an incredibly good dancer, the best she'd ever seen!

Lisa had never been so happy. She'd just discovered that she loved to dance! She'd been so nervous, her legs had been shaking when she'd gone out on the floor with Jerry. But dancing was easy and it was fun, even though she'd never had a lesson in her life.

"You're really terrific, Lisa!" Craig smiled down at her. "My sister's off at college, but I'll take up ballroom dancing again if you'll be my partner."

Lisa's eyes sparkled. "Thanks, Craig. That's a wonderful compliment, but I can't."

"Why not?"

"I just don't have the time." With her work schedule, her studies, and her family obligations, Lisa really didn't have the time. And then there was Jerry. She wanted to spend all her free moments with him.

"Too bad." Craig sighed. "We would have been fantastic together. How about the dance contest tonight? You'll be my partner for that, won't you?"

Lisa was surprised. She hadn't known they were holding a dance contest. But she was Jerry's date and if she entered the contest, it would be with him. "Sorry, Craig." Lisa shook her head. "I'm Jerry's date and that wouldn't be right."

The song ended and Craig walked her back to the table. Jerry was there, waiting for her, and so were Donna and Steve.

"Thanks, Jerry." Craig gave a little bow. "Looks like the best man won."

Jerry looked puzzled. "What do you mean?"

"Lisa's a fantastic dancer. I asked her to be my partner for the contest, but she turned me down for you."

"Really?" Jerry turned to Lisa with a grin. "I'm flattered, but I think you made a big mistake. You could win if you danced with Craig." Suddenly, Jerry had a pained look on his face. "Oh, oh! Not again!"

"What is it, Jerry?" Lisa turned to him in alarm.

"It's my ankle. It's beginning to swell. It's an old football injury and it acts up once in awhile."

"Is there anything I can do?" Lisa looked worried. "Some ice, maybe? Or I could get an extra chair so you could prop it up."

Jerry shook his head. "That's okay. It'll be fine if I rest it. Why don't you enter that dance contest with Craig? I'll stay right here and watch you."

"Good idea." Craig started to grin. "How about it, Lisa?"

"I don't think so."

"Oh, go ahead." Jerry smiled at Lisa. "Really, you'd be doing me a favor. I'd feel guilty if you couldn't compete. You're such a good dancer, and I'd really like to see you win."

Lisa smiled, and then she took a deep breath. Something

strange was happening to her. The band wasn't playing, but her feet were tapping to a wonderfully complicated beat. She wanted to dance. Oh, how she wanted to dance! And even though she tried to keep her feet still, under the table, they kept right on dancing to a beat that no one else could hear.

The trumpets played a fanfare and the bandleader stood up to take the microphone. "You all know about the dance contest, don't you?"

There were cheers from several tables, and a couple of the students started to clap. The bandleader gave a little bow, and then he spoke into the microphone again. "Five of your teachers will be the judges."

As the bandleader began to announce the rules, Craig pulled Lisa to her feet. "Come on, Lisa. We have to sign up and get a number."

"But I'm still not sure if I should—"

"Go ahead, Lisa." Jerry interrupted her. "Get out there and win . . . for me."

Lisa felt her hopes soar. Jerry really wanted her to enter the contest, and her feet were itching to dance. They'd been tapping and moving ever since she'd come back to the table.

"All right." Lisa took Craig's arm. "Let's go out and win it for Jerry!"

As Lisa stepped out on the dance floor, her heart pounded in excitement. The other couples had lined up for numbers, and Lisa's feet tapped as they stood in line. She even did a little twirl, right there in the line, she was so eager to enter the contest. Tonight she felt like dancing was what she'd been born to do, and she could hardly wait until the band started playing.

Just as soon as Lisa and Craig had left the table, Steve turned to Jerry. "What football injury? You don't have any football injury!"

"I know. But Lisa couldn't win the contest with me, and the prize is a hundred dollars. Craig's going to give her his share. I set it up with him, right after that first dance with Lisa."

Donna leaned across the table, and gave Jerry a big kiss on the cheek. "That's really nice of you, Jerry. Lisa could use the money."

"Hey, Donna. How about it? Let's enter the contest." Steve pulled her to her feet.

"Okay, if you want to." Donna nodded. "But I don't think we stand a chance of winning with Lisa and Craig out there on the floor."

Steve waited until they were far enough away from the table so he wouldn't be overheard. And then he turned to Donna and gave her a little hug. "Winning doesn't matter to me, Donna. I just want a chance to hold you in my arms again."

Thirteen

The first song in the contest was a slow love song, and Donna and Steve did very well. When the song ended, both of them were pleased that they'd made it past the first cut.

"We're still in!" Donna smiled as she glanced around her. All through the song, she'd been expecting the bandleader to tap Steve on the shoulder to tell them they'd been eliminated.

"The dance floor was crowded. Maybe they just didn't see us." Steve grinned down at her. "What kind of music are they playing next?"

Donna grinned back. "I think they said it was salsa. You'd better not hold me quite so close if you ever want to use your feet again."

It was a miracle, but Steve and Donna made it past the second cut. When the last note had faded away, Steve turned to Donna with a smile on his face. "We made it! What's next?"

"Retro." Donna started to laugh. "It's like the disco they used to do in the seventies."

"Do you think we should leave now, before it starts?"

Donna nodded. "I think that's the best idea I've heard all night!"

Steve took Donna's arm and they walked off the dance floor. They found Jerry, standing on the sidelines next to the bridge, and Steve clapped him on the back. "That old football injury of yours is much better, right?"

"Right." Jerry grinned. "I've been watching Lisa and Craig, and they're doing great. Let's climb up the bridge and watch from the top."

All three of them walked up the arched bridge and stopped at the highest point. They were about five feet above the dance floor and they could see perfectly.

"Where's Lisa?" Steve glanced out, over the crowd. There were still quite a few couples left on the floor.

"Right over there, next to the platform." Jerry pointed her out. "She's got to be tired. Craig had her spinning all over the floor."

Steve nodded. "I see her, but she doesn't look tired. She's even practicing some steps . . . look!"

They all watched lisa as she practiced a series of complicated steps. And then the band started playing again, and Craig and Lisa began to dance.

"She's great!" Jerry looked proud as he watched Craig and Lisa. "And she really looks good in that outfit. It's perfect with those red shoes."

Steve turned to Donna in alarm. "Where did Lisa get those red shoes? They look exactly like—"

"I know." Donna interrupted him. "But don't worry, Steve. Lisa's red shoes were a birthday present. Her father worked two hours of overtime so he could buy them for her. They came from Delano's shoe store at the mall."

Jerry whistled. "I worked at Delano's last Christmas and their shoes are expensive. The cheapest shoes they carried were over a hundred dollars."

Steve shook his head. "There's no way Lisa's father could have bought her shoes at Delano's. Tow truck drivers don't make that much."

Donna felt an icy shiver run right down her back. She'd forgotten that Lisa's father was a tow truck driver.

"Are you thinking what I'm thinking?" Steve looked very

worried when Donna nodded, and he turned to Jerry with a question. "Do you know if Lisa's father towed Alice's car?"

"Yes." Jerry nodded. "I was studying with Lisa when he came home."

Donna took a deep breath. She hated to ask, but she had to know. "Do you think Lisa's father might have lied about where he got the shoes?"

"Maybe. He might be embarrassed because he can't buy nice things for Lisa."

"Uh-oh." Steve looked even more worried when he turned to Donna. "You were standing right next to Tammy when she bought the red shoes. Do you think you could recognize them if you saw them again?"

"I think so. Let's go out there and ask Lisa to take off her shoes so I can look at them."

"No!" Jerry grabbed Donna's arm. "What if we're wrong? We all heard the rules. If Lisa stops dancing, she'll be disqualified. Let's just watch her and see what happens, okay?"

Donna sighed. Jerry had a point. They all wanted Lisa to win the contest, and they could be wrong about where her father had gotten the red shoes.

"Okay, Jer." Steve nodded reluctantly. "We'll all keep an eye on Lisa. But if there's even the slightest hint of trouble, we've got to stop the contest!"

Lisa was having a wonderful time! Her feet felt like they had wings, and she tapped them impatiently, waiting for the next part of the contest to start. Dancing was simple. She'd been silly to worry about it. Even though she'd never done any of these dances before, her feet just seemed to know the steps. It was a miracle. And it was wonderful to discover that she had a new talent!

"What comes next?" Lisa's eyes were sparkling as she turned to Craig.

"Hip-hop. Do you know how to do that?"

Lisa shook her head. "No, but you don't have to worry. I can pick it up as we go along."

"I believe you." Craig gave her a friendly hug. "You're really incredible, Lisa. I've never seen anyone with so much natural talent."

"Thanks, Craig." Lisa blushed. She wasn't used to compliments. And then the band started to play again, and she rushed into Craig's arms so that she could dance.

Hip-hop was easy. Lisa picked it up in no time at all. Her feet flew across the floor in perfect rhythm, and she smiled and smiled as the bandleader passed them by to tap someone else on the shoulder.

"Oh, man! I'm winded!" Craig was puffing when the dance ended. "Aren't you tired, Lisa?"

Lisa giggled. "Tired? Of course not I can hardly wait to dance again! What's next?"

"More retro. I don't know, Lisa. I haven't danced like this for a long time, and I'm really worn out."

"But you have to dance with me!" Lisa began to frown. "Please, Craig—I really want to dance!"

Craig nodded and wiped his forehead with a handkerchief. "Okay. I can do it, if they just give me a little time to rest up. This should be the last round. Only two other couples are left."

"You're right!" Lisa did a little dance step as she whirled around to survey the dance floor. "I think we're going to win, Craig. I really do!"

The panel of judges conferred for what seemed like hours to Lisa, but she was glad that Craig got a chance to rest. By the time the music started again, his color had returned to normal and Lisa was relieved as he took her in his arms.

Retro took a lot of energy, but Lisa was ready. She felt as if she could dance like this all night! One by one, the two remaining couples were eliminated and then the bandleader stopped the music.

"The winners!" The bandleader walked forward with the microphone. "And just in case you're wondering, it was a unanimous decision by our panel of judges! Come on up here, Lisa and Craig."

Everyone burst into applause as they climbed up the steps to the platform. Lisa did another little dance step, and laughed as she accepted her prize. She opened the envelope and then she gasped as she saw what was inside.

It was a crisp, new hundred dollar bill! Lisa's face lit up in a brilliant smile. It was a whole week's salary for her and she'd earned it by just having fun!

The bandleader held out the microphone and Craig took it first. "I didn't win first prize, my partner did. She made me look good. And that's why I'm giving my half of the prize to the best dancer at Jefferson High, the incredibly talented Miss Lisa Jensen!"

"Oh, thank you! Thank you all so much!" Lisa spoke into the microphone. "I just love to dance, and I'm sorry the contest is over."

"Encore, encore!" One of the guys in the band yelled out. And then everyone in the whole gymnasium took up the cry for an encore.

"I'm all danced out." Craig turned to Lisa. "Don't you want to rest?"

Lisa shook her head. "Not me! I'm just getting started. If you're too tired to dance with me, I'll dance by myself."

Craig put his arm around Lisa's shoulders. "Why don't we just go back to the table? You can show Jerry what you won."

Lisa's eyes snapped with anger and she shook her head. "But I don't want to go back to the table. I want to dance!"

"Come on, Lisa. Let's get a glass of punch and sit down."

"Go away!" Lisa pushed Craig's arm away. "I love to dance and I'm going to dance alone!"

The bandleader overheard Lisa's comment and he stepped up to the microphone. "Lisa's going to dance a solo. What kind of music do you want, Lisa?"

Lisa laughed. "I don't care, as long as it's fast."

Everyone applauded then, and several of the guys whistled and stomped their feet. The band started to play something fast, and Lisa's flying feet carried her out to the middle of the floor.

As Lisa leaped and twirled to the music, an expression of pain crossed her face. What she'd said was true. She did love to dance. But she was beginning to feel the effects of dancing non-stop. Her leg muscles felt as if they might cramp at any second, and her arms were beginning to shake. But she couldn't seem to stop dancing, even though she really wanted to sit down and rest. Something was terribly wrong with her, but she didn't know what it was. It was as if some strange kind of compulsion had taken over her body, and Lisa wondered just how long she could keep it up before she dropped from pure exhaustion.

Fourteen

Craig had come up to join them on the bridge, and he'd told them how weird Lisa was acting. And then Lisa whirled very close to the bridge and Donna was able to see her feet.

"She's wearing the cursed red shoes!" Donna hands were shaking as she grabbed Steve's arm. "Come on! We're got to stop Lisa before the red shoes kill her!"

They ran down the bridge, but a huge crowd of students had lined up to watch Lisa dance, and they couldn't get close to the dance floor. At first they tried to inch their way through, but that wasn't fast enough.

"Hurry, Steve!" Donna tugged at Steve's arm.

Steve nodded, and he turned to Jerry and Craig. "It's like football practice. Let's just sweep them out of the way!"

While Donna followed in their wake, the three guys linked arms and barreled their way through the crowd. Lisa's life was in danger and they had to get to her as fast as they could.

"There she is!" Craig elbowed the last person out of the way and pulled Donna up beside him. Lisa was dancing alone, in the middle of the floor while the crowd cheered her on.

"What is she *doing*?!"

Jerry sounded horrified, and Donna could see why. Lisa was spinning around, leaping and whirling, her feet moving almost too fast to see. The tempo of the music was increasing with every measure, faster and faster as Lisa danced her frenzied solo dance.

"Come on, let's get her!" Steve ran out on the dance floor with Jerry and Craig. "Stop the band, Donna!"

Donna raced up to the platform and shouted for the band to stop. Then she glanced at Lisa, and her eyes widened in horror as she saw that Lisa was still dancing. There was no music, but Lisa was leaping and spinning, faster and faster, like a whirling dervish!

"Stop, Lisa! Stop!" Donna raced across the dance floor, but she couldn't get close enough to Lisa. "Please! You're wearing the cursed red shoes! You've got to stop dancing!"

"I . . . can't!" Lisa's voice was faint as she whirled away, almost knocking Donna down. "Help . . . me! Please!"

"We'll have to surround her." Steve motioned for Craig and Jerry, and they closed in on Lisa from three different directions. But Lisa was whirling so fast, they couldn't get close enough to grab her.

"Tackle her!" Donna shouted out. "You've got to stop her!"

The three guys ran forward to tackle Lisa and drag her down to the floor. Donna raced up to help, but she couldn't grab the red shoes. Lisa's feet were still moving, flying faster and faster, kicking out wildly in every direction.

"Hold her legs!" Donna's voice was high and frantic. "I have to take off the shoes!"

Lisa seemed to have incredible strength, and the guys struggled to hold her. It took precious seconds, but at last Donna managed to pull off Lisa's right shoe. A few seconds later, she had the left and she held them up triumphantly. "It's all right. I've got them!"

"Thank . . . you . . ." Lisa's eyes fluttered, and all the color drained from her face. And then she collapsed completely, crumpling in a heap on the dance floor.

Donna turned to Steve. "Let's carry her to the ladies' room. There's a couch there."

Everyone watched in stunned silence as they started to carry Lisa from the floor. But the bandleader did exactly the right thing. He took the microphone and tapped it loudly.

"The excitement's over, folks. And Lisa needs to rest. Let's all calm down and dance to a song I know you're going to like."

The band began to play a popular love song, and some of the students got up to dance. Others offered to help them with Lisa, but Donna turned them down. Lisa appeared to be sleeping, and Donna knew she'd be terribly embarrassed if she woke up to a crowd of curious faces.

At the door to the ladies' room, Steve turned to Donna. "Do you really think we should go in?"

"You have to. I can't carry Lisa all by myself. But don't worry, Steve. The couch is in the outer alcove. Just put Lisa down, and you can leave."

"Okay. Come on, guys. Here we go."

Donna held the door, and the guys carried Lisa to the couch. They'd just put her down on the cushions when Rita Swensen, the head cheerleader, came in.

"What are you guys doing in here!" Rita was angry and the guys beat a hasty retreat. But then Rita saw Lisa, stretched out on the couch, and she rushed over to help. "Is she all right?"

"I don't know." Donna stuck the red shoes on the shelf under the mirror, and hurried over to the couch.

"I'll take her pulse." Rita sat down and reached for Lisa's hand. "I learned how, last summer."

Donna was quiet as Rita took Lisa's pulse. It seemed to take a long time and when Rita looked up again, she was frowning. "I did it twice, just to be sure, but I got the same count both times. Her pulse is weak, and it's much too fast."

"Can you stay with her while I call a doctor?" Donna was even more concerned than she'd been before.

"Of course." Rita picked up Lisa's wrist again. "I'll monitor her pulse while you're gone."

It didn't take long for Donna to reach Doctor Weston, their family doctor. When she'd explained what had happened to

Lisa, he said he'd be there in less than ten minutes. Donna hurried back to the alcove and waited while Rita took Lisa's pulse again.

"Her pulse is stronger." Rita didn't look quite as worried as she'd been before. "And it's slowed down a lot."

"That's good, isn't it?"

"That's very good. It's still on the high side, but her heart rate is returning to normal."

About five minutes more ticked by in silence. Then the door to the ladies' room opened, and Doctor Weston came in. When he saw Rita, he smiled. "How's my patient, Rita?"

"Better, Doctor Weston." Rita turned to Donna to explain. "I work for Doctor Weston every summer. I'm just his receptionist, but I've learned a lot."

Donna listened while Rita rattled off a series of numbers which Doctor Weston seemed to understand. Then the doctor took out a stethoscope, and listened to Lisa's heart.

"She's going to be all right, isn't she?" Donna asked, her voice shaking.

"She's going to be fine." Doctor Weston gave Donna a reassuring smile. "But it's a good thing you stopped her when you did. Another few minutes of exertion, and it might have been a different story."

Donna gave a huge sigh of relief. "Will she wake up soon?"

"That's not likely." Doctor Weston shook his head. "She'll sleep until morning, and then she'll need a few days of rest. I'll call for an ambulance to take her down to the clinic. I want to run a few tests, just to be on the safe side. If they turn out all right, she can go home in the morning."

Donna jumped to her feet. "I'll go with her. Lisa shouldn't wake up, all alone."

"There's no need for that. My nurse is there now. And I'll call Lisa's parents if you give me her number. You can stay with Lisa until the ambulance comes, and then I want you to go back and enjoy the dance."

Donna jotted down the Jensens' number for Doctor Weston

and the ambulance was there in less than five minutes. Everyone went along as they carried Lisa out on a stretcher and put her inside.

"Come on, Donna." Steve draped his arm around her shoulders. "Let's go back to the dance. You heard Doctor Weston. Lisa's going to be just fine."

Donna nodded. She didn't really feel like going back, but Steve was the class president and they couldn't leave yet. Perhaps dancing with Steve would take her mind off what had happened to Lisa, and how the red shoes had tried to kill her.

Steve noticed the expression of panic that crossed Donna's face. "What is it, Donna? What's wrong?"

"The red shoes! I left them in the ladies' room!"

Donna ran back to the ladies' room as fast as she could, almost bumping into several people. She pushed open the door, and then she gasped as she saw that the shelf was empty!

"Oh, no!" Donna stared at the shelf under the mirror in utter dismay. The cursed red shoes were gone!

The inner door opened, and two girls came out. Donna had never seen them before, but several guys from the senior class were dating girls from other schools. One girl had short, dark hair, and the other was a redhead. Both of them were giggling at something they found terribly funny.

"Did you see anyone else while you were in here?" Donna's voice was shaking slightly.

"Did we ever!" The girl with dark hair nodded, and they both started to giggle again.

"Who was it?" Donna tried not to sound too impatient.

"I don't know, but she was really weird." The redhead looked very amused. "She looked just like a big black crow."

Donna felt her knees start to shake. Could it have been the old woman from the Magical Footwear booth? "This woman— was she dressed in black, with a long skirt and a cape?"

"That's her." The redhead nodded. "Don't tell me she's one of your teachers?!"

"No, she's not. Did you see which way she went?"

"I did." The girl with the dark hair nodded. "She grabbed her things from that ledge under the mirror and went straight out the door to the parking lot."

"Her things? What did they look like?" Donna felt her heart leap up to her throat. If the old woman from Magical Footwear had the cursed red shoes again, she might sell them to somebody else!

"I'm not sure. She just grabbed them and went out the door. All I know is they were red and kind of shiny."

The redhead stared at Donna for a moment, and then she looked concerned. "Is something wrong?"

"Yes." Donna didn't bother to explain. She just turned around and went out to find Steve. The cursed red shoes were gone. And somehow, they had to find a way to get them back!

"It's all right, Donna. Just give me a minute to think."

Steve and Donna were out on the dance floor again, dancing to a long, slow song. It was one of Donna's favorites, but she was much too worried about the old woman and the cursed red shoes to enjoy it.

"I've got an idea." Steve danced Donna close to their table and motioned for Jerry to cut in. "Dance with Jerry while I check on something."

Although Donna tried to pay attention to Jerry, her eyes followed Steve as he walked over to the big faculty table. He talked to Mr. Simon, the principal, for several minutes, and then he moved on to talk to some of the teachers. Steve's conversation with Miss Adams seemed to last a long time, but eventually he headed back to the dance floor. There was a big smile on his face, and Donna felt her hopes rise. Had Steve figured out what to do about the cursed red shoes?

"You can stop worrying." Steve grinned as he took Donna in his arms. "I just talked to Miss Adams, and she wants you to write another section for your article. You're supposed to describe exactly what happened to Lisa, and how the old woman took the shoes."

Donna nodded. "I can do that, but it won't help. Everybody saw what happened to Lisa, and even if they don't believe in the curse, they know that the red shoes are dangerous. No one in Jefferson City will buy them, but the old woman could sell them somewhere else."

Steve nodded, and Donna frowned slightly. He didn't seem at all concerned. "Steve—this is important!"

"I know, but we've got it all figured out. One of Mr. Simon's college classmates owns a big newspaper chain. When you're all done with your article, he's going to publish it in every one of his papers."

"What?" Donna could hardly believe what Steve was saying. She'd never been published in a real newspaper before!

"And Coach Harrison has a friend who works for UPI."

Donna nodded. "United Press International?"

"That's right. And Miss Adams knows somebody at Associated Press. They're going to make sure that every newspaper in the country prints your story."

Donna didn't say anything. She just took a deep breath, and hoped she wouldn't faint. But Steve was still grinning and she had to ask. "There's something else, isn't there?"

"Just one little thing." Steve said. "One of your jobs as the new editor of the *Gazette* is to send copies of your article to every other school in the state. That way you can warn them, too."

Donna's mouth dropped open. "The new editor?! But Steve . . . the contest hasn't even been decided yet!"

"Yes, it has." Even though Donna had thought it was impossible, Steve's grin grew even wider. "The faculty committee was so impressed with your article, it was a unanimous decision. You won the contest, Donna. And Miss Adams thinks you'll be the best editor the *Gazette* has ever had."

"Oh, Steve!" Donna was so excited and so happy, tears started to roll down her cheeks.

"What's wrong, Donna?" Steve looked worried. "Why are you crying?"

Donna wasn't sure what to say. Her best friend, Lisa, was going to be fine, she could stop worrying about the cursed red shoes, and she was the new editor of the *Jefferson High Gazette*.

And to make everything even more perfect, she was going out with the guy of her dreams!

"Donna? What is it?" Steve held her tightly. "Please tell me why you're crying."

"I'm crying because I'm so happy!"

"But that's nothing to cry about." Steve smiled down at her.

"You're right," Donna said, as she threw her arms around Steve and gave him a hug, right there on the dance floor. Steve hugged her back and then he kissed her, a light, friendly kiss that promised much more. And then they started to dance a long, slow dance, and neither one of them even realized that the band had stopped playing.

Epilogue

Two Months Later in a Different State

There was no doubt about it Shirley Conway was having a horrible day. She'd been shopping at the Grand Forks Mall for over three hours, and she hadn't found a single thing to buy.

"Come on, Shirl—let's go, huh?" Ronni James, Shirley's best friend, had reached the end of her patience. "We're already late. We were supposed to meet the guys ten minutes ago!"

"Don't worry, Ronni. They'll wait." Shirley turned to survey the strip of booths in the center of the mall. "My Christmas party's tomorrow night, and I still don't have the right shoes."

Ronni sighed. Shirley was stubborn and she wouldn't leave the mall until she'd found the perfect pair of shoes. "Okay, Shirl. Which booth do you want to try next?"

"That one!" Shirley pointed toward the booth on the end. "Just look at those shoes, Ronni. They're incredible!"

Ronni nodded. The shoes really *were* incredible, and so was the booth. It was a huge tent made of oriental carpets, right next to a big, artificial tree. Pairs of boots, and shoes, and slippers hung from the branches like sparkling jewels, but something about the booth made Ronni feel very uneasy. It was hauntingly familiar, although Ronni was sure she hadn't seen it before. And something about the old woman who ran the booth made Ronni want to turn around and run for her life!

Ronni swallowed hard. "Shirl—listen to me. There's something about that booth that scares me. I don't want to go over there."

"Oh, don't be silly!" Shirley grabbed Ronni's hand. "We have to go. I need party shoes."

Ronni thought about pulling away and running for the safety of the parking lot, but she didn't want Shirley to laugh at her. She was tired after their long day of shopping, and her imagination was playing tricks on her. There was nothing wrong with this booth, nothing at all.

"What have you got that's really fantastic?" Shirley's eyes were sparkling as they arrived at the counter. "I need the most wonderful pair of shoes in the world for my Christmas party!"

The old woman nodded and led them into the tent. "Please come with me, young ladies. My special shoes are in the back. Each pair is one-of-a-kind."

Ronni frowned. Something about the old woman was familiar, too. She wore a long black skirt that swept against the floor, and a huge black cape with flapping arms. She looked like some kind of giant black bird . . . a raven? Or a crow?

Suddenly Ronni remembered, and her throat went dry with fear. She'd read an article in the newspaper about a place called Magical Footwear and a pair of cursed red shoes. This booth and this old woman were almost exactly the same as the writer had described!

The old woman had stepped behind a curtain to get several boxes of shoes. Ronni leaned close to Shirley and spoke very softly in her ear. "Remember that article about the cursed red shoes, and Magical Footwear? I think this is the same booth!"

"Come on, Ronni." Shirley gave a little laugh. "It's not the same at all. I saw the sign and this booth is called Charmed Feet."

Ronni knew she should drop the whole thing before Shirley

got mad, but she had a duty to warn her friend. "I know the name's different, Shirl. But she could have changed it."

"Stop being ridiculous!" Shirley's voice was sharp. "That story was fiction. They just made it up to sell papers!"

Ronni sighed. "Maybe you're right. But don't buy your shoes here, Shirl. I just have a bad feeling."

"I don't know about you, Ronni. You're really weird!" Shirley stopped speaking as the old woman brought out a display case. She set it on the counter and Shirley clapped her hands in delight. "Those shoes are gorgeous, and they're exactly what I need! Let me try them on!"

The old woman smiled as she opened the display case. "Certainly, young lady. I am happy to oblige."

Ronni shivered as she caught sight of the shoes. Their color was so deep, it was almost luminescent. And the shoes were red, the same as the cursed shoes in the article she'd read!

"If they fit, I'll take them." Shirley reached out to grab the shoes.

"Shirl—please don't!" Ronni knew she had to keep Shirley from buying the shoes. Shirley wouldn't listen to another warning about the curse, but she might be swayed by fashion advice. "They won't match your dress. I'm sure of it."

"So what?" Shirley glared at Ronni. "I want these shoes! And if they don't match my dress, I'll just buy another dress."

"But, Shirl—"

"Cut it out, Ronni! I'm getting sick of this. Why don't you just get lost?!"

Ronni turned away with tears in her eyes. They'd been friends for years, and Shirley had never been mean before. As she walked toward the exit, her head hung low, Ronni heard Shirley's voice again. And what Shirley said made Ronni shiver in dread.

"Ring them up, and I'll take them." Shirley's voice was high and excited. "And don't bother to put them in a box. I love these red shoes so much, I'm going to wear them home!"

The Dead Girl

One

The Denver airport was small compared to Heathrow or Zurich, and the customs inspection area was tiny and
cramped. Euro-World Flight 503 had been scheduled to stop for
customs at Kennedy in New York, but they had landed fifty
minutes late. To save time, the passengers who were flying on to
the West had been asked to stay on the plane and go through
customs in Denver.

"Miss Forrester." The inspector looked up at her with a
frown on his face. "Are you here for business, or pleasure?"

Julie felt like saying yes and letting him guess which one she'd
meant, but this wasn't the time for joking around. She'd been
through enough customs checks to know that an inspector wasn't
hired for his sense of humor. "I'm not sure how you'd classify it,
sir. My parents died, and I came here to live with my aunt and
uncle."

"I see." He stamped her passport, but he didn't hand it back.
"And you're seventeen years old?"

Julie nodded. "Yes, sir."

"I'm sorry, Miss Forrester, but we're not allowed to release
minors until we're sure that an adult is here to meet them. Are
your relatives here?"

"Yes, they're here." Julie had a sudden inspiration, and she
turned to wave to the group of strangers who were waiting out-

side. It wasn't exactly a lie. Aunt Caroline and Uncle Bob were supposed be here . . . somewhere.

The customs official turned toward the window, and at that exact moment, an older couple waved at someone who was in line behind Julie. "I see them. All right, Miss Forrester. You can go. And welcome to Denver."

"Thank you." Julie picked up her carry-on and hurried through the door. It was a lucky break. She certainly hadn't wanted to wait like a child until someone had come to claim her. She was perfectly capable of taking care of herself. She'd been on her own for four months now.

As she strode away from the customs area, Julie held her head high. She pretended that she didn't mind that she'll never see her parents again, pretended that she hadn't been kicked out of Europe and shipped back to the States like some sort of undesirable alien, pretended that she loved the fact that her life had been turned upside down. She was playing the role of a supremely self-confident woman, the woman she hoped to become.

At least she looked the part. Julie let a smile cross her face. She'd worn her curly reddish-blond hair loose for the long plane ride. It was more comfortable that way. But right before they'd landed, she'd pulled it up in a twist and secured it snugly with the hammered silver barrette her father had sent her from India. She'd also changed out of her jeans and sweatshirt, and now she was wearing the smart black suit her mother had bought her in Paris during last year's Christmas break. Julie cherished the memory of that Paris trip. It was the last time she'd seen her parents.

Julie's eyes glistened with unshed tears as she remembered the morning of her seventeenth birthday. Her parents had been scheduled to arrive that evening, and she hadn't suspected that anything was wrong when the headmistress had called her into the office. Miss LaFond always presented each of her girls with a birthday present. It was a school tradition.

But when Julie opened the door to the office, there had been no birthday greeting, no gift-wrapped package on the desk. Miss

LaFond had looked very grim as she'd asked Julie to sit down on the couch, instead of in the chair in front of her desk. Then she'd taken a place next to Julie, cleared her throat, and told her the horrible news. Her mother and father had been attending a company meeting in Beijing. They'd taken an early commercial flight, instead of waiting for the company plane, because they'd wanted to get back to Zurich for her birthday. But they hadn't made it; their plane had gone down and there had been no survivors.

The time period immediately following Miss LaFond's shocking announcement was still a complete blank. Julie didn't remember what she'd said, or what she'd done, or how she'd acted, but somehow the minutes had ticked past on the old school clock hanging behind the desk. It had been ten o'clock in the morning when she'd entered Miss LaFond's office. No one was ever late for an appointment with the headmistress. But when she'd looked at the clock again, it was twenty past ten and she'd been gathered in surprisingly gentle arms, her tears soaking Miss LaFond's white silk blouse.

Someone gave a low whistle and Julie was brought back to the present with a jolt. She blinked back her tears and shook off the painful memory. She didn't want to dwell on the past. That was then and this was now. She had to take each day as it came.

Julie turned toward the source of the whistle and saw three guys in college sweatshirts, grinning at her. She let a very small return smile play around the corners of her mouth, but she walked quickly past.

Although Julie had never been in Denver before, she was technically no stranger to America. She'd been born in Dallas, Texas, and she'd lived there for the first six months of her life before her parents had been transferred overseas. She'd traveled from country to country with her parents, attending the various American schools their company had established in foreign countries, and when she'd turned fourteen, she'd gone off to an exclusive Swiss boarding school. Julie had been happy there, although she'd seen her parents only on school vacations. And now her parents were gone; she'd never see them again.

Julie lifted her head and squared her shoulders. The time for grief was past. She'd finished the summer term at her boarding school, and supervised the packing and shipping of her parents' possessions. Now, after almost seventeen years of living abroad, she was back in the States. She'd be living in Crest Ridge, Colorado, with Aunt Caroline, her mother's twin sister. And after she'd completed her senior year of high school, she'd enroll at Vassar, her mother's alma mater.

The thought of attending a coed high school made Julie smile. Of course she was a few weeks late; high school had been in session for almost a month, but she was a good student and she didn't expect to have any trouble catching up with her studies.

The Swiss boarding school had been for girls only. There had been a boys' boarding school five miles away, but the two schools had discouraged dating except at supervised social events. Miss LaFond's girls had strict curfews and regulations. They were required to be in their rooms at ten P.M. on school days and by eleven on weekends. Julie had discovered several ingenious ways to sneak out of her room and back in again, much to the admiration of her classmates.

Julie's eyes swept over the faces in the waiting area, but she didn't spot Aunt Caroline. There was no way Julie could fail to recognize her, even though she hadn't seen Aunt Caroline since she'd come to visit them in Tokyo over thirteen years ago. The reason was simple. Julie's mother and Aunt Caroline had been identical twins, and they'd looked exactly alike. But there could be a big problem if Uncle Bob had come to meet her, alone. He hadn't come along on the Tokyo visit, and Julie had never met him.

There had been an occasional family photograph, and Julie had studied them carefully before she'd packed her parents' photo albums. The most recent had arrived two years ago, and it had shown Aunt Caroline, Uncle Bob, and Cousin Vicki, standing in front of the huge Christmas tree outside their lodge in the mountains. It had been a nice, clear shot, but the photographer had moved back to include the whole tree, and their faces had been tiny specks in the frame.

Julie sighed as she surveyed the crowd. She'd always dreamed of visiting her aunt and uncle's lodge in the mountains, especially since Cousin Vicki had been her age. But now Cousin Vicki was dead, too, killed in a car accident last winter. It had been a year of tragedy for the whole family.

After the crowd had thinned, Julie walked to the airline counter and requested a page. Her aunt and uncle might have been delayed by traffic, or perhaps they'd gotten a late start. Julie wasn't worried; she had enough money to tide her over, even if she had to stay at a nearby hotel for the night.

Paging the party meeting Euro-World Airlines' passenger Julie Forrester—please pick up the red phone. The party meeting Miss Julie Forrester, pick up the red phone, please.

Julie laughed out loud as she heard the page. It was so garbled and full of static, she doubted that anyone could understand it. And the speaker's accent was very thick. She'd ask the airline to try again, in ten minutes or so. Perhaps it would be clearer the second time.

"Sorry. No one's answering." The older man at the counter looked concerned. "Do you want me to try again a little later?"

"Yes, please. I'll wait in the coffee shop." Julie tried not to laugh. His accent was the same as the voice on the loudspeaker.

There was a seat at the counter in the coffee shop, and Julie stashed her carry-on at her feet. The rest of her baggage had been delayed, and the airline had promised to deliver it in the morning. She took the menu the waitress handed her and studied the specials.

"Can I take your order?" The waitress stood behind the counter, her pencil poised over her order pad.

"Yes, thank you." Julie scanned the menu quickly for something familiar. "I'll have coffee and . . . a Danish."

The waitress placed a cup on the counter and poured Julie's coffee. Then she went back to the kitchen and came back with the Danish. Julie cut off a piece with her fork, popped it into her mouth, and frowned. She'd expected to be served something similar to the *Wienerbrod* she'd eaten in Copenhagen, but this pastry wasn't buttery or rich at all. It was what her mother had called a sweet roll, a thin piece of dough with a gob of jam in the center. She took a sip of coffee to wash it down, and her frown deepened. The coffee was also disappointing. It was weak and tasteless, more like colored water than the strong brew she'd grown to love.

"The food here isn't much, is it?"

Julie turned to look at the young man sitting next to her at the counter, and she felt her pulse race. He had an American accent, too, but she liked the sound of his voice. He was in his early twenties, with dark hair worn slightly long in the back. His eyes were a deep blue, so dark that they looked almost purple, and his skin was tanned bronze by the sun. If all American men looked like this, she was sure she'd enjoy her new life in the states.

Since Julie wasn't sure how to respond, she smiled.

"So, where are you from?" he asked.

Julie gave him her best smile. Her heart beat a little faster when he smiled back. "That's a difficult question. I've lived in Tokyo, Beijing, Paris, Hamburg, Warsaw, Prague, Venice, Madrid, Amsterdam, Copenhagen, and most recently, Zurich. But I was born here, so I'm technically an American."

"I guess that explains the accent." The young man laughed. "I was having a devil of a time figuring it out. Excuse me for staring, but you look exactly like someone I used to know."

Julie raised her eyebrows. Was he flirting with her? It was difficult to tell because she wasn't acquainted with the way American men flirted. "This someone you knew, was it a pleasant relationship?"

"Well . . . not exactly." He gave a wry grin and changed the subject. "You've certainly lived all over the world. Was your father in the military?"

Julie shook her head. "No, he worked for a big corporation. So did my mother. The company moved us from country to country, setting up their global communications network."

"Sounds interesting. So you and your parents are back here now?"

Julie hesitated. She wasn't sure it was right to discuss her life with a complete stranger, but he looked nice enough, and his questions weren't all that personal. "I'm here alone. My parents were killed in a plane crash four months ago."

"I'm sorry. I guess I've got a big mouth."

"It's all right." Julie smiled at him. He really did look sorry, so she tried to make a joke. "And I don't think your mouth is too big at all."

He laughed at that, and held out his hand. "I'm Ross Connors, and I live up in the mountains, about twenty miles from here. Are you staying in Denver long?"

"I'm Julie Forrester, and I'm not really staying in Denver." Julie shook his hand. "My relatives own . . ."

"Saddlepeak Lodge." Ross Connors interrupted her. He also looked a bit confused "But I thought you were only seventeen."

"I am . . . but how did *you* know?"

Ross Connors dropped her hand and sat up a little straighter. He was still smiling, but Julie noticed that it was a different smile, the kind of smile you'd give to a child. "I live at Saddlepeak Lodge. I'm your uncle's assistant manager."

"I see. Well . . . I'm very glad to meet you." Julie kept a smile on her face even though her spirits took a nosedive. She was sure he'd been flirting, but now he was only friendly. "Did my aunt and uncle send you to meet me?"

"No, but I'll be glad to give you a ride. I spent the afternoon delivering brochures to the travel agencies, and I just dropped by the airport to talk to the people at the visitors' bureau. Do you know who was supposed to meet you?"

Julie shook her head. "Not really. I just assumed my aunt and uncle would be here."

"You wait right here." Ross got up from his stool. "I'll call the lodge to see if they left yet."

Julie nodded and sipped her tasteless coffee while Ross went out to make the call. She hadn't been alone for more than a minute when a short girl with frizzy blond hair came rushing up. When Julie turned to face her, the girl stopped in midstep and gasped.

"Oh my God! Julie? Are you Julie Forrester?"

The girl looked very upset, and Julie smiled to set her at ease.

Perhaps she'd been sent to meet the plane, and she was worried because she'd arrived late "Yes. I'm Julie. And you're . . . ?"

"Donna Kirby. Sorry we're late. My brother's waiting in the van, and we're in a no-parking zone."

"You're here to meet me?"

"You got it!" Donna grinned, but she still looked upset. "Your uncle sent us to pick you up. They had two busloads of tourists come in at the last minute, and everything's pretty hectic up there. Do you have any baggage?"

Julie nodded and pointed to the carry-on bag at her feet. "All I have is this. The rest has been delayed, but the airline promised they'd deliver it tomorrow."

"Good luck! The airlines always tell you that to get you off their backs."

"And you think they won't deliver?"

"They probably won't. At least, not when they say they will. But don't worry, Julie. I've got gobs of clothes you can borrow until yours come."

Julie couldn't help it. She started to laugh. "I don't think your clothes will fit me, Donna. I have more height."

"That's true." Donna giggled as Julie stood up. "I guess my midis would be minis on you."

Just then Julie saw Ross approaching through the crowd, and she waved. Then she turned back to Donna. "My uncle's assistant manager is here. He offered to take me up to the lodge if no one else came to meet me."

Donna sighed and leaned closer. "You might know it! We're late and *he's* here! Did he try to pick up on you?"

"No." Julie shook her head. "He said he wasn't here to pick me up. He came to the airport to talk to the people at the visitors' bureau."

Donna raised her eyebrows and turned to face Ross. "Hi, boss. Paul and I just got here, so you don't have to bother with Julie."

"You're a little late, aren't you?"

Julie glanced at Ross in surprise. He was very changeable. When she'd first met him, he'd been all smiles, flirting with her and joking. Then, when he'd found out who she was, he'd become almost paternal, treating her as if he were responsible for her welfare. Now he was different again. The moment he'd seen Donna, he'd become as stern as a professor whose favorite student had flunked a test.

"Saddlepeak employees are expected to be reliable, and you're over thirty minutes late." Ross frowned at Donna. "Didn't you read that handout I gave you last week?"

Donna didn't look the least bit intimidated. "I read it. And we *are* reliable. We've got the best reason in the world for being late. We had a flat on the way down, and *someone* forgot to fix the spare tire."

"Oh-oh." Ross looked guilty. "Okay—you made your point. Tell your brother I said to take it down to the station the first thing in the morning."

Donna nodded. "Yes, boss. Did you call the lodge?"

"I couldn't get through. The lines were busy."

"Then you don't know?"

"Know what?"

"Two busloads of German tourists came in."

Ross looked puzzled. "Are you talking about the RTL tour group?"

"That's right." Donna nodded. "They got in an hour ago, and it's a real madhouse up there."

"But they were supposed to spend two days in Salt Lake City and get to us tomorrow night. What happened?"

Donna shrugged. "Your guess is as good as mine. We can't ask them because they don't speak English."

"No English at all?"

"Not that I could notice. And that interpreter you hired isn't coming until tomorrow afternoon."

Ross frowned. "Doesn't anyone on the staff speak German?"

"Well . . . sort of. Mrs. Hudson had a year of German in high school, but I think you'd better get somebody to help her. She couldn't remember how to tell them that dinner would be served from seven to nine."

"Es gibt Abendessen von sieben bis neun."

Julie spoke without thinking, and Ross turned to her in surprise.

"Julie! You speak German?"

Julie nodded. "Yes. I have four languages, not counting English. My conversational German is quite fluent."

"You're just what the doctor ordered!" Ross gave her a quick pat on the back, and then he turned to Donna. "Get Julie to the lodge as fast as you can. I'll run out to the university and see if I can round up some language students to help us out until the interpreter gets here. And Donna? I'm sorry I jumped all over you about being late."

"That's okay, boss. Are you sorry enough to give me a couple of hours off tomorrow, so I can show Julie around Crest Ridge?"

Ross laughed. "Only in your dreams, Donna. You've got Sunday off. You can do it then. Now, hurry up, will you? Mrs. Hudson's probably pulling her hair out by the roots."

Donna grabbed Julie's carry-on, and the two girls hurried through the airport. Outside, Donna led the way to a van parked near the curb. A painted sign on the door identified it as a Saddlepeak Lodge vehicle. She tapped on the window, and the driver rolled it down to smile at them. He was blond and handsome, but his pleasant expression quickly turned to one of shock.

"You're Julie?!"

Julie resisted the urge to step back, he was staring at her so intently. "Yes. I'm Julie Forrester. And you're Donna's brother, Paul?"

"Right." He got out of the van to shake her hand. His lips were smiling, but Julie could tell he was very upset as he took her carry-on and put it in the back of the van. "Why don't you two girls ride in the back? There's more room."

"Good idea." Donna motioned for Julie to follow her, and they climbed into the second seat. But when Paul came back to the driver's side again, he carefully avoided looking at Julie as he slid in behind the wheel.

Donna tapped Paul on the shoulder as he pulled out into traffic. "We have to get up to the lodge as fast as we can. Julie speaks German, so she can help Mrs. Hudson."

"Great!" Paul smiled again. Julie could see him in the rear-view mirror. But it was a polite smile with no real warmth. For some reason, Paul disliked her. And she hadn't done more than introduce herself!

Donna more than made up for her brother's silence. She kept up a lively chatter as they drove up the mountain, pointing out landmarks and telling Julie about the history of the area. Julie was still trying to figure out what she'd done to make Paul angry when they pulled up the driveway.

Julie stared out at the five-story building, nestled in the hollow between two towering mountain peaks, and gave a little gasp of delight. "Oh! It's beautiful!"

"It's the most beautiful building around." Donna looked proud. "Saddlepeak Lodge was built by Mrs. Hudson's great-grandfather before the turn of the century. It's the tallest building in a twenty-mile area, and it's virtually unchanged, except for certain modernizations that were necessary for the comfort of our guests.

"Saddlepeak Lodge has forty rooms, twenty on the second floor and twenty on the third. The fourth floor has been set aside for the live-in employees and the owner's private quarters. The ground floor contains the lobby, a full-service restaurant, several conveniently located shops, and the grand ballroom, which is used for many community functions.

"This lovely lodge, located in the heart of the majestic Rockies, offers a wide range of leisure activities. Depending on the season, Saddlepeak guests can enjoy horseback riding on well-maintained mountain trails, hunting and fishing trips with local guides, skiing and skating in the midst of breathtaking winter beauty, nature walks to explore the flora and fauna of the area, and fine dining in our lovely restaurant.

"If you have any questions or require any item to ensure your comfort, please ask any of our friendly staff members. We're all dedicated to making sure you enjoy your stay with us at Saddlepeak Lodge."

Julie turned to look at Donna in surprise. "You sound like a tour director."

"I am. When we pick up guests at the airport, I ride along to point out the sights. And when we stop in front of the lodge, I get up and make that speech. Ross Connors wrote it."

"I'll go tell the Hudsons you're here." Paul stopped the van and jumped out. He grabbed Julie's carry-on from the back, and before the girls could say another word, he was rushing up the steps.

"Oh, boy!" Donna sighed as she got out of the van. "I bet you think he's pretty freaky, huh?"

Julie nodded. Paul *had* acted very strangely. "Your brother doesn't seem to like me. Did I do something wrong?"

"Not a thing. You can't help the way you look."

"The way I look?" Julie was completely puzzled as she followed Donna up the steps to the lodge.

"I think I'd better clue you in before you meet your aunt and uncle—they might act a little weird, too."

"Why is that?" Julie frowned slightly. Donna looked worried again.

"Because of Vicki. That's why Paul was so strange—he was in love with her, and she dumped him."

Julie frowned. "You're talking about my cousin Vicki?"

"That's right. You look so much like her, you could be her twin."

"I see." Julie nodded. No wonder Paul had been upset!

"I was a little freaked, too, when I first saw you." Donna looked slightly embarrassed. "It was almost like seeing Vicki's ghost."

"I assure you, I'm not a ghost. And it's not really surprising that I resemble my cousin. You see, my mother and Aunt Caroline were identical twins."

"That explains it. At least you don't sound like Vicki. She didn't have an accent."

Julie was amused as she followed Donna into the huge lobby of the lodge. She thought Donna had a very peculiar accent.

And Donna thought Julie's accent was strange. Accents were indeed in the ear of the listener. But it was disturbing to learn that she looked so much like her cousin Vicki. She hoped that Aunt Caroline and Uncle Bob wouldn't be too upset when they saw her.

Donna walked over to the desk in the lobby and pressed a buzzer. Then she smiled at Julie again. "They must be busy, or they'd be here already. Mrs. Hudson was so excited about you coming to live here, she repainted Vicki's room for you."

"That was very kind of her." Julie glanced around the huge lobby, and then she moved closer to examine the wall of pictures behind the desk. "Is there a photograph of my aunt and uncle?"

Donna pointed to a large framed photograph. "Right here. This was taken a couple of years ago. Your aunt's hair is shorter now, but your uncle looks just the same."

Julie moved closer to examine the photograph. Uncle Bob was a well-built man, with dark brown hair and blue eyes. Her mother had once told her that Aunt Caroline had married the best-looking boy in Crest Ridge, and Uncle Bob was still very handsome. Julie also had a vague memory of something else her mother had said, something unpleasant in connection with Aunt Caroline's visit. But since Julie had been only four at the time, she couldn't quite recall the details. "Did your aunt ever come to visit you, Julie?"

"Yes." Julie nodded, but didn't elaborate. She didn't trust her voice. She was still staring at the picture of Aunt Caroline, and it was exactly like looking at a picture of her mother. They'd had the same blond hair, the same green eyes, and they'd smiled at the camera in exactly the same way. Julie was almost sorry her aunt had invited her to come to Saddlepeak Lodge. Living with Aunt Caroline and seeing her every day might make her miss her mother even more.

Suddenly Julie had another thought, and she turned to Donna in alarm. Donna had said she looked just like Vicki. "Do you think that seeing me will upset Aunt Caroline and Uncle Bob?"

"I guess it might . . . at first. But maybe it'll make them feel better. Since you look so much like Vicki, it'll be almost like having her back again. It'll be sort of like giving them a second chance to set things right, you know?"

Julie felt a sense of foreboding. "Set *what* things right? I don't understand."

"Uh . . . well . . . you know about Vicki, don't you?"

Now Julie was confused. "What do you mean? My cousin died in an automobile accident, didn't she?"

"In a way. Her car went off the cliff."

Julie nodded. It was exactly what her mother had told her. "Poor Aunt Caroline and Uncle Bob. It must have been a very difficult time for them."

"It was. Especially with all those unanswered questions. Our neighbor's the sheriff, and he searched Vicki's room. He's the one who found the note."

"The note?"

"Yes. But it didn't really say why. That's what was so terrible for your aunt and uncle."

Julie began to harbor a terrible suspicion. "I think you'd better tell me everything, Donna."

"Well . . ." Donna looked around the room nervously as she heard approaching footsteps. "They're coming!"

"Then tell me now."

Donna was clearly anxious. "Okay. I guess you have to know. And I'm not sure that anyone else'll tell you. You see, Vicki had a mental breakdown. She was acting so weird, her parents sent her to see a shrink down in Denver. That's where she was supposed to be going when she . . . uh . . . died."

"I understand." Julie nodded, but there was clearly more to the story. "And . . . ?"

Donna winced. The footsteps were getting louder. "Put a smile on your face, Julie. I don't want them to know I told you."

"But you *haven't* told me!"

Donna frowned as she leaned closer and lowered her voice. "Nobody's supposed to know, but I heard Sheriff Nelson tell my Dad that Vicki committed suicide."

Two

Julie's head was still whirling from Donna's shocking news when her aunt rushed in. Aunt Caroline's arms were outstretched as she hurried across the lobby. But when Julie turned to face her, she let out a startled cry and stopped short.

"Hello, Aunt Caroline." Julie crossed the distance between them and gave her aunt a kiss. "I hope I didn't alarm you. Donna told me that I look like my cousin Vicki."

Uncle Bob came through the door just in time to hear Julie's comment. He seemed just as shocked as Aunt Caroline, but he recovered much more quickly.

"You *do* look a lot like Vicki." Uncle Bob walked over to shake Julie's hand. "I'm glad to meet you, Julie. Welcome to Saddlepeak Lodge."

Aunt Caroline's face was still white, but she hugged Julie and managed to smile. "We're very glad you're here, Julie."

The moment was awkward, and Julie took a deep breath. It was time to set her aunt at ease. "I can understand why you're upset, Aunt Caroline. I'd be upset, too, if I hadn't seen a picture of you. You look just like my mother."

"Oh, dear!" Aunt Caroline hugged Julie again, and when she stepped back, there were tears in her eyes. But the color was beginning to come back to her face.

Julie crossed her fingers, and hoped her aunt had a sense of humor. "What do you think we should do, Aunt Caroline? Dye our hair so we don't walk around shocking each other?"

It took Aunt Caroline a moment to realize that Julie was joking, but then she smiled. "What a wonderful idea! I've always wanted to be a redhead."

"Hey . . . wait a minute." Uncle Bob frowned as he turned to his wife. "You're not serious, are you?"

Donna laughed. "Relax, Mr. Hudson. They're just putting you on. It's a joke."

"That's a relief. I've got enough troubles with our new guests. Somebody in 204 wants an extra *Decke,* and I don't have any idea what that is."

Julie turned to her uncle. "It's an extra blanket. I speak German, Uncle Bob—I'll be happy to help you translate."

"Good!" He looked relieved as he nodded. "I'll start you off at the front desk. You can handle the calls from the rooms, and translate for the staff. And then, during dinner . . ."

Aunt Caroline put her hand on her husband's arm to interrupt him. "Perhaps Julie's tired, Bob. Most people start yawning when they come up to this altitude for the first time."

"It's all right, Aunt Caroline." Julie smiled at her aunt. "My school was in the Alps, and I'm used to high altitudes."

"But, Julie . . ." Aunt Caroline looked distressed. "You just got here. It wouldn't be fair to put you to work so soon."

"Of course it would! I'd be *happy* to help you and Uncle Bob."

"Well?" Uncle Bob turned to his wife. "I think we'd be foolish to turn down an offer like that."

Aunt Caroline hesitated for a moment, then nodded. "You're right. As usual. I'll get Julie started. Will you go out to the kitchen and tell Mrs. Robinson to start frosting that cake?"

"Whatever you say, Caro. You're the boss." Uncle Bob glared at his wife for a moment, turned abruptly, and walked toward the door. Then he seemed to remember his manners, and he turned back to smile at Julie. "Thanks, Julie. You came at just the right time. See you at dinner."

Aunt Caroline watched him go with a frown on her face. Then

she sighed. "Sorry, Julie. He's been a regular bear today, but it has nothing to do with you. Right, Donna?"

"Right." Donna nodded. "Tell us what you want us to do, Mrs. Hudson. We're your willing slaves."

"That's the best offer I've had in years." Aunt Caroline laughed, and Julie drew in her breath sharply. It was an exact duplicate of her mother's laugh. "I'll show you how to operate the intercom, Julie. We need to tell our guests that dinner will be served from seven to nine in the restaurant."

"I'll be glad to do that, Aunt Caroline. Is there anything else you want me to tell them?"

"Well . . . you could welcome them to the Saddlepeak Lodge and tell them some of the activities we have planned for them. Donna can brief you on that. And if you're not too tired, you could table-hop a bit during dinner."

Julie looked confused, and Donna explained. "Mrs. Hudson wants you to go from table to table to help them order. The menu's in English."

"I'll be glad to table-hop. But are my clothes suitable for dinner? My luggage won't be delivered until tomorrow, and the only other things I have with me are jeans and a sweatshirt."

Aunt Caroline raised her eyebrows as she considered Julie's outfit. "You look lovely, Julie. And very sophisticated. What do you think, Donna?"

"Me?" Donna grinned. "Personally, I'd kill to be able to wear an outfit like that. But you have to be tall and thin, and I strike out on both counts. It's pretty fancy, though . . . especially when the rest of us'll be dressed in sweaters and skirts. Do you want me to see what I can scrounge up, Mrs. Hudson?"

Aunt Caroline hesitated, then shook her head. "Never mind, Donna. I just remembered that I've got the perfect thing for Julie to wear. I did my Christmas shopping early last year, and I bought some sweaters and skirts for Vicki. You're welcome to them, Julie."

Donna nodded. She was obviously pleased. But Julie turned to her aunt with concern. "Won't it bother you if I wear them?"

"No." Aunt Caroline smiled at her. "You'll be doing me a favor, honey. Bob'll be terribly upset if he sees them in my closet and finds out I never got around to returning them."

It was after ten by the time the last of the guests had left the dining room. Julie sighed and pushed her hair back from her forehead. It had been a long evening, but luckily, Ross had arrived, halfway through dinner, with two German-speaking language students in tow.

"Nice job, Julie." Donna patted her on the back. "And everybody enjoyed the cake Mrs. Hudson made for you."

"It was delicious. And it was also very nice of her. I had no idea she was planning a surprise party for me."

"I did." Donna looked smug. "And the German guests loved it, after you explained it to them. Cake is *Kuchen,* right?"

"That's right."

"I learned a lot just listening to you. Chicken is *Hähnchen,* ham is *Schinken,* and roast pork is *Schweinebraten.*"

Julie smiled at her. Even though she'd just met Donna this afternoon, it was clear that she would be a good friend. "That's very good, Donna. And I'm sure you know how to say 'roast beef' in German."

"But I don't. Mrs. Hudson didn't have roast beef on the menu tonight. How do you say it?"

"*Roastbeef.*"

Donna nodded "That's right. I want to know how to say 'roast beef' in German."

"I just told you: *Roastbeef.* Most of the fine restaurants in Germany use the English word now."

Donna laughed. "Okay. I guess that's what I'll order if I ever go to Germany. Of course, I could always have *Wienerschnitzel.* I just love hot dogs."

"But you won't be served hot dogs. *Wienerschnitzel* is a breaded veal cutlet prepared in the Viennese style."

Donna sighed. "Maybe I should've taken German for my foreign language this year. What's your schedule like, Julie?"

"I'm not sure. I'm enrolling on Monday, but I don't have my classes yet. Do you think I'll have any trouble? I'm over three weeks late."

Donna shook her head. "I'll help you catch up. Ask Mr. Zimmerman if he'll put you in my classes and I'll introduce you to everybody. Tell him you've simply got to have first period algebra."

"Thank you, Donna. I'm glad you want me in your classes."

Donna grinned. "Well . . . I *do* have an ulterior motive. You see, your aunt told me you were at the top of your class, and I'm a total airhead when it comes to math."

Aunt Caroline and Julie were about to step into the elevator when a rugged man with a full reddish-blond beard rushed up. He was in his early thirties, and he was wearing a green-and-black checked shirt, blue jeans, and a soft deerskin vest. He smiled at Aunt Caroline, and Julie's eyes widened. She'd seen a lot of American movies in Europe, and this man looked just like Brad Pitt in *Thelma and Louise.*

But the moment he turned to look at Julie, his face turned pale. He blinked, put his hand on the elevator door to steady himself, and blinked again.

"Easy, Red." Aunt Caroline reached out to take his arm. "This is my niece, Julie Forrester. Julie? Meet Red Dawson. He's one of our hunting and fishing guides, and he runs the taxidermy shop in the basement."

Red Dawson began to recover, and a little color came back to his face. "Sorry. For a second there, I . . . I thought . . ."

He seemed to be searching for the right thing to say, and Julie felt sorry for him. He was obviously upset by her resemblance to Vicki. "It's all right, Mr. Dawson. I know I look like Vicki, and you must have been startled."

"Yes." Red nodded, but he didn't smile at her. "Mrs. Hudson? I just wanted to tell you now that I finished that trophy buck tonight. They can pick it up in the morning before they leave."

Aunt Caroline nodded. "Thank you, Red. That'll save us the shipping costs. How's the bearskin rug coming along?"

"It's a tough job. The hunter panicked, and there's a whole lot of holes in that skin. The head's okay, though, and I think I can pull it out."

"If anybody can do it, you can." Aunt Caroline patted him on the shoulder. "Keep at it, Red. It's his first bear."

"And it'll be his last, if I have anything to say about it! That man's a menace with a rifle, and he couldn't hit the broad side of a barn. He's just lucky that Bob's shot went through the eye. If your husband hadn't bailed him out, that bear would've got him, instead of the other way around."

"I know. Bob told me." Aunt Caroline chuckled. "That's why I talked him into a fishing trip for next year."

Red laughed. "Good for you, Mrs. Hudson! We might have to take a couple of hooks out of him, but it'll be a lot safer."

"Will you give Julie a tour of your shop? She'll be helping out on the switchboard and she should be familiar with all the services we offer."

Red didn't look delighted, but he nodded. "Anytime, Mrs. Hudson. Is there anything left in the kitchen? I didn't have time for dinner."

"I'm sure Mrs. Robinson saved a plate for you." Aunt Caroline smiled. "Go ahead, Red. And I'll send Julie down to see you sometime tomorrow."

Red Dawson nodded and headed for the kitchen. Then he seemed to remember his manners, because he turned to wave at Julie. "Nice meeting you."

Aunt Caroline smiled as they got into the elevator. "Red's a little rough around the edges, but he's got a good heart. He's a little skittish around women, though, and I'm afraid we have Vicki to thank for that."

"What do you mean?" Julie turned to stare at her aunt as the elevator doors closed and they began to rise.

"Red thought the sun rose and set in Vicki. Whenever she came into his shop, he used to follow her around with those sad, puppy dog eyes."

Julie was curious. "Did Vicki ever date him?"

"No, but poor Red was so preoccupied with her, I had to have a little talk with Vicki and ask her to stop flirting with him. Bob and I were afraid he'd start thinking about her out on the trail, and have an accident."

Julie nodded, but she didn't ask any more questions. Aunt Caroline looked distressed. Instead, she changed the subject. "Is there a lot of game in the mountains, Aunt Caroline?"

As Aunt Caroline began to tell her about the hunting trips they offered, Julie thought about Red Dawson. She'd have to be very careful around him. She looked like Vicki, and if she gave Red any encouragement at all, he might think she was flirting with him, too.

It was almost midnight, but Julie was too excited to sleep. Her room was beautiful, and it was decorated in her favorite color, delft blue. The furniture was white and it looked lovely against the soft, smoky blue walls. There was a canopied bed, a white vanity with an oval mirror, and a desk where she could study. There was even a white wicker chaise lounge with delft blue cushions where she could stretch out to watch the color television set which was perched on a shelf in the white entertainment center.

Julie walked over to the entertainment center and turned on the stereo. It was tuned to a classical music station, and she wondered if Vicki had preferred classical music. She hadn't wanted to ask her aunt, but she assumed that the contents of the entertainment center had belonged to Vicki.

It was the perfect room for a teenage girl, and Julie wondered if her cousin had been happy here. Obviously not, or she certainly wouldn't have committed suicide! But why *had* Vicki killed herself? It was a mystery, and Julie shivered a bit as she imagined her cousin pacing the floor of this lovely room, attempting to exorcise the demons that had driven her to her death.

It was useless to dwell on a mystery she couldn't solve. She might never know why her cousin had committed suicide, but perhaps she could learn more about Vicki's life. Julie found a jazz station on the radio and set out to explore her new surroundings. The desk was first, and she pulled out each drawer. But there was nothing inside, no trace of her cousin or the life she'd lived within these walls.

The closet was next. Julie found a soft velour robe in a beautiful shade of forest green, but it was brand new. And the matching slippers were still in the box from the store, wrapped in tissue paper. The only thing that might have belonged to Vicki while she was alive was a lavender windbreaker jacket tucked up into the corner of the top shelf.

Julie's heart beat faster as she stood on tiptoe and pulled the jacket down. It smelled faintly of perfume, and she tried to imagine her cousin wearing it. There was a handkerchief in one pocket, a plain white square of linen with nothing to identify it as Vicki's. But when she reached into the other pocket, she found a small piece of colored cardboard.

"Saddlepeak Lodge—Fifth Annual Turkey Trap Shoot." Julie read the words aloud. It was a ticket of some sort. There was a date stamp on the ticket, and Julie gasped as she noticed it was December eighteenth. Donna had told her that Vicki had committed suicide on the night of December eighteenth!

Julie's hands were trembling as she turned the ticket over and saw the message that someone had scrawled on the back. *Vicki—Meet me tonight—R.*

The handwriting was bold, and Julie was almost sure that "R" was a man. But who? And did he have something to do with her cousin's death? Perhaps there was another clue, somewhere in this room.

All thoughts of sleep left Julie's mind as she examined the rest of the room. The vanity yielded nothing of importance, just a perfume sample from a department store, and several hair clips. There was nothing under the cushions of the chaise longue, and the drawers in the bathroom looked as if they'd been recently cleaned. There was a small bottle of aspirin in the medicine cabinet, but the seal on the cover was still intact. And the miniature bottles of shampoo, conditioner, and hand cream all bore the

Saddlepeak Lodge logo. It was clear that someone had removed all of Vicki's belongings. The room was bare, except for the entertainment center.

Julie stared at the collection of records and tapes and CDs for a moment, and then she shook her head. She didn't feel like searching through every record cover, tape box, and CD carrier for something that might not be there. She'd save that task for the morning, when there was more light.

Although she still wasn't sleepy, Julie decided to get ready for bed. Then she could watch television, or listen to music until she fell asleep. She hung her clothes on hangers, and put on the warm flannel nightgown that Aunt Caroline had given her. Then she slipped into the green velour robe and sat down on the bed to pull on the green fuzzy slippers.

Suddenly a thought struck Julie, and she smiled. If Aunt Caroline and Uncle Bob had kept Vicki's things, they might have packed them up and moved them to the fifth floor. Aunt Caroline had mentioned that they used the fifth floor for storage. And she'd told Julie that when her parents' trunks had arrived, they'd stored them there. She could always tell her aunt that she wanted to go through some of her parents' things, and that would give her a perfect excuse to explore the attic.

But perhaps it wouldn't be an excuse. She might be able to use some of her parents' things to decorate her room. Julie tried to recall all the things she'd packed, and she smiled as she thought of their elephant collection. Ever since she'd been old enough to go on shopping trips with her parents, they'd looked for elephants in every corner of the world. There was a beautiful carved wooden elephant from Africa, one made of fine Czechoslovakian glass, a hand-sewn patchwork elephant they'd bought in India, and a delicate bone china miniature from France. There was even one she'd found in Zurich and shipped to her parents, a comical little creature made out of stuffed leather. There were so many, Julie couldn't remember them all. But she did remember all the fun they'd had shopping for new elephants to add to their collection.

But where would she put them? Julie smiled as she saw that

the top shelf of the entertainment center was bare. The elephant collection would add character to her room, and it would be a reminder of all the places they'd lived and visited when her parents were alive.

Moonlight streamed in from the balcony windows, and Julie walked over to the double French doors to look out at the mountains. Since her room was on the fourth floor, she had an unobstructed view of the slopes. Aunt Caroline had told her that every room at Saddlepeak Lodge had a balcony with a mountain view.

Julie had been impressed when Aunt Caroline had shown her their quarters. Heavy antique wooden doors separated their section from the rest of the lodge, and inside was a lovely, spacious apartment with a living room, dining room, kitchen, den, and two bedrooms, each with its own bath.

The view from the balcony windows was too compelling to resist, but when Julie attempted to open the French doors, she found they were stuck. On closer examination, she realized that two long pieces of metal had been installed on the frame, one at the top and one at the bottom, held in place by thumb screws. It wasn't a pretty lock, but it was very effective. With the thumb screws in place, no one could open the doors from the outside.

Had Cousin Vicki been afraid that someone would break into her room? Julie shivered slightly as she gazed out at the mountains. She'd ask Donna about the lock in the morning, but if there had been a break-in at the lodge, it seemed doubtful that it had occurred on the fourth floor.

Julie sighed and loosened the thumb screws. The pieces of metal swung easily to the side, and she stepped out on the balcony. Another mystery. Saddlepeak Lodge seemed to be full of them.

A bright, full moon rode low in the sky, casting dark purple shadows on the silent grounds below. Off in the distance, the mountains loomed so large, it felt almost as if she could touch them. It was the second week of October, and in the mountains, there was frost in the air.

Julie smiled as she looked out at the jagged peaks of the

Rocky Mountains. It was lovely scenery, and she could hardly wait for the snow to fall. Then Saddlepeak Lodge would turn into a ski resort, and Julie was an excellent skier. Perhaps she could help her aunt and uncle by offering her services as a ski instructor.

There was a slight sound, and Julie turned to look at the neighboring balconies. Someone was standing at the rail, one balcony to her right. She tried to remember who had the room next to hers. There were small brass plaques on the doors, and Julie had read the names as she'd walked down that side of the hall with her aunt. Mrs. Robinson, the cook, had the room on the end, next to the elevator. She was a heavy-set woman with a jolly face who had told Julie to come to the restaurant kitchen anytime she pleased. The Larkins were next. They were both tall and thin, with the same shade of dark gray hair. He was a general handyman, and she ran the curio shop on the ground floor.

The third room and fourth rooms were vacant. Uncle Bob had knocked out the connecting wall to make a lounge for the live-in employees with a large-screen television and kitchen facilities. And the fifth room belonged to Red Dawson. His real name was Oliver, but everyone called him Red. With an R. Could Red Dawson have written that note to Vicki? Aunt Caroline had said that he'd been preoccupied with her.

Julie considered it for a moment, and then she shrugged. Vicki had never dated Red Dawson; Aunt Caroline had told her that. There was no reason to think that'd he'd written that note. She peered over at the shadowy figure on the adjacent balcony and concentrated on remembering the name plaques. And then she smiled. It was Ross Connors' room, and he was right next door to her!

Should she make a sound to let Ross know she was out here? He was terribly handsome, and she knew he'd been interested in her before he'd discovered who she was. Julie debated the pros and cons for a moment, and then she decided to stay silent, at least for tonight. She'd ask Donna some questions about Ross in the morning, and find out exactly what sort of guy he was.

Even though her robe was warm, Julie shivered a bit. Ross

Connors . . . he could be the mysterious R on the note she'd found in Vicki's jacket pocket. The time frame was right. Donna had mentioned that Ross had been working at the lodge ever since he'd graduated from high school. And Ross had told her that she reminded him of someone he used to know.

A door closed, and Julie glanced over at the neighboring balcony. Ross had gone back inside. Then she noticed that only a few feet separated her balcony from his. It would be simple for an athletic person to hop from one balcony to the next. And Ross certainly looked like an athletic person. Something had frightened Vicki so badly that she'd installed a lock on her balcony door? Was it possible that her cousin had been afraid of Ross Connors?

Three

Her long blond hair whipped from side to side in the pale moonlight as the night wind blew in the open window. She was driving down a curving mountain road, taking the hairpin turns much faster than safety allowed. Tears filled her eyes and flowed in narrow, glistening streams down her cheeks. There was no help for her, no way out except this.

The white lane markers blurred beneath her tires, stretching into one continuous line in the night. Trees whipped past her at the side of the road, too fast to really see. The world was spinning, and she didn't have the courage to stop it. But she wasn't afraid. She'd made up her mind and this was her final decision. Suddenly she felt powerful and able to defy the earthly bounds of gravity. She was invincible. Nothing could hurt her now. It seemed she could lift the car through sheer force of will and speed away to capture the stars.

Then a sound intruded, a noise that made her breath catch in her throat. The car swerved sharply as the tires blew out. Two of them. And miraculously, that sound brought her back to harsh reality.

She wrenched the steering wheel in an attempt to steer out of the skid. Now that the final moment was here, she knew she'd made a terrible mistake. She wanted to wear the new dress she'd bought last week for the Christmas dance. She wanted to listen to the hottest new band, go to the premiere of a movie and walk down the red carpet, and swim in the ocean at midnight. She wanted to kiss her mother and tell her that she loved her. She wanted to help clear the table, brush her hair, take a shower, polish her nails, do all the little mundane things she'd never thought she'd miss. She wanted to live!

Frantically she pumped the brakes. Nothing there. The pedal went all the way to the floor and the car was racing, swerving, screeching at heart-stopping speed toward the guard rail. There was a splintering crash as the guard rail shattered and the car teetered on the brink of the cliff. She shoved hard on the door. There was still time to jump out. But the door was jammed. She was trapped! And then the earth crumbled away under the weight of the tires and she was hurtling over the edge of the cliff into the darkness, screaming and whimpering, crying out for someone, anyone, to save her!

"Julie? Are you up yet?"

There was a knock on the door, and Julie sat bolt upright in bed. It took her a moment to shake off the nightmare, another moment to remember where she was. Her mother's voice? No, it was Aunt Caroline. And she was knocking on the door of Julie's room at Saddlepeak Lodge.

"Julie? You'd better hurry. Donna just called, and she's coming over to walk you to school."

Julie hopped out of bed and raced for the door. She opened it a crack and smiled at her aunt. "Thanks, Aunt Caroline. I'll be ready just as soon as I can. When is she coming?"

"Right away. It'll take her about fifteen minutes to walk up here. I told Mrs. Robinson to make breakfast for two."

"Great. I'll be down in less than ten minutes." Julie shut the door and raced for the bathroom. She'd always been a late sleeper so she had her morning routine all worked out. She'd take a quick shower, put on the clothes she'd chosen last night, and be downstairs by the time Donna arrived. Luckily, her suitcases had arrived only a day later than the airline had promised. It was disturbing enough to look like Vicki; she didn't want to dress in Vicki's clothes for any longer than necessary.

As she hurried past the balcony doors, Julie looked out and gasped. It had snowed during the night, and the grounds below were covered by a soft, white blanket. The sun was shining brightly and the snow glistened as if it had been sprinkled with diamonds. What a great morning for her first day of school!

Julie didn't think about the nightmare again until she'd dressed in her favorite soft lavender sweater and skirt. It was the same terrifying dream she'd had for the past three nights. It had started on her first night at Saddlepeak Lodge, and each successive night, it had grown in detail.

The first night Julie had experienced the horrifying sensation of falling from a great height, and she'd sat up in bed, heart pounding, with a scream on her lips. The second night, she'd been in the car with Vicki, and she'd heard the guard rail splinter before the heart-stopping fall. Those two nightmares had been horrible. But the one she'd had last night had been even worse.

Julie shuddered as she remembered. Last night she had taken her cousin's place and shared her hopeless, suicidal thoughts. She had driven the car, felt the wind on her face, seen the landscape whip past at shocking speed. She'd changed her mind at the last minute and tried to save her life, but she hadn't succeeded. The car had gone over the cliff with her inside.

Had Vicki changed her mind? Had she wrenched the wheel and pumped the useless brakes? There was no way to know, now that Vicki was dead. And to dwell on the question of whether her cousin had gone to her death intentionally or reluctantly was an exercise in futility.

The intercom beeped twice, her aunt's signal that Donna had arrived. Julie brushed her hair back, secured it with the hammered silver barrette, and sighed as she left her room. She had to find some way to stop these awful nightmares. They were making her jumpy and out of sorts; now she was always dreading the moment when she'd fall asleep for fear the nightmare would come again. And it had, three nights running. It was as if her cousin were trying to send her a message from the grave.

Julie shook off the ridiculous thought, and sighed as she

walked down the hallway to the elevator. She'd never believed in restless spirits or messages from the hereafter, and she wasn't about to start now. But she did want to know why Vicki had chosen to end her life.

Donna had filled in some of the blanks, but what Julie had learned didn't make much sense. Vicki'd had every reason in the world to be happy. She'd been blessed with loving parents, a beautiful place to live, nice clothes, and even her own car. She had been a good student, and Donna had told her that she'd been the most popular girl in her class. Why would someone like Vicki commit suicide?

The elevator doors opened, and Julie stepped inside. As she pushed the button for the ground floor, she thought about Donna's brother, Paul and a fleeting smile crossed her face. Vicki had gone steady with him for over a year, and Paul certainly hadn't made a good impression as far as Julie was concerned. He was handsome enough, but he was definitely unfriendly. He'd frowned at her every time they'd run into each other at the lodge, and when she'd tried to be sociable, he'd acted as if she was poison. If she had to spend all her time with Paul, as Vicki had done, she might just decide to end it all, too!

"Well? What do you think?" Donna picked up a bowl of chef salad and dumped on a huge ladle of honey mustard dressing.

"I like it." Julie dished up some macaroni and cheese, and laughed. "The school, that is. I'm not so sure about this macaroni and cheese."

"It's not bad if you put some pepper on it. Drinks are over here, in the cooler."

Donna led the way to a cooler at the far end of the line where cartons of juice, milk, and soft drinks were kept. "Did you get fifth period history?"

"I got all of your classes."

"Great!" Donna grinned at her. "See that table for four over there? Let's stake it out."

Julie liberated a carton of orange juice and followed Donna

to the table. But two boys were headed for the same table, and the moment Julie recognized the taller of the two, she stopped.

"What's the matter?" Donna turned to stare at her.

"Uh . . . nothing. That's your brother, isn't it?"

"Right. We usually eat lunch together. I save a table for him if I get there first, and he does the same for me."

"Oh." Julie nodded and followed Donna through the crowded lunchroom toward the table. She really didn't want to eat lunch with Paul, but it might offend Donna if she said so.

"Hi, guys." Donna plunked down her tray and grinned at her brother. Then she turned to Julie. "Julie Forrester? Dave Wilkins."

"Hey . . ." The heavy-set, dark-haired boy plunked his tray on the table and turned to look up at Julie. "Glad to meet . . ."

Julie watched as his mouth dropped open. He blinked once, twice, and then he cleared his throat. "Sorry. You look just like . . ."

"Vicki Hudson." Julie supplied the name. Then she smiled at him. He looked like a very nice guy. "I'm Vicki's cousin, and you're the thirty-seventh person to say that today."

"Sorry. But seeing you here really shocked me. For a second, I thought you were . . ."

"Vicki's ghost." Julie smiled again. "And you're the twenty-sixth person to say that."

"At least I'm original." Dave laughed, and then he turned to Paul. "Come on, Rock. They just set out some apple pie. Let's get some before it's all gone."

Paul frowned as he got to his feet. "Don't call me Rock!"

"Okay, okay. I forgot." Dave turned back to Julie. "Want me to bring you a piece?"

"I'd love some, thanks."

"Me, too." Donna glanced at her brother, who was already walking toward the lunch line. His back was stiff, his posture tense. "Watch it, Dave. He hates it when anybody calls him Rock."

Dave gave her the high sign, and hurried to catch up with

Paul. Julie stared after them for a moment, and then she turned to Donna. "Is Rock his nickname?"

"Not anymore. That's what Vicki used to call him. We double-dated a couple of times, and Dave picked it up from her. Nobody's called him Rock since she died."

"I see." Julie nodded. But she didn't have time to ask any more questions. Dave was coming back to the table, juggling two plates of pie.

"Here you go." Dave set one plate down in front of Julie and gave Donna the other. "Paul's coming with ours. He just stopped to find out if there's football practice on Saturday."

When Paul got back to the table, Julie smiled at him. She'd try to be friendly one more time and see what happened. "Dave just mentioned football practice. Are you on the team?"

"He's the best quarterback Crest Ridge High ever had!" Donna gave her brother a fond punch on the arm. "To look at him now, you'd never know he spent two years on crutches."

Paul looked embarrassed. "You don't have to tell her my whole life story. Julie wouldn't be interested."

"Oh, but I am! Tell me, Donna."

Donna grinned as she launched into what was obviously a familiar story. "Paul was in the hospital for a whole year when he was ten. That's why he's older than anyone else in the senior class: He got hit by a logging truck and now he's bionic."

"Bionic?"

Donna nodded. "The doctors replaced his knee. They didn't think he'd ever be able to walk again, but look at him now. He plays football, and baseball, and basketball. And he even dances!"

"Only when I'm forced to by my bratty sister. And that's because she can't find anybody else to dance with her."

Now it was Donna's turn to look embarrassed. "That was only once, when I was in ninth grade. Now I know plenty of boys who are dying to dance with me. Right, Dave?"

"Oh, sure." Dave nodded solenmly. "If we don't ask her to dance, Paul beats up on us."

"He does not!" Donna glared at him. Then she turned to look at Paul. "Do you?"

"Of course."

They burst into laughter and Julie joined in. Paul seemed different here at school. He actually seemed to have a sense of humor. Perhaps she'd judged him too harshly?

Dave smiled at Julie. "What classes are you taking?"

"I have the same schedule as Donna."

Donna nodded. "That's so she can keep me from flunking. She's even promised to help me with French. Did you guys know that the French word for fish is poison?"

"That's *poisson,* not poison." Julie grinned at her. "But it might be hard to tell under all those sauces."

Paul laughed, and Julie noticed that he looked a little friendlier. Perhaps he was beginning to see her as Julie, and not just a carbon copy of Vicki.

Just as Julie popped the last bite of food into her mouth, the bell rang signaling the end of the lunch period. She picked up her tray and carried it over to the counter where Donna was waiting. Then she turned back to get her books. But Paul had them under one arm, and he was waiting for her at the door of the lunchroom.

"Thanks, again." Julie took her books and smiled. And then she said something stupid, something she never would have said if she'd taken the time to think. "Did you carry Vicki's books for her?"

Paul frowned and shook his head. "She never brought her books to lunch. She always left them in her locker."

"Well . . ." Julie thought fast. "J guess that proves I'm not exactly like my cousin."

Paul looked a little uncertain. "Did you mean that about helping Donna with her French?"

"Of course."

"Maybe you're not like Vicki. She never would have helped anybody with anything. Vicki was out for one thing, and that was herself!"

"Come on. Let's go!" Donna rushed up and grabbed Julie's arm. "If we don't hurry, we'll be late. And Mr. Jenkins is a real crab. He'll give us detention if we're not in our seats when the bell rings."

As they rushed down the hall toward their classroom, Julie was smiling. She'd learned an important fact. Paul could be very nice if he wanted to be. The other fact she'd learned at lunch didn't sink in until Mr. Jenkins had launched into a boring lecture about the Civil War. Rock was Vicki's nickname for Paul. Rock . . . with an "R." Paul could be the R who'd written that note, the one who'd met Vicki on the night she'd died. He could even be the person who'd driven her cousin to suicide!

Four

"I don't know if this is such a good idea." Julie glanced down at her feet, as she looped the laces around her ankles and tied them tightly. "I've never skated before."

"Really?" Donna looked surprised. "But you went to school in Switzerland, and I thought they skated on the rivers and everything. Hans Brinker and all that jazz?"

Julie laughed. "Hans Brinker was a fictional character from Holland."

"Oh, well." Donna shrugged. "Maybe, when you coach me in French, you should give me a couple of geography lessons, too. Stand up, Julie, and see if you can skate over here. Hold onto the rail until you get the hang of it."

Julie got up from the bench reluctantly. Then she grabbed the rail that ran all the way around the interior of the warming house as her feet almost slid out from under her. Donna had convinced her that skating would be a breeze since she already knew how to ski. Julie wasn't so sure. While it was true that she had good balance, the blades of her figure skates were a lot harder to balance on than skis.

The warming house was a three-sided building at the end of Saddlepeak Lodge's ice rink, equipped with electricity and a wall phone that was connected to the switchboard at the lodge. It wasn't really warm, but it was a haven from the wind that sometimes howled down from the peaks of the mountains. Long wooden benches were built along the walls, and there were hooks for skates and extra jackets. It had a roof, but no floor, since it sat directly on the surface of the ice.

Ice skating was one of Saddlepeak Lodge's featured activities. There was a sporting goods shop on the ground floor of the lodge where guests could rent skates if they hadn't brought their own. Donna had outfitted Julie there before they'd come to the rink.

"Just get your balance and try to skate over here." Donna encouraged her again. "It's easy. You'll see."

Julie shoved off tentatively, and managed to push herself across the ice to Donna. But she had to grab the rail again to keep from crashing into her new friend. "How do you stop these things?"

"Just drag one toe on the ice. See the little teeth on the front of your blades? They scrape the ice and slow you down."

"Okay." Julie shoved off again and managed to balance on one foot as she executed a clumsy stop. "This isn't so bad. Can we go out to the rink now?"

"Sure. Just follow me. There's a rail around the rink, too. Ross put it up last year for the beginners. But I don't think you'll have to use it very much."

"You've got more faith in me than I have." Julie laughed. "If I don't stay close to that rail, I'll fall flat on my face!"

Donna shook her head. "You won't fall. Just look out there and you'll see why."

Julie skated to the edge of the wall and looked out at the rink. A crowd had gathered, and they seemed to be gliding across the ice effortlessly.

"There's Paul, in the stocking cap. He's skating with Gina Lawrence from our French class. And Dave's over there, in the green Army parka. The guys promised to prop you up until you learn to skate on your own."

"That's nice of them . . . I think."

Julie wobbled out onto the ice with Donna right behind her.

She spotted Ross, who was helping two guests learn how to skate, and she recognized several of her classmates from school.

"Mrs. Hudson lets us skate here anytime we want to. All we have to do is help the guests." Donna's voice came from directly behind Julie, but Julie was wise enough not to turn her head. Her balance was precarious enough as it was.

"Hey . . . Julie!" Dave skated over to take her arm. "Come on. Let's take a swing around the rink."

"Uh . . . okay." Julie smiled at him, and before she had time to be nervous, Donna had grabbed her other arm and they were pulling her forward.

"Glide, Julie. First your left foot and then your right." Donna gave her instructions. "Just do what I do, and we'll hold you up."

Julie followed Donna's lead, putting her weight on one foot and then the other. At first she leaned heavily on Donna and Dave, but gradually she began' to feel more in control.

"I think I've got it." Julie began to smile. "Let me try it once on my own."

Julie set off on her own, staying very close to the rail, just in case. She wobbled once or twice, but swinging her arms for balance seemed to help. She concentrated on her feet. Left, glide. Right, glide. She made her way around the rink once, and then she tried it again. Skating was fun, and it wasn't as difficult as she'd thought.

Suddenly music came from the loudspeakers at the edge of the rink. Strauss's "Skater's Waltz." How appropriate. Julie moved her skates in time to the music and smiled. She moved away from the rail, out toward the center of the rink. This was fun. But she was still watching her feet, and before she realized it, she'd plowed right into another skater!

"Oh! I'm sorry!" Julie looked up as strong arms steadied her. Then she blushed as she realized she'd bumped into Paul.

But Paul was laughing, and he actually looked friendly. "Don't worry about it. Just grab my arms and I'll pull you over to the rail."

Julie grabbed his arms, and Paul skated backwards, steering

her to the rail. When they got there, Julie grabbed on, and gave a deep sigh of relief. "I guess I got too brave. I felt like Dorothy Hamill for at least thirty seconds . . . until I crashed into you."

"She was here once, about ten years after she won the gold at the Winter Olympics. Every kid in town hung out at the skating rink, and she came out and gave us autographs. I've still got mine."

"That must have been a thrill." Julie smiled at him. "Did she skate?"

Paul nodded. "We cleared the rink and she did part of her routine. I think that's what sold Vicki on figure skating."

"My cousin was a figure skater?"

The moment she'd asked the question, Julie knew she'd made another mistake. A frown flickered across Paul's face, and he looked unfriendly again.

"She used to enter the ice-dancing competitions down in Denver."

Julie took heart. At least she'd gotten him to talk about Vicki. That was a step in the right direction. Now she'd change the subject, and maybe he'd smile at her again. "I was watching you skate with Gina. You're very good."

"Not good enough for Vicki. Ryan Stratford was her partner. They won, last year."

"Ryan Stratford?" Julie was curious. "I don't think I've met him."

"That's no great loss. He's over there, in the black jacket. And he's headed our way. Be careful around him, Julie."

Julie turned to look at the skater who was gliding across the rink toward them. She didn't remember seeing him in any of her classes. "Is he a senior?"

"Yeah. When he bothers to go to school, which is once in a blue moon. He's got a private tutor."

"He does?" Julie raised her eyebrows. "But why?"

"His old man's loaded, and he thinks Ryan's the next Jean-Claude Killy."

"You mean, he's a skier?"

"He's *the* skier, our local celebrity. He's trying out for the Olympic downhill team."

"And you don't like him?"

"Right." Paul put on a smile as Ryan came into earshot. "Stratford. You decided to favor us with your presence?"

Ryan Stratford smiled, a flash of perfect white teeth in a face tanned dark by the sun. "You might say that. History repeats itself . . . right, Paul?"

"Not if I have anything to say about it. Julie, this is Ryan Stratford. Ryan, Julie Forrester."

"Vicki's cousin." Ryan Stratford took Julie's hand and squeezed it. "And you're even prettier. Hello, Julie. Do you want to take a turn around the rink?"

Julie looked up into his slate-gray eyes, and felt her heart beat faster. She knew instinctively that Ryan Stratford was dangerous. His eyes were compelling as they assessed her, and the smile on his face held a hint of a sneer. And since his name was Ryan, *he* could be the R in Vicki's note!

"Well? How about it?" Ryan held out his hand.

It took sheer willpower, but Julie managed to break away from his gaze. "Thank you, but no. I'm just learning to skate and I'd only slow you down."

"Maybe. And maybe not. We'll see."

Ryan took Julie's arm and steered her out on the rink before she could refuse again. He slipped one arm around her waist and pressed her up against his side.

Julie felt a blush color her face. He was holding her much too tightly, but she had to admit that she was enjoying it. He was strong and handsome and a very good skater. No wonder Vicki had chosen him for her partner!

Ryan's hand moved across her back, massaging her gently, exploring under the jacket. Julie knew she should pull away. She barely knew him. But she'd never make it back to the rail without falling flat on her face. At least she'd learned one important fact about Ryan Stratford. She'd told him she didn't want to skate with him, and here she was, gliding around the rink with his arm clamped tightly around her waist. Ryan was the kind of guy who wouldn't take no for an answer.

"So, Julie . . ." Ryan leaned over to give her a lazy smile. "How about coming down to Denver with me, Saturday night? A friend of mine's doing a concert."

"Sorry. I have to work."

Ryan kept right on smiling. "You can't get out of work to hear Shane Darrow?"

Julie shook her head, even though her pulse was racing. Shane Darrow was the lead singer with Neon Spider, the hottest new rock group from England.

"Too bad. There's a party after the concert at the Brown Hotel. It's an informal little jam session with the guys from Ded Hero."

Julie swallowed hard. It was very tempting since she was also a Ded Hero fan, but she didn't want to go anywhere with Ryan Stratford, not until she'd learned a lot more about him. Paul had warned her to be careful around him, and there had to be a reason. "I can't make it. Sorry, Ryan."

"Another time, then." Ryan brought her in a full circle, until they were back at the rail again. "I think I'll give you some pointers. You might turn into a good skater."

"Thank you, but not now. This is the first time I've been on skates, and my ankles are tired."

"I've got to run anyway. Ski practice in an hour." Ryan smiled at her again and his glance seemed to probe under her jacket, under all her clothes to her trembling body beneath. Then he gave a casual wave and skated away toward the warming house.

"Julie?" Donna skated up the moment Ryan was gone.

Julie blinked and shook her head, almost as if she were shaking away the remnants of a bad dream. "Yes, Donna?"

"Your aunt just called, and I've got to work tonight. Mr. Stratford reserved the private dining room for a party of twenty."

"Mr. Stratford?" Julie frowned. "Is that Ryan's father?"

Donna nodded "I saw you skating with Ryan. What do you think?"

THE DEAD GIRL   155

"I think he's someone to stay away from."

"Smart girl!" Donna patted her shoulder. "Too bad your cousin didn't feel that way."

"Vicki was more than his skating partner?"

Donna shrugged. "Don't quote me on this, but it sure looked like they had something going besides spins and double axels. All I know for sure is, Ryan's bad news."

"It's a good thing I turned down his invitation, then."

Donna looked shocked. "He asked you out?"

"For the Shane Darrow concert on Saturday night. I told him I had to work."

"Oh, God!" Donna rolled her eyes. "I'd kill for a chance to hear Neon Spider live!"

Julie grinned. "Maybe I should have asked for the tickets in advance. Then you could have killed him and both of us could have gone."

"Don't tempt me. I wouldn't mind killing Ryan Stratford. Or his father. If you think Ryan is bad, just wait until you meet his dad. No wonder Mrs. Stratford divorced him last year!"

Julie frowned. "What do you mean?"

"You'll find out first-hand. Your aunt wants you to work the switchboard tonight, and you'll meet him when he comes in."

One by one, the skating party broke up. Ross escorted the guests back to the lodge, Donna and Paul went home to get ready for work, Gina left with Dave, and Julie found herself alone on the ice. She thought about going back to the lodge, too, but it was a perfect opportunity to practice her skating. No one would see her if she fell down, and she certainly wouldn't bump into another skater since she was the only one on the rink.

The music was still playing, and Julie took one last turn around the rink. She was definitely gaining in self-confidence, and she didn't even wobble as she glided across the ice. Then the music stopped. Someone must have shut it off, up at the lodge. Julie skated in a tight circle in the center of the rink, and watched the purple shadows lengthen on the face of the mountains. The peaceful scene reminded her of the last time her parents had visited her at school. They'd gone skiing and spent almost all day on the slopes. And then, when twilight had begun to fall, they'd gone to a little restaurant with a lovely view of the mountains and watched the purple shadows fall.

It was a warm and beautiful memory, and Julie felt a smile spread across her face. It was the first time since her parents had died that she'd thought of them without sadness. Perhaps that was the key to conquering her grief. When she felt sad, she'd remember the happy times they'd shared, and it would be almost as if her parents were with her again.

The air was lovely, crisp but not too cold, and her winter parka kept her warm. The sun was a huge golden ball, almost touching the peak of the mountains, and mountain blue jays called raucously from the pine trees bordering the far end of the rink. Julie stopped to listen, standing on one skate and balancing with the toe of the other. And then she heard it—the snapping of a dry pine branch, the rustle of a body crashing through the trees.

A deer? An elk? A bear? Julie's eyes swept the edge of the wooded area, and she saw something moving near the base of a large pine. Then she blinked and the shape was gone. Perhaps it had been one of the lodge cats. Aunt Caroline kept several strays to keep down the mice population.

One more lap, and she would go back to the lodge. Julie began to skate again. The blades on her skates made soft shushing sounds against the ice, and she smiled as she fell into an easy rhythm. As she glided past the far end of the rink, she felt an uneasy prickling at the back of her neck. Eyes were watching her. From the trees.

"Hello?" Julie's voice was shaking as she called out. Perhaps one of her classmates had forgotten something and was coming back to get it. "Is anyone there?"

But there was only silence. Silence, and the sensation of breathing, back in the pines where the shadows were deepest. Someone was there. Julie was sure of it. And that someone was watching her!

Suddenly the sun dropped behind the mountain peak and darkness began to fall. She'd forgotten how quickly light faded up here in the mountains. Julie's breath came in ragged gasps as she pushed off from the rail and raced toward the warming house. There was barely enough light to see. And someone was watching her! Waiting for darkness to fall!

Her fingers fumbled frantically with the laces and she pulled off her skates as fast as she could. Where was he? Out there somewhere, waiting for her to come out? But she couldn't stay here. She had to get back to the safety of the lodge!

Then she heard footsteps coming across the ice, straight toward the warming house in a direct path. Heavy footsteps. A man's footsteps!

Julie dropped to her knees and scuttled under the wooden bench. Her heart was beating so hard, she was sure he could hear it. He knew she was in here. And now he was coming to get her!.

Then the footsteps paused, right next to the warming house. "Julie? Are you still here?"

Lights blazed inside the warming house, and Julie blinked in confusion. Ross's voice. Ross was here.

"I'm just . . . uh . . . putting on my boots." Julie slid out quickly and plunked herself up on the bench. There was no way she'd let Ross Connors catch her acting like a terrified child!

Almost immediately, Ross stuck his head around the corner. "Sorry, Julie. I would have turned on the lights sooner, but I thought you came in."

"No . . . I decided to skate a little longer."

"Are you all right?" Ross looked worried.

"I'm fine. And I'm ready to go." Julie pulled on her boots and stood up. "Ross? Were you standing out there by the pine trees?"

Ross shook his head. "I came from the other side of the woods. Why?"

"I . . . uh . . . I just thought I heard something in the trees, that's all."

"And it scared you?"

Ross gave an amused chuckle, and Julie quickly shook her head. "No, not at all. I was just curious."

"Well, it was probably a raccoon. They get pretty hungry this time of year, and they start coming up to the lodge at dusk. That's why we keep our garbage in the shed."

Julie nodded and smiled. "Of course. A raccoon. I should have known."

Ross took her skates and slung them over his shoulder. As they started walking up the trail to the lodge, Julie considered it. No, not a raccoon. And not any other type of animal, either. She was sure that a man had watched her from the shadow of the pine tree. And whoever he was, he'd intended to scare her!

Julie dressed in a red-and-black-plaid skirt and a red sweater, and brushed her long blond hair until it was shining. She pulled it back with a red velvet ribbon and glanced at the clock on her dresser. It was almost six, and she'd told Aunt Caroline she'd be downstairs at seven to handle the switchboard.

Since she was early, Julie took the elevator to the basement and headed for Red Dawson's taxidermy shop. Aunt Caroline had asked her to pick up Red's invoices so the bookkeeper could do the billing. Julie wasn't really looking forward to going into Red's shop after dark. She'd gone down for the guided tour on her second day at Saddlepeak Lodge, and the sight of the realistically mounted animals crowded into the small basement shop, had made her feel nervous and jumpy.

As Julie pushed open the door and stepped inside, she saw that the shop was deserted. Red must be working in the back. Normally, the space was well lit, with spotlights aimed at Red's prize specimens, but now there was only one dim light over the counter. The door to Red's workroom was flanked by two animals that looked powerful and dangerous, even though they'd been rendered harmless by some lucky hunter. There was a mountain bobcat on the left, mounted in a crouching position on a heavy tree branch. Its mouth was open in a snarl of rage to expose its long, sharply pointed teeth. Julie shivered and turned to the right, but she felt even more nervous as she looked into

the small, sightless glass eyes of a wild boar. It seemed to be bar-
reling straight at her, its wicked-looking tusks about to impale
anything in its path.

Julie jumped as the door opened suddenly and Red Dawson
stepped out into the shop. His bulk filled the doorway, and he
was wearing a canvas apron that was covered with stains and
bits of hair and fur.

"Julie. I thought I heard someone out here."

Red didn't look friendly. She'd probably interrupted his
work. Julie tried to smile, but it was difficult. "Aunt Caroline
sent me to pick up your invoices."

"They're in that folder." Red pointed at a manila folder on
the counter. "Tell her the bear rug is finished, and I'll ship it out
tomorrow."

Julie nodded, and picked up the folder. "Thanks, Red. I'll
tell her."

"You want to see it?"

"Uh . . . sure." Julie kept a smile on her face, even though she
didn't have the slightest desire to see the bear rug. "Where
is it?"

"In the back room. Come on."

Julie took a deep breath as she followed Red into the back
room. A combination of harsh smells assaulted her as she
stepped into the huge work space, and she wrinkled up her nose.

"You get used to the smell after a while." Red turned to grin
at her expression. "You want me to turn on the fan?"

Julie shook her head. "No, that's all right. It reminds me of
biology class, that's all."

"That's what Vicki used to say." Red's grin disappeared. "She
didn't like it down here, either."

Julie's eyes widened as she glanced around the workroom.
Banks of fluorescent lights hung over a row of wide tables that
appeared to be made out of giant planks of wood several inches
thick. Their surfaces were scrubbed clean, but Julie could still
see stains. An impressively large array of knives hung in a rack
over the tables, and there were molds in the shapes of animals
stacked up against the wall. Even though the workroom was

clean and well lighted, it still reminded Julie of Dr. Frankenstein's basement laboratory.

"What do you think of my grinning bear?" Red lifted a heavy
bundle up to one of the tables and spread it out.

Julie gasped as she stared down at the huge bear rug. The
bear's head was still attached, and its mouth was open. Its eyes
gleamed yellow in the reflected light and its teeth were long and
sharp. Red seemed to think that the bear was grinning, but it
looked more like a snarl to Julie.

"That's . . . uh . . . very impressive," she said.

Red reached out to stroke the coarse fur. "Can you see any
holes?"

"No I don't see any."

"Good. He's patched in eleven places. I used up almost all the
scrap fur to get a match."

Julie nodded. "Well, I can't see where you patched him. You
did a wonderful job, Red."

"Vicki used to help me sometimes. She had a good eye for
things like that. She seemed to be really interested in taxidermy . . . for a while."

Julie hesitated. Should she ask what had happened? Red
seemed to be in a mellow mood, and she was curious. "Did
Vicki lose interest?"

"You could say that." An expression of pain flickered across
Red's face, but it was gone so quickly Julie wondered if she'd
imagined it. "Are you interested in taxidermy?"

Julie hesitated again. She wasn't, not really, but she didn't
want to hurt Red's feelings. "I think it's fascinating. But it's also
kind of . . . uh . . ."

"Creepy?" Red smiled, and he looked friendly again.

"Yes. Your animals are beautiful, in a savage sort of way. But
don't you get a little nervous, working here alone at night?"

Red threw back his head and laughed. It was a good sound in
the big, silent basement room, and Julie joined him. Then he
slipped an arm around Julie's shoulder and hugged her. "There's
nothing to be nervous about. These animals are dead, and

they're perfectly harmless. It's just like people. It's only the live ones that can hurt you."

On the way up from the basement in the elevator, Julie thought about Red. From what he'd told her, it was clear that Vicki had dumped him. The comment Red had made about dead animals and dead people stuck in her mind, and Julie shivered slightly. Had he been talking about Vicki? Vicki had hurt Red while she was alive, but now that she was dead, she was harmless.

The elevator doors opened, and Julie stepped out into the lobby. It was still early, only six-thirty, and guests wouldn't be arriving for dinner until seven. This was a perfect time to find Donna and see how they'd decorated the private dining room.

Julie let herself in through the double French doors and walked through the deserted restaurant to the small private dining room. One wall was glass, and it had a lovely view of the snow-covered grounds, which were lighted at night with low spotlights. The other walls were wood paneled, and there was a huge stone fireplace with a portrait of the founders of the lodge, Julie's great-great-grandparents, hanging over it.

Julie walked over to the long table which was set up in the middle of the room, surrounded by twenty red leather chairs. Ten standing ice buckets were lined up nearby, champagne chilling in each of them. Julie recognized the distinctive label—Dom Perignon. This must be a very important dinner party. She'd noticed that Dom Perignon was the most expensive champagne on the menu, over a hundred dollars a bottle!

There was a smile on Julie's face as she glanced at the table itself. Three bouquets of fresh flowers had been arranged on the white linen cloth, red roses peeking out from lacy white baby's breath and delicate green ferns. Aunt Caroline had told Julie she'd taken a class in flower arrangement so she could do the centerpieces for the tables.

Silver gleamed and crystal wineglasses sparkled under the soft glow from the recessed lighting overhead. And to add a touch of warmth and comfort, someone had started a cheery blaze in the stone fireplace.

"Nice, huh?" Donna came in, carrying a stack of china plates. "We always go all out for one of Mr. Stratford's parties. You never know who might be coming. I've waited on senators, and movie stars, and a bunch of millionaires. Of course, none of them bring their wives."

"Why not?"

"Dick Stratford supplies the women."

"Dick? That's short for Richard, isn't it?"

Julie frowned as Donna nodded. Another R. There were so many, she'd have to start keeping a list. Ross, "Rock," Ryan, Richard Stratford, Red Dawson, and even Uncle Bob, since his name was Robert!

"Dick Stratford's got a whole phonebook full of gorgeous young girls." Donna looked amused. "And they all want to be invited to one of his parties. You'll see what I mean when they get here."

Julie nodded. She should have guessed. Ryan was smooth, and he'd obviously had plenty of practice with his father's women. "What does Mr. Stratford do?"

"You mean besides drink, and sleep with gorgeous women, and throw money away?"

Julie laughed. "Yes. What does he do for work?"

"He doesn't. Oh, he flies to New York every week or so to check on his magazine, but that's it."

"Which magazine?"

"*Fantasy.* Have you heard of *Playboy,* or *Penthouse?*"

Julie nodded. "Of course. Mr. Stratford's magazine is like that?"

"Sort of. Except it has less articles. Paul's got a stack of them under his bed, and it's mostly just pictures of naked girls."

"And those are the girls Mr. Stratford brings to his parties?"

"You got it." Donna began putting out the plates. "At least he doesn't bring them in naked. Mrs. Hudson wouldn't let him. They're dressed . . . but barely."

Julie raised her eyebrows. "Who's helping you serve to-night?"

"Mrs. Larkin. Your aunt won't let the boys work Mr. Strat-ford's dinners anymore."

Donna was grinning, and Julie had to ask. "Why not?"

"Because Paul dropped a whole bowl of creamed spinach last year, when he recognized September's top model."

The two girls burst into laughter, but they quickly sobered when Julie's uncle came into the room. He was frowning.

"Isn't that table set yet?"

"It's almost ready, Mr. Hudson. All I've got left are the water glasses."

Donna set out the rest of the plates and hurried back to the kitchen. The moment she was gone, Uncle Bob turned to face Julie sternly. "Don't bother Donna when she's working. She's slow enough as it is."

"Yes, Uncle Bob." Julie's eyes flashed with protest, and she quickly dropped her gaze. Donna wasn't slow. Aunt Caroline had said she was the best waitress at the lodge.

"I need you on the switchboard, Julie. One of our guests wants to place a call to France."

"All right, Uncle Bob." Julie turned and hurried to the lobby. There was something wrong with Uncle Bob tonight. He was just as crabby as the day she'd arrived, and this time there were no German guests to frustrate him.

It took only a few moments to place the call. Julie spoke to the international operator in English and the Paris operator in French. At least her foreign language skills were helpful. Uncle Bob couldn't complain that she wasn't pulling her weight here at the lodge.

Julie had just finished answering several reservation calls when Donna rushed into the lobby. She looked up with a smile as Donna darted around the back of the desk and set down a small plate.

"Louisiana Crab Cakes. They're our special appetizer tonight.

But don't let your uncle see them. He doesn't let anybody eat at the desk."

"Thanks." Julie moved a piece of paper over to hide the plate. "What's wrong with Uncle Bob tonight? He's really cranky."

Donna moved closer and lowered her voice. "I think he's drinking again. He went on a real bender after Vicki died, and he hasn't been the same since. Ross says he wanders around late at night, and every couple of months he goes off in the mountains all alone and doesn't come back for days."

"That's awful." Julie frowned. "It must be very hard on Aunt Caroline."

Donna nodded. "I know it is. She told me she's been trying to get him to go back to AA, so he can straighten out his life."

Julie stared after Donna as she hurried back into the restaurant. She'd thought she'd smelled liquor on Uncle Bob's breath this afternoon, but she hadn't been sure. And Donna's comment had explained a lot. She'd wondered why her aunt waved the wine bottle away at dinner, and now she knew: Uncle Bob was an alcoholic. That was why the liquor cabinet in their living room was filled with nothing but soft drinks. And it also explained why Uncle Bob had been so crabby. If he was drinking again, he was probably feeling guilty about his lapse.

Donna's words had jarred some memory, just below the surface. Julie sighed and shut her eyes, trying to remember back to the time when her aunt had visited them in Tokyo. She'd been sent off to bed while the grownups stayed up late to talk. But she'd been curious, and she'd slipped back down the stairs to listen.

Aunt Caroline had cried, and said she was leaving Uncle Bob. Julie remembered that. She'd said something about another woman, and how Uncle Bob had been drinking too much. Julie's parents had recommended Alcoholics Anonymous, and it must have worked, because Aunt Caroline and Uncle Bob had stayed together.

Before Julie could dredge up any more memories, the front door opened and a crowd of people came in. One glance at them and Julie knew exactly who they were. The men looked rich and successful, and they were dressed in expensive casual wear. And the women were exactly as Donna had described . . . and then some! The last time Julie bad seen so much bare skin was on a nude beach in the South of France.

The women were young and beautiful. Their hair was perfect, their makeup was faultless, and they were all smiling up at their dates with identical adoring expressions on their faces. They were dressed in low-cut evening gowns, and to use the new slang phrase Donna had taught her, they all had bodies to die for. Julie thought they looked like they didn't have a brain among them, but they were gorgeous.

The man in the lead was dressed in slacks and a black silk shirt, open at the neck. His jacket was slung casually over his shoulder, and he looked like he'd stepped right out of the pages of a men's fashion advertisement. He had dark, curly hair and a deeply tanned face. Julie recognized him immediately—Dick Stratford. His eyes were the same shade of slate gray as Ryan's.

He strode toward the desk with the bearing of a man who knew exactly where he was going and why. But he stopped cold as he saw Julie.

"Mr. Stratford?" Julie smiled, and her heart beat a little faster. His eyes were every bit as compelling as his son's.

"Yes." His voice was deep and intimate, and Julie shivered. It was a bedroom voice, a voice that would whisper sweet, sexy things in some woman's ear. He stared at Julie, blinked hard, and then smiled. "Ah, yes. The little cousin. Julie, isn't it?"

"Yes, sir." Julie took a deep breath. "Your table is ready. If you'll wait just a moment, I'll call for the hostess to show you the way."

"That's not necessary. We've been here before. Come on, Bunny. Let's go." Dick Stratford tucked his date's hand under his arm, and escorted her toward the private dining room.

Julie stifled a giggle as she watched them leave. Dick Stratford's date was aptly named. She had long, honey-colored hair and huge brown eyes with impossibly long eyelashes. Her lips were pouty, and her walk was a sexy wiggle. Julie could imagine how a powder puff tail would bounce if someone pinned it to the back of her gold cocktail dress.

To make the resemblance even more startling, Bunny was also very short. That meant she had to hop a bit to keep up with Dick Stratford's long strides. As they turned to go into the private dining room, Julie noticed Bunny's dress, and she bit back another giggle. The gold material clung to her figure like a second skin, and it was slit up both sides. It was lucky that Paul was no longer allowed to work at one of Dick Stratford's parties. If he'd served Bunny, he'd have dropped much more than a bowl of creamed spinach!

After Dick Stratford's dinner guests had left, there was a flurry of calls. Julie answered them quickly, connecting one to the housekeeping desk, another to the long distance operator, and a third and fourth to room service. Mixed in with the in-house calls were several requests for reservations, and one inquiry about a tour group which she referred to Ross.

The old adage was true—after the storm came the calm. After the brief flurry of calls, there was a long, silent interval when the phone didn't ring at all. Julie listened to the sounds from the dining room, glasses clinking, silverware clattering, the low hum of polite dinner conversation. That got boring after a while, and she'd just opened her history book to do a little extra reading when the phone rang again.

"Saddlepeak Lodge. This is Julie speaking. How may I help you?"

There was silence and Julie frowned. A bad connection? She could hear noise in the background and a crackle of static, but the sounds were faraway and indistinct. She was about to hang up when she heard a muffled, whispery voice.

"Julie. You look so pretty in that bright red sweater. Don't do what your wicked cousin did or you'll wind up dead, too."

Then there was nothing but silence again, and the faint indistinct noise in the background. Julie shuddered, and her fingers gripped the receiver so tightly, her knuckles turned white.

"Hello? Hello? Who is this?"

But there was no answer, just the faint crackling of a bad connection. And then she heard something that frightened her even more. A low chuckle that grew to an ominous laugh. And then a click. And a dial tone, loud and jarring, as the call was cut off.

The phone slipped from Julie's nerveless fingers and dropped back into the cradle with a thump. A wrong number? He'd known her name, but she'd identified herself when she'd answered the phone. It could have been a prank, a childish attempt to scare her. But why? What had she done to make someone want to frighten her?

She sat behind the desk, face white, hands shaking, trying to imagine why anyone would make such a call. The voice had been deep and gruff. A man's voice. He'd known that she was Vicki's cousin, but everyone in Crest Ridge knew that.

Julie reached out for a piece of paper and forced her shaking fingers to write down the words exactly as he'd spoken them. *Julie. You look so pretty in that bright red sweater . . .*

She was about to continue when she looked down at the bright red sleeve of her sweater. The pen dropped from her shaking fingers and she gasped in terror. He'd known what she was wearing! Her caller was here, and he was watching her!

Julie felt the back of her neck prickle. It was the same feeling she'd had at the skating rink, the feeling of being watched by hostile eyes. She swiveled around to stare out the window. The grounds looked lovely and peaceful, a white expanse of freshly fallen snow that glittered under the spotlights. Perfectly beautiful. Perfectly still. But he could be out there somewhere, peering out from the corner of a building, or hiding behind one of the huge pine trees. He could be anywhere, lurking in any of a thousand dark shadows while she sat here shaking, exposed by the bright lobby lights.

Deliberately, Julie turned her back on the window. She told herself there was nothing out there, no reason to be in such a panic. She'd been sitting at the switchboard for over an hour and there had been a steady stream of guests and employees who had walked through the lobby. Anyone of them might have noticed that she was wearing a red sweater. It was only a prank—a mean, spiteful trick. She should ignore it and go on as if it had never happened.

Although Julie did her best to push down her fear, nothing she tried had any effect. She could still hear the echoes of that muffled voice, and with each passing second her anxiety grew. Her heart pounded hard and adrenaline surged through her veins. Her mind was flashing a message to her trembling body. Scream. Run to the safety of the restaurant. But how would she explain why she'd left the switchboard? Uncle Bob would think she was crazy to get so upset over a crank phone call.

Julie had to write down the rest of the message. She picked up the pen again and forced herself to continue. *Don't do what your wicked cousin did or you'll wind up dead, too.* The words were ominous, and she stared down at them as if they could somehow magically explain themselves. "Wicked" was a strange word to use, almost old-fashioned, the type of word you'd hear in a fairy tale. How had Vicki been wicked? What had she done?

Julie pushed that part of the sentence out of her mind and concentrated on the rest. As she read the words, she felt her panic rise to the surface again. At first she'd thought that Vicki's death was accidental. That was horrible enough, but then Donna had told her that Vicki had committed suicide, something Julie found even more dreadful. This message hinted at something even more frightening, something so gruesome Julie didn't even want to think about it. Vicki had been wicked, and now she was dead. What if Vicki hadn't committed suicide? What if she'd been murdered?

Julie shuddered as she remembered that chilling laugh. And the creepy feeling of being watched. If the man on the phone had murdered Vicki, would he try to kill her, too?

Five

After an hour of nothing but routine calls, Julie began to relax again. She was grateful she hadn't given way to her fear and gone screaming into the dining room. There was no one out there, watching her. She'd just overreacted to a prank call.

"Here's your dinner, Julie." Uncle Bob was frowning as he walked in with a covered platter and set it on the desk in front of her.

"But, Uncle Bob . . . I thought you didn't want anyone to eat while they were working the switchboard. Donna said that was one of your rules."

"That's true, but Caro overruled me tonight."

Julie looked up in surprise, but Uncle Bob seemed to be avoiding her eyes. "Thank you, Uncle Bob. I'll be careful not to spill anything."

"Good. I have to talk to you, Julie. It's about that sweater of yours."

Julie tried not to look surprised. What was wrong with her sweater? "Yes, Uncle Bob?"

"It's much too tight. And that color just calls attention to . . . well, you're a bright girl. You know what I mean."

Julie was so shocked, she almost objected. Her sweater wasn't tight at all. But one look at Uncle Bob's glowering face and she decided to back down.

"I'm sorry, Uncle Bob. I won't wear it again, if you object. Would you like me to go upstairs and change?"

"It's too late for that. Just try to be more modest in the future. If you need some larger clothes, just ask Caro or me, and we'll see that you get them."

"Thank you, Uncle Bob." Julie did her best to smile. She could tell that Uncle Bob was very crabby tonight, and she could smell alcohol on his breath. If Donna was right and he *was* starting in on another bender, she didn't want to do anything to anger him.

"All right, then. Enjoy your dinner." Uncle Bob started for the door, but then turned and came back. "Here's your paycheck."

"My paycheck?" Julie stared down at the envelope he handed her. "But Uncle Bob . . . I never expected you and Aunt Caroline to pay me."

Uncle Bob frowned. "Of course we're paying you. You're working for us, aren't you?"

"Well . . . yes." Julie was clearly embarrassed. "But you and Aunt Caroline are my family. You're already giving me room and board, and it wouldn't be fair if you paid me, too."

"Why not? We paid Vicki when she worked at the switchboard."

"You did?"

"Of course. If she hadn't done it, we'd have had to hire someone else for the job."

Julie could see his point, but she still shook her head. "I can't let you pay me, Uncle Bob. It just wouldn't be right. You've both done so much for me."

"Well . . ." Uncle Bob seemed at a loss for words. He looked down at the envelope, and then he shrugged. "All right. If you're sure . . ."

"I'm sure."

"Maybe I've misjudged you, Julie." Uncle Bob looked flustered as he took back the envelope. "I'm sorry if I gave you a rough time."

"It's all right, Uncle Bob. I understand. And please tell me if you think I'm wearing something inappropriate. I certainly wouldn't want to embarrass you or Aunt Caroline."

"Well . . . I may have been overreacting a bit." Uncle Bob sighed deeply. "It's just that Vicki used to wear things that were totally unsuitable. Too tight. Too short. It was like she was advertising herself to the staff and the guests. And I was afraid you might be starting to do the same thing. I guess I was afraid that you'd end up like . . . like my poor little Vicki."

Suddenly it struck Julie. Uncle Bob was talking about Vicki, the first time he'd really mentioned her. Would it be wrong to ask a few questions? She'd never know unless she tried. Julie took a deep breath and plunged into unknown waters.

"I'm sorry about Vicki, Uncle Bob. And I wish I could have helped her. One of the kids at school said she was very depressed."

"She was." Uncle Bob didn't look angry anymore. He just looked sad. "We tried to help, but she didn't seem to want to talk about what was bothering her. It got so bad, we even sent her to see a psychiatrist, but she wouldn't talk to him, either. And now we'll never know what was wrong."

Julie sighed. It was now or never. She' simply had to ask. "Uncle Bob?"

"Yes!!"

"I don't want to bring up anything that might hurt you, but something's been bothering me. My mother told me Vicki died in a car accident. Is that true?"

An expression of pain flickered across Uncle Bob's face. "Not entirely. It's true that her car went off the cliff, but . . . Caro and I are afraid she committed suicide."

"Oh, Uncle Bob!" Julie reached out and patted his hand. "I'm so sorry. But are you sure?"

Uncle Bob nodded. "We're sure. She left a note for Caro. She said she couldn't stand it here anymore. She didn't want to hurt us, but there was no other way out."

"But maybe it wasn't suicide. Maybe she was . . . uh . . . running away from home."

Uncle Bob shook his head. "I really wish we could believe that. It would be a real comfort."

"Did she have clothes in her car? Anything that might help you to believe that she was just running away?"

"Well . . . that's part of the problem, Julie." Uncle Bob pulled up a chair and sat down. "Vicki's car burned before Sheriff Nelson could get to it. We'll never know what was inside."

"That's too bad. Wasn't anything saved?"

"Just a few personal items she'd picked up at the drugstore that night. A new lipstick, a bottle of perfume, and a pair of designer sunglasses."

"Designer sunglasses?" Julie looked puzzled. "Why would anyone buy a new pair of sunglasses at night, if they were planning to commit suicide before morning?"

Uncle Bob blinked. And then he stared at Julie. "I never thought of that! The note didn't really say she was planning to *kill* herself."

Julie didn't say a word. She just let the theory take root and grow in Uncle Bob's mind. It took a few moments, but then he turned to her again.

"But why would she run away? We gave Vicki everything she wanted."

"Maybe she was just going off on her own to think things over. You said she was depressed. She could have planned to come back home when she'd worked out her problems."

"I suppose that's possible." Uncle Bob looked thoughtful. "Thank you, Julie. I'll mention this to Caro tonight. It might make her feel better. It's been a rough year for us, searching our memories, trying to figure out what made Vicki decide to kill herself."

Julie nodded. "I'm sorry, Uncle Bob. It must have been awful for both of you."

Uncle Bob got up. He walked toward the door, and then he turned again. "Julie? Please don't mention this to anyone else. It

would only hurt Caro. There's been too much gossip and specu-
lation around here, and I don't want to upset her again."

"Don't worry, Uncle Bob. I won't say a word."

"Good." Uncle Bob nodded. "And if you ever want to talk
about Vicki again, come to me. Don't talk to Caro. She's still . . .
well . . . I really thought she was going to have a nervous breakdown, and she's still very close to the edge. I don't think she
could bear it if you tried to talk about Vicki."

"I understand." Julie gave him a sympathetic smile, but she
was puzzled as she watched him leave. Aunt Caroline had
talked about Vicki that first night when she'd given her the
sweaters and skirts. And she certainly hadn't seemed close to a
nervous breakdown.

Three calls came in before Julie had a chance to lift the cover
on the platter, but when she did, she smiled happily. Mrs.
Robinson had sent her a plate of prime rib, and it looked delicious. There was a Caesar salad, a baked potato with sour
cream and chives, and even Yorkshire pudding. It was a feast.

Julie lifted the cover on the last dish. Mrs. Robinson's pine-
apple custard. Then she noticed that an envelope was tucked
under the dish. she opened it, and a tiny pair of gold, heart-
shaped earrings fell out. There was a note, and Julie read it
quickly.

> These belonged to Vicki. I hope you don't mind. They
> were her favorite earrings when she worked the switch-
> board because they were so tiny. I just thought you might
> like to have them.
>
> Aunt Caroline.

The earrings were beautiful, and Julie slipped them on. Then
she thought about what Uncle Bob had told her and frowned.
He'd said it disturbed Aunt Caroline to talk about Vicki. But
she'd mentioned Vicki in the note!

Was Uncle Bob lying? Or was he simply being overprotective
of his wife? Julie wasn't sure. But she'd promised not to talk

about Vicki with Aunt Caroline, and she wouldn't. Perhaps Uncle Bob was right. After all, he knew Aunt Caroline a lot better than she did.

"Julie! Nice sweater!" Ryan Stratford strode across the lobby and leaned over the desk. "Where's the old man? I've got a message for him."

Could Uncle Bob have been right? Was her sweater too tight? Julie felt a blush rise to her cheeks and hoped she wasn't turning the same color as her sweater. "Your father's in the private dining room. Through the restaurant and . . ."

"Never mind." Ryan interrupted her. "I know the way. You know, I think you look even better than Vicki did in a sweater. She wore them so tight, it left absolutely nothing to the imagination . . . not that anybody could have imagined anything better than what she had, but I like your understated look better."

Julie just nodded. She didn't want to discuss her sweater with Ryan, but he had brought up Vicki, and there were some questions she wanted to ask. "You knew Vicki pretty well, didn't you, Ryan?"

"I guess so." Ryan shrugged. "Why?"

"I . . . well . . . I was just wondering if you knew why she was so depressed."

"Why do you care?" Ryan shrugged again. "She's dead."

Suddenly Julie's temper flared. It was clear Ryan hadn't cared a bit for Vicki. If he had, he couldn't be so callous. "I care because she was my cousin! And I'm living here with her mother and father, practically in her shadow. I need to know what happened to her!"

"Hey . . . take it easy!" Ryan grinned. "I can see where you're coming from. Everybody says you're just like Vicki, and you don't want to make the same mistakes and wind up like she did, right?"

Julie nodded, even though that particular reason had never occurred to her. "So are you going to tell me about her?"

"Sure." Ryan hoisted himself up on the desk and gazed down into Julie's eyes. He was so close, she could see the amber flecks in his deep gray eyes. "The rumor is, your cousin slept around . . . a lot. Maybe she inherited her wild streak from your uncle."

Julie winced. She didn't like gossip, but she had to ask. "What do you mean?"

"Your uncle had a mistress for years. Everybody knew about it except your aunt."

"I don't believe it!"

Ryan shrugged. "I'm just telling you what I heard. You asked, remember?"

"All right. I *did* ask. But you're just repeating gossip."

"Maybe. And maybe not." Ryan gave her a lazy grin. "What time do you get off work?"

"Nine o'clock. Why?"

"Meet me by the stone archway at nine-thirty, and I'll tell you everything I know." Ryan tipped her chin up and touched her upper lip with his finger. "And believe me, Julie . . . I know plenty about your cousin."

"I'm sure you do. And what you don't know, you'll make up. Forget it, Ryan—I'm not interested in your kind of dirt."

Ryan laughed as Julie glared at him. Then he hopped off the desk and started for the door. When he got there, he turned and grinned that lazy grin again.

"Goodbye, Julie. It's really too bad you don't take after your cousin. We could have had a really good time."

It was almost eleven by the time Julie was ready to go up to her room. She'd finished her shift on the switchboard at nine, spent some time talking to Dave and Gina, and helped Mrs. Robinson carry trays of leftovers to the walk-in refrigerator in the kitchen.

Julie stepped into the elevator and pressed the button for the fourth floor. The doors were just closing when she spotted Ross hurrying down the hall, and she reached out to hold the doors for him.

"Thanks." Ross stepped in, but his smile turned into a frown as he glanced at Julie.

Julie sighed. "It's perfectly safe, Ross. I don't bite."

"Sorry." Ross grinned, and looked a little sheepish. "I wasn't frowning at you, Julie. I just . . . uh . . . it's those earrings. Vicki had a pair just like them."

"These *are* Vicki's earrings. Aunt Caroline gave them to me tonight. You're the only one who noticed."

Ross sighed. "That's because I gave them to Vicki."

"You did?" Now it was Julie's turn to look embarrassed. She reached up, took off the earrings, and handed them to him. "Here. You'd better take them back. I didn't realize Aunt Caroline had given me someone else's gift."

Ross waved her hand away. "No, you keep them. It's okay, Julie. And your aunt didn't know I bought them for her. I didn't put my name on the tag. It just said, *From Santa.*"

"They were a Christmas present?"

Ross nodded. "It was my first Christmas with the Hudsons and I bought presents for all of them. The earrings for Vicki, gloves for Mr. Hudson, and a scarf for Mrs. Hudson. I was so grateful to be included. It was almost like having a family again."

"You don't have a family?"

"No. Not anymore. My Dad died in 'Nam. I never even knew him. And my mother . . ." Ross cleared his throat and frowned. "She died when I was a senior in high school."

Julie felt tears gather in her eyes. She knew exactly how Ross had felt, because she had felt the same way. Her parents had been there, loving and supporting, and suddenly they were gone. It had taken her weeks to get over that horrible abandoned feeling. "I'm really sorry, Ross. It must have been awful for you."

"It wasn't the best time in my life." Ross tried to grin, but it came out lopsided. "I don't know what I would have done if your aunt and uncle hadn't taken me in. They gave me a job so I could save up the money for college."

"When are you going?"

"Next September. I'll come back here in the summers to work at the lodge. Your uncle promised me a job, anytime I need it.

He's been just like a father to me. And your aunt has been great, too."

Julie nodded. No wonder Ross had been so upset when she'd told him that her parents had died! He'd been through the same thing himself.

The elevator stopped and Julie got out. But she stumbled slightly, and the books she was carrying toppled to the rug.

"Here. Let me." Ross scooped up the books and stuck them under his arm. "Homework?"

"Not really. I just wanted something to read in case it got slow."

Ross smiled as he walked down the hallway with her. "Your uncle says you're very good at the switchboard. Do you like it?"

"Most of the time." Julie thought about the frightening phone call and winced. She certainly wouldn't mention that! "I had eleven calls for reservations tonight. One woman even asked if we could do her daughter's wedding."

"What did you say?"

"I took her number and told her someone would return the call tomorrow. Her daughter's a skier, and she wanted a winter wedding on the slopes."

"That might be fun." Ross looked interested. "And we might even get some press coverage. Do you have her number with you? I'll call her first thing in the morning."

Julie reached into the side pocket of her purse and pulled out a pink message memo. "Here it is."

"Thanks." Ross stared down at the message for a moment and then he frowned. "Julie . . . what's *this?*"

Julie stared down at the memo and winced again. It was the transcript of the prank phone call! She'd forgotten that she'd stuffed it into the pocket of her purse.

"Oh. Uh . . . it was just a crank phone call I wrote down, that's all. It's nothing to get upset about."

Julie tried to grab the paper, but Ross pulled it back. "Do you have any idea who made this call?"

"No. I didn't recognize his voice. It . . . it scared me, until I realized that it had to be a joke."

"Some joke!" There was anger in Ross's voice. "Do you mind if I keep this?"

"You can have it. I'd just as soon forget it ever happened. But please don't show it to Uncle Bob or Aunt Caroline. It would only upset them."

"I won't." When they reached the double doors, Ross handed Julie her books. "Julie?"

"Yes?"

"Yesterday at the skating rink . . . you said you thought you heard someone in the trees?"

Julie nodded. "At first I thought it was a person, but I'm sure I was just overreacting. It could have been a raccoon."

"Well . . . maybe." Ross looked doubtful, even though he'd been the one to tell her about the raccoons. "Do me a favor, Julie. If anything else happens, anything that makes you nervous, tell me about it right away."

Julie nodded solemnly. "All right. I'll tell you. But do you expect anything else to happen?"

"No. Of course not." Ross refused to meet her eyes. "Nice talking to you, Julie. See you tomorrow."

Ross gave a little wave and headed off toward his room. Julie stared after him with a frown on her face. He *did* expect something else to happen, and that was why he'd refused to meet her eyes. But what?

Six

Julie shivered as she got ready for bed. Her room was cold and there seemed to be an icy draft coming from somewhere, even though the windows were tightly closed. She chided herself for being silly, but it reminded her of the night she'd gone to a seance.

Julie's friends had urged her to come along, and Julie had suffered through an evening of flickering candles, dark shadows, and what she'd thought was theatrical nonsense. But there had been one disturbing moment, right after the medium had called for the spirit to come forth. There had been an icy draft, much like the one that was now invading Julie's room at Saddlepeak Lodge.

Julie sighed. If there *was* a draft, something must be causing it. She walked around the room, checking for the source. It seemed to be strongest near the ceiling right over her bed. How strange! Perhaps there was a hairline crack in the plaster and cold air was seeping through from the fifth-floor attic.

She was about to give up and go to bed anyway when she happened to glance at the balcony doors. They were closed, but she'd forgotten to lock them. As she put the bars in place and fastened them with the thumb screws, Julie felt a bit foolish. She was probably being overly cautious, but she'd sleep better knowing that her room was secure.

Since she liked to look out at the moon on the snow-covered peaks of the mountains, Julie opened the curtains. Then she flicked off the lights and climbed into bed. It was almost midnight, and her alarm was set for seven. She'd be tired in the morning if she didn't get right to sleep.

But sleep was a long time in coming. Julie tried to think of something pleasant, and she smiled as she remembered her encounter with Ross in the elevator. He'd told her to keep the earrings he'd given Vicki. That must mean that he liked her. He'd even told her something personal about his family, and that meant they were becoming friends. Friendship was a good start to a relationship. And a relationship with Ross would be wonderful.

Julie sighed as she remembered the way Ross's deep blue eyes had swept over her, taking in every detail. And the way his lips had turned up in a smile when she'd told him that she didn't bite. She shivered a little as she thought about those lips. How would they feel if he pulled her into his arms and kissed her?

Ross thought she was attractive, Julie was sure of that. Now all she had to do was arrange some seemingly chance meetings, preferable in romantic spots. The ski slopes would be nice. She could pretend to stumble and he could catch her. She'd figure out some way to end up in his arms or her name wasn't Julie Forrester!

But even her warm, pleasant thoughts about Ross didn't work to chase away the chill in the air. Julie shivered and pulled the covers up to her chin. Perhaps she'd ask Aunt Caroline for an electric blanket. There definitely seemed to be a draft in her room.

Another few moments, and Julie felt her body begin to relax. The moon cast lovely shadows on the ceiling, but her eyes were too tired to appreciate them. Her eyelids were closing, heavy with the need for sleep. She could hear her own breathing. Slow. Very slow. The rhythm was as deep and peaceful as the lovely darkness that started to claim her.

But there was the draft again. An icy, frigid breeze. It blew in through the open window of the car she was driving, a red Mustang with the window rolled down. Ice particles clung to her hair, and she wanted to shut her eyes. But she was driving too fast down the mountain road, and she had to see the curves ahead.

There was a sense of weightlessness as she whipped around the tortuous bends. Her headlights were a golden ribbon piercing the darkness. The ribbon was on a giant spool, and it was unwinding at breathtaking speed.

But there was something wrong. And now the ribbon was tangled, weaving and veering in a crazy pattern. Danger! There was danger ahead! And she was flying too fast to stop!

The fence was just ahead, a white fence to stop her, to keep her from danger. The golden ribbon snagged against it, pulling it in, faster, faster. There was a horrible scraping noise, as it bumped along, clumping louder and louder until . . .

Julie's eyes flew open and she stared at the moon-swept balcony. Then she screamed, a high, thin sound of terror. A face! There was a disembodied face on her balcony! It looked like a death's head, and it was grinning a terrible smile!

She tried to get out of bed, to run, to hide, but her body seemed incapable of movement. The hollow eye sockets seemed to stare at her, pinning her to the bed as securely as a butterfly in a specimen box.

"Julie! Are you all right, Julie?"

There was a loud knock on the door, and miraculously the spell dissolved. Julie stumbled from her bed and raced for the door, her fingers fumbling frantically with the lock. It seemed to take forever, but at last she had it open, and she raced into her aunt's arms. "Aunt Caroline! There was someone on my balcony! I saw him!"

Aunt Caroline turned toward the balcony, and Julie turned with her. Nothing there. No face. No grinning death's head. Nothing but the beautiful, peaceful moonlight.

"Are you sure, Julie?" Aunt Caroline frowned as she walked to the balcony doors and looked out. "There's no one there now."

"The fire escape! Maybe he went down the fie escape!"

Aunt Caroline loosened the thumbscrews and swung the bars

aside. Then she stepped out on the balcony in her robe and slippers and peered down at base of the fire escape. "Put on your boots, honey. And then come out here. I want you to see for yourself."

Julie went to her closet and pulled on her boots. Then she stepped out on the balcony, shivering in her blue flannel nightgown. There were no footprints in the snow at the base of the . fire escape, just an unbroken sheet of icy snow.

"Mrs. Hudson? Is something wrong?" Ross appeared on his balcony, dressed in a bathrobe.

"No, Ross. Julie just thought she saw someone on her balcony."

Ross nodded, but Julie noticed he didn't look surprised. "Do you want me to check it out, Mrs. Hudson?"

"Thank you, but there's no need. If someone climbed up here, he'd have left footsteps."

Julie stepped back inside her room, away from Ross's sympathetic gaze. She was terribly embarrassed. "I'm sorry I woke you, Ross. I guess it was just a nightmare."

Aunt Caroline gave one last look and then came back inside Julie's room. "Go back to bed, honey. And try to sleep. Do you want me to stay for a while?"

Julie shook her head. "I'm okay, Aunt Caroline. And I'm sorry I caused such a fuss."

"Don't worry about it." Aunt Caroline smiled at her. "Sometimes dreams can be very frightening. And very real. Vicki used to have nightmares, too. That's why we put these bars on the doors. We thought it might help if she knew that no one could get in."

"She thought she saw someone on her balcony?"

Aunt Caroline nodded. "We sent Ross out to check the grounds the first couple of times, but he didn't find any evidence of an intruder. Tell me about your dream. You thought you saw a man?"

"No—at least, not a whole man." Julie sighed as she remembered the face. "It was only his face. And he was ... uh ... grinning at me."

"Was there a sound? Something that woke you?"

"I think I heard a screeching noise. Something scraping, like nails on a blackboard."

Aunt Caroline sighed. "That's exactly what Vicki described. There's got to be a real sound that occurs this time of night. I just wish we could figure out what it was."

"Maybe it's a branch scraping against a window," Julie suggested.

"That's possible. I'll have Ross check it out tomorrow. Do you think you can go back to sleep?"

"I think so." Julie smiled at her aunt. It was clear that Aunt Caroline was worried. "I'm all right, Aunt Caroline . . . really. It was just a dream, that's all."

After Aunt Caroline had left, Julie locked her balcony doors again and climbed back into bed. She was terribly embarrassed. It was bad enough that she'd awakened Aunt Caroline, but now Ross knew about her nightmare, too. That made Julie doubly humiliated. Ross had been friendly when they'd ridden up in the elevator. He'd complimented her on her work, he'd carried her books, and he'd even confided in her about his family. Tonight had been a breakthrough, the first time Ross hadn't treated her like a child, and Julie was sure he'd been interested in her as a date, not just as his employer's niece. She'd hoped this would be the start of a new relationship, perhaps even a lasting romance. But now she'd blown it. Two hours after Ross had finally shown some interest in her, she'd awakened him with her silly, childish nightmare!

Seven

Saturday morning dawned bright and sunny, a perfect day for skiing. Julie got up refreshed, and she smiled as she dressed in her cousin's beautiful blue ski outfit. There had been no more nightmares since the one on Sunday night. Perhaps the gruesome death's head had driven all the lesser nightmares out of her system.

Julie had established her basic duties earlier in the week, telling her aunt that she'd like to volunteer to work on the ski slopes if Ross thought her skills were adequate. Aunt Caroline had immediately agreed. Just as Julie had hoped, her aunt had asked Ross to take her out on the slopes this morning, to show her the trails and test her skills. Saddlepeak Lodge was opening its ski season tomorrow, and the switchboard had been swamped with calls for reservations.

Unfortunately, Julie's skis had arrived damaged by their long overseas trip. They were being repaired in the pro shop, but they wouldn't be ready in time. Aunt Caroline had dismissed the problem with a wave of her hand. Julie could use Vicki's skis. Since she was the same size and weight as her cousin, Vicki's skis would be perfect for her.

Yesterday afternoon, when she'd come home from school, Julie had found a large box in her room. She'd opened it and gasped as she'd examined the contents. Vicki had owned an expensive, customized pair of compounds by Rossignol. But that was only part of the package. Vicki's boots had been molded to fit her feet, and the bindings had been especially fashioned to fit the boots.

Julie's hands had trembled as she'd pulled on the boots and stood up. If she couldn't wear Vicki's boots, she wouldn't be able to use these marvelous skis. She'd taken a couple of steps, and then she'd smiled happily. Vicki's boots fit her perfectly!

Julie had taken Vicki's skis to the pro shop last night, and watched while they were being waxed. They were in flawless condition, and she was almost glad her skis had been damaged in transit. There was an old saying, "The better the skis, the better the skier," and Julie hoped it was true. She knew she was a good skier, but she wanted to look like an expert when she went out on the slopes with Ross.

The thought of Ross sent a flurry of butterflies dancing in her stomach. She wasn't nervous about her performance. She knew she was good. The anxious fluttering had started only when she'd thought of being alone with Ross.

As she waited in the pro shop, to pick up her skis, Julie felt a familiar, prickling sensation at the back of her neck. Someone was watching her; she was sure of it. She turned, but there was no one in the hallway outside, and the other shops in the lobby were virtually deserted. Most of their guests would arrive tonight, turn in early, and be out on the slopes for the opening run in the morning.

Julie was just inspecting her skis when she felt eyes watching her again. She whirled and saw the shape of a man standing across the hallway in her aunt's office. The miniblinds were half closed and he had turned his back to them, but Julie was sure he'd been watching her only moments before.

It took just a few minutes to pick up the rest of her equipment. Julie left the pro shop and headed across the hall to her aunt's office. There was only one way to find out who the man was. She'd confront him face-to-face.

Julie opened the door and stepped inside. The man turned and greeted her with a smile. Julie's eyes widened, and then she smiled back rather sheepishly. "Hi, Mr. Stratford."

Mr. Stratford smiled back at her. "Please, call me Dick. I wasn't sure that was you, Julie. You look very professional."

"Uh . . . thank you. Does my aunt know you're here?"

Dick Stratford nodded. "Caro had to leave for a minute, and I'm waiting for her to get back. That's a lovely ski outfit, Julie. Is it one of Reneé Clusong's?"

Julie nodded, and touched the fabric reverently. Reneé Clusong's designer ski outfits were terribly expensive. "It belonged to my cousin, Vicki. Aunt Caroline said I could use it."

"I thought I recognized it!" Dick Stratford nodded. "You know, I think it looks even better on you."

An alarm went off in Julie's mind. Dick Stratford must have seen Vicki wearing this outfit. "Did you know Vicki well, Mr. Strat . . . I mean, Dick?"

"Of course. My son brought her to the house several times. Charming. And beautiful. Just like you, Julie."

"Thank you." Julie felt the color rise to her cheeks. Was Mr. Stratford trying to pick up on her? But that was ridiculous! He was much too old to be interested in someone her age. But he certainly was staring at her. And his eyes were very warm and friendly.

Julie took a deep breath. Now was the time to ask some questions. Mr. Stratford had claimed to know Vicki well. "Was my cousin dating Ryan?"

"I believe so. Of course, Ryan never tells me anything about his personal life. I've taught him that Stratford men never kiss and tell. I do know that your cousin and Ryan were together quite often, and they were skating partners. But you probably knew that."

Julie nodded. "Someone told me they won a trophy."

"Yes. And we had a celebration that night. Vicki and Ryan were the guests of honor at one of my house parties."

"How nice." Julie nodded, and tried not to blush! Donna had told her all about Mr. Stratford's house parties. Sometimes they lasted the whole weekend. "Were Aunt Caroline and Uncle Bob there?"

Dick Stratford burst into laughter. "Of course not. And I don't think your little cousin told them she was there, either. Let's keep that secret, all right?"

"That's probably a very good idea." Julie frowned slightly. "Did you like Vicki, Mr. Stratford?"

"Tremendously. Such a tragedy. She was just beginning to live her life to the fullest when it was taken away from her."

"Yes. That's true." Suddenly Julie felt terribly uncomfortable. She had the feeling that Mr. Stratford was playing with her, like a cat with a mouse, and she didn't like it at all.

"Shall I invite you to one of my parties, Julie?"

Dick Stratford smiled, but his smile reminded Julie of a predator, and she quickly shook her head. "No, thanks, Mr. Stratford."

"I'm sure you'd have a very good time."

"I might. But I think I'd be playing way out of my league." Julie took a step toward the door. "Sorry, Mr. Stratford. I have to run. I hope Aunt Caroline doesn't keep you waiting too long."

"Oh, I never mind waiting for a beautiful woman." Dick Stratford smiled again. "If you change your mind, Julie, I'm in the book."

Julie turned and walked through the door. Her legs were shaking and she felt almost dizzy as she walked down the hall toward the lobby. Dick Stratford was very handsome, and he was even more dangerous than his son. Had Vicki really gone to one of his parties? Julie wished she could ask her cousin. It was another question that would never be answered, another mystery that would never be solved.

"Hi, Julie!" Donna jumped up from the couch as Julie walked through the lobby. She was dressed in bright yellow ski wear and she looked like a plump, round canary. "Are you ready?"

Julie frowned slightly. "Ready for what?"

"Skiing. I can hardly wait to get back on the slopes. Paul and

I haven't skied since last winter, and the first day out is always the best."

Realization dawned, and Julie felt her spirits sink. "Ross asked you and Paul to come along?"

"Yes. He told us to meet him here at nine." Donna pulled up her sleeve and glanced at her watch. "It's only eight-thirty. Do you want a quick cup of coffee to perk you up?"

Julie nodded, although she doubted that coffee would do anything to elevate her sinking spirits. It was very clear that Ross hadn't wanted to be alone with her.

"Hi, Julie." Paul came in, dressed in a dark green jacket and matching ski pants.

Julie smiled and her heart gave a little lurch. Paul was very handsome when he smiled, and he was smiling at her now. Julie smiled back. She was beginning to think she'd been wrong about Paul. He'd been very nice to her lately. But then he noticed her skis and his pleasant expression turned into a glower.

"What are you doing with those?"

Paul pointed to her skis, and Julie sighed. She should've known Paul would notice. "My skis are being repaired, and Aunt Caroline said I could use these today. They belonged to Vicki."

"I know." Paul nodded, but his expression didn't lighten. "I'll go see if I can help Ross."

Julie frowned as Paul strode out through the door. Then she turned to Donna. "What's wrong with him? He practically bit my head off."

"It's the skis." Donna sighed as she explained her brother's reaction. "Paul worked for three solid months to earn the money to buy them."

"Paul gave them to her?"

Donna nodded. "They were a birthday present."

"Maybe I should run down to the pro shop and rent another pair." Julie was still frowning. "I don't want to hurt Paul's feelings."

"Don't be silly. He'll get over it. There's no reason why you shouldn't wear those skis. *Somebody* should appreciate them."

"Vicki didn't use them?"

"She dumped Paul before ski season started. Go ahead and enjoy them, Julie. It's time Paul got over being so touchy about Vicki. And seeing you wear those skis might help."

The sun glistening on the hard-packed snow was gorgeous. Julie's spirits took an abrupt upswing as she followed Ross to the ski lift. So what if he hadn't wanted to be alone with her? She was going to ski again, and that was enough to make anyone feel wonderful!

Julie smiled as she gazed up at the jagged peaks towering above her. Then she noticed a beautiful, unbroken slope, right at the edge of a stand of pine trees, and pointed it out to Ross. "Look at that marvelous natural run!"

Ross laughed at her bubbling excitement, but he shook his head. "Looks are deceiving. See that scrub pine about halfway down? Just to the left of it is a nasty drop. You can't see it from here, but the landing's flat, not sloped. It's a real killer."

Julie shivered. She knew it was possible to make a very steep jump if you landed on a downward slope, but flat landings were extremely dangerous. One of her classmates had broken her leg on a four-foot jump when she'd landed on flat ground.

"It doesn't look very dangerous from down here, does it?" Ross smiled at her.

"No. It looks so gentle, I thought it was a beginner's slope."

"That's part of the problem." Donna spoke up. "It looks great from down here. And it's just as deceptive at the top. A skier might start down that slope, thinking he was in for an easy run. He wouldn't realize he was in trouble until it was too late."

Julie nodded and turned to Ross. "Has anyone been hurt since you've been here?"

"No. We're very careful about marking our slopes. That's why I asked Paul and Donna to come with us today. We had the slopes groomed yesterday. The crew is supposed to replace the flags, but sometimes they miss a few. We always doublecheck each slope, especially that one."

"I'm glad you told me." Julie felt her spirits rise again. Ross had asked Paul and Donna to work this morning. That was the reason they were here.

Paul came up just in time to hear the end of their conversation, and he turned to Julie. "That's Dead Man's Run, and the name's no joke. Five people have lost their lives on that slope. I don't care how good you *think* you are, stay away from there!"

"Oh, I will." Julie nodded, but she felt more like frowning. Paul didn't have to be so nasty. And the implication behind his words made her do a slow burn. She'd never claimed that she was an expert skier. All she was doing was trying to help out on the slopes.

Donna gave her brother a withering glance, and did her best to soften his words. "Dead Man's Run is our biggest worry. We warn the guests, and we never let them out on the slopes alone. Ross even stations one of us up at the top to make sure no one ignores the signs."

Ross nodded. "We tape it off at the top, and flag it as far as we can. But that's a bad slide area, and we have to check every morning to make sure the warnings are still up."

"You're certainly very safety conscious." Julie gave Ross an approving smile. Then she glanced up at the dangerous run again, and grabbed his arm. "Look, Ross! Someone's skiing up there!"

Ross shaded his eyes with his hand. He watched for a moment, and then he nodded. "It's all right, Julie. That's Ryan Stratford."

"But he's skiing right down toward the drop!"

"Don't worry. He'll veer off. Ryan's been skiing these trails all his life, and he knows the terrain."

Julie watched for a moment, her heart in her throat. But Ryan was in perfect control. He veered off, just as Ross had said he would, and she breathed a sigh of relief. "He's really good!"

"Depends on your point of view."

Paul muttered his comment in an undertone, but Julie was standing near enough to hear him. She turned around to frown at him. "You really hate him, don't you?"

"Let's just say we don't get along."

Ross checked his bindings, and then he turned to Julie. "Are you ready?"

Julie nodded, and Ross motioned to Paul and Donna. "You two go first. Split up when you get to the top. I want Donna to check Sleeping Giant. Paul? You take Spruce Ridge."

"Okay, boss." Donna grinned at him. "Did you bring the flags?"

Ross nodded, and pointed to two ski packs. "You know the drill. Green circles on the beginner slopes, blue squares for the intermediate, and black diamonds to mark the expert runs. We'll all meet back here when you're through."

"Which slope do you want me to take?" Julie turned to Ross as he strapped on a ski pack.

"You're going to the beginner slopes with me. I want to make sure you can handle yourself."

Julie sighed. Ross was certainly being cautious. Of course, that could mean he was beginning to care for her. "How about Dead Man's Run? Does that have flags?"

Ross nodded. "We use two black diamonds for extremely dangerous, but that's not enough. We also have black with a white skull and crossbones. Even if people don't know the color code, they recognize that symbol."

Julie shuddered. A skull and crossbones would certainly keep her away! "If I prove that I'm a good skier, will you let me replace some of the flags?"

"Sure." Ross smiled at her. "If you can ski as well as your aunt says, we'll split up when we finish the beginner slopes. I'll take Sky Top. That's our most difficult run. And I'll let you try your hand on Camel Back."

Julie nodded, and watched him ski away to start the lift. Then she turned to Paul with a pleased expression. "Is Camel Back very challenging?"

"Oh, definitely." Paul grinned at her in his exasperating way. "It's got a couple of jumps that are at least six inches high."

Julie felt her face burn, and she turned away. Paul was a despicable person, and she was glad she hadn't had time to change to another pair of skis. She hoped he was miserable, seeing her wear the skis he'd given to Vicki. He deserved to squirm, and then some, after putting her on about Camel Back!

Loose snow rose up like a bright white cloud as Julie skied to a stop. She laughed, a pure sound of exhilaration in the crisp mountain air, and turned to watch with sparkling eyes as Ross skied down the gentle decline.

"Well? Do I pass?" Julie laughed at the shocked expression on his face. It was clear he hadn't realized she was such a good skier.

"And then some." Ross draped a friendly arm around her shoulder as they walked to the ski lift again. "I don't think I've ever seen anybody get so much speed out of Old Betsy."

"Old Betsy?" Julie giggled and snuggled a little closer. Ross's arm felt warm and wonderful, resting against her shoulders.

"It's our name for the baby slope. Old Betsy's like a ancient swaybacked mare, gentle and completely toothless."

Julie sighed. "From what Paul tells me, Camel Back doesn't have any teeth, either. How about letting me try something with a little more oomph?"

"Oomph?" Ross laughed. "I can give you oomph, but you might not like it."

"Why not?"

"Because I'm half tempted to put you to work, now that I know what a good skier you are. Somebody has to check out Hannah's Folly."

"Hannah's Folly?" Julie grinned up at him. "I like it already. What color flags?"

"Black diamond."

"That's expert." Julie felt a shiver of excitement. "I'll do it, Ross. I'd love to!"

"If you're sure you don't mind . . ."

"I don't. Please, Ross . . . I'm just dying to do some real skiing."

Ross nodded. "All right. I was going to have Paul do it, but this way we'll all finish up about the same time."

Ten minutes later, Julie had her own pack of flags and she was riding up the ski lift again. Her spirits were soaring. Ross had taken the most difficult slope for himself, but he'd trusted her enough to give her the next best thing. When she got to the top of the ridge, she met Paul and Donna, who'd just finished their assignments.

"Going to Camel Back?"

Paul grinned at her, but this time it didn't bother Julie. Ross had given her the ammunition to really get back at him. She managed to stifle her urge to laugh, and shook her head dejectedly. "Ross said he didn't want me to ski Camel Back."

"But why?" Donna looked shocked. "Nobody's ever been hurt on Camel Back. It's practically a baby slope! Do you want me to talk to him, Julie? He might let you ski it if I go along to help you."

Julie winked at Donna, and did her best to keep a straight face. "No, thanks. It's all right. Ross said I could ski another slope, if I promised to be very careful."

"He's the boss." Paul shrugged. "Is he going to let you try Lazy Boy?"

"No." Julie shook her head, and tried not to laugh. Ross had told her the names of all the slopes and she knew that Lazy Boy was another, very gentle beginner's run.

"Rocking Horse?"

Paul guessed again, and Julie shook her head. It was impossible for her to keep a straight face for much longer, especially since Donna was obviously holding in a giggle. Paul frowned. "But we only have three beginner slopes."

"I know." Julie nodded. She could hardly wait to see the expression on Paul's face when she told him. "I'm not skiing on a beginner slope. Ross asked me to replace the flags on Hannah's Folly."

"Hannah's Folly?" Paul's mouth dropped open. "But that's an expert slope!"

"So I hear." Julie slung her ski pack over her shoulder, and grinned at him. His mouth was still open, and she almost told him to close it before he froze his tongue.

Paul must have read her thoughts, because he closed his mouth with a snap. He blinked once and then started to frown.

"I don't know what he's thinking of! I'd better go with you. Somebody's got to keep you out of trouble."

"Thanks for the offer, but you'll be much too busy to ski with me. You see, Ross has a very challenging job for you."

Paul looked slightly mollified. "What does he want me to do? Check out Sky Top?"

"Oh, no." Julie shook her head. "It's much more challenging than that. He told me he wants you to replace the flags on Camel Back."

Eight

Julie skied away with Donna's laughter ringing in her ears. So far, this had been a marvelous day. She'd managed to put Paul firmly in his place, but that was only part of her pleasure. She'd also made some real headway with Ross. It was clear he thought she was a good skier. He'd told her to replace the flags on Hannah's Folly, a very difficult slope. But even more important than that, he'd hugged her. Sort of.

A smile spread over Julie's face as she found the sign for Hannah's Folly and began to ski down the steep slope. Perhaps it hadn't really been a hug, but remembering the warm, close feeling of Ross's arm resting on her shoulders made her shiver in delight.

"Oops!" Julie skied dangerously close to the edge of the run and slowed to a panic stop. Hannah's Folly was steep and filled with sharp hairpin turns. This wasn't the time to think about Ross. The headway she'd made with him would come to a screeching halt if she did something foolish like break a leg on her way down the slope.

Ross had told her to replace only damaged flags, and Julie checked each flag to make sure it was intact. She was only about a third of the way down when she found one that was tattered. She skied to a stop, took a new flag out of her ski pack, and tied it on securely.

It was difficult to ski slowly on Hannah's Folly. The steep slope was built for speed, and Julie was dying to let loose and soar down the steep incline. She decided to go just a bit faster. There was no reason why she couldn't have fun and get her task done at the same time.

She was just rounding a bend when she heard it, a sharp explosion like someone was firing a gun. A split second later, there was a low rumbling directly above her. It was every skier's nightmare—an avalanche!

Julie didn't turn around to look up. There wasn't time. She just veered off sharply and cut through a stand of pines, skiing around trees with as much speed as she could gather, using her poles to jump obstacles, and praying that she could get to a place of safety before the heavy wall of snow caught her and swept her away.

The noise was deafening as tons of snow roared down the mountain, uprooting trees and burying markers so deep they might never be found. Julie skied on the edge of the white death, almost caught in its path as it roared down Hannah's Folly. Somehow she had to stay on her feet and keep veering away from the hurtling snow. If she fell, she'd be buried alive!

Almost as suddenly as it had come, the avalanche was gone. Now there was only an eerie stillness, a quiet so intense it hurt Julie's ears. She turned to look back and shuddered. The spot where she'd been only seconds before was buried under tons of unforgiving snow.

Julie leaned against the trunk of a pine tree, trembling uncontrollably as she stared at the destruction the avalanche had left in its wake. Hannah's Folly was gone, completely erased, as if it had never existed, by the crushing power of one of nature's most destructive whims.

She stood there shaking, thankful to be alive, when she suddenly realized that her troubles were far from over. There was no safe way down the mountain, now that the markers were gone. The mountainside was treacherous, and Ross had warned her not to leave the slope. If she tried to ski down over unknown terrain, she could wipe out on a hidden boulder, or ski over the edge of a drop. And it was impossible to climb the steep slope to the top. She was trapped!

Julie took a deep breath and let it out, trying to force down her panic. There was no cause for alarm. She was warmly dressed, and the stand of pines was a good windbreak. All she had to do was wait, and someone would come to look for her.

But would they find her? She was a small speck of humanity and the mountainside was huge and heavily wooded. They knew the slope she'd been skiing, but Hannah's Folly was gone. No one could ski down the path the avalanche had made. Of course they'd search the area by helicopter, but she was well hidden, here in the pines. Would they take one look at the place where Hannah's Folly had been and then write her off as the first casualty of the winter ski season?

Julie shuddered. They might never find her if she stayed here. Nights were cold on the mountain, and she could freeze to death before morning. She couldn't just sit here and hope that help would come to her. She had to think of a way to get down the mountain safely.

Suddenly, the drawing she'd seen in the pro shop flashed through her mind. The slopes all started from a central area on the ridge, and ran down the mountainside in roughly parallel lines. All she had to do was ski horizontally across the mountain until she ran into another slope!

Julie picked up her poles and smiled in relief. If she was lucky and ran into another slope quickly, she could be back at the lodge before they even sent out a search party.

But the task was harder than she'd anticipated. The ungroomed ground was rough, and Julie had to pick her way carefully. This wasn't the time to suffer a mishap. The farther she skied from Hannah's Folly, the less chance she'd have of being spotted.

Julie skied until her legs were aching, and her lungs burned with the cold mountain air. She was doing cross-country skiing with downhill skies, and that was difficult. She was about to take a break and rest for a while when she spotted a slope in the distance. It hadn't been groomed, but perhaps the crew still had a couple of slopes left to do.

It took at least fifteen minutes to reach the slope, and Julie arrived breathless. She glanced around for markers, but none were visible. Perhaps the crew had taken them out, intending to replace them when they'd finished their grooming. It really didn't matter. The slope was wide and it looked gentle. It would be an easy trip down.

As she started her downhill descent, Julie realized her legs were trembling from fatigue. She told herself that the sooner she made it down, the sooner she could rest, and she dug in her poles and forced herself to go faster. This was practically a baby slope, although it was quite steep. She'd be at the bottom in no time at all.

Suddenly she heard a shout above her, and she turned her head quickly to see who was there. A figure in black was streaking toward her, and she recognized Ryan Stanford.

Julie smiled as she dug in her poles again. Ryan obviously wanted to race. Of course, she wouldn't be much competition in her weakened state, but she'd do her best to give him a run for his money.

Then there was a terrible jolt, and Julie felt herself flying through the air. She landed heavily and started to skid down the icy slope, but Ryan clamped his arms around her. She rolled several feet, tangled in Ryan's embrace. His arms were like steel bands around her, and she couldn't get loose. Finally they came to a stop, sprawled in a heap in the center of the slope.

"What . . . what do you think you're doing?" Julie glared up at him. He'd knocked her down on purpose, and now he was holding her so tightly, she couldn't move. She was pinned down, his body covering hers in a way that made her blush and then steam with anger.

Julie's leg throbbed where he'd barreled into it, and she knew she was bruised all over. She started to struggle, but there was no way she could get to her feet.

"Let me go!" Julie glared at him again, and then she drew in her breath sharply. Ryan's face was a pasty shade of white, and his gray eyes blazed with something that looked almost like fear.

"Don't move a muscle." His voice was tight. Clipped. "Just inch back with me, up the slope."

Julie's eyes widened. Had he gone mad? "But . . ."

"Do it! Now!"

Julie did it. She had no other choice. Ryan was holding her so tightly, his fingers were digging into the tender skin on her arms.

"More. Come on! Wiggle your hips and scoot backward!"

Julie did as he said. This really wasn't the time to argue. They managed to move a foot or so up the slope, and then Ryan seemed to relax.

"Thank God! I thought you were a goner!"

"What do you mean? I was just skiing back to the lodge." Julie frowned at him. His eyes had lost their fierce gleam, but he was still holding her tightly.

Ryan shook his head, and laughed. "Well, you wouldn't have made it. You owe me one."

Before Julie could do more than gasp, Ryan's lips had clamped over hers. They were cold at first, chilled by the winter air, but then they warmed and Julie sighed softly. How could firm lips be so soft? And why was she trembling? She really should stop him. He'd been terribly rude. He'd knocked her down like a battering ram, just so he could kiss her. If he thought these caveman tactics would impress her, he was dead wrong.

Julie tried to twist away, to open her mouth to tell him to stop. But Ryan seized the opportunity to kiss her more deeply. His tongue flickered into her mouth, and she felt her pulses race. She'd never been kissed this intimately before, and she shuddered as she began to respond to him.

And then he stopped. Abruptly. Julie blinked and then she shivered. What had gotten into him? And what was the matter with her? She thought about the sensations he'd evoked with his hot, wet tongue, and she shivered again. She was almost disappointed that he had stopped!

Ryan pulled back and laughed at the confusion in her eyes. "You still don't know what happened, do you?"

"I . . . I certainly don't!" Julie did her best to sound outraged, but her voice was shaking. Ryan's kiss had affected her much more than she wanted to admit.

"You're on Dead Man's Run. And I stopped you about six inches before you went over the drop!"

Julie was trembling as she approached the group that awaited her at the base of the slope. Naturally, her two near brushes with death had terrified her, but Julie wasn't thinking about the avalanche, or how she'd almost gone over the drop on Dead Man's Run. Ryan's kiss had been her real undoing, and she couldn't seem to stop thinking about the way his lips had claimed hers, and how his tongue had teased the moist, hot depths of her mouth.

After Ryan had helped her to her feet, Julie had tried to thank him. After all, he'd saved her life. But Ryan had just grinned and told her that the kiss had been his reward. The gleam in his intense gray eyes had made her tremble even more as he'd checked to make sure she wasn't injured, inspected her skis and bindings, and shown her a trail through the trees to Lady Luck.

Lady Luck was an expert run, and he'd skied at her side most of the way down, watching her critically for signs of fatigue. He'd forced her to stop several times to rest, and the last time they'd stopped, she'd asked him to keep her near accident a secret.

"Why should I do that?" Ryan had raised his eyebrows.

Julie had winced, and tried to think of a good excuse, but finally she'd settled for the truth. "It's embarrassing. They warned me about Dead Man's Run, and I should have realized where I was when there were no markers."

"You don't want to admit you made a mistake?"

Ryan had chuckled, and Julie had felt a blush spread over her face. She'd nodded and glanced down at the ground, rather than meet his eyes.

"It's our secret, then." Ryan had reached out to raise her chin, until she had to meet his eyes. "But don't forget you owe me another one."

Julie hadn't asked what he meant. She didn't want to know. She'd just nodded and started to ski again, almost hoping he wouldn't follow her.

But Ryan did follow her, and he'd skied at her side almost all the way down Lady Luck. He'd only veered off when he'd spotted the group waiting for her at the bottom. And here she was, only a little worse for wear, despite her frightening experiences.

Julie did her best to smile, but it was a pitiful effort. She was so tired, her legs were shaking. Suddenly she remembered Donna's comment. The first day on the slopes was the best. Julie hoped her friend was wrong. She couldn't imagine a day any worse than this!

"Julie!" Ross looked alarmed as he skied to meet her. "Are you all right?"

"I . . . I'm fine." Julie nodded, and quite unexpectedly, the terror of her near brush with death caught up with her. She swayed, and Ross caught her in his arms. And then Paul was there, too, taking her other arm and helping her the last few feet down the slope.

Donna came up to hug Julie, and Julie noticed that there were tears in her eyes. "We thought for a minute that . . ." Donna's voice broke and she swallowed hard. "We're so glad you're all right! You'd better sit down, Julie. You look like you're ready to pass out."

"I'm fine . . . really." The moment the words were out of her mouth, Julie really did begin to feel better. She was safe. She was with friends. And now that Ross and Paul were supporting her, her legs steadied and stopped their trembling.

"Sit down over here." Ross propelled her toward one of the rustic benches near the bottom of the slope. "I'll call the lodge and tell them what happened."

"They don't know?" Julie looked up at him in surprise.

"Not yet. We skied over to Hannah's Folly to see if we could spot you. And then we had to cut over to Sleeping Giant to get down. I was just dialing the emergency rescue team when Paul and Donna saw you skiing down Lady Luck."

"Don't call the lodge." Julie's voice was firm. "They'd only worry."

"But, Julie, you were almost killed up there!"

"I know." Julie shivered at the grim reminder. "But it was just a freak accident. There's no reason to upset them, now that it's over. I'd really rather you didn't tell anyone."

Donna reached out to grab Ross's arm. "She's right, Ross. Think of how Mrs. Hudson will feel if she finds out Julie was almost killed. It'll be almost like . . . well, *you* know."

Ross thought it over for a moment, and then he nodded. "All right. We won't mention it. Tell me exactly what happened, Julie."

"It won't be easy." Julie sighed deeply. "Everything happened so fast. I was about a third of the way down Hannah's Folly when I heard the avalanche. I skied off into the trees as fast as I could and it just missed me."

Donna shivered. "It must have scared you practically to death!"

"Not really." Julie frowned slightly. "It was all over before I had time to be scared."

"You didn't look back?" Paul looked surprised, when Julie shook her head.

"No. The minute I heard that cracking noise, I knew what was happening. All I could think of was to get away as fast as I could."

"Tell us about the noise." Ross looked worried.

"It was . . . loud. And sharp. Almost like a rifle shot. And then there was a roaring noise, like a thousand freight trains rumbling past me."

"An ice pack?" Paul looked at Ross and frowned.

"I guess so." Ross didn't seem to be pleased with that explanation, but he nodded reluctantly. "I didn't think we had that much ice, but we'd better set off the cannon, just to be sure. If there's any more loose snow, we want it down before we open tomorrow."

Donna looked puzzled as she turned to Julie. "How did you get over to Lady Luck?"

"I took a trail through the woods. I knew I'd run into another slope if I just kept going. There was a map on the wall at the pro shop and I remembered that they were roughly parallel."

"You must have skied right past Dead Man's Run!" Donna shivered again. "You're lucky you didn't try to get down that way."

Julie nodded. "I saw it, but it wasn't groomed. And there were no markers. I wanted to be safe, so I went on to Lady Luck."

"Smart girl!" Ross smiled as he knelt down and snapped loose Julie's bindings. Then he held out his hand and pulled her to her feet. "Let's go back in and have some lunch. You need to warm up."

Julie's mind was whirling all the way back to the lodge. Ross's arm was around her shoulder, and she was nestled close to his side. It felt wonderful, but Julie knew she hadn't deserved his praise. Ryan just had to keep his word and not tell anyone she'd made the mistake of trying to ski Dead Man's Run. If Ross ever found out she'd made such a stupid mistake, he'd never smile at her again!

Nine

Julie was so excited, she could hardly sit still as she worked the switchboard. It was Saturday afternoon, and tonight was the night of Saddlepeak Lodge's annual Halloween costume dance. Aunt Caroline had explained that the dance was a lodge tradition, started by Julie's great-grandfather. Everyone in Crest Ridge was invited to attend, and almost everyone did. Of course, the lodge guests were welcome, too, and an enterprising costume rental place in Denver had set up a temporary shop in the lobby this morning.

The phone rang and Julie reached out to answer it. "Saddlepeak Lodge. This is Julie speaking. How may I help you?"

Julie listened for a moment, but there was only a distant crackling on the line. The indistinct background noise reminded her of the other call she'd received, the one that had frightened her so badly.

She frowned and forced herself not to panic. Perhaps it was just a bad connection. "Hello? Is there someone on the line?"

Without conscious thought, Julie reached for a pen and the message pad. If this was another threatening call, she was determined to take down every word.

"*Julie.*" The word was a harsh whisper, spitting and crackling through the line. "*I warned you, but you're wicked, just like she was.*"

Julie shuddered. It was the same hissing voice. And he'd used the word "wicked," just as he had before. Her fingers shook as she scribbled down the words. What should she do? Call for help?

Suddenly Julie knew. She'd pretend she couldn't hear him and ask him to call back again. That would give her time to find someone to listen in, someone who might recognize his gravelly, whispery voice.

Julie took a deep breath, and spoke into the receiver. "Hello? I'm sorry, but we must have a bad connection. Could you call back, please?"

"*You heard me!*" The whisper was even harsher, filled with hateful venom. "*I watched you with him, and I know what you're doing. You've adopted her wicked ways!*"

Julie frowned. She hadn't done anything he could possibly think was wicked, unless he was referring to that kiss on the mountain with Ryan. But he couldn't know about that!

"*I saw you flirting with him. Stop right now before it's too late!*"

Julie's fingers were shaking so hard, she almost dropped her pen. There was no way she could pretend to be calm any longer. She was too frightened. But if she could keep him talking, she might get a clue to his identity. "I don't believe you! You're not watching me."

"*Oh, but I am. You're wearing her earrings, little gold hearts. You can't hide from me.*"

Julie whirled around and glanced out the window, but no one was there. She had to calm down. He was trying to scare her, and she couldn't let him know how well he was succeeding.

"*Such a wicked girl.*" The voice sighed deeply. "*I warned you up on the mountain. Next time I won't be so nice. Mend your ways before I have to punish you, too.*"

"Who are you? What do you want?" Julie's voice was shaking. But the whispery voice just laughed, the same chilling sound she'd heard over and over in her dreams. The awful laugh reached a screeching crescendo, and then it trailed off, leaving only the sound of any empty line. And then there was a click as the connection was broken. And a dial tone, loud and droning in her ear.

Julie's hands shook as she replaced the phone in its cradle. She was shaking so hard, her teeth were rattling. She tried to tell herself that the caller was just a harmless prankster, someone who got his kicks by scaring women on the phone. But he knew too much about her to be a random caller. He had to be someone she knew.

Julie glanced down at her scribbled transcript. He'd said he was watching her, and to prove it, he'd described Vicki's earrings. But she wasn't wearing Vicki's earrings. She'd forgotten them on the dresser this morning, and she hadn't had time to go back to her room to get them. She'd worn them every other time she'd worked the switchboard, but not today.

He had made an error, and that made Julie feel slightly better. He'd lied about watching her, but what did he mean about warning her on the mountain? Julie shivered as she remembered how puzzled Ross and Paul had been about the avalanche, especially when she'd mentioned the loud crack she'd heard right before it had happened. Was it possible he'd started the avalanche to scare her?

Julie's heart pounded hard, and she turned to her scribbled notes again. She hadn't flirted with anyone . . . except Ross. It was true that she was trying to get him to notice her. Would Ross make a whispered phone call to warn her to stay away from him?

That thought was so ridiculous that she almost laughed in spite of her fear. If Ross didn't want to be around her, he'd just tell her to leave him alone. But how about Paul? There were times when he acted as if he hated her. But she *did* look like Vicki, and Donna claimed that Paul had been in love with Vicki. What if Paul hated her and wanted her, all at the same time? Would he make a whispered phone call to warn her to stay away from Ross?

Julie sighed. No. Paul didn't seem to be the type to hide behind a phone call. He'd be nasty to her face. But no one else had been on the slopes except Ryan. Why would Ryan call her wicked?

The kiss! Julie shivered as she thought about their secret moment of passion. Did Ryan think she was wicked because she'd responded to his kiss? He was very intense, and Donna had said she thought he was weird, but Julie couldn't believe Ryan would resort to making a whispered phone call.

"Hey, Julie!" Donna walked in, and hurried to the desk. "Your aunt said to tell you that . . . what's wrong?"

"Oh . . . nothing. Nothing at all."

Donna raised her eyebrows. "You look freaked, Julie. Did you get a prank call?"

"What do you mean?" Julie tried not to looked as shocked as she felt. How had Donna known about the call?

"It's Halloween. I worked the switchboard last year and it was ridiculous. Vampira asking to speak to Frankenstein, the Wolf Man howling, all sorts of kid stuff like that."

Julie seized the opportunity Donna had given her and nodded. "No wonder! I forgot people would be making calls like that on Halloween."

"Well . . . don't let it get you down. Just remember that tonight's the biggest party of the year. What costume are you going to wear?"

"I don't know yet. Aunt Caroline said she'd send someone to relieve me so I could go to the costume shop before all the good ones are gone, but she must have forgotten, because . . ."

"Say no more." Donna interrupted her. "That's what I started to tell you when I came in. I'm supposed to relieve you. Go ahead, Julie. And when you come back, I'll go."

Julie got up and gave Donna her chair. "Does everybody unmask at the end of the evening?"

"Not unless they want to. Last year I danced with a totally incredible pirate, and I still don't know who he was."

"You never found out?"

"No." Donna shook her head. "Vicki taped the whole thing, and she was going to let me borrow it, but . . ."

"Vicki had a camcorder?" Julie interrupted.

"Sure. Your aunt gave it to her when she started competition skating. She was supposed to use it to improve her routine, but she spent more time taping parties, and dances, and stuff like that. I'd give anything to see some of those . . . what's the matter, Julie?"

"I wonder what happened to Vicki's tapes. I went through the things in the entertainment center, but there were no personal tapes."

Donna shrugged. "They're probably packed up with the rest of her things. I know Paul carried a bunch of boxes up to the fifth floor."

"Are you working tomorrow?"

"No." Donna frowned slightly. "You know Sunday's my day off."

"Can you keep a secret?"

"Sure, if I have to. What's up?"

Julie began to smile. "I think I'll go through some of my parents' things tomorrow. They're on the fifth floor, too. Do you want to help me?"

"I'd love to!" Donna began to grin. "And if we happen to stumble across some of Vicki's videotapes, we might just decide to watch them, right?"

Julie nodded. "You got it!"

The costume shop was deserted and Julie frowned as she went through the costumes still hanging on the rack, looking for something in her size. She had just pulled out an old-fashioned nun's habit that was much too large when she felt an uncomfortable prickling at the back of her neck. Someone was watching her.

Julie turned and tried to keep the pleasant expression on her face as she saw who had just entered the shop. It was Ryan Stratford, and he was grinning at her.

"Are you sure you want to rent that?" Ryan laughed as he saw the costume Julie was holding. "You have to take a vow of chastity to wear something like that."

"Maybe that wouldn't be such a bad idea." Julie blushed, and turned away. She knew Ryan was referring to the kiss they'd shared on Dead Man's Run.

Ryan walked up, close to her side, and reached out to touch the bulky material. "I think it would be a terrible waste of natural resources. And it's much too big for you, anyway."

"That's true." Julie put the costume back on the rack and sighed. She didn't want to get into any sort of personal conversation with Ryan, but she had to be polite to him. He'd saved her life up there on the mountain, and he hadn't told anyone about her embarrassing mistake. He hadn't mentioned the kiss, either. She was sure she'd have heard some gossip if he had. Perhaps Mr. Stratford had been right when he'd told her that Stratford men didn't kiss and tell.

"Ryan?" Julie moved away slightly. It was hard to think when he was so close to her. "I ran into your father the other day, and he said you'd dated my cousin Vicki."

Ryan raised his eyebrows. "You're really curious about her. Are you sure you should be asking all these questions?"

"I told you the other night. I really want to know more about her. Did you date her?"

Ryan shrugged. "I'm not sure 'date' is the right word. Let's just say I was one in a long line of guys."

Julie did her best not to react. At first she'd been sure that Ryan was lying when he'd told her that Vicki had slept around, but now she had doubts. Uncle Bob had mentioned Vicki's sexy clothes, and Mr. Stratford had told her that Vicki had been at one of his parties without her parents' knowledge. There was a possibility that Ryan was telling the truth.

"A long line of guys?" Julie frowned as Ryan nodded. "Who were they? I want to know."

Ryan closed the space between them, and slipped his arm around her shoulders before Julie could react. "Meet me at the stone archway tonight, and I'll tell you."

"Oh, sure!" Julie pushed his arm away, and stepped out of reach. "Come on, Ryan . . . I'm really serious. Who else did Vicki date?"

Ryan stared at her for a moment, and then he seemed to make up his mind. "Look, Julie . . . I'm telling you this for your own good. Give it a rest, huh? A lot of people are very touchy about Vicki's death."

Julie frowned as Ryan turned on his heel and walked away toward the clerk at the other end of the costume shop. Was Ryan right? Was she asking too many questions about Vicki? A few minutes later, he was back, carrying an armload of harlequin costumes. Aunt Caroline had told her that all the men who worked at the lodge would dress as harlequins tonight. They could still have fun in their masks and costumes, but the guests could identify the male employees without benefit of name tags.

"I like you, Julie." Ryan was very serious. "But I think you're a little too curious for your own good. I'll tell you one more thing, but that's it. And then I want you to promise to drop it."

Julie nodded, although she had no intention of dropping anything. "What is it, Ryan?"

"Your cousin slept around. I already told you that. And used to have this crazy alphabet thing. Vicki was only interested in guys whose name started with the letter 'R.' "

Julie frowned as she adjusted her veil so that only her eyes were visible. Since she'd arrived at the costume shop so late, there had been only one costume left in her size—a harem dancer's. It consisted of a very skimpy bright pink bikini covered by a see-through veiled skirt. It was terribly revealing, and Julie felt a blush rise to her cheeks as she turned from side to side, watching the diaphanous veil float around her body. She looked good. Her reflection confirmed that fact. But there wasn't enough cloth in her whole costume to cover a decent-sized throw pillow!

There was no help for it, and Julie sighed as she turned from the mirror. Thank goodness everyone was required to wear a mask of some type. If she was lucky, no one would recognize her under her the veil that almost covered her face. Julie was just walking through the living room, feeling naked and exposed, when she heard a knock on the door.

"Who is it?" Julie resisted the urge to rush back into her room, and headed for the door instead. Perhaps Aunt Caroline had forgotten her key.

"It's Paul." His voice was muffled by the heavy wooden door. "Your aunt sent me up to get her camera."

Julie winced. She didn't want Paul to see her like this, but she had to let him in. Aunt Caroline always took pictures of the best-dressed guests, and put them up on the lodge bulletin board.

"Just a minute." Julie unlocked the door, and took a deep breath. Then she pulled it open and faced Paul.

Paul's mouth dropped open and he stared at her. He swallowed hard, and then he frowned. "You're wearing *that?*"

Julie was very glad she was wearing the veil. At least he couldn't see the color rise to her cheeks. She'd wanted to keep her identity a secret, but now that Paul knew, he'd probably tell everyone that she was the harem dancer.

"What's the matter? Don't I look good enough to suit you?" Julie did her best to act nonchalant. Paul was still staring at her, and his frown was deepening by the second. He didn't have to be so disapproving. She certainly wouldn't have chosen this costume if there'd been anything else left.

Paul dropped his eyes, but not before he'd given her a very critical glance. "Why don't you change into something else? I don't want you to wear that!"

"Why not?" Julie challenged him. "I happen to think I look good."

"Wear something else. Just take my word for it, okay? You're only going to cause trouble if you go to the party dressed like that!"

Julie gave an exasperated sigh. What in the world was wrong with him? He looked angry, and sad at the same time. "Grow up, Paul. I'm not going to cause trouble. And I can't wear something else. You're just going to have to put up with me the way I am!"

"Please?" Paul's voice was hoarse with emotion. "Trust me, Julie. Don't go down to the party like that."

"Why not?"

Paul winced, and Julie knew he didn't want to tell her. They stared at each other for a long moment, and then Paul sighed and gave in. "You shouldn't wear that because . . . Vicki wore it last year."

"Oh." Julie's voice immediately lost its challenging tone. She noticed that Paul looked really upset, and she reached out to put her hand on his arm. "Thanks for telling me, Paul. I never would have picked it, if I'd known. But what am I going to do? I got to the costume shop late, and this was the only thing they had left in my size."

Paul nodded and Julie noticed that he looked very relieved. "Is there any way you could . . . uh . . . remodel it? Change it into something else?"

"Change what? There isn't enough here to change!"

Paul laughed and the tension between them was broken. "You're right. Do you have anything else you can use as a costume?"

"I don't know. Come on and help me look."

When Paul first entered Julie's room, she noticed that he was a little nervous. Julie assumed it was because the room had belonged to Vicki, and his memories of her cousin were bound to be painful. But they had a common problem, and Paul seemed to relax as they tried to fashion a costume out of the contents of Julie's closet.

"How about this?" Paul pulled out a denim skirt, and a red and white checked blouse. "If you have boots, you can go as a cowgirl."

Julie nodded, and found a pair of fringed buckskin boots. "Will these do?"

"Sure. Put your hair in braids and I'll see what else I can scrounge up."

When Paul left, Julie got dressed and braided her hair. She'd barely finished before he was back.

"Here's a cowboy hat. I borrowed it from Red. The Larkins

sent you this string tie, and Donna came up with a bandanna you can tie around your neck."

"Thanks, Paul." Julie smiled at him. "Did you find a mask?"

"Right here. The costume shop had a couple of extras. I thought the red would be nice. It'll match your blouse. And you can keep this denim vest. It's a present."

Julie's eyes widened as she picked up the vest. It was hand embroidered with red roses and it was gorgeous. "It's beautiful! Where did you get it, Paul?"

"Mrs. Larkin made it. She does custom work."

Julie was confused. "But why would Mrs. Larkin give me a present?"

"It's not from her. It's from me. I ordered it last year for Vicki. And then we broke up, and . . . well . . . I just never got around to picking it up. Until tonight."

"But won't it bother you if I wear it?" Julie was concerned.

Paul shook his head. "Take it, Julie. Vicki probably wouldn't have liked it anyway."

"Thank you, Paul." Julie didn't know what else to say. She was beginning to have serious doubts about her cousin. From the comments she'd heard, Vicki sounded as if she'd been a very ungrateful person.

"Go ahead. Try it on."

Julie nodded and slipped into the vest. It fit her perfectly, and she smiled. She'd always admired the embroidered shirts and vests of the American West.

Paul's voice shook slightly as she turned to face him. "It looks great on you, Julie."

Suddenly, Julie felt very sorry for Paul. He was smiling, but the sad look was back in his eyes. She stood on tiptoe and put her arms around his neck. And then she kissed him to thank him for the present.

The kiss took Paul by surprise. His arms slipped around her waist, but he held her stiffly, as if he wasn't quite sure what was expected of him. There was a tense moment when neither of them moved. Then Paul groaned softly, and his arms tightened around her waist.

Julie gasped as their kiss deepened. Her knees began to tremble, and her mind spun in dizzy circles from the unexpected passion of his embrace. She'd never dreamed that being in Paul's arms would be this wonderful. She was trembling so hard, she could barely think.

Paul sighed, and Julie's sigh echoed his. Her lips parted, and she snuggled even closer into his arms. Paul's blustery, hardboiled act was a sham. Buried beneath that prickly exterior was a sweet, tender, and caring guy.

She could feel his fingers moving, slipping under the vest to massage her back. Then her fingers moved, too, as if they had a will of their own, rubbing the back of his neck and moving up to brush through his thick, curly hair.

She could smell his cologne, a hint of musk that made their caress even more exciting. Had he worn that cologne with Vicki? And had her cousin's knees gone weak when he'd wrapped her in his arms? His tongue was like liquid fire, sending her senses reeling as he tasted the secrets of her lips. Had he taught Vicki to kiss this passionately? Or had she taught him?

There was no way that Julie could think while his tongue was moving and his lips were claiming hers. She just sighed again, and met his passion with her own, nibbling his lower lip with sharp little biting caresses until he groaned, deep in his throat.

His hands moved over her back, and his fingers spread out to almost touch her breasts. She heard herself whimper at the exquisite pleasure, and a flush of heat rose to her cheeks. She wanted him to go further, to love her as much as he'd loved Vicki.

Then she remembered that whispery voice, and her passion ebbed as quickly as it had risen. *I saw you flirting with him. You've adopted her wicked ways . . .*

Paul must have sensed her withdrawal, because his arms dropped to his sides. His lips lifted from hers, and he stared down at her in consternation. He looked just as surprised by his reaction to her as she'd been by her response to him.

Julie pulled back and refused to meet his eyes. She was suddenly cautious, and more than a little perplexed. She'd lost her head for a brief moment, and so had he.

"I . . . I think you'd better go." Julie's legs were shaking as she turned from him and began to gather up the accessories to her costume.

Paul nodded. He swallowed hard, took a deep breath, and did his best to apologize. "I'm sorry, Julie. I don't know what got into me. But don't worry. I promise, it'll never happen again. Are we still friends?"

"Of course." Julie nodded, and tried to smile, but her smile was wobbly and she knew she was blushing. "Don't forget Aunt Caroline's camera."

"Right." Paul's voice was brisk as he headed for the door. But when he got there, he stopped and turned toward her again. "Uh . . . Julie?"

"Yes, Paul?"

He frowned. It was clear he wanted to say something, but he couldn't seem to find the words. "I'll . . . uh . . . I'll see you at the party, okay?"

"Sure." Julie tried to be casual, but that was difficult when her knees were still shaking and she felt weak all over. Ryan's kiss on the mountain had been exciting, but Paul's was pure dynamite!

Paul nodded and gave her a little wave. Then he opened the door and went out, forgetting entirely about closing it behind him. Julie waited until she was sure he was gone, and then she crossed the room to shut the door. Her emotions were in a turmoil, and she wasn't sure whether she felt like laughing, or crying, or groaning in frustration. Since she didn't seem to be capable of deciding on any one reaction, she just sank down on the bed and sighed.

Paul had been a real gentleman. He could easily have taken full advantage of her, but he hadn't. And she almost wished he had! She was disappointed and relieved at the same time, a very uncomfortable state of mind to be in.

Julie sighed again. Maybe the whispery voice had been right.

She'd enjoyed Ryan's kiss on the ski slope. She wouldn't deny that. And she had initiated the kiss with Paul. Of course, it was only meant to be a friendly kiss. She'd had no idea things would get so out of hand!

A slow smile spread across Julie's face as she remembered the delightful sensations Paul's kiss had evoked. It had been totally wonderful, losing her head and finding herself wrapped tightly in his warm, strong arms. Perhaps the whispery voice on the phone had been right. Perhaps she was wicked . . . especially because she really hoped that Paul would break his promise and kiss her again!

Ten

Julie was having the time of her life. She'd never known costume parties could be so much fun. She'd danced with a prince, a Southern gentleman in a white suit, a scuba diver, a skeleton, Dracula, and three harlequins. And she'd only been at the party for an hour.

"Julie?" A Gypsy fortune teller tapped her on the shoulder and Julie whirled around. "It's you, isn't it?"

Julie laughed as she recognized Donna's voice. "It's me. Is your pirate here?"

"No." Donna sounded very disappointed. "At least, I don't *think* he's here. He could be wearing something else this year."

"Check out the prince. He's a great dancer. Maybe he's your pirate."

Donna shook her head. "No, that's Larry Berman. He's one of the weekend ski instructors. Have you danced with the ghost?"

"Not yet. But the night's young and so am I. Be careful of that green-and-black harlequin, though. He's got two left feet."

"Dave." Donna nodded. "I saw him putting on his mask."

"How about the one in pink and black? He's very fast on his feet . . . and I say that deliberately."

"I don't know who that is. We've got over a dozen harlequins here tonight, and they're all wearing different colors."

Julie stared at the pink-and-black harlequin, but she had no clue to which employee was under the mask. Then the color rose to her cheeks as she realized that she could have been dancing with Paul. "Which one is Paul? He's wearing a harlequin costume, isn't he?"

"Sure, but I don't know which color he picked. The yellow-and-black is Ryan. He's helping out tonight."

"How can you tell?" Julie was puzzled. The harlequins were wearing full-face masks.

"I danced with him, and nobody but Ryan would have the nerve to put his hands where he did! Take my word for it. Avoid him like the plague."

"Thanks. I will." Julie nodded, and tried not to blush. It was a good thing Donna didn't know about the way Ryan had kissed her on Dead Man's Run, and the two times he'd tried to get her to meet him at the old stone archway that marked the driveway to Saddlepeak Lodge.

"I think that's Paul in the red, over there by the fireplace. Or maybe he's the one in blue. That looks like him, too. Or the orange. They're all tall enough to be Paul."

"How about the one in purple? Do you think that's Ross?" Julie's heart beat a little faster. She knew that purple was Ross's favorite color.

"Search me." Donna shrugged. "I can't tell, once they put on their masks. And they love to confuse us. It's fun, isn't it?"

Julie nodded, but her eyes lingered on the purple-and-black harlequin, trying to will him over to her side. She'd been watching him all evening as he'd danced and mingled with the guests. He was an excellent dancer, and he never seemed to miss a step. He'd been attentive to every partner, even when he'd danced with several very elderly ladies. It just had to be Ross. His eyes met hers briefly and she saw him smile. Then he nodded to a turquoise-and-black harlequin, and they started to move across the crowded dance floor.

"Here they come!" Donna grinned as the two harlequins approached them. "I think the one in the turquoise is John Jaeger. He went to high school with Ross."

Julie's heart beat faster as the two harlequins approached them. The one in purple-and-black bowed in front of her and held out his hand. The other harlequin dipped his head toward Donna.

"You want to dance, right?" Donna laughed as her harlequin nodded. "Okay, I'd love to. Just whirl me past that refreshment table, so I can grab a cookie on the way."

Julie's heart beat a rapid tattoo as the purple-and-black harlequin took her in his arms. She was almost sure it was Ross. He was the right height and weight, and she could feel the muscles ripple in his arms as he held her. Yes, it was Ross.

The song ended, and Julie turned to leave the dance floor. But her harlequin shook his head and held her arm, so she couldn't back away. Then the band started playing again, a slow, dreamy love song, and the harlequin pulled her into his arms and held her close as they moved around the crowded floor.

Julie felt as if she were floating in the strong circle of Ross's arms. It had to be Ross. Her heart pounded wildly as he reached out to fondle a lock of her hair. But the memory of Paul's kiss intruded, the way he'd stroked her hair, the expression of caring in his eyes. Deliberately she put that memory out of her mind. She was dancing with Ross, and that was exactly what she'd wanted, wasn't it?

They approached the open doors to the terrace, and he moved her smoothly through them. And then they were dancing on the smooth stone floor, embracing in the velvety darkness illuminated by thousands of brilliant stars.

The dance ended on a clear, sweet note, fading away into breathless silence. Julie waited for the moment he would release her, but he didn't seem to want to let her out of his arms. She looked up with a question in her eyes. And then his lips came down to meet hers.

His kiss was bold, a confident declaration of his passion for her. Julie felt a jolt of surprise. It was a man's kiss, the blazing caress of an experienced lover who was aware of his power to seduce an attractive woman. But that shouldn't really surprise her. Ross was almost four years older than she was, and he'd obviously had experience.

Julie's mind spun in dizzy circles. How far should she let him go, now that she'd gotten his attention at last? Would Ross be satisfied with one kiss, a single caress in the shadows, when he was obviously used to much more?

Her mind spun in crazy circles. She'd done everything she could to attract Ross, hoping for this very moment. And now that the moment was here, she found she really didn't like it. His kiss was expert, and she should have been enjoying it, but she couldn't help thinking about Paul and how disappointed he'd be if he knew that Ross was kissing her.

Julie pulled back, stepping out of his embrace. "I . . . I think we should go inside now." The harlequin nodded, and Julie saw the flash of his smile in the darkness. Then he inclined his head, and offered his arm.

Julie stared at him for a moment, and then she took his arm to let him escort her back inside. But suddenly, she felt that curious prickling at the back of her neck. Was someone watching them? She turned to look back at the dark shadows where he had kissed her, but it was too dark to see. And then they were inside, under the lights, where people were laughing and talking.

The purple-and-black harlequin led her to the refreshment table where Donna was waiting. Then he bent one knee in a sweeping bow, and left her.

"Was that Ross?" Donna's voice was eager.

"What?"

"The purple-and-black harlequin . . . was it Ross?"

Julie nodded, barely registering Donna's question. His kiss had been so intense, her legs were shaking.

"You look weird. What did he do, try to hit on you?"

Julie hesitated. She trusted Donna not to spread gossip, but she didn't want anyone to know about the kiss. Not yet. Not now. Not until she'd sorted out the strange feelings she'd experienced.

"Well?" Donna grinned as she waited for Julie's answer. "Did he?"

"No. Of course not. We just went out for a breath of air, that's all."

"Oh, sure." Donna raised her eyebrows, and gave Julie a knowing grin. "And Santa Claus is alive and well at the North Pole. But I think I should warn you. You had an audience. I saw another harlequin follow you out there."

"What color was he?"

"I didn't notice. Is it important?"

"No . . . not really. I was just curious, that's all." Julie took a glass of punch and followed Donna to an empty table. They'd only been sitting for a moment when a skeleton and a scarecrow came to ask them to dance. The skeleton was an excellent dancer, and Julie did her best to concentrate as he whirled her around the floor. But all she could think about was the other harlequin who'd seen her kissing Ross, and hope that he hadn't been Paul.

The rest of the dance passed in a fog. Julie was sure she'd danced with every single one of the two hundred male guests. And then it was midnight, time for the unmasking and the awards for the best costumes.

There was a drum roll, and Aunt Caroline stepped up on the bandstand. Donna came over to stand beside Julie, and they listened as Aunt Caroline explained the prizes. There were three trophies, one for the best-dressed woman, another for the best-dressed man, and a third for the best-dressed couple. The first runners-up in each category would receive season ski passes, and the second runners-up would be entitled to free dinners in the lodge restaurant.

As Aunt Caroline awarded the prizes, Julie's eyes scanned the crowd for the purple-and-black harlequin. It was almost time, and she wanted to see Ross pull off his mask. But the purple-and-black harlequin wasn't mingling with the crowd. He'd disappeared right before the unmasking.

There was another drum roll and everyone unmasked. Julie

gasped as Donna pointed toward Ross. He was wearing a black-and-white harlequin costume!

"But who was in the purple?" Julie's voice shook slightly as she remembered the kiss with the harlequin she'd thought was Ross.

Donna grinned. "All I can say is, it's a good thing you didn't kiss him. I saw him drive off in his car."

"Who was he?"

"There's only one Rolls Royce Silver Ghost in town, and it belongs to Dick Stratford."

The Halloween costume party was over and the guests had left. Julie helped to clear the tables, and as she was carrying the last tray of dishes into the kitchen, she spotted Donna putting away the leftovers from the party platters.

"Hi, Julie." Donna finished covering a platter with plastic wrap, and set it on the counter.

"Donna? I know you have to help clean up, but I really need to talk to you."

"No problem. I'm due for a break." Donna shoved the tray to the back of the counter. "What's the matter?"

Julie glanced around. There were several other people in the kitchen. "Can we go somewhere private?"

"Sure. Let's go into the lobby. We can talk there."

A moment later, both girls were seated on one of the over-stuffed leather couches. Julie took a deep breath and blurted out her confession.

"You were right, Donna. I kissed the purple-and-black harlequin. But I really thought he was Ross."

Donna started to laugh. "You kissed Dick Stratford?"

"Yes. I never would have done it, if I'd known who he was. And now I feel so . . . so cheap."

"You just kissed him? That's all?" Donna looked puzzled when Julie nodded. "I don't see why you're so upset. It was just a harmless kiss at a party."

"I know. But I don't want to be like Vicki. I heard she was . . . uh . . . a little wild."

"Forget it, Julie." Donna reached out to pat her on the shoulder. "There's no way you could be like Vicki. She used guys, and then she dumped them. You're not like that at all."

"But . . . I've kissed three different guys since I moved here. And I liked it, Donna! All except for Dick Stratford. He was so good at it, he scared me."

"I'll bet! Dick Stratford's had plenty of practice." Donna laughed, and then she turned serious. "You're really worried, Julie?"

Julie nodded. "Aunt Caroline and Uncle Bob have been great, but I miss my parents. And I keep remembering all the happy times we had. I'm afraid that I'm going to throw myself at some guy because I miss the love and affection my parents gave me."

"Thank you, Miss Freud." Donna grinned at her. "Look, Julie . . . I don't think that the fact you kissed three guys has anything to do with missing your parents. Did you date a lot at your school in Switzerland?"

"No. It was a girls' school, and we were supervised almost every minute. I only went out on my own a couple of times, and I never really had a boyfriend. It was just friends of friends, that sort of thing. And I never met anyone I was serious about."

"So you never had this much freedom before?"

Julie shook her head. "No."

"Well, that's it, then!" Donna grinned at her. "There's absolutely nothing to worry about." Julie frowned.

"Are you sure?"

"Of course I'm sure." Donna laughed. "You're just making up for lost time. If I'd been locked up in a girls' school for almost five years, I'd go absolutely wild when I got out. And kissing three guys isn't exactly wild, especially when you thought one of them was someone else."

Julie breathed a big sigh of relief. "Thanks, Donna. I was really worried, and you helped a lot. If there's ever anything I can do for you, all you have to do is ask."

"Well . . . there is one thing."

"What is it?"

"Tell me who else you kissed. I'm dying to know."

Julie sighed. She was trapped. She had to tell Donna, now. "I kissed Ryan. He took me by surprise up on the ski slope."

"Ryan?" Donna began to grin, and she leaned forward. "Was he as good as his father?"

"Almost."

"And you liked it?"

"Yes." Julie could feel herself blushing again. "I liked the kiss, but I'm not sure I like Ryan. And I'm not going to kiss him again."

"That's good. Ryan's not right for you. Who's the third?"

Julie took a deep breath. She had to tell, and she didn't really want to. "You've got to promise not to say anything to anybody."

"Okay. I promise. Who was it?"

"Paul."

"My brother, Paul?"

Donna looked shocked, and Julie winced. Perhaps she shouldn't have told her. "I'm sorry, Donna. It just sort of happened."

"Don't be sorry. I think it's fantastic! Did you like it?"

Julie nodded, and began to blush again. "I liked it a lot. And I think he did, too, once he got over being shocked. That's one of the reasons I didn't like kissing Mr. Stratford, even though I thought he was Ross. I kept thinking about your brother."

"That's the best news I've had all year!" Donna absolutely beamed. "Did Paul ask you to go out?"

"No. He apologized. And then he promised me it wouldn't happen again."

"Right." Donna's grin grew wider. "My brother, the gentleman. Give him a little time, Julie. Paul's dense sometimes, but he'll come around. And I can almost guarantee you that if he kissed you once, he'll kiss you again."

It was three in the morning, and Julie still couldn't sleep. She'd tried all the usual tricks, counting sheep, watching a bad movie, reading a boring book, but none of them had worked. The talk she'd had with Donna had helped a lot, but she was still worried about having kissed Dick Stratford. He'd assured her that Stratford men didn't kiss and tell, but the other harlequin had followed them out on the terrace. It would be horribly embarrassing if he told anyone what he'd seen.

There was no sense staying in bed when sleep was impossible. Julie got up and flicked on the light. It only took a moment to dress in jeans and a Saddlepeak Lodge sweatshirt, and then she grabbed her key and let herself out of the apartment. Since she was awake, she might as well work. Mrs. Robinson would be grateful if she tidied up the kitchen before breakfast had to be served.

The elevator doors opened the moment she pressed the button. Julie rode down and walked through the silent lobby. Dave had night clerk duty, and Julie grinned as she caught him sleeping at the desk. She didn't blame him. It had been an exhausting party, and the phone would wake him if one of the guests had a middle-of-the-night request.

There wasn't as much to do in the kitchen as she'd thought. The work crew had washed the dishes and put them away. Julie ran soapy water in the sink and wiped down the stainless steel counters until they were clean and shining. She was about to go back upstairs when she noticed that there was a platter of cold cuts sitting-out on the butcher block worktable in the center of the room.

The kitchen was chilly, and the meat would probably be all right until morning, but since she was here, Julie decided to put it away. She picked up the heavy platter and carried it to the huge walk-in refrigerator before she realized that it was locked. Restaurant personnel had the combination to the lock, but she didn't. And the big serving platter would never fit in Aunt Caroline's refrigerator upstairs. What should she do?

Julie stared down at the platter. There was Black Forest ham, choice smoked turkey breast, delicious rare roast beef, and an array of expensive cheeses. It was a shame to take a chance that all this good food would spoil. Uncle Bob was always complaining about waste in the kitchen.

Suddenly Julie realized who'd been assigned to put away the

party platters. She'd heard Uncle Bob tell Donna to do it. Her friend might be in danger of losing her job if Uncle Bob discovered the forgotten plate of cold cuts. She had to do something. But what?

Julie glanced around the kitchen again and began to smile. It would be breaking a rule, but she'd cover the platter with several extra layers of plastic wrap and put it the game cooler for the rest of the night. The game cooler was never locked. Of course, restaurant food wasn't supposed to be kept in there, but Donna could sneak it out again in the morning.

It took only a few moments to wrap the platter. Julie carried it to the game cooler and hesitated. No one was allowed to open it from the kitchen entrance—it was a health regulation—but the inspectors would never know.

The game cooler had been the original walk-in refrigerator for the lodge, when her great-great-grandparents had owned it. Since those early years, the restaurant refrigerator had been replaced with successively newer models. The walk-in refrigerator Mrs. Robinson used now was state-of-the-art, with lights that went on automatically, doors that couldn't lock from the inside, and handy, moveable shelves and hooks. The game cooler was ancient, but it was perfectly adequate for its purpose. When hunters brought in their kill, it was stored in the original cooler until the town butcher came to cut and wrap it for the successful sportsman. The trophy animals were stored there, too, until Red Dawson skinned or mounted them.

She frowned as she thought of Red. Julie had caught him staring at her several times, and she hoped he wasn't beginning to feel the same way about her as he'd felt about Vicki. She liked Red even though he was a little strange, but she wasn't at all interested in going out with him. If he asked her, she'd have to turn him down. And she'd have to be very careful how she worded her refusal. Vicki had hurt him badly, and he might be very sensitive.

Julie balanced the tray in one hand and pulled on the door. It was very heavy. There were two entrances to the cooler. The game was brought in through an outside door to avoid the kitchen. There were several official signs posted on the kitchen entrance, warning about potential contamination, and it was never used. Julie had heard Uncle Bob tell Mr. Larkin to board it up as soon as possible, to comply with health regulations. But Mr. Larkin had been busy replacing floors in several of the guest bathrooms. Thank goodness he hadn't done it yet!

The heavy door creaked as it swung open, and Julie shivered slightly. It was dark inside. She felt around on the wall for the light, and found a knob, but no switch. How odd. But then she remembered the old-fashioned light switches she'd encountered in an old hotel on the West Bank, and she turned the knob it until it gave a resounding *click*.

A dim bulb lit up, and Julie shuddered as she saw several carcasses swaying on hooks in the center of the long room. It was best not to look too closely. Julie stepped in to place the platter on a wooden shelf near the door, but the shelf was old, and the wood had warped with age. The platter slid dangerously close to the edge, and Julie caught it just in time.

Averting her eyes from the swinging carcasses, Julie moved deeper into the cooler. She managed to find a solid shelf, and she set down the platter carefully. Then she checked to make sure the plastic wrap was tightly in place, and turned to leave. That was when she heard it, a sound that made her gasp in fright. The cooler door was creaking shut.

Julie sprinted toward the bright, safe light of the kitchen. She should have propped the door open! But she hadn't, and she reached the door just as it shut with a heavy thud.

Frantically, she reached for the handle. No reason to panic. She'd just open it from this side. But there was only a smooth panel of metal. No handle. No way to open the door.

She screamed then, a thin, high scream of terror. No one knew she was here. No one would dream of opening the game cooler to look for her. She was trapped, and there was no way out!

It could have been minutes. It could have been hours. Julie's panic was timeless. She knew she'd been pounding on the door for some time. Her hands felt hot and bruised, a startling contrast to the rest of her body, which was chilled and shaking. Unanswered questions flashed through her terrified mind. Would she suffocate? Was there enough air? Or would she freeze to death first? There was a thermometer hanging right next to the door. Thirty-seven degrees. Could she freeze to death when the temperature was above the freezing point?

Then she thought of the other door, the door that led to the outside. Perhaps it had a handle on the inside. She'd come in through the original door, and safeguards like inside handles might not have been required when the cooler was built. But the outside door had been added later. She wasn't sure exactly when it had been installed, but it might conform to the new safety standards. If so, it would have an inside handle!

There was only way to find out. Julie got to her feet, and frowned. Why was she kneeling on the floor? She couldn't remember. Then she turned to face the other end of the cooler and the narrow corridor that led to the outside door. Her eyes swept past the hanging carcasses, and she shuddered. To get to the other door, she'd have to walk past all those awful gutted shapes, those horrible, huge, frightening animals. But she had to do it. It was her only hope of escape.

It was a scene straight out of a nightmare. Even though Julie tried not to look, her eyes were drawn to the grotesque shapes and the monstrous shadows they cast. She forced her trembling legs to move past the deer, gutted and bloody, with their heads still attached. Their eyes stared sightlessly down at her, and their antlers looked as sharp as the meat hooks that were forced through their necks.

Julie took a deep, shuddering breath and moved past the elk. More sharp antlers cast crazy, nightmarish patterns against the walls of the freezer. And the wild boar, with evil-looking tusks that seemed ready to pin her to the wall, pierce her trembling body, and stare down in sightless fascination as the life ran from her veins and stained the floor red. The bear was horrible with its shaggy, dark bulk. One swipe of its razor-sharp claws and her face would be cut to ribbons. Even the Rocky Mountain sheep, normally stately and taciturn in a natural setting, looked sinister and frightening now.

There was a sudden noise, and a blast of air that made her heart jump to her throat. Julie opened her mouth to scream, but she was too terrified to make a sound. The carcasses were swinging, swaying, taking on a life of their own. They looked ready to grab her, devour her, as she stood helpless and trembling, rooted to the spot in paralyzing fear.

But it was only a powerful blower. The cooling unit had kicked in. Julie sighed, a ragged little sound that emerged from her throat as a moan of terror, and made herself move past the bodies of the dead animals. At least there was air. Or was there? It could be a closed unit, merely recycling the frigid air that would soon lose its oxygen. But it was best not to think of that.

She was almost there, only a few feet to go. She had to keep her legs moving, force her imagination to stay in check. These huge animals couldn't hurt her. They were already dead. As dead as she'd be if she didn't get out of here soon.

That was exactly the impetus she needed. Julie broke into a shambling, awkward run, and reached the door with a thankful sob. Her hands reached out, searching, searching . . . and finding nothing. No handle. No way out. She was trapped like those awful dead animals. Trapped with them to become just another unfortunate victim.

It was colder here, near the outside door. But she couldn't go back to the other end of the cooler. She couldn't force herself to pass all those hideous carcasses again. It would be over sooner here. There was no reason to try to hang on. No one would find her. No one would save her. She was doomed.

"No!" Julie's cry of protest bounced against the walls. She would not willingly become a victim. She'd fight until she couldn't fight any longer. She'd walk the length of the cooler again even if she died of fear. At least it would be quicker than freezing to death.

This time she watched her feet, one in front of the other, trying to ignore the swaying shadows on the floor and the wall.

Step and step again, steady and straight. She had nothing to fear except fear itself.

Julie smiled then, although it was more of a grimace. The quote was from Franklin Delano Roosevelt, and she was willing to bet he'd never been locked inside a game cooler. But the smile seemed to help to keep her feet moving forward. She'd head for the warmest spot, right by the door that led into the kitchen, and hope that someone would find her.

At last she reached the door, and Julie gave a thankful sigh. She had to think positively. She couldn't actually freeze to death. It was above thirty-two degrees. Of course she could suffer from hypothermia, but she wouldn't think about that. The butcher could come before then, if he worked on Saturday. Or Red Dawson. He always did taxidermy work on his off hours. She had to keep the faith. She had to believe that someone would find her. Any other possibility was too horrible to contemplate.

Julie shivered, and then she yawned. She was so tired. Unusually tired. All she wanted to do was curl up near the door and go to sleep. But she couldn't do that! She remembered a story she'd read about a man falling asleep in the snow and freezing to death. She had to keep moving, keep her body generating warmth. But she was so tired, she could barely raise her arms.

She'd pound on the door. She'd pound with her arms, raise them and lower them. That would keep her body warm. Julie raised her right arm and whacked the door. It hurt and that was good. She couldn't give up and go to sleep if her arm was hurting. She raised her left arm and banged it even harder. How long could she keep this up? It had been almost four in the morning when she'd decided to put away the platter, and Mrs. Robinson was always in the kitchen by six-thirty. Two and a half hours to go.

Long minutes passed as Julie raised and lowered her arms, pounding and knocking until her arms wouldn't obey her mind's command. She slipped to her knees, and then to a tired, huddled crouch. She knew she couldn't give way to exhaustion. She had to keep pounding so Mrs. Robinson would hear her.

Heat rises. The moment the thought occurred to her, Julie tried to stand again. But she was so tired, she could barely pull herself up to a kneeling position. She'd lean against the door, and pound on it with her fists. That was a very good idea. She'd do it, in just a minute. But first she'd close her eyes, just for a second, to gather her strength.

Julie knew she was making a mistake as her eyes flickered shut. But she couldn't seem to open them. Just a moment more, and she'd be ready to stand up. It seemed much warmer now, almost toasty warm. Snug and cozy, with the heat register open, huddled beneath the blankets in her warm, safe room with the lovely blue walls and the . . .

Julie's eyes snapped open and she pulled herself to her feet. She'd almost gone to sleep! She had to fight the lethargy that stole over her. It would be a battle to stay awake, but she would do it.

Julie propped herself against the cold metal door and pounded hard with both fists. They were already bruised and sore, and the pain would help to keep her alert. Just as she felt her strength beginning to ebb again, the door flew open. And she tumbled out. Right into Donna's arms.

"Oh, my God!" Donna's mouth fell open. "What were you doing in there?"

"I . . . I think I was freezing to death." Julie gave a shaky laugh. She was so glad to see Donna, she almost cried.

Donna helped her to a stool. Then she poured a mug of left-over coffee, popped it into the microwave, and turned to face Julie with a bewildered expression. "But . . . why did you go into the game cooler in the first place?"

"Somebody left a platter of cold cuts out on the counter. I didn't know the combination, so I couldn't put it away where it belonged. So I put it in there." Julie pointed to the game cooler and shuddered. "The door closed behind me and I . . . I couldn't get out!"

Donna nodded, but Julie noticed that her hands were trembling as she handed her the steaming mug of coffee. "It's my fault, Julie. I left that platter out. That's why I came back here. I figured I'd better put it away before your uncle found out."

"What time is it?" Julie knew there was a clock on the kitchen wall behind her, but she couldn't seem to gather the energy to turn around.

"It's almost five-thirty. How long were you in there?"

Julie blinked. She was so tired, she could barely do the simple subtraction. "Over an hour. I . . . I don't think I could have lasted much longer, Donna. You saved my life."

"But you wouldn't have gone in there if it hadn't been for me." Tears welled up in Donna's eyes, and she looked terribly guilty. "I almost killed you!"

Julie managed a grin. "Okay. You almost killed me, but you saved my life. It all cancels out. That's what friends are for, yes?"

Donna frowned, and then she gave a shaky grin. "You must be all right. That's two jokes you've made since I let you out. But how did the door close when you were in there? There's a little rubber thing on the wall to hold it open."

"I . . . I'm not sure." Julie took a sip of the scalding coffee and studied the door. Donna was right—there was no way the door could have closed on its own. "Maybe I didn't open it all the way?"

Donna looked dubious, but she nodded. "That must be what happened. You sit right there and warm up. I'll get the platter and put it away."

Julie watched as Donna opened the cooler door and stepped inside. The rubber door-catcher held it securely. She was almost sure she'd opened the door all the way, and she thought she remembered the rubber catcher engaging. But her memory must be faulty. If she'd done it correctly, the door couldn't have closed, unless . . .

The whispery voice! Julie shivered in spite of the warm air blowing down from the heat register directly above her. He'd said that he was watching her. And he'd warned her to mend her wicked ways. What if he'd found out that she'd kissed Paul or Dick Stratford, and decided to punish her by locking her in the cooler?

"Okay. All done." Donna came back with the platter of meat and stored it in the walk-in refrigerator. "Do you want some more coffee? I can make a fresh pot."

"No, thanks. I'm fine now. Why don't you come up to my room? We can sleep for a couple of hours, and then we can look for those tapes in the attic."

"Okay." Donna grinned at her. "I won't let you go upstairs alone, anyway. You're accident-prone. First the avalanche, and then this. The next thing I know, you'll end up stuck in the elevator."

Julie laughed, but her laughter sounded weak, even to her own ears. Too many accidents. The avalanche. The game cooler. And Donna didn't even know about her brush with disaster on Dead Man's Run. Perhaps Donna was right—she could be accident-prone. Either that, or the whispery voice on the phone was trying to kill her!

Eleven

"Yuck!" Donna brushed aside a cobweb, and shivered. "It's creepy up here!"

Julie nodded. The fifth floor was more than a little scary, although she didn't think anything could frighten her as much as the avalanche, or Dead Man's Run, or the time she'd spent locked in the game cooler. "Do you have the flashlights?"

"Got 'em." Donna handed her one of the large flashlights she'd borrowed from the storeroom. "If somebody cleaned those windows more than once a year, it might help."

Julie glanced at the clouded windows and frowned. It was obvious no one came up here unless they absolutely had to, and she could understand why. There was no electricity, and only hazy light streamed in the windows. Dust and cobwebs were the order of the day, and bulky furniture, hidden under white canvas dust covers, looked like ghostly shapes. To make the attic even more inhospitable, the wind was howling and moaning and shrieking around the eaves. She'd expected to spend a pleasant Sunday afternoon going through old trunks and mementos with her best friend in Crest Ridge, but this wasn't going to be fun at all!

"Maybe this isn't such a good idea." Donna shivered slightly. "It's chilly up here, and I don't want you to catch a cold."

Julie turned around to grin at her. "It was a lot colder than this in the game cooler. Come on, Donna. Vicki's things have to be up here somewhere."

Donna sighed. "If you're really determined, count me in. I just hope we hit pay dirt soon. I really despise spiders!"

Julie pulled off a dust cover and promptly sneezed as the dust flew everywhere. Not only was this unpleasant, it was dirty. She'd have to make sure to be through long before Uncle Bob and Aunt Caroline got back. She'd need to shower and so would Donna before they could appear in public again.

"This is neat!" Donna pulled back a dust cover and smiled as she found an old console radio. "My grandparents had one of these. I wonder if it still works."

Julie shrugged. "There's no way to tell unless we lug it downstairs. No electricity, remember?"

"Right." Julie replaced the dust cover, and then she looked puzzled. "You're going to think I'm crazy, but . . . it's warmer right here. I think I can feel warm air on my ankle."

Donna bent down to look. "No wonder—it's a floor vent. I can see the fourth-floor hallway, right next to the elevator. And here comes . . . it's Ross! He's unlocking the door to his room. I wonder what he'd do if I moaned or something."

"Don't do it!" Julie grabbed Donna's arm and pulled her to her feet. "I don't want him to know I'm up here. He might tell Uncle Bob."

Donna looked disappointed, but she nodded. "I wonder if you can see into any of the rooms through these vents. Ross's room would be right over there."

"Let's check it out." Julie grinned and moved to the spot Donna indicated. "Help me move this rolled-up rug. It's in the way."

Julie got on one end of the rug, and Donna took the other. Working together, they moved it out of the way. There was a small hole under it, and Julie motioned for Donna to look first. It had been her idea.

Donna crouched down and peeked through the hole. She let out a gasp and stood up. "Hurry up. Take a peek. He's changing his shirt!"

Julie knelt down and put her eye to the hole. She gasped as

she realized that she could see right into Ross's bedroom. He was standing at the closet, taking out a fresh shirt, his skin rippling and gleaming under the overhead light.

"Did he take off his pants?"

Donna whispered, but Julie heard her clearly. She jumped to her feet, blushing wildly. "Of course not!"

"Well, I was wondering what was keeping you so long. Do you think he knows there's a vent right over his room."

"I'm sure he doesn't." Julie bent down to look again, and when she straightened up, she was frowning. "It's not a vent; it's a peephole! I think somebody drilled a hole in Ross's ceiling deliberately!"

"Vicki?" Donna began to grin. "That sounds like something she would have done. She was always getting into one scrape right after another. And let's face it. Ross is a hunk. I noticed that you were pretty interested when you saw him without his shirt."

Julie fought down the blush that was rising to her cheeks, and nodded. "You're right. I can understand why Vicki did it . . . *if* she did it. Let's see if we can find any more peepholes."

"This must be your room." Donna walked over and pointed to the floor. "No sense looking here. Vicki certainly wouldn't have drilled a hole in her own . . . oh-oh!"

"What's the matter?" Julie felt her heart beat faster as Donna whisked aside a crumpled dust cover and knelt down. When she stood up, she was frowning.

"What did you see?" Julie began to frown, too.

"It's your room. And the peephole is right over your bed. But there's no reason Vicki would drill a hole in her own ceiling!"

"That's true." Julie nodded. Now she understood why there had been a cold draft over her bed. It hadn't been a visitation from Vicki's ghost. She'd known that idea was ridiculous when she'd thought about it the next morning. It had been cold air from the attic, seeping down through the peephole!

Donna seemed to be intrigued by the puzzle. "We know Vicki didn't drill those peepholes. And neither did Ross. Who do you think did it?"

"I don't know. We're assuming those holes were drilled recently, but they could have been there for years. For all we know, my great-great-grandfather did it. Or someone who worked for him."

"Very true. But why?"

Julie shrugged. "Was the fourth floor ever used for guests?!"

"Never. It was always for the help. Of course, your great-great-grandfather might have had some very pretty girls working for him."

Donna was grinning, and Julie grinned back. "Are you suggesting my great-great-grandfather was a Peeping Tom?"

"Maybe. Did you see the portrait of your great-great-grandmother, hanging over the fireplace in the private dining room?"

Julie nodded. "I saw it."

"Then you can understand why your great-great-grandfather drilled those holes!"

"Donna! That's mean!" Julie giggled in spite of herself. But she had to admit that Donna had a valid point. Her great-great-grandmother had looked very prim and proper.

"So what shall we do?" Donna looked serious. "Shall we squeal on your great-great-grandfather?"

Julie thought it over for a moment and then she shook her head. "Let's not. But I do think we ought to plug up those holes. Let's move something heavy over them."

"How about this for yours?" Donna pointed to an old steamer trunk. "It'll take both of us to move this."

But Donna was wrong. The trunk moved quite easily, sliding over the hole with a screech of metal casters against the wood floor. The sound was very familiar and Julie shivered. Was that the sound she'd heard in her dream the night she'd seen the face on her balcony?

"Oh, my God! Pay dirt!"

Julie whirled to look at Donna, who had raised the lid of the trunk. "What did you say?"

"These are Vicki's things. That's the sweater she wore in her school picture. And this is her backpack. I'd recognize it anywhere. We found it, Julie! They stored all Vicki's things in this trunk!"

Julie's hands were trembling as she helped Donna lift out her cousin's things. And way down in the bottom, under all those beautiful, expensive clothes, was a rosewood box with a lock.

Donna pointed to a zippered makeup case on top of a pile of sweaters. "Find me a pair of eyebrow tweezers, will you? Anything narrow and sharp will do. I'll pick the lock."

"You can do that?" Julie was amazed.

"Of course. I used to pick the lock on Paul's bicycle all the time. No problem."

Julie watched as Donna slipped a scissor blade into the hole on the lock and twisted. There was a soft *click* and the lid lifted.

"Oh, boy!" Donna grinned as she turned the box so Julie could see. "Here's Vicki's videotape collection. You've got a VCR in your room, don't you?"

Julie nodded, a bit reluctantly. She wasn't sure it was right to watch her cousin's personal videotapes.

"What's the matter? Having an attack of morals?"

Julie sighed. "Just a slight attack. But don't worry about it, Donna. I want to see those tapes every bit as much as you do!"

Twelve

Julie gasped as her cousin's picture appeared on the screen of the color television set in her bedroom. Now she understood why everyone had been so upset the first time they'd seen her. She *did* look exactly like Vicki!

Donna and Julie had concealed the rosewood box in a carton and carried it up the back stairs to Julie's room. Feeling like two conspirators, they'd sorted out the tapes and stacked them in neat piles, according to the dates on the labels. They'd decided to play them chronologically, and now they were sitting in front of the entertainment center, Donna on a chaise longue, Julie on the bed, watching Vicki's oldest tape.

"I really hate to write things down, so this is my diary. I decided it would be a lot more fun to tape it." Vicki smiled at the camera. *"I grew up right here at Saddlepeak Lodge. I'm almost seventeen, and I'm going steady with Paul Kirby. We're not exactly in love, but we're in lust . . . at least, I'm in lust. Paul's a nice guy, and he buys me lots of neat stuff, but he's so straight, he's getting on my nerves. I hate to think how bored I'd be if I didn't have R."*

Julie reached for the pause button. "Who did she say?"

"She said 'R.' Like an initial, you know?"

"That's what I thought." Julie clicked off the pause, her mind racing. It must be the R who'd written the note. She just hoped Vicki would give his full name.

"*R's so great in bed, the best lover I've ever had! Of course, he's the first, so I really don't have any standard of comparison. He makes me feel like . . .*"

"Oh, my god!" Donna hit the pause button. "She was going steady with Paul, and sleeping with *him!*"

Julie nodded. "But who is he? Who's 'R'?"

"I don't care! If she wasn't already dead, I'd strangle her! Paul saved all his money to buy her nice things, and that cheap little . . ."

"Hold it." Julie reached out to take her friend's arm. "It won't do any good to get mad now. Maybe she's just making it up for the camera, playing a part, or something like that. We don't know for sure that it's true, so let's just listen, okay?"

Donna took a deep breath and let it out again in a long sigh. Then she nodded reluctantly. "Okay. But I think it's true. Vicki wasn't the type to play a part. She was in the junior play and she was a lousy actress."

"Let's back it up a little." Julie took the remote control out of Donna's hand and hit the rewind. "We'll make up our minds when it's over."

"*. . . the best lover I've ever had! Of course, he's the first, so I really don't have any standard of comparison. He makes me feel like the most beautiful woman in the world. He's slept with so many women, it really means something when he tells me that I'm the best. Let me tell you, he's taught me things I never read in any book!*"

Donna flinched, and Julie hit the pause again. "Come on, Donna. Forget about your brother for a minute, and just listen. Pretend it's a movie or something if it upsets you so much."

"Okay, okay. Go ahead."

"*I'm meeting him tonight at his place, so I'd better get ready. Maybe I'll take along my camcorder and shoot some tape of him. I ought to preserve my first lover for posterity, don't you think? And then I'll come back and tell you all about it.*"

The screen went blank, and Donna sighed again. "I can't be-lieve Paul was dumb enough to fall in love with her!"

"Shhh!" Julie motioned for silence. "It's on again!"

"Okay. I just parked and now I'm getting out of the car." The camera tilted, and there was a shot of a fountain, sur-rounded by rosebushes. *"And now I'm ringing the doorbell. I'd better shut this off, or R'll get freaked. And I'd better ask if it's okay to tape him. I don't want to get him mad at me. He might cut me off. Later, okay?"*

The screen went dark again, and Julie put the tape on pause. "Did you recognize the house?"

"No. It looked like one of those fancy places in Denver. I don't think anybody local has a fountain like that."

"The door was very distinctive." Julie nodded thoughtfully. "Did you see that stained glass? Two blue cranes, facing each other."

"Play the rest. Maybe he let her tape him. Hurry up, Julie. I want to see if I recognize him."

Julie hit the play button again, and they watched as the screen flickered. There was a shot of a sunken living room, and a mahogany coffee table holding a beautifully carved antique chess set.

"Whoever he is, he's got money!" Donna sighed deeply.

Suddenly a man's hand loomed up to cover the lens of the camera. *"Shut it off, Vicki. And put it away."*

The screen went blank, and Donna sighed. "Damn! I know that voice, but I can't quite place it."

"Me, too." Julie hit the fast forward button, but the rest of the tape was blank. "I guess he didn't want to be taped. And she didn't feel like telling us about it. Now we'll never find out who R is."

Donna look thoughtful. "Don't give up yet. I think I know who can tell us if that stained glass window is anywhere around Crest Ridge. Can I use your phone?"

Julie nodded, and watched as Donna dialed a number. "Hi, Mr. Wilkins. It's Donna Kirby. No, that's all right. I know Dave's working. I really wanted to talk to you."

Julie lifted her eyebrows. She had no idea why Donna wanted to speak to Dave's father.

"I think you're much cuter than Dave, too . . . but don't tell him I said that." Donna laughed. "I need some help on a homework assignment, and I thought maybe you'd know. Are there a lot of stained glass windows in Crest Ridge?"

Julie frowned. Why in the world would Mr. Wilkins know that?

"That many, huh? But we're not talking major expensive here, are we?"

Donna nodded again, and she seemed pleased with the answer Mr. Wilkins gave her. "Three. I see. Which one would you say is the best? I need to know for an art project."

Julie began to grin as Donna nodded, and made an occasional comment to Mr. Wilkins. She was very good at getting information.

"Thanks a lot, Mr. Wilkins. You have no idea how much you've helped me. Say hi to Mrs. Wilkins for me, okay?" Donna hung up the phone and turned to Julie with a grin. "The Stratford mansion has two blue cranes on the door."

"Dave's father was a guest in the Stratford mansion?"

"No. He runs a window-washing business. I figured that if anybody remembered that window, it would be the guy who had to clean it. Bingo, Julie! We've got Vicki's R. It's Ryan Stratford."

Julie shook her head. "I don't think so. The minute you mentioned the Stratfords, I knew. That voice wasn't Ryan's. It was his father's."

"Dick Stratford? But why would Vicki call him R, if his name is . . ." Donna stopped in mid-sentence and thumped the side of her head with her hand. "Dick is short for Richard, right?"

"Right. Vicki's first lover was Dick Stratford. Do you want to play another tape?"

"Why not?" Donna raised her eyebrows. "This is just getting juicy. I want to find out if she ever slept with Paul."

"Donna!"

Donna laughed at Julie's shocked expression. "You want to know, too. Don't you?"

"Well . . ." Julie couldn't help it. She started to grin. "Of course I want to know. But for purely academic reasons."

"And what would those be?" Donna looked amused.

"I want to find out if your brother's as good as Dick Stratford."

Donna sighed as Julie slipped the second-to-last tape in the machine. "I still can't believe it. Four different guys in less than three months."

"And they all had names starting with R. I wonder if she did that on purpose."

Donna shrugged. "Who knows? Vicki was weird, sometimes. And don't forget that Paul's name didn't start with an R until she started calling him Rock."

"Well . . . let's just hope there's not another one! All these Rs are getting confusing." Julie sighed as she picked up the remote control. "Did you happen to notice the date on this one?"

"October thirty-first, the night of the Halloween Party. She broke up with Paul in the middle of October and Ross was her date."

Julie felt her spirits fall as she pressed the play button. Vicki had been wild, and she doubted that Ross had tried too hard to resist her. And he was an R.

"Tonight's the big night." Vicki twirled in front of the camera, showing off her harem dancer's outfit. *"I picked this for R because it's straight out of a fantasy. And just to help matters along, I've got this!"*

"A bottle of vodka?" Donna turned to Julie, but before she could ask what it was for, Vicki's voice answered her.

"I'm going to spike his beer. R doesn't like the taste of hard booze, but he'll never notice. I'll wait until after the party. They're depending on him to keep everything running smoothly. Mom says she can't get along without him, but neither can I. I need him, and I need him bad!"

Donna reached out and pressed the pause button. "She's go-irig to go for Ross!"

Julie nodded. It certainly sounded like that was what Vicki was planning.

"Just a little for me, so I don't lose my nerve." Vicki raised the bottle to her lips and took a swig. *"He'll never know what hit him. He's perfect for me, absolutely perfect! He's got ambition, and character, and he'll do the right thing. I'd stake my life on it. I am staking my life on it! But I won't tell you about that now. I'll tell you on my next tape, my last tape."*

The screen went blank and Julie turned to Donna. "What is she talking about?"

Donna shrugged. "I don't know. Play the last tape. It's dated December eighteenth."

Julie shivered as she put the tape in the machine. December eighteenth was the day Vicki had died. Would this be a deathbed confession of some sort? Or was it just another tape? The only way to tell was to play it, and her hands were shaking as she pressed the play button.

Both girls gasped as Vicki's face came on the screen. She looked haggard, and there were dark circles under her eyes. In sharp contrast to the other tapes, she was dressed in an old shirt and jeans, rather than a designer outfit. She looked as if she hadn't had any sleep in days, and her hair was lank and knotted.

"Oh, my God!" Donna shivered. "She looks like hell! Do you suppose she had the flu? I never saw her looking so awful!"

"I have to tell you about something." Vicki's voice was weak and trembling. *"I made up my mind, and I'm going to do it tonight. R sent me a note today, and I don't have a choice any-more. I have to go through with it."*

"The suicide?"

Julie shivered as Donna nodded. "It sure sounds like she's going to kill herself, doesn't it?"

"I feel bad for him. And I feel even worse for Mom. Poor Mom. She doesn't know what I'm going through, and she's been

so sweet and patient with me. I want to tell her, but I can't! I just can't do that to her!"

"Tell her *what?*" Donna looked terribly confused, but Vicki's next statement didn't help.

"When she finds out what I've done, she's going to be so upset. She might even hate me, but I don't know what else to do. And R's going to hate me, too, when he finds out how I lied to him. But I've got to do it! I just can't take it anymore!"

"Take *what?*" Julie almost shouted, she was so excited. Vicki just had to say why.

"They all think I'm crazy. The shrink. Mom. Maybe even R. But I'm not crazy. I'm perfectly sane. And I know somebody's out there, trying to get me!"

"Whoa!" Donna reached out the stopped the tape. "What did she say?"

"She said somebody was out there, trying to get her."

Donna nodded. "Sure, but she's paranoid, right?"

"Maybe." Julie pressed the play button again. She didn't think Vicki was one bit paranoid, but she couldn't tell Donna how she'd reached that conclusion.

"I'm going to tell you exactly what's been happening. Maybe it'll calm me down so I'm not so scared. I know someone's been watching me. I caught a glimpse of him a couple of times, and I can feel him, even when I can't see him. And I know his voice, at least when he whispers. And his laugh. It's a horrible laugh. I hear it in my dreams every night. The stalker's the one who's crazy, not me!"

Julie leaned forward anxiously and stared at her cousin's face. She clasped her hands tightly together to keep them from shaking and waited for Vicki's next words.

"He's the reason I can't stand to work the switchboard any-more. You see, there's that big open window, and I know he's out there somewhere in the dark. And I'm inside, under the lights, all lit up like a target!"

"What is she talking about?"

Donna looked shocked, and Julie reached out to take her hand. "Shh! Maybe she'll tell us!"

"He can see me, but I can't see him. And just when I convince myself that the shrink is right, that I'm just imagining things and nobody's really out there, he calls me to tell me he's watching!"

"Who calls?" Donna looked intrigued. "Is she talking about another R?"

"I don't know. Listen."

"He says I'm wicked, and if I don't change my ways, he's going to have to punish me. That's why I've been so freaked. He's been scaring me for a long time now, and I just can't take it anymore!"

Both Julie and Donna stared at the screen in horrible fascination as Vicki began to cry. This was no act. She was truly frightened.

"R. sent me a note. It's all set for me to meet him tonight. I saw him this afternoon, at the turkey shoot, and he looked so worried, I thought I'd cry. I don't want to do it, but I don't have any other choice!"

Without really realizing what she was doing, Julie reached out to grab Donna's hand. This was scary! She still didn't know whether Vicki had committed suicide, or whether that mysterious someone she'd told them about had killed her.

"Sometimes I dream about R. I see that awful, trapped expression on his face the night I told him I was pregnant. He . . ."

"What?" Donna hit the pause button. "I didn't know she was pregnant!"

Julie shuddered. "Maybe they . . . uh . . . couldn't tell. The car burned and . . . well, they probably weren't able to . . ."

"Right." Donna interrupted. "You don't have to say anymore. I get the picture. But R knew. And he never said anything."

"That's true, but he could have been protecting Uncle Bob and Aunt Caroline. After all, Vicki was dead. And the baby was dead. Maybe he thought it would only make them feel worse."

"Maybe . . . but he might have been thinking about saving his own skin." Donna was clearly outraged. "If Vicki killed herself because she was pregnant with his baby, it would have looked pretty bad for him. I hope she tells us who he is! It's too late for Vicki to get even with him, but I was her friend and I can do it for her!"

"Donna . . . no! You shouldn't think like that. Maybe it wasn't R's fault. And you promised we wouldn't tell anybody what we heard on these tapes."

Donna turned to look at Julie. "You know, don't you? You know who R is!"

"No, I don't know." Julie sighed deeply. "He could have been anybody. Dick Stratford, Ryan, Red Dawson, Ross . . . even your brother."

Donna's face turned white as she realized that Julie was right. "But Paul would have told me . . . wouldn't he?"

"Maybe. But maybe not. He didn't tell you he'd slept with Vicki, did he?"

It took Donna a moment, but then she shook her head. "No, he didn't say anything about it. Oh, my God! She's just got to tell us! We can't go around asking every guy in Crest Ridge whether he got Vicki pregnant!"

"Calm down, Donna. Back up the tape a little, and let's listen. Even if she doesn't tell us his name, maybe she'll give us a clue to who he is."

Donna nodded and backed up the tape. "Okay. You're right. I'm fine now. It was just a shock, that's all."

"*. . . dream about R. I see that awful, trapped expression on his face the night I told him I was pregnant. He's always been really good to me, and he actually told me he was glad about the baby. I don't think he really meant it, but he tried to make me feel better. But maybe he really is glad about the baby. He said he wanted it, and he'd do his best to be a good father. And that makes what I'm going to do even worse!*"

Vicki broke down in tears again as the two girls watched her.

Julie wished there were some way she could comfort her cousin, but it was too late. Too late for Vicki. Too late for the baby. And too late for "R," too. Vicki was dead, and there was no way to change that.

"*I . . . I've got to get ready.*" Vicki sighed deeply and wiped the tears from her eyes with the sleeve of her sweatshirt. "*I wish I could tell Mom, but I can't. She'd only try to stop me. If the shrink found out what I'm planning to do, he'd lock me up in a mental institution. Mom would sign the papers. I know she would. She'd be trying to help me, but I just couldn't stand it!*"

Vicki faced the camera and gave a sad little wave. "*I'm sorry, Mom. I'm sorry, R. Maybe I should have listened to that whispery voice on the phone. You were right, you know. I am wicked. I tried to be good, but I didn't make it. And I can't change now. It's too late to change.*"

Vicki stood up and walked toward the camera. There were tears rolling down her cheeks. "*That's it. That's the end of my diary. Say goodbye to Vicki Hudson. She'll never be back again.*"

The screen went blank and Julie shivered. It was over. There were no more tapes. Vicki had left this room never to return. But had she committed suicide?

"That's awful!" Donna shivered as she rewound the tape and put it back in its box. "Poor Vicki. I should've tried to be nicer to her. All that stuff about a guy watching her, and calling her on the phone. She was really going nuts, and I never really realized it. And then getting pregnant on top of it! No wonder she killed herself!"

Julie raised her eyebrows. "But did she? I listened very carefully, Donna. And Vicki never said she was going to commit suicide."

"*Say goodbye to Vicki Hudson? She'll never be back again?*" Donna repeated the last words on the tape. "Of course she was going to kill herself! What else could she mean?"

"She could mean she was running away from home, leaving for good and planning never to come back. I'm still not convinced, Donna. Don't forget about those things she bought at the drugstore before she left. Lipstick, sunglasses, perfume . . . that really doesn't make any sense."

Donna thought about it for a minute, and then she nodded. "Okay. I thought it was pretty clear, but there's a one-in-a-million chance you're right. So maybe it *was* an accident, but we'll never know for sure. And even worse, we'll never know who R is, either!"

Thirteen

It was almost ten-thirty when they put on their coats and took the elevator down to the lobby. Donna had been surprised when Julie had offered to walk her home, but she hadn't said no. Julie could tell that Donna was upset. She was upset, too, despite the crystal-clear night and the glorious stars overhead.

When they got to the road, Donna stopped and turned to look at Julie. "You don't have to walk me home. There's no crime in Crest Ridge."

"I need the walk to clear my head." Julie smiled at her friend. "Watching Vicki's diary was really depressing."

"I know. It got to me, too. You know . . . I can watch a depressing movie and it doesn't affect me at all, but this . . . this was real! I mean . . . I knew her! And it was almost as if she was right there in the room with us. I kept wanting to ask her questions, and hoping I could talk some sense into her, but all the time, I knew it was too late."

Julie nodded, and they walked in companionable silence, each of them thinking their own private thoughts about Vicki. Their footsteps crunched through the thin film of ice that glazed the deep snow, and their breath came out in puffy white clouds, turned silver by the bright moonlight. It was a lovely night, very calm, very peaceful. And gradually, Julie began to lose the anxious feeling she'd had when they'd watched Vicki's tapes.

"I feel a lot better," Donna announced, turning to Julie w.
a smile. "Did you ever see such a beautiful moon? It must be ful.
tonight."

"It must be." Julie gazed up at the round silver globe peeking
through the tall, graceful pines. The snow on the branches glistened with a soft, silver sparkle. The peaceful evening was a
time for confidences, a time for sharing intimate secrets. But she
couldn't tell Donna about the stalker. Donna might think she
was cracking up, like Vicki.

They walked on in silence that was broken only by the sound
of their own footsteps until they reached the houses at the edge
of town. Snow was falling softly, and the old-fashioned street
lights looked like the halos of very tall angels, circles of warm
light in the deep, dark night. The sidewalks were covered with
snow and they stayed on the street, walking at the edge of the
plowed snow, skirting the mammoth white humps of parked
cars.

Julie smiled as she passed a house with light spilling out of an
upstairs window. She saw the shadows of a man and a woman
against the curtains, embracing. How nice to be married and
live in a snug little house in a lovely town, where you were surrounded by all your friends and relatives.

Suddenly Julie had a thought that made her shiver. Perhaps
her parents would still be alive if they'd settled down at Saddlepeak Lodge. They could have helped Aunt Caroline and Uncle
Bob run the business, and she could have grown up with Vicki.
Things might have been very different then. But Julie's parents
hadn't wanted to stay in the States. They'd enjoyed the excitement of moving from country to country, and Julie had enjoyed
it, too. Until now. Until she realized what she'd missed. Her life
with her parents had been temporary, dictated by the whims of
a large corporation. She'd never really had a hometown.

Children who grew up in Crest Ridge had a sense of con-
tinuity. They knew their grandparents, perhaps even their
great-grandparents. When Julie touched the stones of the huge
fireplace in the lobby, she knew that her great-great-grandfather
had placed them there. And when she walked down the street in

Crest Ridge, her feet traveled over the same path her ancestors
had taken. In Crest Ridge, a house might stay in the same family for generations, passed on from the old to the new, complete
with the memories of family history.

She said goodnight, waited until the front door had closed
behind Donna, and then she walked back up the street. It was
clear that Donna wouldn't believe her if she told the truth about
the man she thought was stalking her. Donna hadn't believed
Vicki when she'd said the same things on the tape. But thinking
about the stalker made her very nervous, and she tried to concentrate on the beautiful night, instead.

Julie passed the houses on the outskirts of town, and walked
up the hill in the direction of the lodge. The road stretched out
before her, empty and desolate, a pristine white ribbon tied
around a huge, silver package decorated with stark black pines.
Black and white. There were no colors at night. Just the white,
glistening snow and the dark silhouettes of trees lining the road,
standing straight and tall like sentinels.

Black and white. They made such a sharp contrast. They
were such complete opposites, like wicked and good. Vicki hadn't
been wicked. Julie didn't believe that. But she certainly hadn't
been good, either. She'd been somewhere in-between, a troubled
person who'd had the same dreams as every other woman. Vicki
had just longed desperately to be loved.

Julie sighed as she remembered her cousin's face, tearful and
frightened, facing the camera. Her voice had been shaking, and
she'd barely choked out the words when she'd talked about the
man who was stalking her. Vicki had been terrified.

Was the stalker still out there somewhere? Was she his new
target? Julie shivered and walked a little faster. Perhaps it had
been foolish to walk home alone. Paul would have driven her, if
she'd let Donna ask him.

Julie stopped as she reached the pine grove that grew at the
side of the lodge. There was a path through the trees, a shortcut
Donna had shown her, but she didn't want to walk through the
grove alone. She'd stick to the road, where it was safer, where a

passing motorist might see her and stop, if she needed help. But there hadn't been a car on the road all night. The snow was unbroken, except for the two pairs of descending boot prints she'd made with Donna when they'd walked to town.

Without warning, a sudden gust of wind whipped up, lifting Julie's green stocking cap from her head and sending it flying toward the pine grove. Julie dashed through the snow in pursuit, entering the pine grove without a second thought. Aunt Caroline had given her the stocking cap, and she didn't want to lose it.

It took a moment before Julie found it, caught on a low branch of a huge pine. She pulled it down, dusted off the snow with her gloves, and clamped it back on her head again, making sure to pull it down snugly over her ears. Then she looked around, surprised at how far she'd had to run to catch it. She could barely see the road from here, and it was dark and frightening under the trees, their heavy branches blocking the moonlight. There was very little snow under the trees. The thick branches that blocked the moon had also kept the snow from falling to the ground.

The pine grove smelled like Christmas, an exciting, sharp, heady aroma. Julie knew she would have enjoyed the scent if she'd been here during the day. But this was night, and the wind that sighed through the branches sounded like a thousand lost souls moaning.

There was a sharp crack and a branch came crashing down, overloaded with its burden of snow. Julie cried out and ran toward the road, gasping in the cold night air. She felt rather foolish when she broke through the trees and turned to see that no one was behind her. Thank goodness no one had seen her run out from the trees like a scared rabbit!

Julie knew the driveway was only a short distance ahead. She felt like running, but she forced herself to stay calm and walk at a sedate pace. The driveway was steep. If she wore herself out now, she'd be gasping by the time she got to the lodge.

It was then that she heard it, the crunch of footsteps behind her. Julie whirled, but she couldn't see anyone following her. It was just her imagination, playing tricks on her. That falling branch had made her jumpy.

Even though she knew she was being ridiculous, Julie walked a little faster. But the footsteps seemed to speed up, too. She picked up her pace again and the footsteps matched hers, faster and faster as she crunched through the snow.

Julie panicked for a moment, almost breaking into a full-scale run. Then she realized that she could be hearing the echo of her own footsteps. Sound did strange things up here in the mountains. She'd put it to the test and see if she was right.

Julie slowed. The footsteps slowed. She stopped. They stopped. A wave of pure relief washed over her, so strong it took her a moment to catch her breath. It was definitely an echo. She had nothing to worry about.

Another few minutes of walking, and Julie spotted the huge stone arch that marked the entrance to the lodge drive. It was twenty feet high at the tallest point, spanning the two-lane driveway. Because it sloped gently up and then down again, the guests sometimes climbed it in the summer, to have their pictures taken. Although no one had ever fallen from the arch, Julie's grandfather had installed a railing on either side to make sure no accidents would occur.

As Julie drew closer, she gazed at the arch in fascination. The stones were all sizes and shapes and colors, but every one had been found on Saddlepeak Lodge land. She remembered Donna telling her that it had taken a four man crew an entire summer to complete the arch to her great-great-grandfather's satisfaction. He'd designed it to be a tourist attraction, and it still was, even today.

The arch gleamed cold and stately under the moon. It looked almost medieval, and Julie could imagine oxcarts laden with straw and produce, passing under its immense stones. It could be a remnant left by a forgotten civilization, or a tribute to an ancient god, a primitive symbol to ward off evil and keep all who lived within its boundary safe and secure from· harm.

Julie knew she was giving way to her imagination again, and she smiled. The arch was simply an arch, nothing more, nothing less. It was a way of marking the road so that tourists could find the lodge. But it was beautiful nonetheless, and Julie felt small and vulnerable as she looked up to see it looming over the driveway.

Then she noticed something glittering brightly under the curve of arch—icicles. A long row of them, hanging down like giant, sharply pointed teeth. They looked like gleaming daggers, and she shuddered at the thought of walking beneath them. She hadn't seen them when she'd passed through the archway with Donna.

Did icicles ever fall? Julie walked closer, her eyes riveted on the glittering spears of ice. They would be a perfect murder weapon, striking with killing force and then melting away in the bright sunlight. As sharp as a pick, as heavy as a club, and capable of being reduced to harmless water before the victim was found.

Julie stopped and looked up. She knew she didn't want to walk under the row of jagged icicles, but there was no way around them, unless she went back to the shortcut. Which was worse? The pine grove, or the icicles? Walking through the pine grove would take much longer, and she'd worry every step of the way. If she ran under the icicles as fast as she could, she'd be through the archway in a heartbeat.

It was the archway, then. Julie sighed and squared her shoulders. She'd never heard of anyone being killed by an icicle, and they'd been around since the beginning of time. It was silly to think that she might be the first.

There was a scraping sound high above her, and Julie glanced up at the top of the arch. Was someone hiding up there? She'd managed to convince herself that the footsteps she'd heard had been only an echo. But what if the stalker had been following her, and he'd taken a shortcut to climb the arch? He could be waiting for her, waiting to knock the icicles loose as she walked through the archway!

Julie stopped, uncertain, frightened, filled with the dread possibilities. But she couldn't stand here all night, shivering with the cold, hoping that someone would come along to help her out of her quandary. She'd stick to her original plan and run through the archway. If the stalker was up there, he wouldn't have time to knock the icicles loose before she got through.

Zero to sixty in seven point three seconds: a line from a new car commercial popped into her mind. That's what she needed—-a car. An icicle might dent the roof, but it certainly wouldn't pierce through metal the way it would do with human flesh. But she didn't have a car. And the road was dark and deserted behind her. If she didn't make her move soon, her legs would stiffen up with the cold. If all she could do was hobble through the archway, she'd end up being a target for that much longer.

Julie took a deep breath and prepared herself for the dash. She'd count to three and then she'd run. One . . . two . . . three!

Julie lunged forward and raced toward the archway. Too fast to change her mind now. She was almost there. Almost through. Almost . . .

Her foot hit a patch of ice and she slipped, tried to right herself, slipped again, and fell so hard it knocked the breath from her body. Right under the arch! My God! She had to get up!

But before she could move, she heard a sharp crack and something hurtled down so close to her body, she felt a whoosh of air as it passed. They were falling! The icicles were falling! She had to get out of the way!

Julie tried to roll, but she couldn't seem to move. Something was pinning her down, holding her fast. And then there was a series of sharp cracks, and descending spears of ice began to puncture the snow, crashing all around her, hammering the ground with the dull thuds of heavy weights dropping from a great height. One massive, gleaming spear landed just inches in front of her nose, its tip as sharp as a stiletto.

It seemed to go on forever, the stark terror of knowing that she could be skewered any moment. Julie couldn't move, and she was too frightened to cry out. All she could do was bury her face in the frigid snow and pray that she wouldn't be killed. Not now. Not yet. Not like Vicki!

Then it was over. Julie's heartbeat sounded deafeningly loud in the total silence. And then she realized that if her heart was still beating, she was . . . alive!

Julie twisted from side to side, trying to pull herself free, but something was holding her down. She raised her head and shuddered as she saw that an icicle had pierced the right sleeve of her jacket, narrowly missing her arm. She reached out awkwardly with her left hand to try to jerk it out, but it was embedded too deeply for her to dislodge.

But she had to get up! She had to get to her feet and run! He was still up there, up on the archway. She had to escape before he climbed down!

And then she heard footsteps crunching through the snow. Coming fast. Running toward her. Footsteps that approached like the hoofbeats of doom.

Julie shut her eyes. She couldn't bear to look! But then she heard the fabric of her jacket tear and she could move again. She opened her eyes to face Vicki's murderer, and the man who would surely kill her, now that his plan had failed. And her mouth fell open in shock.

"Paul?" Julie's voice was tentative and shaking, like the mewl of a frightened kitten.

"Jesus, Julie!" Paul dropped to his knees, and put his arms around her. "Are you hurt?"

"Uh . . . no." It took a moment for his words to sink in. He'd asked if she was hurt. You didn't ask someone a question like that if you were going to kill them.

"Here . . . let me help you up." Paul lifted her gently to her feet. "My God, Julie! You were almost killed!"

Julie nodded, sagging against Paul's arms in relief. Paul was here. Everything was all right now. She was safe in the protective circle of his arms. And then she remembered the stalker. And how the icicles had fallen.

"He's up there! Paul! On top of the arch!"

Paul stepped back, and looked up. "Who's up there? I don't see anyone."

"He was up there a minute ago! He knocked the icicles loose! He tried to kill me, Paul!"

"Who?"

"I . . . I don't know. But I saw someone up there, right before I went through the archway. That's why I was running. I thought maybe I could get through before he could do it!"

"Julie . . . honey. You're getting hysterical." Paul wrapped her in his arms again. "There's no one up there. I guarantee it. And I didn't see anyone come down."

"He must have climbed down when you were pulling the icicle loose. He's still out there, Paul! And now he's going to try to kill me again!"

"Hold on. Just take it easy, okay?" Paul helped her over to the side of the archway where there was a place to sit down. "Just rest for a minute and catch your breath. You're safe, Julie. I won't let anyone hurt you."

He didn't believe her! Julie felt tears come to her eyes, and then she began to sob. She had to convince him that she was in danger. He had to believe her!

Paul pulled her close and patted her back. "Come on, Julie. I know you had a bad scare, but you're not making any sense right now. Why do you think that someone's trying to kill you?"

Between sobs, Julie told him about the face she'd seen outside her balcony, the scare she'd had at the ice rink, the whispery voice on the phone, the avalanche, and her near-accident on Dead Man's Run. She even told him about last night, when she'd been locked in the game cooler. The only thing Julie left out was Vicki's taped diary. And when she was finished, she looked up at him with tears in her eyes. "Doesn't that prove someone is after me?"

"Oh, Julie." Paul bent down and kissed her softly on the lips. Then he brushed back her hair and put her stocking cap back on her head. "Everything's all right, Julie. You had a horrible scare, and you're not thinking straight."

"You don't believe me!" Julie broke into fresh sobs.

"Of course I believe you. I just think you're jumping to conclusions. I know you've had a rough time. It must have been horrible to lose your parents, and it's bound to be hard to adjust to life in a small place like Crest Ridge. Just take it day by day, and try to calm down. The kind of stress you've had would be enough to drive anybody a little batty."

Paul wrapped his arm even tighter around her shoulders and kissed the side of her neck. "Please, Julie . . . if you can relax, everytbing'll fall into place. I absolutely guarantee it. And promise me you won't mention any of this to your aunt and uncle."

"Why not?" Julie was so surprised, she stopped crying.

"You'd make them feel awful, Julie. You're beginning to sound just like Vicki. Mrs. Hudson told me that Vicki thought someone was after her, too. It got so bad, they sent her to a psychiatrist, but it didn't seem to help. Vicki just got more and more paranoid. You may not know this, but Vicki's death wasn't accidental. She flipped out, and drove her car off the cliff."

"I know." Julie nodded. "Donna told me, my first night here. And Uncle Bob mentioned it, too. The only one who hasn't talked about it is Aunt Caroline."

"It's hard for her to talk about it. I think she still blames herself for refusing to lock Vicki up."

"Lock her up? You mean, like . . . in a mental institution?"

Paul nodded. "Your uncle wanted to commit her, but Mrs. Hudson just couldn't do it. And now she feels guilty because she refused to sign the papers. If she'd agreed to lock Vicki up, it would have saved her life."

"I see." Julie's mind was whirling. "Can I ask you a personal question?"

"Sure. What is it?"

Julie took a deep breath and blurted it out. "Did you love Vicki?"

"I thought I did." An expression of pain flickered across Paul's face. "I always thought we'd get married when I graduated from college, and we'd settle down right here in Crest Ridge. But Vicki didn't like small-town life. She wanted to make lots of money and travel around the world. She used to talk about the wonderful life your parents had, and how lucky you were because you weren't stuck in Crest Ridge."

Julie's eyes widened. "Really? And I thought she was the lucky one! I always wanted to grow up in a town where I knew everyone and everyone knew me, surrounded by lots of relatives and friends. I guess we were very different."

"I guess so." Paul nodded.

"Is that why you broke up with Vicki? Because you had different goals in life?"

"That's part of it." Paul looked sad again. "I wanted to stay here and she didn't. And I wanted a family when the time was right. But Vicki told me she never wanted to have kids."

"Never?"

"Never. Vicki hated kids. She didn't have any patience with them. I always thought I could change her mind, but it didn't work out that way. How about you? Do you feel the same way Vicki did?"

"No." Julie's eyes turned misty. "I'd like to work with children, maybe teach . . . I'm just not sure. And I definitely want a family of my own. But that's a long way in the future, after I finish college and work for a while. Are you really sure Vicki didn't want children someday? Maybe when she was older?"

Paul shook his head. "I know she didn't. But maybe that was because she couldn't have any of her own."

"What?"

"I shouldn't have said that." Paul winced. "Look, Julie . . . you've got to promise you'll never tell anyone, okay?"

Julie's heart was pounding a rapid tattoo as she nodded. "I promise."

"Vicki and I were sleeping together. And once she thought

she was pregnant. I drove her down to a clinic in Denver, and a doctor examined her. That's when we got the bad news." Paul gave a bitter laugh. "At least, it was bad news for me. It was probably very good news for her. He said Vicki had some kind of blockage, and she'd never be able to have children."

Fourteen

By the time she'd taken a hot shower, Julie was feeling much better. But she was still reeling from the bombshell Paul had dropped. Vicki hadn't been pregnant. She couldn't get pregnant. There was no reason for Paul to lie about it . . . unless he was R, and he was covering up for getting Vicki pregnant! But why would he do that when he'd admitted that he'd slept with Vicki? He'd even told her about the scare they'd had, thinking she was pregnant. The whole thing just didn't make sense. And if Vicki wasn't pregnant, why had she said she was on her tape? Or had she?

Julie got out the rosewood box and put Vicki's last tape in the machine. She had to hear her exact words. She fast-forwarded to that section, and frowned as she listened. *"Sometimes I dream about R. I see that awful, trapped expression on his face the night I told him I was pregnant."* Maybe Vicki hadn't been pregnant. She could have been lying to R. But there was also the possibility that Paul was lying when he said Vicki couldn't get pregnant.

Julie shook her head. She was so confused, she really shouldn't think about it anymore tonight. But something seemed to be driving her, some compelling need to know more about her cousin and why she'd died. At first, idle curiosity had entangled her in the mystery surrounding Vicki's death. But now she'd seen

Vicki's videotapes, and she'd watched her cousin degenerate from a beautiful, self-confident young woman to a terrified, desperate girl. Julie just *had* to know what had happened to change her cousin so drastically.

The box of videotapes was still sitting out on the shelf. Julie frowned and tried to concentrate. She knew that there was something she should do, but she wasn't quite sure what it was. And then she remembered—Vicki had said she'd come back to erase her diary. But she'd died before she could do it.

Julie turned on the television and switched to an all-night movie channel. Then she put Vicki's first tape into the VCR and started to record over her cousin's diary. It wasn't until she'd slipped the final tape into the machine that she realized which movie was playing. It was *Life Stinks* with Mel Brooks.

The irony struck her, and Julie began to laugh. And as she laughed, she had the feeling that someone else was laughing with her. Vicki's spirit? It no longer seemed impossible. If Vicki was still out there somewhere, she'd be sure to appreciate which movie was recorded over her diary.

Julie sobered quickly as she had a frightening thought. During her first week at Saddlepeak Lodge, she'd experienced horrible nightmares about her cousin. But the frightening dreams had stopped abruptly on the day she'd begun to ask probing questions about Vicki's life and death. Perhaps Vicki really *had* been trying to contact her, to warn her about the stalker. Unless she learned Vicki's secret and solved the mystery surrounding her death, she might share Vicki's awful fate.

The final tape was finished. Julie put it back into the box and closed the cover. She was tired, and she knew she'd be able to think more clearly after a good night's rest, but there was no way she could sleep with all with these puzzling questions running through her mind. Which R had written the note to Vicki? That was the place to start.

It took only a moment to pull on a green velvet sweatsuit and take Vicki's note out of the desk again. She'd peek at Paul's notebook at school tomorrow, and compare his handwriting to the writing on the note. And she'd go down to the pro shop and look at the autographed picture of Ryan that was hanging on the wall. She could get a sample of Dick Stratford's signature from his credit card receipts. And Red Dawson had invoices ready to be sent out. She could go to her aunt's office and look at his writing. The only other candidate was Ross, and she'd take care of that right now. She'd knock on his door with some kind of excuse, and get a sample of his handwriting.

Julie shivered. She had to be very careful. The author of Vicki's note could be the whispery voice on the phone, the stalker who had followed her and knocked the icicles from the archway. He could have been trying to scare her off, to make her stop asking questions about Vicki. But if he suspected that she had Vicki's note and she was collecting handwriting samples, he'd have to kill her.

Should she go to the sheriff? Julie thought about it for a moment, and then she realized that it wouldn't do any good. There was no proof she was being stalked, and Sheriff Nelson wouldn't believe her. He'd probably think she was flipping out, and he'd be sure to tell her aunt and uncle. Then Uncle Bob would want to lock her up in a mental institution, and after what had happened to Vicki, Aunt Caroline might just agree with him! She had to do this on her own, identify the stalker and prove that she hadn't been imagining things. And getting a sample of Ross's handwriting was the perfect place to start.

Her hands were shaking as she gathered up a notebook and pen. She still didn't know what excuse she'd use, but the first thing to do was to see if Ross was still awake.

Julie loosened the bars on her patio doors and opened them quietly. She stepped out and glanced over. There was Ross! Out on his patio!

"Hi, Ross." Julie spoke softly, so she wouldn't wake her aunt and uncle. "I'm glad you're still awake. Can I talk to you for a minute? It's important."

Ross nodded. "Sure. What is it, Julie?"

"Would you come inside for a minute? It's cold out here."

Ross nodded again, and then he laughed. "Your place, or mine?"

"Your place. Give me a couple of minutes, okay?"

Julie glanced down at her sweatsuit. No need to change clothes. Perhaps it wasn't entirely proper to meet Ross in his room, but she hadn't wanted him to come to hers. If Aunt Caroline or Uncle Bob happened to see him coming out of her room, she'd have a lot of explaining to do.

Less than a minute later, Julie was knocking on Ross's door. He opened it, and she stepped in. "Hi. I know it's late, but I forgot all about this school project I have to turn in tomorrow. It'll only take a couple minutes, if you'll help me."

"Sure." Ross grinned as he noticed her notebook. "What is it, Julie? An interview?"

"Well . . . sort of. It's for history class. We're . . . uh . . . studying historical buildings in the area, and I decided to use Saddlepeak Lodge. I wrote out some questions. Could you just answer them for me?"

"No problem. Have a seat, Julie." Ross motioned her to one of the two chairs that were arranged by a low round table. Then he took the notebook, and read the first question aloud. "*What is the address of this site?* You know the answer to that, Julie."

Julie nodded, and handed him the pen. "I know, but could you write it down for me, Ross? It's supposed to be in the source's handwriting. It's one of Mr. Haskell's rules. That's to prove I really interviewed you."

"Mr. Haskell?" Ross looked at her in surprise. "When I went to Crest Ridge High, Mr. Haskell taught math."

"Right. I meant to say Mr. Jenkins." Julie nodded, but she blushed bright red. She'd never been a good liar.

"What's this about, Julie?" Ross put down the pen and stared at her. "It's not a school project, is it?"

Julie sighed. As Donna would say, she was busted, caught dead to rights with her hand in the cookie jar. "Uh . . . no. It's not. It was a trick to get a sample of your handwriting. But I should have asked you honestly. That would have been a lot better."

Ross nodded. "Why do you need a sample of my handwriting?"

"So I can compare it to this." Julie pulled the ticket stub with the message out of her pocket, and handed it to him. She noticed that Ross's hand trembled as he took it.

"I can save you the trouble. I wrote this note. Why?"

"Because the date on the ticket is December eighteenth. Did you meet Vicki on the night she died?"

"No. She didn't show up. I waited for hours, and then I drove back here. That's when I found out she . . ." Ross's face had turned white and he cleared his throat. " . . . that she was dead."

"Where was she supposed to meet you?"

Ross looked as if he didn't want to answer, but he did. "In Denver. At a justice of the peace's house. Vicki was pregnant, and we were going to get married."

"And you think she killed herself, rather than marry you?"

An expression of pain flickered across Ross's face. "I made all the arrangements, and she drove off the cliff on the way to the wedding. What would you think?"

"I'd think it was a terrible accident or . . . or something like that." Julie stopped herself short. She had almost said, *or maybe someone murdered her,* but she didn't want to burden Ross with that suspicion, not until she'd gathered all the facts.

"It wasn't an accident. Vicki left a suicide note for her mother. Mr. Hudson showed it to me."

"I know. Uncle Bob told me about it. But it didn't say anything about suicide." Julie faced him squarely. "I don't think Vicki intended to kill herself. The only reason she left that note was because she was running off with you, and she wanted to say goodbye."

Ross didn't look convinced. "Look, Julie. I'd like to believe that, but it doesn't make sense. Vicki knew that road. She'd driven it thousands of times before. She barreled right through the guard rail on a curve that wasn't even dangerous. What makes you think it *wasn't* suicide?"

"She bought new sunglasses right before she left. And a new lipstick she never even got a chance to wear. And a brand-new bottle of perfume. Why would she buy all those things if she was planning to kill herself?"

Ross frowned deeply, and then he shook his head. "I don't know."

"Because she *wasn't* planning to kill herself. She was planning on running away with you, and wearing that lipstick and perfume at her wedding, and putting on those sunglasses the next morning. That's why."

Ross blinked. And then he gave a deep sigh. "I wish I could believe that. God knows, it would make me feel a lot better."

"Then believe it." Julie's eyes met his. "There's no evidence to the contrary, none at all. I'm convinced that Vicki really wanted to marry you."

The color began to come back to Ross's face, and he nodded. "That's why I couldn't understand it. I thought she wanted to get married. And she *said* she did. I was going to do the right thing by her, Julie. I really was. We barely knew each other, but we could have made it work for the sake of the baby."

"You never told anyone that you were going to get married?"

"No. I wanted to tell Vicki's parents, but she was afraid they'd try to stop her. They could have, you know. She was under age. And to make matters even worse, she was having some tough emotional problems."

"I heard about that." Julie seized the opening Ross had left for her. "She thought someone was after her, right?"

Ross sighed. "That's right. She got a couple of crank phone calls when she was working the switchboard. And she had several nightmares about a face at her window. That's why I asked you to tell me if anything else happened. For a moment there, I thought that there was really something to it. But you haven't had any more nightmares like that, have you, Julie?"

"No. Not like that." Julie shook her head. She pushed down the impulse to tell Ross about the other things that had happened to her, and decided to ask him a question, instead. "Do you think Vicki was crazy?"

"Of course not! She was just under a lot of stress. I thought taking her away from Crest Ridge might help. She hated it here. But . . . it just didn't happen that way."

"How about after she died?" Julie asked the question even

though she thought she knew the answer. "Did you tell anyone that you'd planned to get married?"

"I wanted to tell Mrs. Hudson. I thought maybe she'd understand. But I never got up the nerve. And then I decided I shouldn't say anything at all."

"Why not?" Julie held her breath as she waited for his answer.

"I thought it would only make Mrs. Hudson feel worse to know she'd lost a grandchild, too."

"Yes. You were probably right." Julie sighed deeply. She wished she could tell Ross that Vicki had lied about being pregnant. That might make him feel better. But she still wasn't sure whether Paul had been telling her the truth. "When did Vicki tell you she was pregnant?"

"December twelfth. I'll never forget it. I got off work, and Vicki was waiting for me in my room. I remember how shocked I was when she told me. I was so grateful to Mr. and Mrs. Hudson for giving me a job, and then I did something like that!"

"What do you mean?"

"I showed my gratitude by getting the boss's daughter pregnant. It's right out of a cheap movie! I was so mad at myself, I could hardly stand it. But then Vicki started crying. She thought I was mad at her. It took me an hour to convince her that I wasn't."

Julie sighed. If Paul was right, and Vicki had been lying to Ross, it was even worse than a cheap movie. "Did you love her?"

"How could I? I barely knew her! But I liked her. And I thought maybe that was enough."

"Tell me what happened." Julie's voice was soft. She wanted to know, and it might make Ross feel less guilty if he talked about it.

"It happened the night of the Halloween party. Vicki had just broken up with Paul, and she didn't have a date. She'd rented a costume and everything. So I played Sir Galahad, and offered to take her."

Julie nodded. "What happened at the party?"

"I danced almost every dance with her, and she seemed to have a good time. Don't get me wrong, Julie—I had a good time, too. Vicki was a great dancer. But it all started out as a favor to her parents. I knew they'd be upset if she didn't show up at the party."

Julie remembered the bottle of vodka that Vicki had shown on the tape. "Did you have a lot to drink?"

"No. I had a beer right after the party started. And another afterward, out on the patio, with Vicki. I guess I was really tired because that second beer hit me like a ton of bricks. I don't even remember going up to my room. But when I woke up the next morning, Vicki was in bed with me."

"You don't remember sleeping with her?"

Ross winced "No, but I didn't tell her that. It would have been a terrible insult. And Vicki was scared enough as it was. She said she'd never slept with anyone else before, and she . . . well . . . she cried."

Julie kept her expression carefully neutral. Vicki had set him up! But she couldn't tell Ross how she knew that. "And that was the start of your affair with her?"

"What affair?" Ross looked puzzled. "It was only that once. Six weeks later, she told me she was pregnant. And a week after that, she was dead."

It was almost one in the morning when Julie let herself back into the apartment. There were no lights on in the living room, Aunt Caroline and Uncle Bob had gone to bed hours ago, and she was careful not to make any noise as she tiptoed past the couch toward the hallway. Suddenly, the swivel chair creaked and someone grabbed her arm roughly. Julie gasped in shock, and whirled to face her uncle. "Uncle Bob!"

"What are you doing out this time of night?"

Julie could see his face in the moonlight, and his eyes blazed with rage. She gulped, and tried to explain. "I . . . I couldn't sleep so I . . . I took a walk."

"Don't lie to me, Victoria! I know you were in his room!"

His fingers dug into her arm and Julie winced. Uncle Bob was so angry, he'd called her "Victoria." And she could smell liquor on his breath. "That's true, Uncle Bob. I couldn't sleep, so I went out on my balcony. And Ross was out on his. We started talking, and it was so cold out there, he invited me to come to his room. I didn't tell you that, because you were so angry. And I didn't want to upset you any more."

"I told you to stay away from him, and I meant it!"

Julie frowned. He'd never told her to stay away from Ross. "No, you didn't, Uncle Bob. I had no idea you wanted me to stay away from Ross."

Uncle Bob looked confused. He stared at her and blinked. And then he dropped her arm. "Julie?"

"Yes, Uncle Bob?"

"Julie." Uncle Bob shook his head, as if he were shaking off a bad dream. "I'm sorry, honey. I must have fallen asleep in the chair. When you came in, you woke me up. I guess I was dreaming about Vicki. And for a minute there, I . . . I thought you were Vicki."

Julie gave a big sigh of relief. Of course! Poor Uncle Bob. From what she'd learned about Vicki and her boyfriends, he had a perfect right to be angry.

"Can you forgive me, Julie?" Uncle Bob looked very upset. "I didn't mean to grab you like that. I hope I didn't hurt you."

Julie's arm was smarting and she knew she'd have bruises, but she didn't want to admit it. It would only make him feel guilty. "It's all right, Uncle Bob. And there's nothing to forgive. I understand."

"Thank you, Julie." Uncle Bob looked very relieved. "How about a glass of milk and one of Mrs. Robinson's chocolate chip cookies?"

Julie nodded, even though she was exhausted. All she really wanted to do was go to sleep, but Uncle Bob seemed to want to talk. "I'd like that, Uncle Bob."

A few moments later, they were sitting on the couch with a plate of cookies between them. Julie munched a cookie and smiled. Mrs. Robinson's chocolate chip cookies were the best she'd ever tasted. "Can I ask you a question, Uncle Bob?"

"Of course."

"Why did you want Vicki to stay away from Ross?"

Uncle Bob sighed. "Ross was all wrong for her. And I knew that if she started going out with him, there'd be trouble."

"You thought he was too old for her?"

"That's part of it. And Vicki could be . . . uh . . . very distracting. I saw Red Dawson almost cut off his finger when Vicki watched him skin a buck."

Julie nodded. Aunt Caroline had told her about Vicki and Red. And the night she'd talked to Red in his workroom, he'd seemed upset when he'd mentioned Vicki. But she didn't want to know about Vicki and Red. She wanted to know more about Ross. "Do you want me to stay away from Ross, too?"

"I'm not really in any position to order you around, Julie. Would you stay away from Ross if I asked you to?"

"Yes, I would . . . if you told me why."

Uncle Bob sighed again. "All right. I'll tell you. But don't repeat it."

"I won't."

"Ross's mother, Marsha, was a very sad case. Her family was poor, and they lived in a little shack up in the mountains. Her mother died when she was quite young, and Marsha's father used to beat her every time he got drunk. She ran away from home when she was fifteen, and your grandparents took her in."

"Did she work here at the lodge?"

Uncle Bob nodded. "She waited tables in the restaurant, and she went to high school with us. Caro was in her class. She worked here until she was twenty."

"Why did she leave?"

"She ran off with a soldier. He was sent to Vietnam for the mop-up operation, and he got killed. Marsha came back here the next year with her baby boy."

Julie nodded. Ross had told her that his father had been killed in Vietnam. "Did she work at the lodge again?"

"No. Caro and I told her she could have her old position back, but she found another job as a cocktail waitress down on Main Street. And then we started hearing rumors that she was involved with some of the married men around town. We didn't believe them at first, but it was pretty obvious that Marsha was getting a lot of extra money from somewhere. Caro didn't think we should get involved, but I tried to help Marsha. I used to drop by every week or so, to make sure that little Ross was all right."

"That was very nice of you." Julie smiled at her uncle, but inside, she was seething. Ryan had told her that he'd heard Uncle Bob had a mistress. That just showed how hateful gossip could be. Those vicious rumors were probably based on Uncle Bob's visits to check on Ross!

"Marsha died when Ross was a senior in high school, and there wasn't much of an estate. So we did what your grandparents did—we took Ross in until he graduated, and then we gave him a job so he could save up money for college."

Julie nodded. "That's a wonderful story, Uncle Bob. But I still don't understand why you want me to stay away from Ross."

"It's because of his family background, Julie. As much as I hate to say it, Marsha wasn't from the best stock. And nobody knows Ross's father. I believe that heredity has a lot to do with the type of person you eventually become. I like Ross. He's a fine young man. But he may carry some very undesirable genes."

"Oh. I see." Julie tried not to look shocked, but she thought Uncle Bob's theory was completely crazy. And it was terribly unfair to Ross.

"Well . . . it's time to turn in." Uncle Bob stood up and yawned. "Don't worry about these dishes, Julie. I'll put them away. It's late, and you'd better get straight to bed."

Julie was exhausted as she got into bed and turned off the light. Uncle Bob had been weird tonight, and she hoped he wasn't going on another bender. All that talk about Ross's family and bad genes. No wonder Vicki hadn't told him that she was planning to marry Ross!

Julie had thought of arguing when Uncle Bob had asked her to stay away from Ross. But then she'd reconsidered. She didn't really want to date Ross now, she just wanted to be his friend. She wasn't exactly sure how that had happened, but it had.

Naturally, she'd promised to keep Ross's secret, and not tell anyone what he'd told her. Ross had been through hell, and in Donna's words, he'd been royally dumped on. He'd been trapped by an expert schemer . . . or had he?

Even though she didn't want to mistrust Ross, it was possible that *he* was the expert schemer. Vicki had set out to trap him. She'd admitted as much on the tape. But what if he'd slept with her anyway, and believed her when she'd told him she was pregnant? And what if he'd thought of a way to get out of a marriage he didn't want by killing his bride-to-be on the way to the wedding?

The possibility was chilling. Julie tried to erase it from her mind, but it held a terrible fascination. Ross could have been the stalker Vicki had described. The loss of his mother might very well have affected his mind. He was the poor boy from the wrong side of the tracks, totally unsuitable for the boss's beautiful daughter. Ross might have spied on Vicki, jealous that she was sleeping with Ryan, and Mr. Stratford, and Red Dawson, and Paul. He could have called her "wicked" on the phone, warned her to mend her ways, and threatened to punish her if she didn't. Then Vicki had slept with him, or at least, he'd thought she had. And Ross could have killed her when he believed she was pregnant with his child, tricking everyone into believing that Vicki had been crazy enough to take her own life.

Julie sighed deeply. She felt like a traitor. She didn't want to believe that Ross was the stalker, but it all made sense . . . except one thing. Why was Ross stalking her?

The answer came in a flash, and Julie shivered beneath her warm blankets. It was simple. And reasonable. And totally believable. Ross was afraid she'd ask too many questions about Vicki's death. And she had. Now he was stalking her, trying to get everyone to think she was crazy, and setting the same kind of trap for her!

Julie thought back to day at the ice rink. He'd seen her skating with Ryan, asking him questions. He could have watched her from the trees at the ice rink, and then appeared to escort her home. Of course he'd told her she'd heard a raccoon. He couldn't very well tell her that she'd heard him!

Ross could have started the avalanche, and when that hadn't worked, he'd been in a perfect position to move the warning flags to lure her over the fatal drop on Dead Man's Run. He'd probably seen her kissing Ryan, after Ryan had saved her, so he'd called her at the switchboard again, warning her to stay away from the men who might know too much about Vicki.

Ross could have been the face on her balcony. That would explain why there were no tracks at the bottom of the fire escape. He could have found that peephole in Vicki's room, and he could have been spying on her all along. He could be the person who'd locked her in the game cooler, and he could have knocked down the icicles on the arch, in an attempt to kill her!

Julie shuddered. If Ross was the stalker, how far would he go? Would he keep on trying to kill her until he succeeded?

Fifteen

"I'm sorry, but we're not accepting any reservations for this weekend." Julie tried to sound as friendly as possible as she read the prepared notice Aunt Caroline had given her. "We're completely redecorating our guest rooms. Would you like to visit us next week, and stay in one of our beautiful new suites?"

The woman on the other end of he line sounded very disappointed. She told Julie that her husband had managed to get a week's vacation, and they'd decided, on the spur of the moment, to go to Saddlepeak Lodge for their wedding anniversary. She'd been hoping to get last-minute reservations, but now that was impossible.

"I'm so sorry." Julie thought fast. Aunt Caroline had told her that this was their slow season, and she wanted to make the reservation. "If you can just wait until Monday to come, we'll reserve the bridal suite for you. At no extra charge, of course."

The woman seemed delighted, and Julie repeated the reservation. "Monday through Sunday in the bridal suite? We'll be looking forward to seeing you then."

What had started as a weekend reservation had turned into a full week. Julie jotted it down in the book, and when she looked up, she found her aunt standing by the desk, smiling at her.

"Good work, Julie. I couldn't have done it better myself! Now tell me . . . which one is the bridal suite?"

Julie giggled. "I'm not sure. The biggest one, I guess. How about three-oh-one? I took a peek today, and it looks beautiful."

"I'll have someone make up a plaque for the door." Aunt Caroline sounded amused. "Whatever gave you an idea like that? We've never had a bridal suite at Saddlepeak Lodge."

"I don't know. It just sounded more romantic."

Aunt Caroline nodded. "Well, it was a great idea! Why don't you take a lunch break, Julie? There's a plate of cold cuts in the cooler, and the bread is on the counter."

"How about you?" Julie smiled at her aunt. "Shall I make you a sandwich?"

Aunt Caroline nodded. "Thank you, honey. That would be nice. How about a ham and cheese with plenty of mustard? And if you don't mind, we can eat right here in the lobby."

Julie nodded, and headed for the kitchen. The lodge was quiet and deserted, except for the workmen who would leave at dusk. Aunt Caroline had given the staff the weekend off, since they were closed for redecorating.

It seemed strange to be in the huge kitchen alone. The only staff member who had stayed behind was Ross. The Larkins were visiting their married children in Greeley, Red Dawson was spending the weekend in Colorado Springs, and Mrs. Robinson was staying with her sister in Denver. Even Uncle Bob had taken advantage of the break to go on a weekend hunting trip. Last night had been eerie, with just Aunt Caroline, Ross, and Julie rattling around in the five-story lodge.

Julie made two ham-and-cheese sandwiches with plenty of mustard, and set them on a tray. Then she poured two cups of coffee, black for her, and one with cream and sugar for her aunt.

When Julie got back to the lobby, her aunt was on the phone. She carried the tray to the huge round table in front of the leather couch, and set it down quietly.

"Of course . . . yes. I understand." Aunt Caroline's pen flew across the pad as she made a hasty note. "Five-fifteen. But you don't know the flight number or the airline?"

Julie grinned at her aunt. It sounded like another reservation. Saddlepeak Lodge provided service to and from the airport.

"No, that won't be a problem. We have a sign, and we'll meet all flights in the waiting area. Do you have a list of names?"

Julie watched as her aunt wrote down the names. It looked like a very long list.

"No, that's not a problem, either. We'll bring them in every morning, and pick them up every night. And you said the convention lasts through Saturday?" Aunt Caroline jotted down another note, and winked at Julie. "Thank you for thinking of us. We'll be there. And try some hot lemonade for that sore throat of yours."

Aunt Caroline hung up the phone and jumped to her feet. "Panic time, Julie. How many rooms do we have ready?"

"You mean . . . right now?"

"By tonight."

Julie frowned. "They did twelve yesterday, and they planned to finish the second floor by noon. That's twenty. What's happening, Aunt Caroline?"

"I'm going to need every one of them. We've got a party of twenty-two arriving at the airport at five-fifteen. That means they'll be up here by six-thirty. There's one married couple, and two of the women want to share, so we can put them all on the second floor. Do you think we can get the rooms ready in time? Or did I bite off more than we can chew?"

Julie shook her head. "We can do it, Aunt Caroline. All we have to do is dust and vacuum, and make up the beds. And it's only a little past one."

"Let's go see how many rooms are finished." Aunt Caroline grabbed her sandwich, and motioned for Julie to follow her. "I guess I'm greedy, Julie. I should have told them we were closed for remodeling, but it's twenty-two paying guests for a whole week. I just couldn't pass on an opportunity like that!"

"Of course you couldn't." Julie grabbed her sandwich, and hurried off after her aunt. "But Aunt Caroline? What will we do for food? The restaurant's closed."

"Sandwiches will be fine for tonight. I explained all that, and these people are delighted just to find a place to stay. There's some sort of big convention in Denver, and all the hotels are full."

"How about breakfast tomorrow morning?"

"No problem." Aunt Caroline reached the elevator and pressed the button. "I had them hold while I called Mrs. Robinson on the other line. She'll be here at the crack of dawn to open the restaurant."

The elevator doors opened, and they stepped in. As soon as the doors closed behind them, Aunt Caroline started to laugh. "When the rest of our reservation comes in on Monday, we'll be only two rooms short of full occupancy. And I thought this was my slow season!"

They were through with five rooms and starting on the sixth when Ross came up in the elevator. "I gassed up the van and your station wagon. Is there anything else I can do to help?"

"I thought you'd never ask. Hold out your arms." Aunt Caroline reached into the linen closet, grabbed a stack of new towels, and plunked them into Ross's arms. "Follow Julie. She's working on this end of the hall. Every bathroom gets four towels, two on the rack and two on the shelf."

Julie was uncomfortable as she walked down the hall with Ross. They hadn't been alone together since Sunday night, when he'd broken down and told her about Vicki, and she was embarrassed she'd suspected him of being the stalker. She'd been so tired that night, everything had seemed to point to Ross. But when she'd awakened the next morning, she'd changed her mind. If there was a stalker, he could be any of Vicki's boyfriends. Jealousy was definitely a motive to spy on someone. The stalker could be Ryan, or his father, or Red Dawson, or even Paul. And there was another possibility she had to consider. Perhaps there wasn't a stalker at all. It was entirely possible that Vicki had imagined the whole thing, except for the phone call. And that could have been just a recurring prank.

Even though she didn't like to admit it, Julie knew she might have been imagining things, too. Paul had been right. She'd been under a lot of stress with her parents' deaths, and her move to the States. She could have been unknowingly buying into Vicki's paranoia. After all, she was in a strange town, surrounded by people she'd only met a few weeks ago, and it was natural to feel like everyone was watching her. They might be. People in a small community always watched newcomers with suspicious eyes. She'd gotten the phone calls, too, but there were lots of sick people out there who called the same number over and over. For all she knew, the other girls who'd manned the switchboard might have gotten similar calls.

The next two hours passed in a frenzy of work. Julie made the bed while Ross vacuumed. He cleaned the mirrors and glass, she dusted. He put out the towels, and she made sure the bathrooms were spotless. And then they went on to the next room and did it all over again.

"All through?" Aunt Caroline looked up as they appeared in the doorway of 219.

Julie nodded. "Everything's done. Shall we start on the sandwich platters?"

"Ross and I'll do that. Did you call Donna and Paul?"

"I tried, but the answering machine was on."

"Try again. And if you can't get an answer, call Dave. Or even Ryan. We could use some help tonight."

Julie went down to the switchboard and dialed again. She left a message explaining the situation, but it was Saturday afternoon, and Donna had mentioned something about shopping for new furniture. Their grandmother was coming to stay with them for six weeks while she recovered from knee surgery. The whole Kirby family had been busy all week, getting the guest house ready for her.

There was no answer at Dave's house and his parents didn't have an answering machine. She'd have to try again later. Ryan was next, and Julie called the Stratford mansion. The housekeeper answered, and told her that Ryan and his father had gone to New York for the weekend. Julie went to the kitchen to report to her aunt, but Aunt Caroline didn't seem very worried. They could manage on their own if they had to.

It was almost four when Ross and Aunt Caroline were ready to leave for the airport, and Julie went out on the steps to wave goodbye. Ross went first, driving the lodge van. As soon as he'd started down the driveway, Aunt Caroline rolled down the window of the station wagon and motioned Julie closer.

"Are you sure you'll be all right here alone?" Aunt Caroline looked worried.

"I'll be fine."

"You're welcome to ride to the airport with me. We can manage to squeeze you in."

Julie shook her head. "No thanks, Aunt Caroline. You need someone here to man the switchboard."

"That's true. But I don't like to leave you all by yourself. There's a storm blowing in, and this big old place can be scary at night. Will you promise to keep calling Donna until you get her? She can come over and keep you company until we get back."

"I'll call her again, right after you leave." Julie gave her aunt a reassuring smile. "Go ahead, Aunt Caroline. You don't want to be late."

"All right . . . if you're sure."

"I'm sure. I'm not a child, Aunt Caroline. I've stayed alone before. And you'll be back soon."

Aunt Caroline nodded and started to drive away. Then she backed up and stuck her head out the window again. "If I see anybody on the way through town, I'll send them up. And Julie? It wouldn't hurt to lock the doors until we get back."

Julie was grinning as she went back inside the lodge. She was perfectly capable of staying here alone. She'd lock the doors, as Aunt Caroline had told her, put some good music on the lodge stereo system, and read that new thriller she'd picked up at the gift shop.

One glance at the cover of the thriller, and Julie decided to read something else. The story was about a serial killer who attacked young women who lived alone. She'd promised to write an article for the school paper, and she'd work on that instead. There was certainly nothing frightening about the field trip the

French class had taken to the new bistro. Of course, Donna wouldn't agree. She'd turned as white as a sheet when she'd discovered that the *escargots* Julie had ordered were snails.

Julie had just finished her article when she realized that she could barely see the page. Dusk was falling, and huge purple shadows crept across the base of the mountains. She switched on the light and glanced at the clock. It was almost five-thirty. If the plane had arrived on time, Ross and Aunt Caroline would be loading their passengers and starting the long drive up the mountain.

The outside lights flickered on, and Julie glanced out over the peaceful grounds. It wouldn't be long now. They'd be here in less than an hour. Then she remembered her promise to call Donna and she dialed again. One, two, three rings, and the answering machine picked up. Julie waited for the beep, and then she recorded her message.

"Hi, Donna. It's Julie. I'm here all alone, and Aunt Caroline made me promise to call you. They're at the airport, picking up a party of twenty-two. Call me back the minute you get in. Aunt Caroline wants you and Paul to work tonight."

Five minutes later, it was completely dark outside. The phone rang again, and Julie picked it up with a smile on her face. It was probably Donna, saying she was on the way. "Saddlepeak Lodge. This is Julie. How may I help you?"

"You've been a very bad girl, Vicki. You thought you could hide it from me, but you can't. I saw you with him. I know what you're doing. I warned you, and you refused to listen. I love you, baby, and I don't want to hurt you again, but you've given me no other choice."

There was a click and then a dial tone. Julie sat in stunned silence for a moment, and then she leaped up from the desk. He was out there, watching her, and she was all alone!

The big front door was securely locked, but how about the back? And the side? Julie ran to the side door and slid the bolt home with a resounding *clunk*. Then she raced to the outside door in the kitchen and breathed a sigh of relief as she saw it was securely locked.

Her heart was pounding, and she sagged against the wall in relief. She was safe. There was no way he could get inside. Then she thought about the words that whispery voice had spoken, and she grabbed Mrs. Robinson's chef's knife, just in case. He was insane. He'd called her "Vicki," even though she'd said her name plainly when she'd answered the phone. In his deranged mind, he thought she was Vicki, come to life again!

Julie shuddered. She'd go back to the switchboard and watch the front door. And if he tried to get in, she'd call Sheriff Nelson.

She was just entering the lobby when she heard it, a creaking noise in one of the rooms upstairs. The doors were securely locked, but what if someone was in the lodge with her? What if the stalker had been inside all along? He could have made the call from an inside phone!

Julie took a deep breath and forced herself to remain calm. The lodge was an old building, and old buildings sometimes creaked in the wind. Aunt Caroline had warned her that it could be scary at night, especially if the wind picked up.

She glanced out the window and saw the pine trees swaying, their branches whipping back and forth in the wind. The storm had arrived. But it was almost six-thirty, and they should be back any minute. She'd sit at the switchboard, her finger on the one-button emergency code for Sheriff Nelson, just in case.

She had almost reached the switchboard when the lights went out. Julie gasped and stopped in her tracks. The moon cast huge, looming shadows through the lobby windows, and even the overstuffed leather couches looked menacing. But it wasn't unusual for the power to go out during a storm, and the wind was blowing even harder now.

Julie clutched the knife and tiptoed silently around the desk. The icy snow pelting against the glass sounded like snare drums, rattling faster and faster until they reached a frightening crescendo. The wind was howling now, screeching around the corner of the building, moaning and shrieking like some giant, prehistoric animal in pain.

Then she heard it again, and she huddled behind the desk. She hadn't been imagining things. There was someone on the second floor, moving toward the main staircase. The top step creaked, and Julie's heart pounded hard in her chest. One of the workmen? No, they'd loaded their truck and left at five o'clock. It was the stalker! And he was inside the lodge!

Then, as if to confirm her worst nightmare, the whispery voice floated down from the top of the staircase. *"Come out, Vicki. I know you're here. You've been a very bad girl."*

Julie reached up and grabbed the phone. She had to call Sheriff Nelson. But there was no dial tone. The stalker had cut the phone line!

"Come out, Vicki." The voice was nearer now, and Julie heard a footstep on the second stair. *"It won't do any good to hide. I checked all the rooms, and I know you're down here. Come to Daddy, and take your punishment like a good girl."*

Daddy? Julie's mind whirled in dizzy circles. It was Uncle Bob! And he thought she was Vicki! Julie was so shocked, the knife clattered from her hand. And then she heard another stair creak, and then another. He was coming down to get her!

Julie knew she didn't have time to look for the knife. It was very dark, and it might take her precious moments to find it. Instead, she forced her trembling legs to move, across the floor toward the back staircase. She had to sneak up the back stairs and hide in her room. It was the safest place. He'd already checked it and found it empty.

Quietly, stealthily, Julie opened the door to the staircase. This was a deadly game of hide and seek, and she was "it." She couldn't let Uncle Bob find her, not if she wanted to live. He'd kill her, just as he'd killed Vicki!

The narrow stairwell had no windows, and now, with the power out, it was pitch black. It was also unheated, and Julie shivered as a blast of cold air came out to meet her. Thank goodness Donna had shown her this staircase! They'd used it to carry Vicki's tapes to the fourth floor, and it had been scary even with the lights on. Since no one used it anymore, it was cleaned only once a year, and Julie shuddered as she remembered the dust and spiderwebs that they'd encountered.

Julie stepped into the dark, cold space and shut the door

silently behind her. She shivered as she reached out and grabbed the banister. Spiderwebs were creepy, but she was glad the back staircase was in such disreputable condition. Uncle Bob would never think to look for her here.

She seemed to remember that the staircase had creaked, and she stayed close to the wall, trying to avoid the center of the steps. The back staircase had never been intended to be used by guests, even when the lodge was first built. It was an employee staircase, and since the elevator had been installed, it hadn't been used at all. Julie held tightly to the rail with one hand while she brushed the wall with the other. How many steps until she reached the landing? It seemed she'd been climbing forever in this cold, dark, airless place.

The banister ended abruptly, and Julie stumbled slightly. Seventeen steps. She'd count them from now on, and hope that there were the same number between each floor. She stepped out on the second-floor landing, her heart beating so rapidly she was afraid she might faint. What if Uncle Bob had heard her? He could be lurking behind the door that led to the second-floor hallway, ready to leap out and grab her as she crept by.

Julie hesitated, shrinking back against the wall. But she couldn't stay here forever. She had to get up to her room, where she could lock the door. Crossing the landing was a chance she had to take. It was only way she could get to the next flight of stairs.

She held her breath as she tiptoed across the landing and turned the corner. She'd made it! There were seventeen more steps to climb to the third floor, and Julie counted as she climbed. She didn't want to stumble again.

It seemed to take forever to reach the third-floor landing. She tiptoed across it, trying to calm the rapid tattoo of her heart. Another seventeen steps and she was on the fourth floor landing. Now all she had to do was open the hallway door, slip inside, and race to her room.

Julie grasped the doorknob and turned it. But nothing happened! It was locked! She swallowed down her sudden panic and tried again. It was no use. The doorknob wouldn't turn.

What would happen if she stayed here on the stairs? Would Uncle Bob find her before Ross and Aunt Caroline got home?

Suddenly a horrible thought flashed through Julie's mind. What if the reservation had been a fake, a trick to lure Aunt Caroline and Ross to the airport? Uncle Bob could have used his whispery voice as a disguise, so Aunt Caroline wouldn't recognize it. If Uncle Bob had made that call, there would be no guests at the airport. And Ross and Aunt Caroline might wait for hours for a plane that would never arrive!

Frantically, Julie tugged at the door. It flew open with a jerk, and she almost fell. The knob had never been designed to turn. It was just a handle to pull the door.

The hallway was as dark as the stairwell, and Julie peered into its inky blackness as she took a tentative step inside. The moon would have seemed as bright as day right now, but its light was blocked by two outside walls.

Julie felt her way down the hallway, touching the wall as she went. Distances were deceiving, and she almost crashed into the double antique doors. The key was in her pocket and she unlocked them quickly. Then she stepped inside, comforted by the bright moonlight streaming in the living room window, and hurried to her room, stepping in and locking her door behind her. But Uncle Bob was strong, and the flimsy lock wouldn't keep him out for long. Julie glanced around the room, her eyes stopping at the heavy dresser that was only a few feet from the door.

The dresser scraped as she pushed it across the floor. If luck was with her, he wouldn't hear it. But even if he did, it would take him precious minutes to break· the lock on her door and push the heavy piece of furniture out of the way.

Now there was nothing to do but wait. Julie sat down on the edge of the bed and stared at the door, her heart pounding in fear. How long would it take for Uncle Bob to find her? Aunt Caroline and Ross just had to get here before he broke into her room and killed her!

Sixteen

"Was that the phone?" Donna frowned as she unplugged the vacuum.

"Don't worry about it. I turned on the answering machine." Paul climbed down from the ladder and stood back to survey the paint he'd just applied to the walls. "Do you see any spots I missed?"

"It looks good to me. I think Grandma's going to love this color. Mom says she's always wanted a pink bedroom."

"It looks like the inside of a Pepto Bismol bottle to me." Paul sighed as he began gathering up his painting supplies. "I just hope it dries before the furniture gets here tomorrow."

Donna nodded and smiled at him. "It'll dry. We'll leave the window open. I'm getting hungry. Do you want to go out for a hamburger?"

"Sure. You finish up in here and I'll put the painting stuff away."

Donna glanced around the room with pride. They'd really worked hard today. The guest house had never been used for anything except storage, and they'd moved what seemed like hundreds of boxes into the garage.

"Ready?" Paul appeared in the doorway.

"Almost." Donna walked over to the basket under the mail

slot and picked it up, intending to take it into the kitchen to clean it. Then she noticed that there was an envelope inside.

"Oh, great. Grandma's already getting junk mail." Donna pulled out the envelope, and frowned as she saw the name written on the front. "It must be for you, Paul. It's addressed to Rock."

Paul reached over and grabbed the envelope out of Donna's hand. His face had turned a pasty white, and Donna stared at him in alarm. "What's wrong?"

"It's got to be from Vicki."

"But . . . how? Vicki's dead!"

"She must have left it here on the night she died. She always dropped notes here for me. I checked it every morning, but I stopped the night I heard she was dead."

Paul's hands were shaking as he ripped open the envelope and pulled out the letter inside. He held it for a long moment, without unfolding it.

"Go ahead." Donna nudged him. "Read it, Paul. It might be important! Don't you want to know what it says?"

"Not really." Paul stared down at the letter as if it were a bomb ready to explode.

"Well, I do!" Donna snatched it from Paul's hand and unfolded it quickly. "I'll read it to you. Sit down."

Paul looked dazed as he sat on the edge of the bed. His face was still white, and Donna couldn't blame him for being freaked. Reading a letter from a dead girl was like getting a summons from the grave.

"Relax. It's probably nothing." Donna patted him on the shoulder. She could understand why Paul was upset, but there was no way she was going to pass up an opportunity to know what Vicki had been thinking on the night she died.

" 'Dear Rock.' " Donna's voice was hushed as she read the words. " '*I know I hurt you, and I'm really sorry. But you're still my best friend, and I have to tell someone. Maybe you'll understand, but if you don't, C'est la vie.*' "

Paul frowned, and Donna explained. "*C'est la vie* means, 'That's life.' Vicki took French last year, remember?"

" *'I'm leaving tonight to marry Ross. He's waiting for me down in Denver. I set him up, Paul. Right after the Halloween Party, I spiked his beer with vodka. And then I sneaked into his room, so I'd be there when he woke up the next morning.'* "

Donna turned to look at Paul, but he was just sitting on the bed, staring off into space. She turned back to the letter again.

" *'Of course, nothing happened. He was out like a light. I know it was mean, but I had to do something. And then I waited six weeks and told him that I was pregnant. I figured he'd do the right thing and ask me to marry him, and he did. So I'm going to. And that'll get me out of here, to someplace that's safe.'* "

Donna turned to look at her brother again. He looked absolutely miserable. Maybe reading Vicki's letter out loud wasn't such a good idea. "You look sick, Paul. Do you want me to stop?"

"No. Finish it."

" *'I know you didn't believe me when I told you about the stalker. Mom didn't, either. Everybody thinks I'm crazy, but I'm not. He's out there, and he's going to kill me if I don't get away. I'm going to wait a couple of weeks, and then I'll tell Ross I lost the baby. Then I'll get a job, and I'll work really hard to be a good wife. I owe him that for taking me away from this horrible place!'* "

Donna glanced at Paul again, and they locked eyes. "This doesn't sound like a suicide note, does it?"

"No." Paul shook his head. "Go on, Donna. Read the rest of it."

" *'I think I know who the stalker is. It's so freaky, I almost don't want to tell you. But I can't tell Mom, and somebody should know the truth. It's Dad. I'm almost sure of it!* "

"Mr. Hudson?" Donna looked shocked. "I don't believe it! Why would her own father spy on her?"

"I don't know." Paul looked just as puzzled as Donna.

" *'He used to love me when I was little. I can remember how he used to carry me around on his shoulders and tell everybody that I was his baby. But then I started to grow up, and he didn't like that. He used to buy me these awful dresses with ruffles and lace. Mom and I even laughed about how he wanted to keep me a little girl forever.' "*

"That's weird, huh?" Donna looked over at Paul.

Paul shrugged. "Not really. Lots of fathers don't want their little girls to grow up. Remember how Dad pitched a fit when you bought your first bikini?"

"Yeah, but Dad was just old-fashioned. Mr. Hudson sounds like he had some kind of a hang-up. Listen to this."

" *'He hated it when I started dating. He kept saying that I was too young. Mom had to practically get down on her knees and beg so he'd let me go to that first school dance with you. And I had to be home at ten-thirty. He waited right there at the door for me, remember?' "*

Paul nodded. "It's true. We had to leave before the dance was over so I could take her home. And Mr. Hudson was right there, checking his watch when I drove up. He was really strict."

" *'I'm sorry I dumped you, Paul. But really, it was for your own good. I know you loved me. I loved you, too. But your family's here, and you love Crest Ridge. You would have been miserable if I'd asked you to marry me and leave here forever. I didn't want to force you to make that choice. Maybe I was afraid you wouldn't choose me.' "*

Donna turned to Paul. "What if she'd asked you? Do you think you would have run away with her?"

"I don't know." Paul sighed deeply. "I loved her, but . . . I just don't know."

" *'Ross is my ticket out of here forever. And the funny thing is, Dad is the one who gave me the idea. He heard me tell Mom that I thought Ross was cute, and he hit the roof. He told me to stay away, that Ross wasn't right for me and I shouldn't even consider going out with him. He was so serious about it, I started to get interested. You know how contrary I can be. And the more I learned about Ross, the more I realized that he was perfect.' "*

"Oh, boy!" Donna sighed. "I never realized she hated Crest Ridge that much."

"I did. She could hardly wait to graduate and move out. We argued about it a lot. She wanted to leave for good, and I wanted to come back here after I finished college."

" *'I totally freaked when you gave me those skis. I'd already decided to pick up on Ross, and I knew I didn't deserve a wonderful present like that. That's why I never took them out of the box. I wanted to give them back, but you would have asked all sort of questions. And I didn't want anyone to know what I was planning. Take them back, Paul. Maybe you can get a refund. And find someone else to love. I was never right for you. You deserve someone better, and I hope you find her.'* "

"I think she really loved you." Donna looked up at Paul in surprise.

"Maybe she did." Paul looked grim. "Read the rest. I have to know about the stalker."

" *'I didn't know the truth about the stalker until tonight. I was just getting ready to leave when Dad caught me. I'd told him I was going to a group meeting in Denver and staying overnight with one of the group. I never dreamed he'd call the shrink and find out we didn't have a meeting scheduled for tonight.'* "

"Oh-oh!" Donna winced. "He checked up on her."

Paul nodded. "He always did. A couple of times, when I took her to the movies, he called the theater to see if we were there. Go ahead, Donna. Keep reading."

" *'Dad was really mad that I'd lied to him. And he demanded to know where I was going. So I told him. I guess I just wanted to see the expression on his face when he found out that I was marrying Ross. I told him I was pregnant, too, so he wouldn't try to stop me.'* "

Paul winced. "Go on, Donna."

" *'He really tried to talk me out of it. He even made up this incredible story about Ross being my brother, and how the baby would turn out deformed! I guess that shows you how desperate he was.'* "

Donna blinked and looked down at the letter again. "I remember something I heard when I was just a little kid. Mom said she felt sorry for Mrs. Hudson because her husband was having an affair."

"I heard some rumors, too. And they were about Ross's mother. Go on, Donna."

"*'Then Dad said something that totally freaked me. He called me a wicked girl and said he'd have to punish me! That was when I realized that he was the stalker. Those were the exact words the stalker used when he called me at the switchboard!'*"

"Oh, my God!" Donna gasped. "Do you think it's true?"

"I don't know. Does she say any more?"

Donna nodded, and began to read again. "*'I ran for the kitchen as fast as I could. Mrs. Robinson was cooking, and I sat down at the table and wrote this note to you. I just got up to look out the window, and he's gone. I'm going to run for it now. I'll drop this off in our usual place, pick up some stuff I need at the drugstore, and then I'll leave Crest Ridge for good. Goodbye, Paul. I'll always love you.'*"

Paul's face was as white as a sheet as he jumped off the bed. "Call Julie! Right away!"

"But . . . why?"

"Because Julie told me she was getting the same kinds of calls! And I didn't believe her! Hurry up, Donna!"

Donna leaped up from the bed and ran for the phone. Paul was right behind her. Her fingers were shaking as she dialed the lodge.

"What is it?" Paul reacted to the alarmed expression on his sister's face.

"The line's out. It's not ringing or anything. And she said she'd call me this afternoon."

The red light was flashing on the answering machine, and Paul pressed the button to play the message. It was Julie's voice, telling them about the convention, and asking them to help with guests who were arriving tonight.

Donna frowned. "But there's no convention in Denver. I read

the paper this morning, and it didn't say anything about any convention."

Their faces were tense as they waited for the second message. It was Julie again, asking them to meet her at the lodge as soon as possible. She was there alone, and Aunt Caroline and Ross had already left for the airport.

"You get Sheriff Nelson!" Paul fairly shoved Donna out the door.

"But where are you going?"

"To the lodge. If Mr. Hudson faked the whole thing to get Julie alone, she could be in terrible danger!"

Seventeen

J ulie bit back a scream as she heard the door to their private quarters bang open. He was here! But did he know that she had locked herself in her room? She had to be very quiet and hope he hadn't heard her.

But her hopes vanished abruptly when she heard his heavy footsteps coming down the hall to her room. They stopped, and his horrible, whispery voice seeped in through the crack at the bottom of the door. *"I've got you now, Vicki. Daddy knows where his wicked little girl is hiding. I heard you up here in your room."*

His breathing was labored. He'd climbed the stairs. The elevator wouldn't work, now that the power was out. Julie held her breath and said a quick prayer for someone—anyone—to come. She knew exactly how a trapped animal must feel as she crouched by her bed and watched the doorknob turn.

"You can't keep me out, you know." Uncle Bob gave a chilling laugh. *"Come to Daddy and take your punishment like a good, brave girl."*

There was a snap as the metal lock sheered off and the doorknob began to turn. Julie stared at it in terrible fascination. He'd broken the lock with his bare hand! But the heavy dresser was in front of the door. He'd have to move it before he could get her!

And then the dresser began to slide back, slowly, but steadily, as he put his shoulder to the door. One inch, two inches. Julie didn't wait any longer. There was only one way out of her room, and she had to take it. She raced for the balcony doors and opened the locks.

A gust of wind howled around her as she stepped out onto the balcony. But Julie was too terrified to feel the sharp ice crystals that pelted against her skin. The fire escape was only a foot from her balcony, but it seemed like much farther as she reached out and grabbed it, pulling herself onto the slippery metal stairs.

She was wearing tennis shoes, a bad choice, since the metal steps were crusted with ice. But there wasn't time to think about that now. Julie grabbed the cold metal railing and hurried down the fire escape, slipping and sliding until she got to the third floor. Frantically she tugged on the window, but it was locked tightly. And the window on the second floor was locked, too. The fire escape ended at the second floor landing, with a metal ladder that was designed to slide down the rest of the way. Julie tugged on the ladder, trying to make it slide down to the ground. But it was stuck tight, covered with a solid sheet of ice.

She glanced down and shuddered. The sidewalk that ran around the lodge had been swept clean by the biting wind. There were no soft piles of snow below, only an expanse of rock-hard concrete. No, she couldn't jump down and risk breaking her leg. She had to climb up the fire escape again, past her window to the fifth floor. There was no other choice.

Julie almost fell as she climbed past the third-floor window. She could hear the dresser screeching against her floor, and she knew Uncle Bob was struggling to push it out of the way. Still, she didn't hesitate as she rushed up the steps that led past her window. All she could do was pray that the dresser would keep him out until she could get past.

She glanced in her window as she rushed by, and gasped in fright. The dresser was moving back and Uncle Bob was trying to squeeze through the opening. He was coming in!

Julie almost flew up the steps to the fifth floor. Her fingers were numb with the freezing cold, but she tugged on the win-

dow as hard as she could. It opened! An inch! And then it refused to go any further. There was only one place left to go. The
roof!

As Julie stepped onto the snowy expanse of the roof, she
heard heavy footsteps clanging against the metal steps of the fire
escape. But they were going down! If Uncle Bob thought she'd
jumped down from the fire escape, she'd be safe!

Quickly Julie crossed the steeply slanted roof and huddled
behind the huge chimney. The bricks were slightly warm and
she pressed her chilled body against them. Her terrified mind
was chanting a litany of hope: *Please think I jumped down . . .
Please think I jumped down . . . Please, please, please think I
jumped down!*

But she hadn't fooled him! The heavy footsteps clanged upward again. She could hear them, louder and louder as he
climbed up the metal steps of the fire escape.

The wind was blowing harder now, whipping up sheets of
snow to send them sweeping across the expanse of the roof.
Would it erase her footsteps in time? Julie felt her hopes rise as
the clanking footsteps stopped at the fifth floor. She'd left the
window slightly open. He might think she'd climbed in and
pulled it down from the inside. *Please think I climbed in . . .
Please think I climbed in . . . Please, please, please think I
climbed in!*

But no. He was coming up to the roof! And she was trapped
behind the chimney. There was no other place to hide!

What would he do? Julie's horrified mind ran through the
possibilities. Would he stab her with the chef's knife she'd left in
the lobby? Or shoot her with one of the guns he used for hunting? Or would he shove her down the steeply slanted roof and
roll her over the edge? She thought about that frightening five-
story drop and her heart beat hard in terror. Somehow she had to
stall him, and keep hoping that someone would come to help her!

"You've been a bad girl, Vicki!" His voice was loud now, an
enraged roar that she could hear over the screeching howl of the
wind "Come out and take your punishment!"

Julie huddled against the bricks. Just a few more seconds and he would find her. What could she say to stall him? Then she remembered the picture she'd seen in the family scrapbook of Uncle Bob holding Vicki when she was a little girl. He'd been smiling down at her, proud that she was his beautiful daughter, and there had been a clear expression of love in his eyes. She had to make him remember that love. It might save her life.

She could hear his labored breathing as he climbed up the steep incline of the roof. He was almost here! It wouldn't do any good to tell him she wasn't Vicki. He was insane, and he wouldn't listen to reason. She'd be Vicki for him, a younger Vicki, the Vicki he'd loved.

Julie took a deep breath, and prayed that her plan would work. And then she called out to him in a tiny, quavering voice. "Daddy? I'm scared, Daddy. Please come and get me."

The footsteps stopped, and there was absolute silence. Even the wind stopped blowing for a moment. And when he spoke again, his voice was softer.

"Vicki? Where are you, baby?"

"I'm here. I'm sorry, Daddy. I've been a bad girl and I'll never climb up here again. Take me down, Daddy? I'm tired and I want you to tell me a story."

He laughed and Julie held her breath. It wasn't a frightening laugh. It was an amused chuckle, the sort of laugh you'd use if your favorite child had done something charming and a little bit foolish. "Which story do you want, baby?"

"I want my favorite. You know the one, Daddy. You tell that one so good."

"Cinderella?"

"Yes, Daddy. Please tell me Cinderella. Please?"

Julie held her breath. Had it worked? Then she breathed a sigh of relief as he started to tell the story. She could hear his voice plainly. He was standing on the other side of the chimney, so close he could take one step and grab her, but he was caught up in the fantasy, immersed in the memory of a happier time . . . for now. But what would he do when he finished the story? Would he decide to kill her then?

*   *   *

Paul skidded to a stop in the driveway and hurtled out of his car. The lodge loomed up in front of him, dark and deserted. Were they in there? Was he too late? But then he heard voices on the roof, snatches of conversation between the howls of the wind. A small voice was asking a question, and Mr. Hudson was answering. She was keeping him busy, talking. That was good. It would give him time to get up to the roof and save her.

As Paul raced to the door, he caught one phrase, something about a glass slipper. And then it struck him. Vicki had been right. Mr. Hudson was truly insane. He was telling Julie the story of Cinderella!

The front door was locked, and Paul hurried around the side of the lodge. His mind was focused on one thought. *That's right, Julie . . . keep him talking. Just keep him talking until I can get there.* But the side door was locked, too. And the kitchen door. Paul raced for the big ladder that was kept by the side of the building and propped it up against the fire escape. Then he climbed quickly, hoping the old wooden rungs would hold until he could step out on the metal stairs.

As he climbed up the rickety ladder, Paul wished he'd listened more closely when his mother had read fairy tales to Donna. Was the glass slipper near the end of the story? Then he was on the metal stairs, and he caught another phrase as he raced upward. The wicked stepmother had locked Cinderella up and one of the ugly stepsisters was trying to shove her foot into the glass slipper. If he remembered right, the story was almost over. He had to hurry!

"And there was a big royal wedding. The prince married . . . married . . ." Uncle Bob's voice faltered. And then he let out a howl of anger. "You tricked me, Vicki! You're not a little girl anymore. You're a wicked woman, and I have to stop you before it's too late!"

"No, Daddy. I'm not wicked." Julie felt her heart thud against her ribs. "I'm just a little girl, and you're telling me all about Cinderella."

For a moment she thought her ploy had worked. And then he

grabbed her. His face was twisted into a snarl of rage, and his voice was loud in her ear.

"I killed you once, and now I have to kill you again! You can't marry your brother and have his child! I won't let you!"

Julie's mouth opened, but she was too terrified to scream. All she could do was stare at him in open-mouthed horror. And then he smiled, a smile that made her blood run cold, because it was so full of love, and kindness, and total insanity.

"I love you, baby. And that's why I have to kill you. You're an abomination, don't you see? I gave you life, and now I'm going to take it away. It's only right."

"But . . . but . . . I don't understand!"

"Ross is your brother." Uncle Bob explained in a patient voice. "I told you all that. And I fixed your car so you couldn't drive down the mountain. But you didn't listen, did you, Vicki? You tried to run off with him anyway. I didn't mean to kill you, darling. I just wanted to keep you here, where I could watch over you. And now it's starting all over again!"

"Wh . . . what do you mean?" Julie gazed up at him in stark terror.

"I saw you coming out of his room. You're devious, Vicki. Devious and wicked. You're going to trap him into running off with you again. But I won't let you do it. I stopped you last time, and I'll stop you this time, too."

"I promise I won't run off with Ross." Julie's voice was shaking. "Really, I won't. Just let me go, and I'll be good."

"Lies. All lies." Uncle Bob sighed deeply as he looked down at her. "And you're not alone, Vicki darling. I know that now. I lied, too. I lied to your mother when I told her I wasn't seeing Ross's mother. And I lied about why you died. My whole life has been a deception, just like yours. It's bad seed, Vicki. You inherited the evil from me. And now we both have to die!"

"No!" Julie put up a valiant struggle, but Uncle Bob was just too strong. He pried her away from the chimney, and started to drag her across the roof. She kicked out at him, scratched him with her nails, pounded his heavy back with her fists, but she was no match for his demented strength.

Then there was a loud shout, and Julie looked up to see Paul standing in their path. Paul had come to save her! He looked solid, and strong, and very determined.

"Stop, Mr. Hudson! She's not Vicki! She's Julie!"

Julie felt her uncle's grip slacken for an instant, and she took full advantage of that momentary lapse. She kicked out hard and managed to free herself, scrambling away through the snow to Paul.

"Stay back!" Paul pushed her to the side. Then he stood there, watching, waiting, anticipating Mr. Hudson's next move.

The move came much quicker than Julie had thought it would. For a big man, Uncle Bob moved with lightning speed. He let out a terrible yell and charged through the snow toward Paul, his arms sweeping wide to knock him off the edge of the roof.

Julie watched with horror as Paul stood frozen in place. He had to get out of the way! But then, at the last instant, Paul sidestepped quickly, throwing Uncle Bob off balance.

Julie screamed then, a high, thin sound of terror, as Uncle Bob hurtled toward the edge of the roof, slipping and sliding, trying to regain his balance. But he was going too fast to stop, and the downward slope was steep. He let out a terrible howl, full of insane rage. And then he was gone, disappearing over the side of the roof with horrible finality.

"Oh, my God!" Julie's knees sagged, and she was about to sink down in the snow, when Paul caught her in his strong arms.

"Are you all right?"

"I . . . I think so." Julie's eyes were wide with horror. "Is he . . . dead?"

Paul's arms tightened around her and he cradled her against his chest. "He's dead. There's no way he can hurt you now."

"Oh, Paul! Thank God you came! Uncle Bob was the stalker! And he killed Vicki!"

"I know, Julie. I know."

They stood in the blowing snow, huddled in a tight embrace, until they heard Sheriff Nelson's siren. Then Julie turned to Paul with tears in her eyes. "He was crazy, you know. He didn't mean to kill her. He just wanted to keep her here so she couldn't marry Ross."

Paul nodded, and led her toward the fire escape. There would be questions to answer, explanations to give. But just before they started down the metal stairs, Julie turned to Paul and kissed him. He'd saved her life, and she wanted to tell him how grateful she was. She also wanted to tell him that she was beginning to fall in love with him. But this wasn't the time. Or the place.

"Paul?"

"Yes, Julie."

"Will you take me to one of your football games?"

"Uh . . . sure. I'd like that, Julie. But what made you think of football now?"

Paul was looking at her as if the strain had unhinged her a mind, and Julie actually managed a shaky smile. "I saw how you sidestepped when Uncle Bob tried to tackle you. And I think you're my favorite quarterback in the whole world!"

Epilogue

Ross pulled the Saddlepeak Lodge van into a parking place in front of the small community hospital, and turned to look at his passengers. "Are you ready to go in?"

"I'm ready." Julie smiled at him. A week had passed and Aunt Caroline was ready to come home from the hospital. She'd collapsed when she'd learned the truth about Uncle Bob, but now she was fully recovered.

Julie opened her door and got out of the van. Donna was right behind her. Then Paul got out and motioned to Ross. "Come on. You're coming in, aren't you?"

Ross looked worried. "I think I'll just wait here."

"Oh, no, you don't!" Julie opened the driver's door and grabbed his arm. "Aunt Caroline specifically asked for you."

As they went through the door and walked down the hall, Julie thought about how they'd all pulled together the night of Uncle Bob's horrible death. Since Aunt Caroline had been taken to the hospital, Paul and Donna had wanted Julie to spend the night at their house. Julie had refused. It wasn't right to leave Ross at the lodge alone. Donna had called her mother and they'd all stayed the night at the lodge, sitting in the lobby until long past midnight, sipping hot chocolate and talking about what had happened.

It had been a night for confessions. Ross had told them he'd had no idea that Uncle Bob was his real father. His mother had always talked about the handsome soldier who'd died in 'Nam, and she'd insisted that Uncle Bob was just a former employer and a family friend.

Paul had read them the letter that Vicki had left in the guest house for him, and Ross had been very relieved to learn that it was all a trap. Vicki hadn't been pregnant, and she hadn't chosen to commit suicide rather than marry him. Vicki had been desperate, and she'd tried to use him as a way to escape the stalker.

Then it had been Julie and Donna's turn. They'd told Ross and Paul about the videotaped diary, and Vicki's fascination with men whose names started with the letter R. That had cleared up a mystery for Paul. He'd always wondered why Vicki had called him Rock.

Now that they knew that Uncle Bob had been the stalker, the peepholes made sense. Uncle Bob had drilled them in the attic floor to spy on Vicki and Ross. Even the disembodied face at Julie's balcony window was explainable, now that they knew about Uncle Bob's obsession. The face had belonged to Uncle Bob. Julie hadn't been able to see the rest of his body, because he'd been leaning down from the fire escape to peer in her window. If Ross and Aunt Caroline had thought to look up at the fire escape, instead of down, they would have seen the footsteps he'd left when he'd climbed back up to the fifth story attic.

The only things they hadn't been able to explain were Julie's nightmares, the terrifying dreams where she'd *been* Vicki, and taken her place in the car. There were only two possible solutions. Either Vicki had really reached out from the grave to warn her about Uncle Bob, or the nightmares had been the product of Julie's own overactive imagination. It really didn't matter, now that Uncle Bob was dead. If Vicki's spirit had been restless, it was now at peace. And if Julie's own imagination had been prompting the nightmares, she couldn't possibly imagine anything more horrible than what had actually happened.

They'd all agreed on one thing, and Julie was glad. They would keep Vicki's secrets, and not tell anyone what had actually happened. Vicki had done some terribly selfish things, but she hadn't really meant to hurt anyone.

As they approached Aunt Caroline's room, Julie took Ross's arm. She could tell he was very nervous. He wasn't sure how Aunt Caroline would react to him, now that she knew he was Uncle Bob's son.

"Hey . . . it'll be okay." Donna came up to slip an arm around Ross's waist. They'd been spending a lot of time together in the past few days, and Julie couldn't help hoping that they'd start dating. Ross was such a hard worker, he'd never learned how to relax and have fun. If anyone could teach him to loosen up and be a little less serious, it was Donna.

They found Aunt Caroline ready to go, dressed in a beautiful powder-blue suit. She looked strong and healthy, totally unlike the pale, confused woman who'd been taken to the hospital on a stretcher.

Julie rushed over to hug her aunt. And so did Donna. And even Paul. But Ross stood in the doorway, looking very out of place.

"Aren't you going to hug me, Ross?" Aunt Caroline held out her arms.

"Sure. But I didn't think you'd want me to . . . I mean, after what happened and all."

"Come here, Ross." Aunt Caroline patted the spot next to her on the bed, and Ross sat down. Then she slipped her arm around his shoulders and smiled at him. "I'm only going to say this once, and then I don't want to hear another word about it. We've all had a terrible shock, but it's over. Bob killed Vicki, and that was the act of an insane man. And his insanity almost cost Julie her life. When they did the autopsy, they found a brain tumor that had been growing slowly for years. That explains the horrible things he did. Bob's disease drove him mad."

Julie nodded. What Aunt Caroline said made sense. "If they'd found the tumor earlier, could they . . ."

"No." Aunt Caroline interrupted her. "It was inoperable,

honey. And that's one of the reasons I asked you to bring Ross here today. I wanted him to know that his father wasn't a bad man."

Ross nodded. Then he took a deep breath and let it out. "I didn't know that he was my father, Mrs. Hudson. My mother never told me."

"Of course you didn't know. I didn't know, either. But now we do, and I'm glad you're here with me. I lost Bob's only daughter, but I still have his son. I hope you'll stay, Ross. It'll make me very happy if you're here to help me run Saddlepeak Lodge."

Tears came to Ross's eyes, and he blinked them back. "You really want me to?"

"I certainly do. Vicki had a college fund, and I'd like you to have it. You can commute if you like, or you can live on the campus in Denver. Either way is fine with me. But when you graduate, I want you to come back as the manager of Saddle-peak Lodge."

They all saw the expression of delight that crossed Ross's face. He'd told Julie that he loved Saddlepeak Lodge. He'd been there for almost five years, and it had become his home.

Ross reached out to hug Aunt Caroline. "I'll stay at the lodge, and I'll commute to Denver. Donna's going there in the fall, and we can car-pool. Thank you, Mrs. Hudson."

"Caro." Aunt Caroline smiled at him. "You really have to stop being so formal, now that you're my stepson."

Julie felt tears of happiness fill her eyes, and she blinked them back. It was a touching scene. And then Paul slipped his arm around her shoulders, and she looked up to see that he was blinking back tears, too.

Aunt Caroline stood up, and Ross took her arm. Then she smiled at all of them. "I think we should have a little celebration tonight. This is a new beginning for all of us."

Donna took Aunt Caroline's other arm, and they all began to walk out to the van. The day was perfect for a homecoming. The sky was a brilliant blue and the sun was shining brightly, reflecting off the banks of glittering white snow. Julie took a deep breath of the clear, chilled air and smiled.

"Julie?" Paul pulled her back, as Donna and Ross helped Aunt Caroline into the car. "Is it a new beginning for us, too?"

Julie knew what Paul was asking. Could she forget that he'd been involved with Vicki? Was she willing to put all this grief and trouble behind her, and make a fresh start?

Paul looked a little nervous as he waited for her answer, and Julie could tell that he really cared about her. She cared about him, too.

Julie smiled even wider as she reached out to shake his hand. "I'm Julie Forrester, and I'm very glad to meet you, Paul. I have the feeling we're going to be very, very good friends."

WHERE INNOCENCE DIES . . .

Expectant parents Karen and Mike Houston are excited about restoring their old rambling Victorian mansion to its former glory. With its endless maze of rooms, hallways, and hiding places, it's a wonderful place for their nine-year-old daughter Leslie to play and explore. Unfortunately, they didn't listen to the stories about the house's dark history. They didn't believe the rumors about the evil that lived there.

. . . THE NIGHTMARE BEGINS.

It begins with a whisper. A child's voice beckoning from the rose garden. Crying out in the night. It lures little Leslie to a crumbling storm door. Down a flight of broken stairs. It calls to their unborn child. It wants something from each of them. Something in their very hearts and souls. Tonight, the house will reveal its secret. *Tonight, the other child will come out to play . . .*

**Please turn the page for an exciting sneak peek of Joanne Fluke's
THE OTHER CHILD
coming in August 2014!**

Prologue

The train was rolling across the Arizona desert when it started, a pain so intense it made her double over in the dusty red velvet seat. Dorthea gasped aloud as the spasm tore through her and several passengers leaned close.

"Just a touch of indigestion." She smiled apologetically. "Really, I'm fine now."

Drawing a deep steadying breath, she folded her hands protectively over her rounded stomach and turned to stare out at the unbroken miles of sand and cactus. The pain would disappear if she just sat quietly and thought pleasant thoughts. She had been on the train for days now and the constant swaying motion was making her ill.

Thank goodness she was almost to California. Dorthea sighed gratefully. The moment she arrived she would get her old job back, and then she would send for Christopher. They could find a home together, she and Christopher and the new baby.

She never should have gone back. Dorthea pressed her forehead against the cool glass of the window and blinked back bitter tears. The people in Cold Spring were hateful. They had called Christopher a bastard. They had ridiculed her when Mother's will was made public. They knew that her mother had never forgiven her and they were glad. The righteous, upstanding citizens of her old hometown were the same cruel gossips they'd been ten years ago.

If only she had gotten there before Mother died! Dorthea was certain that those horrid people in Cold Spring had poisoned her mother's mind against her and she hated them for it. Her dream of being welcomed home to her beautiful house was shattered. Now she was completely alone in the world. Poor Christopher was abandoned back there until she could afford to send him the money for a train ticket.

Dorthea moaned as the pain tore through her again. She braced her body against the lurching of the train and clumsily made her way up the aisle, carefully avoiding the stares of the other passengers. There it started and she slumped to the floor. A pool of blood was gathering beneath her and she pressed her hand tightly against the pain.

Numbness crept up her legs and she was cold, as cold as she'd been in the winter in Cold Spring. Her eyelids fluttered and her lips moved in silent protest. Christopher! He was alone in Cold Spring, in a town full of spiteful, meddling strangers. Dear God, what would they do to Christopher?

"No! She's not dead!" He stood facing them, one small boy against the circle of adults. "It's a lie! You're telling lies about her, just like you did before!"

His voice broke in a sob and he whirled to run out the door of the parsonage. His mother wasn't dead. She couldn't be dead! She had promised to come back for him just as soon as she made some money.

"Lies. Dirty lies." The wind whipped away his words as he raced through the vacant lot and around the corner. The neighbors had told lies before about his mother, lies his grandmother had believed. They were all liars in Cold Spring, just as his mother had said.

There it was in front of him now, huge and solid against the gray sky. Christopher stopped at the gate, panting heavily. Appleton Mansion, the home that should have been his. Their lies had cost him his family, his inheritance, and he'd get even with all of them somehow.

They were shouting his name now, calling for him to come back. Christopher slipped between the posts of the wrought-iron fence and ran into the overgrown yard. They wanted to tell him more lies, to confuse him the way they had confused Grandmother Appleton, but he wouldn't listen. He'd hide until it was dark and then he'd run away to California where his mother was waiting for him.

The small boy gave a sob of relief when he saw an open door-way. It was perfect. He'd hide in his grandmother's root cellar and they'd never find him. Then, when it was dark, he'd run away.

Without a backward glance Christopher hurtled through the opening, seeking the safety of the darkness below. He gave a shrill cry as his foot missed the steeply slanted step and then he was falling, arms flailing helplessly at the air as he pitched forward into the deep, damp blackness.

Wade Comstock stood still, letting the leaves skitter and pile in colored mounds around his feet, smiling as he looked up at the shuttered house. His wife, Verna, had been right, the Appleton Mansion had gone dirt cheap. He still couldn't understand how modern people at the turn of the century could take stock in silly ghost stories. He certainly didn't believe for one minute that Amelia Appleton was back from the dead, haunting the Appleton house. But then again, he had been the only one ever to venture a bid on the old place. Amelia's daughter Dorthea had left town right after her mother's will was read, cut off without a dime——and it served her right. Now the estate was his, the first acquisition of the Comstock Realty Company.

His thin lips tightened into a straight line as he thought of Dorthea. The good people of Cold Spring hadn't been fooled one bit by her tears at her mother's funeral. She was after the property, pure and simple. Bringing her bastard son here was bad enough, but you'd think a woman in her condition would have sense enough to stay away. And then she had run off, leaving the boy behind. He could make a bet that Dorthea was never planning to send for Christopher. Women like her didn't want kids in the way.

Wade kicked out at the piles of leaves and walked around his new property. As he turned the corner of the house, the open root cellar caught his eye and he reached in his pocket for the padlock and key he'd found hanging in the tool shed. That old cellar should be locked up before somebody got hurt down there. He'd tell the gardener to leave the bushes in that area and it would be overgrown in no time at all.

For a moment Wade stood and stared at the opening. He supposed he should go down there, but it was already too dark to be able to see his way around. Something about the place made him uneasy. There was no real reason to be afraid, but his heart beat faster and an icy sweat broke out on his forehead as he thought about climbing down into that small dark hole.

The day was turning to night as he hurriedly hefted the weather-beaten door and slammed it shut. The door was warped but it still fit. The hasp was in workable order and with a little effort he lined up the two pieces and secured them with the padlock. Then he jammed the key into his pocket and took a shortcut through the rose garden to the front yard.

Wade didn't notice the key was missing from his pocket until he was out on the sidewalk. He looked back at the overcast sky. There was no point in going back to try to find it in the dark. Actually he could do without the key. No one needed a root cellar anymore. It could stay locked up till kingdom come.

As he stood watching, shadows played over the windows of the stately house and crept up the crushed granite driveway. The air was still now, so humid it almost choked him. He could hear thunder rumbling in the distance. Then there was another noise—a thin hollow cry that set the hair on the back of his arms prickling. He listened intently, bent forward slightly, and balanced on the balls of his feet, but there was only the thunder. It was going to rain again and Wade felt a strange uneasiness. Once more he looked back, drawn to the house . . . as though something had been left unfinished. He had a vague sense of foreboding. The house looked almost menacing.

"Poppycock!" he muttered, and turned away, pulling out his watch. He'd have to hurry to get home in time for supper. Verna liked her meals punctual.

He started to walk, turning back every now and then to glance at the shadow of the house looming between the tall trees. Even though he knew those stories were a whole lot of foolishness, he felt a little spooked himself. The brick mansion did look eerie against the blackening sky.

"*Mama!*" He awoke with a scream on his lips, a half-choked cry of pure terror. It was dark and cold and inky black. Where was he? The air was damp, like a grave. He squeezed his eyes shut tightly and screamed again.

"*Mama!*" He would hear her footsteps coming any minute to wake him from this awful nightmare. She'd turn on the light and hug him and tell him not to be afraid. If he just waited, she'd come. She always came when he had nightmares.

No footsteps, no light, no sound except his own hoarse breathing. Christopher reached out cautiously and felt damp earth around him. This was no dream. Where was he?

There was a big lump on his head and it hurt. He must have fallen . . . yes, that was it.

He let his breath out in a shuddering sigh as he remembered. He was in his Grandmother Appleton's root cellar. He'd fallen down the steps trying to hide from the people who told him lies about his mama. And tonight he was going to run away and find her in California. She'd be so proud of him when he told her he hadn't believed their lies. She'd hug him and kiss him and promise she'd never have to go away again.

Perhaps it was night now. Christopher forced himself to open his eyes. He opened them wide but he couldn't see anything, not even the white shirt he was wearing. It must be night and that meant it was time for him to go.

Christopher sat up with a groan. It was so dark he couldn't see the staircase. He knew he'd have to crawl around and feel for the steps, but it took a real effort to reach out into the blackness. He wasn't usually afraid of the dark. At least he wasn't afraid of the dark when there was a lamppost or a moon or something. This kind of darkness was different. It made his mouth dry and he held his breath as he forced himself to reach out into the inky depths.

There. He gave a grateful sigh as he crawled up the first step of the stairs. He didn't want to lose his balance and fall back down again.

Four . . . five . . . six . . . he was partway up when he heard a stealthy rustling noise from below. Fear pushed him forward in a rush, his knees scraping against the old slivery wood in a scramble to get to the top.

He let out a terrified yell as his head hit something hard. The cover—somebody had closed up the root cellar!

He couldn't think; he was too scared. Blind panic made him scream and pound, beating his fists against the wooden door until his knuckles were swollen and raw. Somehow he had to lift door.

With a mighty effort Christopher heaved his body upward, straining against the solid piece of wood. The door gave a slight, sickening lurch, creaking and lifting just enough for him to hear the sound of metal grating against metal.

At first the sound lay at the back of his mind like a giant pendulum of horror, surging slowly forward until it reached the active part of his brain. The Cold Spring people had locked him in.

The thought was so terrifying he lost his breath and slumped into a huddled ball on the step. In the darkness he could see flashed of red and bright gold beneath his eyelids. He had to get out somehow! *He had to!*

"*Help!*" the sound tore through his lips and bounced off the earthen walls, giving a hollow, muted echo. He screamed until his voice was a weak whisper but no one came. Then his voice was gone and he could hear it again, the ominous rustling from the depths of the cellar, growing louder with each passing heartbeat.

God, no! This nightmare was really happening! He recognized the scuffling noise now and shivered with terror. Rats. They were sniffing at the air, searching for him, and there was nowhere to hide. They'd find him even here at the top of the stairs and they would come in a rush, darting hurtling balls of fur and needle teeth . . . the pain of flesh being torn from his body . . . the agony of being eaten alive!

He opened his throat in a tortured scream, a shrill hoarse cry that circled the earthen room then faded to a deadly silence. There was a roaring in his ears and terror rose to choke him, squeezing and strangling him with clutching fingers.

"Mama! Please, Mama!" he cried again, and then suddenly he was pitching forward, rolling and bumping to the black pit below. He gasped as an old shovel bit deeply into his neck and a warm stickiness gushed out to cover his face. There was a moment of vivid consciousness before death claimed him and in that final moment, one emotion blazed its way through his whole being. Hatred. He hated all of them. They had driven his mother away. They had stolen his inheritance. They had locked him in here and left him to die. He would punish them . . . make them suffer as his mother had suffered . . . as he was suffering.

One

The interior of the truck was dusty and Mike opened the wing window all the way, shifting on the slick plastic-covered seat, Karen had wanted to take an afternoon drive through the country and here they were over fifty miles from Minneapolis, on a bumpy country road. It wasn't Mike's idea of a great way to spend a Sunday. He'd rather be home watching the Expos and the Phillies from the couch in their air-conditioned Lake Street apartment.

Mike glanced uneasily at Karen as he thought about today's game. He had a bundle riding on this one and it was a damn good thing Karen didn't know about it. She'd been curious about his interest in baseball lately but he'd told her he got a kick out of watching the teams knock themselves out for the pennant. The explanation seemed to satisfy her.

Karen was death on two of his pet vices, drinking and gambling, and he'd agreed to reform three years ago when they were married. Way back then he'd made all the required promises. Lay off the booze. No more Saturday-night poker games. No betting on the horses. No quick trips to Vegas. No office pools, even. The idea of a sportsbook hadn't occurred to her yet and he was hoping it wouldn't now. Naturally Mike didn't make a habit of keeping secrets from his wife but in this case he'd chosen the lesser of two evils. He knew Karen would hit the roof if he told her he hadn't gotten that hundred-dollar-a-month bonus after all, that the extra money came from his gambling winnings on the games. It was just lucky that he took care of all the finances. What Karen didn't know wouldn't hurt her.

"Cold Spring, one mile." Leslie was reading the road signs again in her clear high voice. "Oh, look Mike! A church with a white steeple and all those trees. Can't we just drive past before we go home?"

Mike had been up most of the night developing prints for his spread in *Homes* magazine and he wasn't in the mood for extensive sightseeing. He was going to refuse, but then he caught sight of his stepdaughter's pleading face in the rearview mirror. Another little side trip wouldn't kill him. He'd been too busy lately to spend much time at home and these Sunday drives were a family tradition.

"Oh, let's, Mike." Karen's voice was wistful. Mike could tell by her tone that she'd been feeling a little neglected lately, too. Maybe it had been a mistake insisting she quit her job at the interior decorating firm. Mike was old-fashioned sometimes, and he maintained that a mother's place was at home with her children. When he had discovered that Karen was pregnant he'd put his foot down insisting she stay home. Karen had agreed, but still she missed her job. He told himself that she'd be busy enough when the baby was born, but that didn't solve the problem right now.

Mike slowed the truck, looking for a turnoff. A little sightseeing might be fun. Karen and Leslie would certainly enjoy it and his being home to watch the game wouldn't change the outcome any.

"All right, you two win." Mike smiled at his wife and turned left at the arrowed sign. "Just a quick run through town and then we have to get back. I still have to finish the penthouse prints and start work on that feature."

Leslie gave Mike a quick kiss and settled down again in the back seat of their Land-Rover. When she was sitting down on the seat, Mike could barely see the top of her blond head over the stacks of film boxes and camera cases. She was a small child for nine, fair-haired and delicate like the little porcelain shepherdesses his mother used to collect. She was an exquisite child, a classic Scandinavian beauty. Mike was accustomed to being approached by people who wanted to use Leslie as a model. Karen claimed she didn't want Leslie to become self-conscious, but Mike noticed how she enjoyed dressing Leslie in the height of fashion. Much of Karen's salary had gone into designer jeans, Gucci loafers, and Pierre Cardin sweaters for her daughter. Leslie always had the best in clothes and she wore them beautifully, taking meticulous care of her wardrobe. Even in play clothes she always looked every inch a lady.

Karen possessed a different kind of beauty. Hers was the active, tennis-pro look. She had long, dark hair and a lithe, athletic body. People had trouble believing that she and Leslie were mother and daughter. They looked and acted completely different. Leslie preferred to curl up in a fluffy blanket and read, while Karen was relentlessly active. She was a fresh-air-and-exercise fanatic. For the last six years Karen had jogged around Lake Harriet every morning, dragging Leslie with her. That was how they'd met, the three of them.

Mike had been coming home from an all-night party, camera slung over his shoulder, when he spotted them. He was always on the lookout for a photogenic subject and he'd stopped to take a few pictures of the lovely black-haired runner and her towheaded child. It had seemed only natural to ask for Karen's address and a day later he was knocking at her door with some sample prints in one hand and a stuffed toy for Leslie in the other. The three of them had formed an instant bond.

Leslie had been fascinated by the man in her mother's life. She was five then, and fatherless. Karen always said Leslie was the image of her father—a handsome Swedish exchange student with whom Karen had enjoyed a brief affair before he'd gone back to his native country.

They made an unlikely trio, and Mike grinned a little at the thought. He had shaggy brown hair and a lined face. He needed a shave at least twice a day. Karen claimed he could walk out of Saks Fifth Avenue, dressed in the best from the skin out, and still look like an unemployed rock musician. The three of them made a striking contrast in their red Land-Rover with MIKE HOUSTON, PHOTOGRAPHER painted on both doors.

Mike was so busy thinking about the picture they made that he almost missed the house. Karen's voice, breathless in his ear, jogged him back to reality.

"Oh, Mike! Stop, please! Just look at that beautiful old house!"

The house was a classic; built before the turn of the century. It sprawled over half of the large, tree-shaded lot, yellow brick gleaming in the late afternoon sun. There was a veranda that ran the length of the front and around both sides, three stories high with a balcony on the second story. A cupola graced the slanted roof like the decoration on a fancy cake. It struck Mike right away: here was the perfect subject for a special old-fashioned feature in *Homes* magazine.

"That's it, isn't it, Mike?" Leslie's voice was hushed and expectant as if she sensed the creative magic of this moment. "You're going to use this house for a special feature, aren't you?"

It was more a statement than a question and Mike nodded. Leslie had a real eye for a good photograph. "You bet I am!" he responded enthusiastically. "Hand me the Luna-Pro, honey, and push the big black case with the Linhof to the back door. Grab your Leica if you want and let's go. The sun's just right if we hurry."

Karen grinned as her husband and daughter made a hasty exit from the truck, cameras in tow. She'd voiced her objections when Mike gave Leslie the Leica for her ninth birthday. "Such an expensive camera for a nine-year-old?" she'd asked. "She'll probably lose it, Mike. And it's much too complicated for a child her age to operate."

But Mike had been right this time around. Leslie loved her Leica. She slept with it close by the side of her bed, along with her fuzzy stuffed bear and her ballet slippers. And she'd learned how to use it, too, listening attentively when Mike gave her instructions, asking questions that even Karen admitted were advanced for her age. Leslie seemed destined to follow in her stepfather's footsteps. She showed real talent in framing scenes and instinctively knew what made up a good photograph.

Her long hair was heavy and hot on the back of her neck and Karen pulled it up and secured it with a rubber band. She felt a bit queasy but she knew that was natural. It had been a long drive and she remembered getting carsick during the time she'd been carrying Leslie. Just a few more months and she would begin to show. Then she'd have to drag out all her old maternity clothes and see what could be salvaged.

Karen sighed, remembering. Ten years ago she was completely on her own, pregnant and unmarried, struggling to finish school. But once Leslie was born it was better. While it had been exhausting—attending decorating classes in the morning, working all afternoon at the firm, then coming home to care for the baby—it was well worth any trouble. Looking back, she could honestly say that she was happy she hadn't listened to all the well-meaning advice from other women about adoption or abortion. They were a family now, she and Mike and Leslie. She hadn't planned on getting pregnant again so soon after she met Mike, but it would all work out. This time it was going to be different. She wasn't alone. This time she had Mike to help her.

Karen's eyes widened as she slid out of the truck and gazed up at the huge house. It was a decorator's paradise, exactly the sort of house she'd dreamed of tackling when she was a naïve, first-year art student.

She found Leslie around the side of the house, snapping a picture of the exterior. As soon as Leslie spotted her mother she pointed excitedly toward the old greenhouse.

"Oh, Mom! Look at this! You could grow your own flowers in here! Isn't it super?"

"It certainly is!" Karen gave her daughter a quick hug. Leslie's excitement was contagious and Karen's smile widened as she let her eyes wander to take it all in. There was plenty of space for a children's wing on the second floor and somewhere in that vast expanse of rooms was the perfect place for Mike's studio and darkroom. The sign outside said FOR SALE. The thought of owning this house kindled Karen's artistic imagination. They *had* mentioned looking for a house only a week ago and here it was. Of course it would take real backbreaking effort to fix it up, but she felt sure it could be done. It would be the project she'd been looking for, to keep her occupied the next six months. With a little time, patience, and help from Mike with the heavy stuff, she could turn the mansion into a showplace.

They were peeking in through the glass windows of the greenhouse when they heard voices. Mike was talking to someone in the front yard. They heard his laugh and another, deeper voice. Karen grabbed Leslie's hand and they hurried around the side of the house in time to see Mike talking to a gray-haired man in a sport jacket. There was a white Lincoln parked in the driveway with a magnetic sign reading COMSTOCK REALTY.

Rob Comstock had been driving by on his way home from the office when he saw the Land-Rover parked outside the old Appleton Mansion. He noticed the painted signs on the vehicle's door and began to scheme. Out-of-towners, by the look of it. Making a sharp turn at the corner he drove around to pull up behind the truck, shutting off the motor of his new Continental. He'd just sit here and let them get a nice, long look.

This might be it, he thought to himself as he drew a Camel from the crumpled pack in his shirt pocket. He'd wanted to be rid of this white elephant for years. It had been on the books since his grandfather bought it eighty years ago. Rob leased it out whenever he could but that wasn't often enough to make a profit. Tenants never stayed for more than a couple of months. It was too large, they said, or it was too far from the Cities. Even though the rent was reasonable, they still made their excuses and left. He'd been trying to sell it for the past ten years with no success. Houses like this one had gone out of style in his grandfather's day. It was huge and inconvenient, and keeping it up was a financial disaster. It seemed nobody wanted to be stuck with an eight-bedroom house . . . especially a house with a reputation like this one.

Rob finished his cigarette and opened the car door. Maybe, just maybe, today would be his lucky day. He put on his sincerest, most helpful smile and cut across the lawn to greet the owner of the Land-Rover. He was ready for a real challenge.

Leslie and Karen came around the corner of the house in time to catch the tail end of the sales pitch. Mike was nodding as the older man spoke.

"It's been vacant for five years now, but we check it every week to make sure there's no damage. It's a real buy, Mr. Houston. They don't build them like this anymore. Of course it would take a real professional to fix it up and decorate it but the price is right. Only forty-five even, for the right buyer. It's going on the block next week and that'll drive the price up higher, sure as you're standing here. These old estate auctions bring people in from all over; you'd be smart to put in a bid right now. Get it before someone buys the land and decides to tear it down and put in a trailer court."

"That'd be a real shame." Mike was shaking his head and Karen instantly recognized the thoughtful expression on his face. She'd seen it enough times when he was in the market for a new camera. He really was interested. Of course she was, too, she thought, giving the house another look. They'd already decided to get out of the Twin Cities and Mike could work anywhere as long as he had a studio and darkroom. The price was fantastically low and there was the new baby on the way. They couldn't stay in their two-bedroom apartment much longer. Out here she could raise flowers and enjoy working on the house. They might even be able to swing a tennis court in a couple of years and Leslie would have lots of room to play.

"I'd really have to think about it for a while," Mike said, shrugging his shoulders. "And I'd have to see the inside, of course. If it needs a lot of work, the price would have to come down."

"No problem, Mr. Houston." The real estate agent turned to smile at Karen and Leslie. "Glad to meet you, ladies. I'm Rob Comstock from Comstock Realty and I've got the keys with me, if you folks would like to take a look. We've got at least an hour of daylight left."

Karen had a sense of inevitability as she followed Leslie and Mike inside. She'd been dying to see the interior and here she was. One look at the huge high-ceilinged living room made her gasp. This room alone was bigger than their whole apartment! Stained-glass panes graced the upper sections of the floor-length windows and the hardwood floors were virtually unblemished.

"Oh . . . lovely," Karen murmured softly. Her voice was hushed as if she were in a museum. She began to smile as she followed Rob Comstock up the circular staircase and viewed the second floor. Huge, airy bedrooms with polished oak moldings, a separate dressing room in the master suite with an ancient claw-footed dresser dominating the space—-the interior was just as she had imagined. If only they could afford it.

"The furniture on the third floor is included." He was speaking to her now and Karen smiled. Rob Comstock could see she was interested. There was no denying Karen's excitement as she stepped up on the third-floor landing and saw what must have been the original ballroom, filled with old furniture covered by drop-cloths. What she wouldn't give to poke under the shrouded shapes and see the intriguing pieces that were stored and forgotten in this enormous shadowed space.

A small staircase with a door at the top led to the cupola and Leslie was scrambling up before Karen could caution her to be careful. The steps were safe enough. The whole house seemed untouched by time, waiting for some new owners to love and nourish it, to bring it back to life again. Karen could imagine it was almost the same as it had been when the original occupants left, with only a bit of dust and cobwebs covering its intrinsic beauty.

"Plenty of real antiques up here, I'll bet!" Rob Comstock was speaking to her, but Karen only half heard him. She anticipated squeals of delight from Leslie over the view that stretched in all directions from the windowed cupola. Strange that there was only silence overhead.

Karen excused herself reluctantly. "I'd better go up and check on Leslie." A prickle of anxiety invaded her mind as she started up the narrow staircase into the dusty silence.

Karen was convinced there was something wrong when she reached the landing and pushed open the door to the cupola. Leslie was standing at one of the twelve narrow windows, staring out blankly. She looked preoccupied and started as Karen spoke her name.

"Kitten? What's the matter?" The still, stiff way Leslie was standing made Karen terribly nervous. She rushed to put her arms around her daughter.

"Huh? Oh . . . nothing, Mom." Leslie gave her a funny, lopsided smile. She looked miserable. "I'm afraid Mike won't buy it!" There was a quaver in her voice. "This house is perfect for us, Mom. We just have to live here!"

"Now, don't be silly, darling." Karen gave her a quick squeeze. "This is the first house we've seen and it really is awfully large for us. We'll probably see other houses you like just as much."

"No! We have to live here in this house!" Leslie's voice was stronger now and pleading. "You know it's the right house, Mom. We can't live anywhere else. This house was built just for us!"

"I think you should have Mr. Comstock's job." Karen said, smiling down indulgently. "You're an even better salesman than he is. But really, kitten, we have to be sensible. I know you love this old house and I do, too, but the final decision is Mike's."

Karen was firm as she turned Leslie around and guided her toward the stairs. "Come on now, honey. We have to get back downstairs before it gets dark. The power's not turned on, you know."

"But you'll help me convince Mike to buy it, won't you, Mom?" Leslie asked insistently, stopping at the top step. "You know it would be perfect for us."

"Yes, I'll help you, silly," Karen promised, brushing a wisp of silvery-blond hair out of Leslie's eyes. She breathed a sigh of relief as her daughter smiled fully and hurried down the stairs in front of her. Leslie would be persistent and she might just manage to convince Mike. Leslie was right. It was almost as if the house had been waiting all this time just for them.